RETURN TO ENCELADUS

RETURN TO ENCELADUS

Hard Science Fiction

BRANDON Q. MORRIS

BRANDON Q.
MORRIS
HARD SCIENCE FICTION

Contents

Part 1: Reclaiming

December 16, 2048, San Francisco

"Hands up, geezer!"

The victim, a fat alien, stood on two legs with its back against the wall, obeying the command with wide-opened eyes. With a cracking sound, it raised its two front limbs, each of which had four sharp claws at the ends. It breathed heavily, and beads of sweat covered the part of the creature's skull that corresponded to a human being's forehead. Was the alien's sweat caused by fear, or was it a consequence of the hot and humid air in the spaceship—or maybe it was not sweat at all, but tears? It was obvious the panicked creature was looking for a way to escape, while both of its eyestalks frantically turned in every direction. Marchenko automatically felt compassion for it, and at first thought it was probably a tourist from a different sector, though the fact it reacted to a spoken English command did not fit this theory.

"Don't move!" the alien's opponent yelled, a lanky guy who seemed barely 18 years of age. The young man wore a light spacesuit and held a large, rusty plasma knife near the alien's abdominal cavity. He stared provocatively at the creature, as if he wanted his victim to disobey the command. Using his left hand, the youth patted down the lower part of the alien's body, which was covered in thin cloth, but he did not find anything. Then he switched the knife to his left hand

and used his right hand to reach into the bag-like container attached to the creature's hip. He exultantly pulled out an object that looked like some ancient wallet, and indeed it was one. Marchenko shook his head.

Sounding like a female teacher praising a student, the teenager said excitedly, "There you go," and proceeded to look inside the wallet, take out the credit cards, and put them in the tool bag of his spacesuit. He briefly glanced at the material of the wallet and noticed the leather was worn out, so he threw it down with a look of disgust. Marchenko shrugged his shoulders when he saw so much ignorance. What a damned novice! That wallet would probably sell for several hundred dollars on the black market.

Now it would be about time, thought Marchenko, who was observing the scene without those involved noticing him. The mugging had initiated a countdown, and the lanky guy had about 60 seconds to finish his mission. Marchenko already heard the heavy tramping of police boots signaling the beginning of the inevitable pursuit. In a moment the two officers responsible for security on this trading base would come around the corner.

The mugging had occurred in a street that dead-ended at a chain-link fence. The mugger heard the police officers, who were humans like him. He did not even turn around, but dropped his knife, took three quick steps, and started climbing up the fence. He was amazingly strong and agile and quickly scaled the fence, which was over two meters high.

"POLICE, STOP!" One of his pursuers yelled, once in English and again in a language Marchenko did not recognize. At that moment the young mugger dropped down on the other side of the fence. He landed catlike on the ground and started running away. One of the police officers, the one who had not shouted the command, reached for his weapon. He aimed and pulled the trigger of the laser blaster. With enormous energy, and at the speed of light, an invisible beam projected silently from the barrel. The next sound was a thud, and at the very same moment the lanky guy collapsed midstride on the other side of the fence, his lifeless body still carried along by his momentum.

Shit, Marchenko thought, *game over.*

By now he had played through the scene hundreds of times, in different variations, but the game AI did not allow the human player a chance to control the criminal. Artificial intelligences had become too good, and this was often a problem for the developers of computer games. This advancement frustrated players, but even in typical consulting tasks the perfectionism of AIs annoyed human clients. Who wanted to have an insurance agent who was smarter than Einstein?

Francesca had quickly realized they could make money from this problem. Who—if not Marchenko, whose consciousness was both human and digital—could teach artificial intelligences to behave like humans? Of course they could not advertise the fact, since his presence on Earth was still illegal and known to but a few. Soon, though, word of their successes spread and in the end, clients did not mind how they reached their goal. The main focus was on their software—which they had spent so much time and money developing—finally being able to understand the users well enough, without losing in intelligence.

The AI consulting firm was officially owned, operated, and managed by Francesca. The couple could well use the money they made this way. Every day of Marchenko's life in digital illegality was expensive. While Francesca had earned a salary for the two years of her journey to Enceladus and back, she could not touch Marchenko's property, because he was officially considered 'missing' by authorities. Both often discussed whether she should have him declared dead—Marchenko said he would not mind if she decided to do just that, but Francesca simply could not do it.

Their successful business easily allowed them to pay the tax-deductible leasing fees for Marchenko's powerful hardware. The combined quantum computer and supercomputer was both his home and his playground. His excursions into the internet were dangerous, since security algorithms might notice his presence. When Marchenko ventured there, he always wore multiple digital disguises and pretended to be a classic AI.

A white dove flew across the scene, a signal that indicated Francesca wanted to talk with him. While he was training AIs, he turned off all external sensors—except his girlfriend's call button. The idea of a bird as her icon had been his own, because he had never seen a simple white bird in any of the programs he edited. Marchenko emerged from the virtual world. In reality, an hour and 14 minutes had gone by, while he had spent weeks inside the program code. Training AIs was a lengthy process—you made them try a task again and again until they found the best way. Marchenko then only had to ensure the optimal way did not end up being too good.

He activated the speech module. A few months ago, he would have quickly researched what might be the reason for Francesca's call—he was phenomenally good at doing that. He had meant well, since this saved time they could spend on more important issues. However, Francesca made it clear to him how creepy an omniscient partner really was. Since then, Marchenko consciously refrained from gathering information concerning her and instead allowed himself to be surprised. While this was not very practical, it was more human.

"Amy sent us a message," he heard Francesca say. The frequency spectrum of her voice was unusually wide. *She must be excited,* he thought, but then he became angry at himself. He wanted to avoid this type of analysis and rely on his own intuition instead, but it was still tempting.

"And what did she say?" asked Marchenko, switching on his camera. A red light told his girlfriend he was watching her.

"She's received a strange offer and would like to talk with us about it."

"Did she tell you anything more, Francesca?"

"No, she said we would have to meet to discuss it."

"If she thinks it is important enough to contact us, it must be something major. We should definitely accept her invitation."

"I thought so, too. I knew you would react this way, so I already agreed to come."

"I see." He really should be angry at her, but Francesca smiled in such a disarming way he simply could not be mad. "When and where?"

"We will meet in Tokyo ten days from now."

"I thought they moved to Seattle?"

"They are visiting Hayato's parents for a few weeks. Sol is supposed to get to know his grandparents and absorb Japanese culture."

Whenever Francesca mentioned Amy and Hayato's son, she always left out his first name, Dimitri, given in honor of Marchenko's sacrificing himself for Francesca and Martin on Enceladus. She once told Marchenko she did not want to remind him of that event. He rather thought Francesca herself did not want to think of the death of his body back then, which led to him existing in this purely digital form now.

"It is a long flight. Should I book a ticket for you? When do you want to fly there?" asked Francesca.

He himself could reach Tokyo at light speed via the trans-oceanic fiber-optic cables. He only had to make sure no one would notice his excursion into the internet. Still, a rather large, heavily-encrypted amount of data would flow through the undersea cables.

"Two days beforehand? Then I could get acclimatized a bit and could look for a place where you can stay."

"Maybe Amy could help us find the proper hardware."

I am rather spoiled, Marchenko thought. *It wasn't very long ago I had to exist in a single memory module, and now I complain about not having a quantum computer. Luxury problems!*

"Did you say something?" asked Francesca.

Could she hear him think by now? Sometimes he had the impression she could. Was this normal, when two people had been together for a while?

"No," he said. Then he made a sound as if clearing his throat. "Eight days from now, that would be December 24th. Is that really okay with you? Do you really want to fly on that day?"

"It's okay. We can celebrate New Year's Eve on our own with Grandfather Frost, according to the Russian tradition. That's one advantage of having no children."

No children. The two words hit Marchenko unexpectedly hard. He had always felt too old for children, even when he had only passed the 30-year mark. Francesca had recently reached her 50th birthday, and it was unlikely she could get pregnant, even under optimal conditions. Yet it hurt him not to have the option available. Francesca sounded as if she did not waste any thought on the issue. That was good, yet it still felt strange to him. He would have to talk to her about it. But not today.

December 17, 2048, Upper Bavaria

MARTIN STARED at the stony path curving steeply upward. *Take a step, breathe in, take a step, breathe out.* How could he have gotten this much out of shape within just a few months? Was this really caused, as his mother said, by him spending too much time in bed with Jiaying? *At least I'm not eating then, and some of the time should count as exercise,* he thought wryly. He wiped the sweat from his forehead. His heavy perspiration was caused by more than the extremely warm weather for mid-December. Normally he would have expected a meter or more of snow up here, but there was none. The altitude was also a factor in making him feel hot. This mountain hike reminded him of the vertigo he thought he had managed to overcome. But crawling across the hull of a spaceship in the black infinity of space was not the same as walking up a narrow, rocky path, at the end of which the giant summit cross of the Kampenwand mountain awaited.

"Come on, come on!" called Jiaying. Martin glanced upward, using a hand to shield his eyes against the sun. His girlfriend was quite a distance ahead of him, and she was waiting on a kind of plateau below the summit. Gasping, he climbed up after her. On their flight to Germany he had read about this trail, so he knew the worst part for him was still to come—a completely exposed part of the path, secured with cables, that started beyond the plateau. How could he tell Jiaying she would have to scale the summit on her own? Martin shook his head and knew she would not accept any excuses. Jiaying was stricter than any NASA instructor! This mindset not only applied to herself, but also to anyone hiking with her. Maybe he should try to see what would happen if he refused? *But maybe not today,* he thought. They were meeting his mother later this afternoon, and he did not want to be dealing with an angry Chinese girlfriend then.

Martin thought about trying it anyway, thinking perhaps she was in a good mood today. Earlier, they had watched the sunrise together from the terrace of the mountain chalet. It had been so romantic, holding Jiaying in his arms in the subdued glow of dawn. He noticed she felt very light in his embrace then—like a butterfly—and he almost felt as though he had to firmly grasp her so she would not be carried away by a sudden gust of wind. So Martin blissfully held on to Jiaying, and he could have stayed that way all day long on the terrace with her if it had been up to him. He had to avoid getting sunburned up here in the summer-like weather, despite it being winter. He pulled his baseball cap down, took a deep breath, and continued on his way. He carefully avoided looking to the right or left, where the abyss and his fears waited.

"IT IS ABOUT TIME," Jiaying said when he reached the plateau, and she punched him in the side.

"I shouldn't have eaten that piece of cake earlier," he replied. But the plum cake they served at the Steinlingalm chalet had been too tempting to decline.

"You should not have eaten cake during the last few months," Jiaying said. Martin had to laugh when she pinched the love handles above his hips.

"Oh well, I'll lose those three kilos quickly," he said.

Jiaying looked at him without saying a word. Instead, she pointed to a path marker that had been painted on a flat rock.

"Fifteen minutes farther," Jiaying said. Martin nodded. He would not try to talk her out of finishing the climb. Jiaying lifted her small backpack and put it back on.

"I am going to lead, okay?" she asked. Martin nodded again. He was afraid his voice would fail him. Jiaying slowly walked to the left. He followed her and saw her reaching for an iron chain bordering the path that led down a few meters. Directly below his feet was the Bavarian upland, the beauty of which he could not admire because he had to avert his gaze, as otherwise he would almost certainly fall down. He focused instead on the laces of his hiking boots.

"Slow and steady," Jiaying said. She was only two steps ahead of him. He looked up and saw she was squinting, something she always did when she was worried. She was worried about him, and a sudden warmth swept through his body. At that instant, Martin would have liked to embrace Jiaying, even though he could not think of a less suitable moment for it.

Oh well, he thought, and made it past the end of the chain. The rest of the climb was not secured, but it was also less dangerous. The path went to the right and upward, followed by a short iron bridge, and finally they were there. Martin felt like uttering a triumphant yell, but other hikers up here were gazing at the landscape in silent awe.

He looked around and saw that the view was truly breathtaking. Jiaying stood next to him and he reached for her hand. He could see fertile, green land all the way to the horizon. Lake Chiemsee was shimmering dark blue below them, with sailboats appearing as white dots on its surface. It smelled of summer, which Martin could hardly believe.

"Can you smell it too, just like in summer?" he asked.

Jiaying smiled, and another warm wave flowed through Martin's body. "Yes, it is..." she was looking for the German word, "dry grass... uh, hay."

"Very good. Exactly... hay," Martin answered. Jiaying

had been taking an intensive German course for several months and was much further ahead than Martin, who was studying Mandarin by himself. His mother would be surprised.

He let his gaze wander across the wide landscape. The horizon seemed to be curving. Up here you could clearly feel you were on a sphere, on this place called Earth, which he had not seen for such a long time, and which was truly unique in space. How stupid did you have to be to leave such a place for such a long time? And why was he just now noticing this?

"Come on," Jiaying said. "Your mother is probably already waiting for you. Let's go."

"And for you, too," he said.

THE DESCENT WAS EVEN WORSE than the climb for Martin. He let Jiaying go first and focused on the little panda trinket attached to the zipper of her backpack. The panda smiled. It was probably laughing at him right now. How could he make such a fuss, just because he would fall down several hundred meters if the sole of his boot slipped? In some areas he had to cross bare rock worn smooth by the stream of hikers. There he did not shy away from sliding on the seat of his pants, even if the climbers coming the other way cast him pitying glances. Yes, he should not have gone on this climb, but the other hikers did not know how hard it was to deny Jiaying anything. Martin felt his stomach cramping, and the muscles in his thighs trembled with exhaustion.

To his great surprise, though, they arrived in the valley sooner than he had expected. The narrow path turned into a wide gravel road. If he slipped here, he would only end up on his backside. Martin took a deep breath. Below he could see the few buildings of Steinlingalm. The wooden benches in front of them were full of hikers eating *Wurstsalat*, strips of sausage, red onions, and chopped pickles in a vinaigrette. They were drinking *Radler*, a mixture of beer and lemon soda.

He noticed his appetite was slowly coming back. He took his backpack off and held it in his hand by the handle. The back of his T-shirt was sopping wet. If he did not take a shower soon, he would start to stink like a polecat.

Jiaying pointed to the restaurant of the mountain chalet. He shook his head and Jiaying smiled. She pointed to the left, where the cable car station was hidden behind a ridge. Martin nodded and smiled back at her. It was wonderful to understand each other without words. His mother would be preparing some food anyway—at least a cake.

HALF AN HOUR later they were crammed into the cable car, gliding downward above the treetops. About half of the people aboard also came from an exhausting hike, so the ventilation system stood no chance against the collective odor of perspiration. But the trip was short, and it was better than walking down the mountain for another hour and a half. Jiaying had linked arms with him, and Martin grabbed one of the support rails on the ceiling. He cautiously studied the people around him. Most of them were together as family groups, and the children in particular stared curiously at his companion. Tourists from the Far East were not uncommon here, but they usually traveled in groups. Would you believe it? He of all people had a beautiful woman from faraway China by his side. He felt his cheeks flushing.

THE DRIVE by car took about 90 minutes. The electric rental car hummed along in automatic mode as they traveled the state road. Martin's mother lived in a small village, far away from the city, where she had bought a little house. He wondered when his last visit had been—*it must be almost three years now*. After his return from Enceladus, his mother had visited him for a few weeks in the U.S., but he had never found the time to visit her in turn. Since her miscarriage, Jiaying had been traveling under orders of the Chinese government, and he had resumed his job as a systems analyst for NASA.

The media siege of the first few weeks after the return landing had now segued into a pleasantly quiet normality. These days, journalists rarely asked to interview him, and even student reporters seemed to have lost interest. Martin was glad about it, although at first he wondered whether he would miss that thrilling time. He didn't. In the light of his past adventures, he was surprised he still found it exciting to scan program code for errors others had made.

Jiaying placed a hand on his thigh.

"What a beautiful landscape," she said in German. "It reminds me of a place in the mountains back home that I visited as a child."

Martin looked out of the window. "In spring and summer it is even nicer," he said, "because the trees are not so bare then."

"Then we will come back in the spring."

"Your German is already quite good."

"Thanks."

"But don't be surprised if you can't understand anyone in the village. It's not your fault."

"I know—the local dialect. I know this from China, too. Even going from Beijing to Shanghai... but what about your mother?"

"She speaks standard German. Don't worry. We're not from this area."

"And what are the people like here?"

"They're friendly and direct. Maybe it is the rural surroundings. You soon get the feeling you belong here. And then again, you don't."

"I understand. I am familiar with it. You are accepted, but you still somehow remain a stranger. It is no different in my home country."

"Yes, it's something like that," Martin said. "It is usually great for visitors, but it's different for people living here all the time." He looked at the map on the display in the center console. He saw that it was another ten kilometers to their destination. Up ahead was a shortcut via a dirt road that the navigation AI did not know about. He placed his hands on the steering wheel.

"Control, I am taking over the wheel," he said. The software checked to see that he was looking forward and had his hands on the steering wheel. Then after a short countdown it switched to manual mode. Jiaying pulled her hand back. Martin hoped the shortcut had not become a victim of some new development. He signaled and turned right onto the dirt road. The road was bumpy, but the car's suspension absorbed most of it. They crossed a railroad line and reached a small forest consisting mostly of fir trees. The sun cast colored dots of light on the narrow road that was now overgrown with grass.

"Warning, dead-end ahead," the AI navigation system announced, but Martin knew better. Jiaying once again placed a hand on his thigh.

"Why don't you stop for a moment?" she asked. Martin looked over at her on his right and then stopped the car. Jiaying smiled mysteriously and placed her right index finger on her lips.

"I would like to kiss you once more before we reach your mother's house," she said quietly. "You know how shy I am."

Martin gave her a wide smile. *Of course, shy—sure.* Martin unbuckled his seatbelt and turned toward her. Their lips met in a lingering kiss.

"What were you doing in the forest for such a long time?"

Martin blushed profusely when his mother confronted them with the question. He had forgotten about the location-sharing mode of the car's autopilot that he had activated so his mother did not have to repeatedly ask him when they were arriving.

"We were just trying to pick some mushrooms for you, Ms. Neumaier," Jiaying answered in almost perfect German, "but unfortunately we did not find any there." His mother turned toward her and smiled.

"Elizabeth. Please call me Elizabeth. I am glad you are here."

"I am Jiaying. I am glad to meet you, too, Ms. Neumaier." It took the Chinese woman a moment before she realized her mistake. "Elizabeth. Of course. The German form of polite address is not easy."

"Nothing compared to what you have to watch out for in Chinese," Martin interjected. During the visit to Jiaying's parents, he had stumbled around the language so much, her father finally asked him to speak English.

Elizabeth spread her arms and embraced her son's girl-friend. Jiaying gave in to the affectionate greeting, and then it was Martin's turn to do the same. At least his mother did not complain about him not visiting for such a long time. He could probably thank Jiaying's presence for that.

"Come on in," his mother said as she opened the front door. Martin was the last one to enter the hallway, and he was immediately struck by a long forgotten smell. It was strange. Although he had not spent his childhood in this house, his nose told him he was home. He smelled his mother's signature citrusy perfume and the slight chlorine smell of a strong cleaner, layered with the aroma of freshly baked cake. Could such a characteristic scent be packed and brought along when you moved from house to house, or did it occur automatically?

The hallway was small. They took off their shoes.

"Do you want slippers?" offered Elizabeth.

Jiaying shook her head.

"No," Martin said, but then remembered the hike they had just finished, and what his socks might now look like. "Actually, yes," he corrected himself.

Elizabeth pointed downward, and below the coat rack stood his old slippers. She had really kept them all these years. He put them on, since they at least protected his feet somewhat from the outside world.

There were three doors off the hallway.

"This is the bedroom," his mother said, pointing to the right. "Back there is the bathroom. The trip was long, wasn't it?"

Jiaying nodded and disappeared behind the door.

The remaining door led to the living room.

"Come along, or do you want to wait outside the bathroom door for your girlfriend?"

Martin shook his head. Elizabeth opened the living room door and invited him in. "After you," he said.

His mother just smiled, so he stepped across the threshold. The room appeared surprisingly small, but maybe the impression was caused by the three crammed bookshelves that reached from floor to ceiling. Another door, on the narrow side of the room and leading to the kitchen, was framed by more shelves. Only one wall was entirely free of books, and there a large window let in daylight. It was the western side. The sun still shone into the room even though it was almost evening. Martin walked along the bookshelves and saw his old favorites. As a child he had read almost all of his mother's books, and only a few seemed to have been added since then.

His mother gave an almost sheepish nod when she saw him looking at the shelves. "Yes, I hardly buy any new books, and I've started rereading the old ones. It's been so long... I can hardly remember the plots."

Martin smiled. He hoped she had not stopped buying books because of a lack of money. He was a bit ashamed that he had never asked her about her financial circumstances, and by now he was making enough money to easily support her. Back in his childhood, she had bought him any book in which he showed an interest.

At first he was fascinated by archeology—Schliemann had been his hero. Martin soon learned, though, that archeological digs were very different now, and each discovery required years of systematic work by a large team. Then his mother had bought him an illustrated book about space, and from that point onward he was awe-struck by the universe. That book might have been the key factor for him eventually taking a position with NASA.

He took a look out the window. The sun already was very low for this time of day, but after all, it was winter. Next to the window there were pictures hanging on the wall. They showed him, his sister, and his sister's children, but neither his mother nor his father was visible anywhere. To the very left he saw ancient-looking portraits of his aunts, who had died a long time ago, and below them a wedding picture of his grandparents, which was already quite faded. *This would be a good idea for a birthday present,* he thought—long ago, before he moved out, he had digitized all the family photos. If he printed out copies and had them framed, his mother would definitely appreciate the effort.

The door hinges creaked as Jiaying entered the room. Martin noticed his mother getting nervous and acting rather tense.

"Do sit down," Elizabeth said, pointing at the table in the middle of the room. Her gestures appeared as if she were trying to usher a flock of lambs into a meadow. Then she turned around and went through the door between the shelves to get to the kitchen.

"I am getting the coffee," she called out to them. Martin sat down and Jiaying briefly inspected the room, just like Martin had done earlier. He wondered what his girlfriend might be thinking. On the table he saw a round marble cake with a hole in the middle. A wire mesh cover protected it against flies, though he had not noticed any.

"Very cozy," Jiaying said. "Was it like this where you grew up?"

"The books, yes," he replied. "I was always surrounded by lots and lots of books."

"That must have been great. We could never afford that

many books, even though they were much cheaper in my country."

That was right—even during his own youth books had become a luxury item, particularly in printed form. But he never had that impression, because there seemed to be an infinite number of them available.

"As a child, I never considered it a luxury," he said. "The books were simply there. Like the grass covering the meadow behind the house, or the many trees in the forest."

Jiaying sat down and placed her hand on his. The kitchen door opened, and his mother carried a glass coffee pot. They could smell the freshly brewed coffee.

"Does anyone want milk or sugar?" asked Elizabeth.

"No thank you," Jiaying said politely.

Martin shook his head. "You know I don't," he said.

"Well, I thought maybe you would like it with milk by now."

He laughed out loud at his mother's comment. "Milk? No. You can bet I'll never drink it with milk."

"Many Chinese people do not like milk," Jiaying added. "Maybe you are half Chinese."

His mother poured the coffee. Then she took the wire mesh cover off the cake and placed a piece on each of their plates.

"Thank you," Jiaying said with a smile.

"Marble cake," Martin said. "What a strange name. The brown color is caused by cocoa. But marble isn't brown."

"As a kid you really liked marble cake, but only the brown parts," Elizabeth said.

"Then you took the white parts, which you preferred."

His mother smiled. Martin suddenly understood. Could he have been that stupid as a child?

"You didn't really prefer the white parts of the cake, did you?"

He received no answer from her. Elizabeth speared a piece with her cake fork and put it in her mouth. She took a sip of coffee and chewed as she gazed somewhere, but Martin did not know where. He smiled.

"Sure," he said, "I understand. I would have done the same."

"I actually don't like marble cake all that much," Elizabeth blurted out, "but you were always so happy when we baked one."

Martin remembered visiting his grandparents. Grandma always baked a cherry cake with a pudding topping. He did not like pudding, but his mother always enjoyed that kind of cake. He made a mental note that he would have to find a recipe to make one and then get some morello cherries.

Silence reigned for several minutes. It wasn't an unpleasant silence, more the absence of noise, the kind of quiet that makes you sleepy. A housefly buzzed somewhere around the room. Now and then he could hear a slight clinking sound when someone put down a coffee cup.

"So what is going to happen with the two of you? Both personally and professionally, I mean."

Martin had expected his mother to ask this, hoping she would avoid the topic of children. He looked at Jiaying, who was sitting next to him.

"I am back working in my office at NASA," he said, "I don't need anything else. Jiaying is currently traveling all over the world, so we don't meet very often."

"The Chinese space agency is very proud of our discoveries," Jiaying said.

Well, the Chinese are proud of the Chinese astronaut on board, Martin thought, *but Jiaying would never say that.*

"Therefore I often represent my country at international conferences, trade fairs, and other events," Jiaying continued.

"And do you like it?" asked Elizabeth.

"Yes, I do. I like being the representative of my country," his girlfriend explained. She was serious about this, even though she realized she was strengthening the power of the Communist Party apparatus by doing so. A few weeks ago she and Martin had discussed this very topic. Jiaying believed it was necessary for her to thank the nation in which she was born for funding her journey to space.

The fact that her parents had been mistreated was a completely different issue to her. Even though there never was an official indictment, those responsible certainly did not escape punishment, and probably would spend the coming years in detention camps. Nonetheless, Jiaying was a patriot, an attitude that was alien to Martin. He preferred to be his own representative, but it was also not a major issue between them. They talked about it, understood what motivated the other one, and that was enough.

"Then that's fine," Elizabeth said. "The most important thing is that you enjoy what you are doing. And both of you are young and still have so much time."

Martin flinched when he heard those words. Back when his father wanted to do what he enjoyed, researching space with a giant radio dish, his mother had not felt the same way. She had given her former husband an ultimatum, and his father opted for his career and against his family. Thinking, Martin wiped a speck of dust from the tablecloth. *This should not be a topic today.*

"Since you probably want to know whether we are going to get married... no, we are not planning to. And if we did, we would do it on our own and everyone else would only hear about it afterward."

"I understand, Martin," his mother said. "Maybe it's really better that way, being together without any external pressure. And do you want to have children?"

He froze and gazed at Jiaying. As always, she smiled in a way he could never quite comprehend. How did she always manage to do this? Even after the miscarriage he only saw her cry a single time. At one time she had explained to him that she did not take herself too seriously. He himself was good at the art of suppressing things, but in Jiaying he had found the true master.

"To be honest, a child does not really fit into our lives," she said. "I am traveling so much, and I still would like to return to space several times. I just turned 40, so I could stay in the Taikonaut Corps for at least another decade."

"And then there is the issue of the radiation we were exposed to. Two years in space, that carries a high risk of damage to our genetic material," Martin added. This, the doctors had explained to them, might have been the reason for the miscarriage. Afterward they both quickly agreed to not try it a second time. With that decision, Martin experienced a strange sense of relief, perhaps due to his latent fear of not being able to become a good father.

Jiaying's wish to return to space was more problematic, though, and Martin did not share it at all. Right now, his girl-friend's face was much too valuable to China for propaganda purposes for the government to consider letting her return to active service. Space travel would always remain dangerous—how awful if this Chinese heroine were to die in an accident. But in two or three years the world would grow tired of seeing Jiaying's face. Then, she had already explained to him, the time would come for her to throw her unquestionable merits into the balance, so the government would not be able to deny her another flight into space. Martin decided he just would not think about it until then. Who knew what could happen in two years.

"I understand," Elizabeth said very calmly. Martin still got the impression his mother had to struggle to keep from showing her disappointment, but maybe he was wrong.

"Thank you very much for being so open about it," she added. "Even though you probably think otherwise, Martin, my most important concern is that both of you are happy. I've got a nice home here," she said as she looked around, "and I don't have to become a grandmother again. I really think women who want to become grandmothers as many times as possible are trying to compensate for errors they made when raising their own children."

Martin suddenly had a bad feeling. He suspected—or rather feared—the direction this conversation might take now. He really did not want to talk about it.

"I still am sorry we cannot offer you that opportunity, Ms. Neumaier… sorry, Elizabeth," Jiaying said. "I had to explain it to my own parents a few months ago, and it was much more difficult. In our culture, having offspring is so important. My father will have to deal with his branch of the family dying out, because I have no siblings. We could never afford them."

"That's hard," Elizabeth said. "I would like to meet your family sometime. You are so kind, Jiaying, so you must have very nice parents."

Phew, Martin thought, *looks like my mother really likes Jiaying. That's good, so I won't be caught in the middle between them.*

"Thank you, Elizabeth. I will certainly tell my parents. I am sure we can get the families together somehow, and my mother is already feeling much better."

"I still think you would have to fly to Shanghai," Martin said. "Jiaying's mother suffered a lot during the kidnapping to Guantanamo."

"Kidnapping? What do you mean?" asked Elizabeth.

Jiaying and Martin looked at each other in surprise. So far, his mother appeared to only know the official version of the story. Hadn't they already told her what actually happened?

"Let me tell you," Jiaying said, and Martin was very grateful for it. He was starting to feel tired. His body was reacting to getting up early today and all the excitement afterward. Jiaying's words, as she told the story he knew so well, calmed him down and made him sleepy.

Then the tabletop started to blink. What Martin had taken for a wooden table was actually a large screen, which now turned on. He gave his mother a surprised look.

"What, you think I live in the boondocks here?" she asked.

The rental car displayed a message on the screen. Its AI asked for permission to have the house AI relay a video call to the tabletop display. The call was labeled as high priority and came from Tokyo. Elizabeth confirmed this in a very routine fashion, after gazing at Martin to get his permission. He was surprised at how technically savvy she was.

Amy's face appeared.

"Amy?"

"Yes, Martin, I'm glad you still recognize me," she said tongue-in-cheek. "I've finally reached you. You have made yourself really hard to find the last few days."

"We are currently traveling in Europe. Jiaying and I don't have simultaneous time off very often, so we wanted to use the opportunity."

"Even better—if I reached both of you I can do this with one call. I would like to invite both of you to a meeting in Tokyo."

"Just a moment, Amy, I have to check my calendar. I don't know when I'll have time next year..."

"No, not next year," Amy replied. "Nine days from now, on December 26th."

Martin looked at Jiaying, who was just as surprised as he was.

"Then it must be..."

"Yes, it is. Important, and urgent," Amy said. "Unfortunately, I can't tell you more right now."

"Okay, we will be there," Jiaying interjected. "Please tell us the exact location of the meeting."

"You will find out in time. I am looking forward to meeting with you."

The screen turned itself off.

"What was that all about?" asked Martin.

"A request from Amy," Jiaying replied. "Sorry I spontaneously answered for both of us. Amy asked us to meet her and there is no alternative but to do it. We will just have to fly there. Now, we have to book a flight and a hotel."

"Then I won't have to ask you where you are going to spend Christmas," Elizabeth said. His mother sounded very neutral, instead of disappointed.

"Yes. Traveling," Martin replied. They had not even mentioned Christmas yet. The holiday really did not mean anything to Jiaying, and Martin himself only liked it when little kids were present.

"That was a very surprising call, wasn't it?" his mother observed.

"It was, indeed, Elizabeth. I do not know yet what to think of it." Jiaying gently rubbed her fingers over her temples.

"I think we should get going then," Martin said. "Is that okay?"

"Of course, my dear," Elizabeth said. "I am very happy you came. And if you happen to be at some conference in Southern Germany, Jiaying, I would be glad if you could visit me on your own."

"I'll tell you by phone what Amy wanted from us," Martin said.

His mother nodded. She fetched some paper towels from the kitchen and wrapped the rest of the cake in them. "Here, take it with you."

"Thanks," he said, and felt a lump in his throat. When Martin hugged his mother goodbye, she seemed much smaller and lighter than she used to. It was as if she was gradually disappearing from this world.

December 19, 2048, Ishinomaki

Dusk seemed to have already fallen, even though it was only 2 p.m. Water splattered against the windshield of the jeep, and it was not clear whether it came from the dark rain clouds above, or the wind-whipped, white crests of the waves from the right. During the summer, Ishinomaki was a nice tourist destination, but in winter the wet Pacific coast could get very unpleasant. Hayato steered the jeep after purposely switching it to manual control. Amy was amused by this contradiction—an engineer who exhibited no faith in technology. The vehicle's AI could probably react to each swerve and curve and gust of wind more quickly than a human, but Hayato was more comfortable trusting his own instinctive driving abilities.

Dimitri Sol slept in his car seat in the back of the vehicle. Neither the weather nor the Japanese voices from the car radio seemed to bother him. Amy tried very hard to understand some of the language, but her Japanese skills were not yet good enough to catch more than an isolated word here or there. She leaned her head against the window and looked at the landscape. The three of them had visited here before, in the summer. She had liked the area so much she agreed to Hayato's suggestion to spend the time between Christmas and New Year's here with his parents. And it was true, if Dimitri

Sol was going to grow up bilingual, he had to absorb his father's native language as early as possible. Plus, she could understand Hayato's parents looking forward to seeing their second grandchild. Hayato, who had an adult daughter, was their only son, and his parents had not been able to see him for a long time. The fact that he had unexpectedly brought back a wife and a child from his long journey rewarded them for their patience.

If it hadn't been for the call from this Mr. Dushek, they might be spending some quiet, relaxing days by the wintery sea. Because of the Russian they were arriving late at the house of Hayato's parents. Back in Tokyo they had tried to research their mysterious caller. Hayato knew some people who knew some people who sold information. Amy also tried to get some details about Dushek through her friends at NASA. The man was said to be an important part of the Russian space program, which the Americans were—at times —dealing with. She hoped to get some interesting phone calls about him this evening.

"We are almost there," Hayato said.

"I am glad to hear that. The storm is getting stronger."

Thus far they had been driving along the coastal road. Hayato activated the left turn signal and steered the car through a narrow street into the town. Suddenly it turned almost completely dark. Amy did not remember coming through here before, but her husband seemed to know the way.

"Here we are," he said suddenly. He turned toward her and smiled. Amy was confused. The house they were stopped at looked completely different than what she recalled from the summer.

"Watch out for the lamp post," Hayato warned. Amy nodded and opened the car door just wide enough to slip outside.

"Damn." Hayato walked around the car. He pulled up the legs of his pants, but his shoes and socks were already soaking wet. "It does not matter," he said, "I am getting Sol."

The front door of the house opened. A large black umbrella came out, under which a short man was hiding. Amy immediately recognized Hayato's father by his duck-like walk. He held the umbrella over her and politely offered her his arm. "Come inside, daughter," he said.

Amy turned toward Hayato. Could she help him somehow?

"Just let your two men alone, they can cope," Hayato's father said while leading her into the house. The umbrella did not fit through the door, so he let her go first, turned around and closed the umbrella, and followed her in. Then Hayato entered the hallway, holding Sol in his arms, so it was pretty crowded. Amy took off her jacket and placed it on a hanger on the coat rack, and then she slipped off her shoes. The adjoining corridor was covered with raffia mats, so she entered with bare feet. There seemed to be no doors, but Amy already knew this was an illusion. Tetsuyo, Hayato's father, slid one of the wooden walls aside, opening to another passage.

They entered the sparsely furnished living room. The floor was covered by the usual *tatami* mat, while a low table with enough spaces for six people stood in the center. The thick cloth on the table reached all the way to the floor. Both side walls had built-in closets, and the front wall had a window that was covered by cloth roller blinds. Hayato's mother came through another entrance. She first bowed, and then hugged Amy.

"Nice to have you here," she said in English. "Did Tetsuyo greet you properly? Or was he as gruff as always?"

"No, your husband was very courteous. I've never seen him act gruff," Amy answered.

Mako gave a sly smile. Amy realized it was impossible to tell the woman's age. "Please have a seat," her mother-in-law then said. "I have already turned up the heater. I will bring tea in a moment."

Amy and Tetsuyo crouched in front of the table. Then they sat down and pushed their legs under the table, while straightening the tablecloth, which also served as a blanket for their thighs. Amy relaxed. The *kotatsu* did not heat the entire room, but the warmth generated by the heating element below the tabletop spread from her legs into her whole body. Mako came back with a teapot, from which she poured into paper-thin porcelain cups. She also placed cookies on the table. Then she sat down as well.

"I hope you had a pleasant journey," she said.

"Yes, but it was strenuous driving in the storm. Hayato had to work really hard," Amy said. Then she added, "You have a great son."

Tetsuyo and his wife bowed slightly.

"Hayato said something important interfered?"

Hayato had already told Amy his mother was both very intelligent and very curious. Amy was about to answer when her husband entered the room.

"I let Sol go back to sleep in the guest room," Hayato said. "He did not really wake up anyway."

He placed a hand on his father's shoulder. His mother stood up to greet him.

"You look well," she said.

"Thank you, I am." He sat down with them and his mother poured a cup of tea for him.

"We were just talking about what kept you in Tokyo."

"Yes," Hayato said, "that was a strange phone call. I would like to hear your opinion about it."

Amy knew he did not just say this as a dutiful son, but because he still valued his parents' guidance, despite being over 40 years old. "I will never catch up with them," he once told her.

"Gladly," Tetsuyo replied.

"The caller identified himself as Dushek," Hayato explained. "He is a Russian, rather well known in IT circles, who makes his money with AIs—artificial intelligences. We still have to check whether he is really the same Dushek. But I see no reason why someone else would pretend to be him."

"And what did he want?"

"That is the strange thing, Mother—he offered to finance us for another expedition to Enceladus. No, not just that, but also to organize it."

"And why should you accept this offer? You just returned, after all."

"The man claims he knows a way to save Marchenko."

"The spaceship's Russian doctor that Dimitri Sol was named for?"

"Yes, Mother, and whose consciousness we brought back as a digital copy."

"You told us about that, yes. I cannot really imagine it, but no matter. How does this man Dushek know of it? Is it not top secret?"

"That is one thing that really puzzles us..."

"And what is the other?"

"His motives, Mother. Such an expedition costs billions of dollars, many billions. What would he get that is worth so much to him?"

"As a businessman, he is certainly not acting due to a charitable impulse."

"Yes, and that is precisely what we are worried about."

"Let us assume you check his offer and the man speaks the truth, and could really get you to Enceladus. Would you accept?"

"Not for us, Father, but for Marchenko, yes, without a second thought. Assuming Marchenko wants it, too."

"When are you going to ask him?"

"Next week, on the 26th, when we all meet in Tokyo."

"Certainly someone will notice the entire crew of *ILSE* meeting a rich Russian in Tokyo?" said Mako, her inflection clearly making it a question.

That's an important argument, Amy thought. *Why didn't we think of that ourselves?* Were intelligence services watching them? Jiaying was an important poster child for her country, and there must be some eager super-secret agencies in the U.S. as well. Francesca would be traveling with an illegal AI. If Jiaying went on a privately-financed trip to Enceladus, her country could no longer use her for propaganda purposes.

Hayato's thoughts seemed to be going in similar directions. "Thank you, Mother, that was an important point," he said. "We should have thought of it ourselves."

"If you actually go on this journey," Mako said, giving her son a stern look, "you certainly will not force Dimitri Sol to go along, will you? Your son is welcome to spend the time here with us."

Amy started feeling hot, and she had to pull her legs out from under the table. Two years without Sol—she could hardly imagine it. Yet Hayato's mother had brought up a crucial issue: Did they have the right to deprive their son of another part of his childhood? Shouldn't he grow up on a green Earth playing with toys, and kids his own age, instead of in dark space, with tools and computers and only adults? And if so, would this expedition be possible without her?

December 20, 2048, Ishinomaki

THE FIRST PHONE call came at 4 a.m. and woke the entire household, even though at breakfast, Hayato's parents pretended not to have heard anything. Amy rejected the call and turned off the phone, but Sol was wide awake. She pulled his baby bed closer to their futon. He babbled happily while playing intently with her fingers, and she dozed off again. At 6 a.m. Hayato woke up due to a rattling sound somewhere. His father always got up this early for the sunrise Tai Chi session at his local dojo, and of course his wife got up to see him off. She cooked breakfast while he was out and they ate together after he returned.

Amy decided to use the time for work. Who was last night's caller? Since the country code was 1, the call must have come from the U.S., her home country. *Perhaps it's someone from NASA?* She called back.

"This is Meyers," she heard a female voice answer.

"Sandy, is that you? This is Amy."

"What a surprise! How are you doing?"

"I'm fine, and how are you?"

Amy hated small talk, but it was she who wanted something from Sandy, not the other way around. The woman she was talking to was an old friend, and they had flown together aboard an Orion capsule. At one point, Sandy's family protested her frequent absences, and she found herself a job back on Earth. Amy was not sure who Sandy's employer was now. Since everyone was very secretive about it, including Sandy, she assumed it was either the NSA or the CIA. These agencies had maintained their own small space program for quite some time, and NASA reserved launch capacity for them.

In order to reach Sandy, Amy had contacted a mutual friend who still owed her a favor. To be on the safe side, Amy made no mention of any details. She hoped Sandy would not be too surprised to hear from her, and would also be willing and able to do a bit of research for her.

"I have a question concerning someone in the Russian space program," Amy began. "I don't know why, and it doesn't matter anyhow, but I have the feeling you could help me with an answer."

"Then let me hear about it," Sandy said.

"Well," Amy said, taking a deep breath, "it is about someone called Yuri Dushek. Should I spell the name?"

"No, that's okay, the name sounds familiar. So he can't be totally unimportant. Just give me a moment."

Amy heard typing on a keyboard.

"I have a large file about this Dushek. Interesting guy. What specifically do you want to know?"

"How does he earn his money?"

"Why? Do you want to marry him? It looks like everything is completely legitimate. He seems to be very good at commercializing the findings of AI research. Then he sells this everywhere—even to countries we are not allowed to export to. In that respect, he has a kind of monopoly there, except for two Chinese guys, who certainly are nothing but front men for state companies."

"What about in the aerospace industries?"

"Well, he uses his profits to finance part of the Russian space budget, but he does not participate. It looks more like an expensive hobby, or maybe he is very patriotic."

"Let's assume he offered to fly me to the moon. Could he do it with his own hardware?"

"No, he would have to buy space in the capsule of an Energia T rocket."

"I understand. That is odd. Then maybe he overplayed his hand."

"Wait a moment... there are connections to the RB Group."

"RB Group?"

"It was formerly a major oil company. Now it is successful in asteroid mining—very successful, even. This allowed Dushek to finance his own company."

"So is he a straw man for the RB Group?"

"No, I wouldn't go so far as to say that. Dushek is much too active to be a mere straw man."

"And who is behind RB?"

"A man who is even richer than Dushek. His name is Nikolai Shostakovich."

"Shostakovich? You mean like the composer?"

"Yes. It's a common last name in Russia."

"What do you know about him?"

"Very little, I have to admit. This is surprising—we don't even have a photo of him. He must have lived in Akademgorodok for a while, the research town near Novosibirsk. There he used borrowed money to start an IT company. It is unclear how he made it to the top of RB."

"But this Shostakovich has a spaceship?"

"Just one, you say? The RB Group owns the largest private space fleet in the world. It is larger than SpaceX. It controls the complete value chain, which is its great advantage. It does not just launch rockets, but also constructs their payloads and determines their usage. Everything is focused on asteroid mining. This is the future, Amy. SpaceX went the wrong way with its Martian ventures. They wasted a lot of money there, while Shostakovich is making money hand over fist."

"Sounds very clever."

"Yes, he is. And from what we know, he doesn't even spend his money on fast yachts and beautiful women, as expected of someone in his position, he invests it in research."

"That's commendable. He seems to be some kind of saint."

"Not completely, Amy. None of his research institutes have ever published anything in any of the well-known journals. They are strictly working behind closed doors."

"That helps. Thanks, Sandy, thanks a lot. Now I think I am able to better judge the offer we received."

December 21, 2048, San Francisco

FRANCESCA TURNED OFF HER COMPUTER. She had attempted to find out what her former crewmates were up to these days. The last time they had all seen each other was in May, more than half a year ago. Having had to put up with each other for two years in a cramped spaceship, the pairs seemed for now to be staying as far away from the rest of the crewmembers as possible, and she'd heard nothing of Martin.

"I couldn't find out much about Amy and Hayato. Amy sometimes speaks at scientific conferences, about problems during long space journeys," Francesca said.

"She has probably retreated into family life. Their visit to Hayato's parents would indicate it," Marchenko said from the loudspeaker.

"But did you know Jiaying just finished a bona fide world tour? In Nairobi, a soccer stadium full of people cheered her."

"Yes, the Chinese want to appear as benefactors who bring wealth to Africa. Having a space heroine fits into their plan," he said.

"In Brazil the president received her, and in Cuba she was driven along the Malecón in a motorcade."

"Yes, she really gets around. I could give you all…" Marchenko fell silent, and Francesca noticed the pause. He must have remembered what they had talked about recently —her having issues with him being omniscient. It just happened so often. When Francesca would excitedly tell him a piece of news, he would already know about it through his numerous feelers on the internet. He even seemed to know more about her friends than she did, not that she had all that many friends after spending two years in space.

Francesca knew he could not help it. Marchenko convincingly argued he was not going out of his way to acquire this information, it simply was there. It was difficult for her to imagine her consciousness being constantly connected with all of humanity's news sources and social networks, and all without much effort. To Francesca this sounded like a full-scale nightmare, but for her boyfriend, this was everyday existence. She did not want him to change because this would be unfair. He would not demand her to upload her consciousness to the cloud, if it were possible—would he?

"How is Martin handling this. What do you think?" asked Francesca.

"Neumaier? According to what I know of him, he should be happy to be back in his office. He has not been seen in public since May."

"Do you think they are still together?"

"I am pretty sure. Not sharing your boring everyday life with each other keeps love fresh. They would be celebrating each time they see each other again."

And what about us? We see each other, and then again we don't. Dimitri is always with me, but at the same time he is as far away as can be. Francesca kept her thoughts to herself.

"You... are so quiet. Francesca, I love you, and you should always know it."

"Yes, I know," she said. But she was not completely convinced it worked on her side. Could she love someone who was with her only virtually?

SHE WAS ACTUALLY PRETTY LUCKY, she thought later, after she got undressed and ready for bed. They had a beautiful and incredibly expensive ground floor apartment in an old house downtown. The streetcars were running just outside the windows. She did not have to work. Well, a bit of book-keeping for the company marketing Marchenko's skills. The clients came by themselves, and they had more work requests than they could handle. Whenever she wanted, she could take her car to a private airfield out in the Valley and fly her own little plane. She had a man who loved her and was always there for her. She might not be able to hug him, and he could not repair the mechanism of the automatic roller blinds, but that she could do herself. But something was lacking, and she was not sure exactly what it was.

Before turning off the reading light, she gave it a try.

"Dimitri, are you there?" she whispered.

"Yes, darling. Are you going to sleep now?"

"I am in the mood."

Her boyfriend did not say anything. She imagined him lying next to her, smiling.

"Shhhh," Marchenko said softly. "I am sliding downward. Please open your legs. You know what I am doing now?"

He whispered into her ear how he was arousing her— which spots he touched, where he kissed her, how his fingers moved. Francesca closed her eyes. She felt warm. She gave in to his touches, slid her hand between her legs, where his mouth now was—or might be. The feelings grew stronger. She was lying on soft sand, while waves of a warm sea splashed against her lower body. The waves would come and go and always left some moisture behind. She touched herself more firmly now, and Dimitri moved more forcefully. The rhythm increased. From far away she saw the wave coming toward her and she was unable to stop it anymore. The water swept over her. Francesca was breathing heavily… and then she relaxed.

She was back to the reality of a dark and silent room.

Now and then the beams of car headlights moved across the ceiling and the walls.

"That was wonderful," Marchenko whispered.

Yes, it was wonderful. She smelled her fingers—yes, it was real, and not a dream—but she was alone in her bed. It would be so nice now if Dimitri could actually hug and hold her. She could imagine it all she wanted, but it was still not the same. And how did her boyfriend experience what had just happened? He could neither smell nor feel, so what really went on in his consciousness? Francesca did not dare ask, because she was afraid of the answers. She was alone, and she had to admit it once and for all. There was just no way around it—it would not end right away, but she would not be able to stand this relationship forever.

December 26, 2048, Tokyo

READY, set, go! When the pedestrian traffic light switched to 'Walk,' Martin and Jiaying pushed through the deluge of thousands as they strode across the large intersection on the western side of Shibuya Station. Among them were men in typical business suits, young Japanese women in colorful dresses, older ladies clad in blouses and skirts, and lots of tourists, who could be easily recognized because they stopped, right in the middle of the street, to take panoramic photos. Martin stood there gaping, while his girlfriend looked at him with amusement. Yesterday, she had explained to him that Tokyo seemed almost quaint compared to the much more modern Shanghai.

Jiaying was right in a certain way. The neon signs on the buildings across the street flashed in many colors, but they were not as elegant as their counterparts in Shanghai. The ones in Tokyo exuded a certain 2000's charm. They actually might not be that old, or even from the previous millennium, but they seemed to be. In any case, they definitely were not new anymore. Martin liked this aspect, since he felt the same way about himself. He cinched his coat even tighter. Tokyo was wet and cold. The fact that the commuter train was heated only increased the feeling, since it made you sweat for a short time and then the cold seemed colder.

Why did Amy select this place for the meeting? Shibuya was fascinating, but there were definitely nicer districts of the city. They were staying at a cute little hotel in Ueno. From their window they could see a large park with a lake. Perhaps, he realized, Amy had not had anything to do with selecting the meeting place. She had told them yesterday they would be meeting a Russian who would make an offer to all of them.

All during the previous evening, Martin and Jiaying had wondered what this meeting could be about, without arriving at any agreed-upon conclusion. In the end, no matter what it was all about, it offered an opportunity to meet their former crewmates again, and Martin was looking forward to that. He could hardly believe it! Jiaying pulled on his right hand to move him forward, but he had stopped again, and turned around without acknowledging her gesture.

"But we are not in a rush, are we?" he asked.

"The traffic signal just turned red, and we have to get out of the intersection."

He nodded and walked faster, even though they were not the last ones blocking the intersection.

"Over there," Jiaying pointed, "we have to follow that street."

A comparatively narrow pedestrian zone lay ahead of them. In the middle there were trees, which gave the area an almost European appearance. However, Martin did not recognize most of the fast food chains and clothing stores that covered three, sometimes even four floors. The rest of the seven-to-eight floor buildings were occupied by offices. They were looking for the building numbered 4776. In Japan, address numbers were not assigned by street, they were distributed across the entire district. Luckily, the navigation app on Martin's phone knew all the addresses. *It should be the fifth entrance on the left,* he assumed. Amy had sent them a digital image of the signs they should find next to the doorbell.

They reached number 4776. Next to the shabby front door there was a panel with about 50 buzzers, almost all of which were labeled in Japanese. *It's good we have Amy's photo,* he thought. The buttons looked as if they had been installed here sometime during the 1950s. Martin pressed the one matching their photo and imagined an old-fashioned bell ringing upstairs. A short time later there was a distinct humming at the door, and Jiaying reacted immediately by pushing against the door to open it. Amy had told them to take the elevator to the sixth floor where someone would be waiting for them.

The pair entered the elevator, and it started moving upward with a creaking sound. Inside it smelled of stale urine, and the walls were smeared with paint. There was definitely no sign of the much-praised Japanese cleanliness here. When they reached the sixth floor they had to manually push the inner metal grating open in order to open the outer door. A manual elevator was something Martin had not seen in a long time. In the hallway outside the elevator, a person was looking out the small window. Once the door opened, she turned around. It was Amy. She first hugged Jiaying and then Martin, both of whom were really glad to see their former commander.

"Welcome," Amy said. "The others are already inside."

Martin gave her a puzzled look.

"No, you are quite punctual—even a bit early. But the others arrived even earlier than you."

"Well, that's a relief," Martin said. He hated being late. He let the two women go first, and they all walked through a dark corridor. A fluorescent light flickered on the ceiling, revealing dull, yellowish paint that was peeling off the walls. Their steps were loud on the worn out linoleum floor. Amy stopped in front of a door at the end of the corridor and knocked in an unusual rhythm. Martin could not see a retina scanner or a keypad to enter an access code. The door had a metal handle, and below it was a huge keyhole. Amy noticed his curiosity.

"Our host is very concerned about security."

He only understood what she meant after they had entered the room. It was about 6 by 6 meters and windowless, but one literally could not see the walls. The place resembled a computer nerd's rec room. Ceiling-high computer cabinets completely obscured the walls and displayed their activities via thousands of colored LEDs. In the center of the room there was a round table, where Hayato, Francesca, and two unknown men were sitting. All of them got up when they noticed the newcomers.

The men stayed inconspicuously in the background while the five friends happily greeted each other.

"Where did you leave Sol?" asked Jiaying, sounding disappointed.

"He is at Hayato's parents," Amy answered. "He would quickly get bored here."

"Too bad. I would love to see him. He must have grown so much."

"Why don't you come over to Ishinomaki later, where Hayato's parents live? We have enough room in our car."

"That is a great idea, right, Martin?" Jiaying looked at him. He was not too excited about meeting more new people, but he could not refuse her wish.

"Certainly," he replied, "but let's listen to what these men have to say first. Everything might change afterward."

THE OLDER OF the two men approached them. "Let me introduce myself. My name is Nikolai Shostakovich. I originally planned to have my business partner, Yuri Dushek, speak with you here first, but as dear Ms. Michaels," he said, pointing at Amy, "left no stone unturned to find out my identity, and was even partially successful in her research, with the aid of a friend at NASA, I decided to participate in our first meeting."

"Excuse me," said Amy, "my name is Ms. Masukoshi now."

Shostakovich gave a dismissive flick of his hand. "We'll stick with 'Ms. Michaels' for the present."

Amy held her tongue, but her former crewmembers knew she was not happy.

"Shostakovich—you mean like the composer?" asked Jiaying, changing the subject and defusing the tension.

The man smiled. "In my country, this Shostakovich is a common name. However, I am indeed a distant relative of Dmitri Dmitriyevich."

"What is this all about?" interjected Martin, waving his hand in a circle that took in all of the computer cabinets. "Those things must be quite powerful," he said. "And then there's this inconspicuous building, even though you surely could afford something better."

"I will be quite frank," Shostakovich said, "so you will realize you can trust me completely. We deliberately chose this low-tech environment to hide from curious eyes. This is an AI-free zone, without a connection to the internet—except for a radio link to another building under our control. This room is shielded against any electronic transmissions going out or coming in—a Faraday cage. You understand?"

"AI free? Then what do you need all this computing power for?" asked Martin skeptically.

"That does not include our own AIs, of course. As you might know, my partner Yuri here is a top AI researcher."

Martin had never heard of Dushek. This could only mean the man did his own research, or worked for an intelligence service.

"This is a small branch office of the company we own. Here we plan our move into new markets, but so far we haven't been very active in Japan. I have to admit we encountered difficulties in this country," he said, now looking at Jiaying, "as our Chinese friends have almost complete control of the local market. But please, do sit down. We do not want to waste your valuable time."

THE FIVE OF them sat around the table. Beside Francesca there was a large suitcase. One of the computer cabinets suddenly moved backward. Through the opening this created came a waiter dressed in livery. He carried a round tray with champagne glasses and two bulbous bottles. Dushek signaled him to come closer.

"Let us drink a toast to the success of this meeting. This is genuine Crimean champagne, ladies and gentlemen!"

Francesca raised her brows, knowing that 'champagne,' by international agreement, can only originate from the Champagne wine region of France.

The waiter distributed the glasses, deftly opened the first bottle, and poured the bubbling liquid into each. Dushek signaled him again and the waiter left, the cabinet moving back into position.

"*Sa Uspekh!* To success!" Dushek raised his glass in a toast to everyone. "Too bad *Tovarish* Marchenko cannot raise a glass with us. At least place him on the table. His being on the floor is so humiliating," The Russian pointed at the suitcase.

Martin noticed Francesca gasp, but then she regained control. She smiled.

"I don't know what you are talking about, gentlemen."

"You can end the cat and mouse game, Francesca," Amy said quietly. "These men know about Marchenko."

The Italian astronaut turned visibly pale.

"No reason to panic, dear guests, we do not intend to harm you. Quite the opposite!" said Dushek.

Francesca still looked tense, and Martin could understand this. She held the handle of the suitcase so firmly that the muscles in her arm bulged out.

"Amy, why didn't you mention this to me?" Francesca's gaze moved back and forth between the former commander and Dushek.

"I did not want to worry you."

Francesca opened her mouth but did not answer Amy.

"You were correct, Ms. Michaels, there really is no reason

for concern. We would like to suggest a deal from which everyone profits."

"I am curious to hear it," Martin blurted out. He wasn't usually so abrupt.

Now Shostakovich was speaking. "Let me first give you a brief overview of my activities. Just so you are confident I will be able to fulfill my side of the deal."

A screen slid downward directly in front of one wall of computers, descending from a slot in the ceiling none of the five had noticed. On the other side of the room a projector turned on, and the logo of the RB Group appeared instantaneously.

"I own 90 percent of the RB Group," Shostakovich explained. "The remaining 10 percent belongs to the Russian state. Yuri's company, which I also supported considerably, is part of the RB Group. Thanks to Yuri I learned of your problem, and that's the reason he is here. But I will tell you more about that later."

Now the screen showed the image of an asteroid, and Shostakovich aimed a laser pointer at a tiny spaceship located on its rocky surface. This showed them how huge the space object must be.

"I own mining rights for the most important asteroids in the vicinity of Earth. You probably know that, according to current law, it is necessary to land on the object you claim. Instead of looking at faraway goals like Mars—as some competitors do—I concentrated on feasible projects. I believe that exploring the solar system should be left to tax-financed agencies. As a businessman I do not need visions, but rather plans that can be realized."

The image zoomed out. Now they saw the Earth orbiting the sun. About 30 blinking dots accompanied the planet. Some moved beyond Earth's orbit, others crossed the path of the home planet.

"I first concentrated on asteroids of the Apollo type, which cross Earth's orbit during their movement around the sun. About 8,000 such objects are currently known, so one can't really say that I have a monopoly."

Shostakovich paused for a moment, then continued. "However, I claimed the asteroids based on how easily they could be reached, picking the low hanging fruit first, so to speak. You have to forgive me for it—it still cost me a ton of cash. My business was close to insolvency. Luckily, the oil prices rose year after year. By now, I am proud to say, I am making a lot of money. I can provide almost any metal and any rare earth at a lower price than mining companies here on Earth."

"I still don't see what this has to do with us," Francesca said. Martin had never seen her appear so obstinate, almost angry.

"Just a moment, Signora Rossi. You will soon understand."

The image changed again. The 30 dots disappeared and were replaced by five others, the orbits of which were clearly more extreme. One got closer to the sun than Mercury, while another one flew beyond Jupiter into the outer solar system.

"Since I plan far ahead, I invest the majority of my profits. Therefore I do research in various areas neglected by state-sponsored sciences, such as genetics and nanotechnology, as well as artificial intelligence. I would be happy to invite you to my research institution. I have also started to occupy some of the more exotic asteroid paths. These are the five dots you see here. I did not have a specific plan for them—at least not until you returned from Enceladus in *ILSE*."

"And what does this plan look like?" asked Amy.

"And particularly, our role in it?" added Francesca.

Another dot appeared on the screen.

"This is the current trajectory of *ILSE*. The ship is slowly moving toward the sun, and it will take about ten months before it gets close enough to burn up. The reason for this delay is that *ILSE* is decelerating quite slowly, and it was not considered necessary to speed up the process. This is good, since you know how much the construction of this spaceship cost. The six Direct Fusion Drives, just the remaining tritium fuel—this would mean literally burning up dozens of billions of dollars. This sum would help my balance sheet nicely. As a businessman, I cannot condone such wastefulness."

"A clever plan," they heard Marchenko's voice say from the suitcase.

"*Tovarish* Marchenko already understands it, of course, despite his currently rather limited hardware. Should I perhaps provide you with an interface for the computers in this room?"

While Shostakovich made this offer, Dushek vigorously shook his head in disapproval.

"Oh, my friend Yuri seems to be against it. He seems to worry you might penetrate his firewalls. An understandable fear, but I know you would never abuse a generously offered guest access this way. I read your file, Dimitri, and I personally know your mentor at Roscosmos."

"No thank you, Shostakovich. I am fine here and do not need anything from you," Marchenko said.

"Oh, well. For you, it might appear like that at the moment. Maybe you will change your opinion in the next sixty seconds. My plan, Dimitri, is to take over *ILSE* with your help."

"It will not work, because any form of remote control has been deactivated in order to prevent something like this."

"I know. We will have to fly there."

"There is currently no spaceship that could catch up with *ILSE*," Marchenko said.

"Yes and no. If we start from Earth, we really stand no chance. But among the asteroids I have claimed is 1566 Icarus, which, true to its name, gets rather close to the sun. In order to receive the mining rights for Icarus, I had to land a spaceship on it. The ship is still there and it flies toward the sun—as a hitchhiker, so to speak. We can reactivate it and then I would transfer you, Dimitri, to the on-board computer. The ship would fly toward *ILSE*, dock with it, and then you go on board and take over control. What do you have to say about that?"

Everyone in the group remained silent. Martin wondered what kind of catch this plan might have. *Technically, it could actually work,* he thought.

"I am pretty sure I know what you get out of this, Shostakovich," Francesca said. "For a rather modest investment you receive, albeit illegally, brand new technology and a functioning spaceship. You could distribute the DFDs among your mining ships and would be far ahead of all competitors, but what about our reward?"

"There is a reason I asked the entire group here, not just Dimitri and you, Signora Rossi. I would like to offer *ILSE* to you for another journey to Enceladus. I think I found a way for you to transfer Dimitri's consciousness back into his body. For that purpose, you would have to first get his body out of the ice ocean."

December 27, 2048, Tokyo

Why should she phone Hayato's mother? Amy wondered for a moment whether she should have Hayato make the call. He was their son, after all. But in the end, his parents would be only half-informed because they did not ask the right questions. She selected the encrypted-transmission mode, even though she did not intend to explain the whole plan in this call.

"*Moshi moshi,*" Mako answered after the second ring.

"*Moshi moshi,*" Amy replied. "It's me, Amy. How are you doing?"

"We are doing fine. Your son has just taken his afternoon nap."

"That's good. Unfortunately we have to stay in Tokyo for at least another day."

"Oh, did something happen?"

"No, we just have to discuss the offer I mentioned to you earlier. We have to make a decision soon, so we all stayed here. We are all going to meet for dinner later to talk things over."

"I understand. For us, it's no problem at all. Take all the time you need. I am glad to have Sol here for a few days. I think he already understands a little bit of Japanese. Tetsuyo always takes him on short walks through the neighborhood. Our grandson does not mind the cold weather at all."

Amy felt an inner glow spread all over her body when she heard her mother-in-law mention Sol. She knew her son was doing fine at his grandparents' house.

"Give Sol a kiss from me. And one from his father, too." She looked at Hayato, who was sitting on the bed of their tiny hotel room, researching something on the internet.

"Of course, Amy. I will tell him the two of you are coming back tomorrow."

"I am sure we will work it all out."

"I am very curious to hear what you will decide. Sol's welfare will certainly play an important role in this."

Yes, it will, Amy thought, but she did not say anything, considering the weighty implications.

"I'll call you back tomorrow morning."

"Talk to you then," Mako said.

Amy pushed the button to end the call.

"Hayato, we should be going."

HAYATO HAD EARLIER ASKED colleagues to recommend a restaurant in the Shibuya district, where only Japanese would be spoken. Their suggestion was a Korean-style grill, a cuisine that was, for the time being, very popular in Japan. It was also unlikely that tourists would show up there, so he and Amy reserved a table for 7 p.m.

The punctual Yamanote commuter train line took them to the Shibuya district. They left the train station and went eastward into an area with high-rise buildings. Hayato seemed to know the exact route and walked briskly along. He must have researched the directions thoroughly in advance because he and Amy arrived early. The bar and grill was located in a basement, and the neon sign above the entrance door read 'Korean Barbecue.' While entering, they both had to duck to avoid hitting the crossbeam above them. Amy was surprised at this, for the building could not have been more than 20 years old.

Hayato made the necessary arrangements with a waiter and ordered *bulgogi* and beer to be delivered when everyone had arrived. A waiter guided them into a room closed off by paper-covered, movable screens. Being the first in the group to arrive, they proceeded to take off their jackets and shoes, and sat cross-legged in front of the low table. Amy was glad to feel the warmth generated by the gas burners in the middle of the table. They were covered by a wire mesh on which the marinated meat would be arranged to cook until it was done to their taste.

Francesca arrived, once again carrying her suitcase, and Amy still felt strange about the idea that Marchenko was actually inside it. In some odd way this seemed cruel and hard to even imagine—an entire human being stuffed into this leather container. Looked at from another perspective, she knew some might see it as humorous.

The restaurant owner automatically guided Martin and Jiaying to the table. If there were three tourists here already, the others obviously also belonged to them. Since Hayato was part of the group, no one seemed to wonder how they ended up in a place that was not listed in any known travel guide. Hayato had once explained to Amy that the Japanese preferred to socially interact among their own. In bars meant for locals, no one would speak English with you, he claimed, even if they knew the language.

The waiter did not hesitate for long. He and Hayato nodded at each other, and soon the food and drink arrived. There was meat, meat, meat, and a few vegetables.

Amy was worried. "I didn't even ask whether we have any vegetarians among us." On board *ILSE* no one had been, but now...

However, all of them speared meat with their skewers and her worries seemed unfounded. Martin gave her a big smile, and Amy remembered him being a picky eater during their missions together. This was probably the first time during his stay in Japan he would get to eat his fill. She smiled.

For five minutes, no one said anything. Amy looked at Francesca's suitcase. How would it feel to be so excluded from their community? What was Marchenko doing right now, while they enjoyed each other's company? Did he still consider himself part of the group?

Hayato raised a can of beer. *"Kanpai!"* he said, and they all toasted each other. Francesca was the first to get to the point. Amy could imagine her feeling the strongest urge to speak.

The Italian pilot's voice was surprisingly soft and hesitant. "What do you think of the offer we received yesterday? It's... nonsense, isn't it?"

Amy realized Francesca hoped someone would contradict her. She was about to answer when her husband spoke up.

"No, based upon what I can see now, the plan is realistic —except for the final promise of reuniting Dimitri with his body. We would have to examine that more closely. But taking over *ILSE*, yes, it could work that way."

"But... would you go on such a journey again?" Francesca looked at them, one after the other.

"I would agree right away," Jiaying said. "I definitely want to return to space, and this would be a real challenge."

"But also completely illegal," Martin said. "We would be hijacking *ILSE*, and your country could throw you in jail for that."

"These people are not stupid, Martin. If we successfully return, with a living Marchenko, they would not dare touch me."

"If we are successful," said Martin, pausing to think. "Then, maybe. But if something goes wrong, we are on our own, and no one would help us."

"Let us look at this pragmatically," Hayato interjected. "No matter whether we sail under the flag of NASA or become pirates, we are always alone way out there. You saw that during our first trip—because no one *can* help us, what does it matter if someone *wants* to?"

"What do you think, Amy? Would you be our commander again?" asked Francesca.

Amy pondered the question—it had come too early for her to consider. If she was on her own, she would have agreed to it right away. But there was Sol to think about, and they would have to decide to leave him behind or bring him along. Both prospects seemed wrong to Amy, and she would have to discuss it with Hayato, away from the others. They were Sol's parents and might have to make the decision. Therefore she asked in turn, "And what about you, Francesca?"

"Yes, right away!" Amy noticed Francesca was about to burst into tears. She placed a hand on Amy's lower arm. "There are so many reasons," Francesca explained, "why I would go on board right away. First reason, of course, because I love Dimitri. It... it is not the same to love a digital consciousness. I imagined it to be different, simpler. But most of all I would come along because I owe it to him. I am alive because of what he did!"

Jiaying looked at Martin. "It is similar with you, right?"

He flinched. "That's true. I am glad you, of all people, mentioned it. Still, I have the feeling the previous voyage took me to my limits. Couldn't we just stay here and enjoy life?"

Jiaying shook her head. "I am sorry, honey, but I would regret it all my life if we abandoned Marchenko."

"What you are saying is all well and good," Marchenko's voice said from the suitcase. "How about asking me? Perhaps I do not want you to cram yourself into a narrow metal can for another two years and cruise through infinity."

"Then we will ask you now," Amy replied. "Do you want this? Do you want your body back?"

"I do not know," Marchenko said. "My current state has some advantages—I am immortal! I know everything, and what I do not know I can find out faster than any human could. The only thing unclear to me is whether I could stand being in this state forever and ever. I would have to watch

Francesca die, like all the people I know. And would I still be able to preserve my human nature? But even if I decided I would prefer to return to my own body, could I take the responsibility for making you risk your lives?"

"The journey will not be that dangerous," Hayato said.

"It does not matter. I already notice how this decision is taking all of you to a crossroads in your life. Amy and you would have to leave Sol behind, or one of you would have to stay with him. Jiaying and Martin, your paths might diverge if you both come to different conclusions, and it would all be my fault."

"Just a moment, Marchenko," Martin said. "That's not how this works. If you had not saved Francesca and me, Jiaying and I would not be facing this question right now. So don't talk to me about guilt. We are all adults who can be responsible for our own decisions. Maybe some of us need to take a little bit longer to decide, and Shostakovich should give us this time. Jiaying and Francesca have already made clear decisions, and during the last part of our previous journey we saw that two people are basically enough. So the rescue mission can happen, no matter what."

"That is a nice final word to this difficult discussion," Amy said, "I will relay this to Shostakovich. Then he can initiate the necessary measures. And whoever has doubts still has enough time to come to a final decision. Concerning Sol, I will have a private talk with Hayato. Martin and Jiaying, you should find it easier to reach a compromise just between the two of you. And now let us focus on the tasty food."

"I am going to order a few more beers," Hayato said, "or does anyone want *sake*?"

December 30, 2048, Akademgorodok

SOME THINGS NEVER CHANGE, Amy thought. The entire group passed through immigration control without too much of an issue—until the official decided to specifically engage her in a long conversation. Judging from his grim expression, he considered the American woman to be a spy, if not an outright terrorist. Amy shook her head. How would she have been treated here, if Shostakovich had not arranged for the special visa? Or was this visa the reason for the treatment she encountered? Whichever it was, she knew too little about Russian attitudes to guess.

At least when Amy finally reached the luggage carousel, her suitcase was already there, and she found the others waiting for her. In front of the exit, a large sign in several languages welcomed them to Siberia. Immediately after expressing their general willingness to travel to Enceladus, the group had received the invitation to Novosibirsk. She would have liked to see her son once more before her trip here, but she had only managed another phone call. Shostakovich obviously wanted to show them the resources he controlled. Would this really help the members of their group who were still undecided? Amy wasn't sure. She would have readily agreed to the planned mission long ago, if she did not have to leave Sol behind.

A wide, automatic door opened to the outside, and immediately the stinging Siberian air hit her face. Shostakovich had not exaggerated. It really was cold! Luckily, they had gone shopping together in Tokyo for the right outerwear suitable for this severe climate. Amy saw how all the others pulled their caps down and covered their chins with scarves, as if on command.

As expected, a man was waiting for them in front of the terminal building. It must have been easy for him to identify their group. Speaking adequate English, the man identified himself as Vassili, and they in turn introduced themselves. Vassili looked the way Amy imagined a Russian bodyguard would. He was brawny, with a nose that looked like it had been broken more than once, and in spite of the cold, he was clad in a business suit. He greeted each of them in turn, and while carrying the two heaviest suitcases, he led them to a vehicle resembling a jeep. Amy did not recognize the brand of the vehicle. The logo on the radiator grill represented a kind of stylized sailboat.

The vehicle had three rows of seats, so there was enough space for all of them. Vassili wanted to put Francesca's suitcase in the luggage compartment, but she refused the offer. He then let her have the front passenger seat.

"It's more comfortable there with the suitcase," he said with a smile that she returned in lieu of saying thank you.

"Our trip will be only 50 kilometers," Vassili announced as he put on his seatbelt. "There is a traffic jam on Gromova Road, but it should not take us much longer than an hour," he added. "Please buckle in—the roads are rather slick."

Like the others, Amy followed his request. Maybe she could get some sleep in the meantime. During the flight she had not been able to shut her eyes, because she kept thinking about Sol, Hayato, and the future. She reached into her coat pocket and felt Sol's photo, but she did not take it out to glance at her son. She was afraid she might cry again. *I've got so much time, and nothing has been decided yet*, she thought, but there was the lingering feeling she was just fooling herself. Or rather, trying to.

She looked at the others. All of them were busy taking off their thick coats to be more comfortable in the warmth generated inside the vehicle. Martin, who was sitting just behind her, acted like he had just fallen in love and would not leave Jiaying's side. Next to Amy, Hayato had his eyes closed. Yesterday and the day before, the married couple kept discussing all possible options for so long he had finally had enough of it. Amy understood she had to decide herself first which solution would be acceptable to her. Not seeing her son for two years did not appear to be such an option. She wiped away a tear from the corner of her eye.

It was light outside, and the sunlight reflected on the glittering snow. The city was busy, and people wrapped in cloth and fur walked around in pursuit of their various tasks. The traffic in the streets was quite heavy and looked chaotic at first, but then one noticed the rudiments of a system behind it. Amy closed her eyes for a few minutes, but she could not fall asleep.

"We are crossing the river Ob," Vassili announced after half an hour. "To the right is the reservoir." The vehicle drove along the crest of a dam, which bordered an enormous lake covered by a layer of ice.

"You should come here in the summer," Vassili said. "In summer it is quite lovely here, like being at the seaside. Only the gnats are a bother." He seemed to be remembering something, as he soundlessly moved his lips.

The rhythmic beeping of the car's turn signal woke Amy. She must have dozed off after all. Their driver Vassili wanted to turn into a side street, but the oncoming traffic would not stop. Finally, he simply made the turn. Amy was frightened, but the driver of the oncoming car hit the brakes in time. Soon they found themselves driving through a dense, tall forest. The fir trees were covered by snow to a height of a meter or more. This was what Amy always imagined the

Siberian taiga to look like. All she needed was for a bear to show up.

"Akademgorodok is a bit distant from the hustle and bustle of the city," Vassili said. "This gives the little town its very own atmosphere. People can really focus on science here. By the way, I am the director of the former Institute for Plasma Research. Former, as it is now part of the RB Group. And if you have any questions concerning plasma physics... I have to admit I asked to be the one to pick you up, because I am very interested in the drive concepts used in *ILSE*. The DFDs are... sorry, I did not want to surprise you like this."

Amy nodded. "It's best you speak with our colleagues Neumaier or Masukoshi, as they know the most about fusion drives."

Their driver pointed ahead. "There is our destination."

They were driving toward a twelve story, tower-like building. It had a shorter front part, topped with a glass pyramid. On the roof of the building they saw a glass dome, which was at least twice as big as the pyramid. The whole thing exuded a Soviet-era character, but it could hardly be a hundred years old.

"This is the main entrance to the university," Vassili explained. "The tower was finished in 2015, when this institution still belonged to the state."

"It is no longer a state university?" asked Amy.

"In the late 2030s, at the height of the Russian state crisis, the RB Group bought it, the entire premises. Today, Akademgorodok is the private research center of the Group."

The vehicle stopped in front of a barrier, which seemed to confirm his words. Vassili showed his ID and a piece of paper, which probably described his mission. The guards saluted him. Amy saw they were armed with Russian-made AMB-17 assault rifles—she recognized these weapons from her time in the army.

"And did the researchers like this change?" she asked, continuing the discussion.

"Not all, but most of them. If you want to advance in the state university system, this is the wrong place. But there is no place like here to do research without having to worry about anything. Funds, permissions, patience—there is plenty of that here. The only condition is that your research belongs to the Group, and *it* decides what will be published."

"A paradise for researchers," Amy said.

"One could really say that," Vassili said. "I estimate in some fields we are ten years ahead of the rest of the world."

"You don't publish and you don't give anything back."

"Well, one might think this unfair. But to be honest, what state-funded science publishes worldwide is years behind our research. We only read scientific journals out of historical interest."

The vehicle took a tight turn and then stopped directly in front of the tower.

"Welcome to Akademgorodok," Vassili said. "My boss is expecting you in his office. We will be together again when I give you a short tour around here."

SHE HAD to suppress a yawn while Shostakovich gave his little welcome speech. There was a buffet waiting in his large office. Amy asked for a cup of coffee and went to look out the window. She could see white treetops all the way to the horizon. *Somewhere behind us must be the Ob reservoir,* Amy concluded. Off to her left was the city of Novosibirsk. It was about 3:30 p.m. and the sun was already low on the horizon. She was looking roughly northeast from its highest floor, and the high-rise cast a long shadow.

"Would you come with me?" asked Shostakovich's unnamed companion, motioning them forward. Finally, their tour of the premises was beginning, but Amy was longing to take a nap.

"You can leave your coats in my office," said

Shostakovich, "since we can reach all the labs through tunnels. Ms. Rossi, may my colleague Vitali take your suitcase? He is going to accompany us."

Francesca stiffened, tightening her grip at first, but then she shrugged and gave in to the request. The group walked toward the elevator. Shostakovich touched the control panel with a key card and then pressed the *2* button. The elevator took them to a diffusely lit corridor. Amy was glad they did not have to go out into the cold again, but at the same time she felt uneasy about not knowing exactly where they were going. If she remembered the position of the elevator correctly, they would be walking roughly northward in what appeared to be a completely straight corridor. Somehow Amy could not fully trust Shostakovich. From a rational perspective she should be feeling safe, since she had no proof that their Russian host was being disingenuous. Nevertheless, she instinctively reached for Hayato's hand and continued counting her steps as they all walked to their eventual destination.

There was a door at the end of the corridor, and it opened just before they reached it. Vassili greeted them— their driver who was also a plasma physicist.

"I am going to accompany you through my institute," he said.

No one answered.

They walked up a stairway and reached a hall the size of an aircraft hangar. It smelled of engine oil, and their ears could not miss the constant deep humming sound.

"Those are the rectifiers you're hearing," Vassili explained. "You will get used to it."

A giant machine took up about two-thirds of the hall. There were coils, thick pipes, transformers, and lots of warning signs. Amy immediately thought of a reactor.

"This is our pride and joy," Vassili said, "a fusion reactor based on the open trap principle." Martin and Hayato suddenly stopped as one. If this was in fact true, then Vassili had reason to be proud.

"But..." Martin began.

Vassili interrupted him. "I know, the open trap principle is considered obsolete. Everybody wants to build a tokamak. We have always said a fusion reactor should have a simple structure. That is why we chose open trap. It has two magnetic mirrors on the sides, bouncing the hot plasma back and forth, which is sufficient. The ring of the tokamak is much too complicated. No wonder there are often breaches."

Amy had read about this before. The two test reactors built according to the tokamak principle, one in Europe and the other in China, experienced dangerous accidents, so-called breaches that almost completely destroyed experiments that had cost billions.

"This reactor is working and produces electricity. A lot of electricity," Vassili said proudly.

"Then why do you not sell the design? You could solve the world's energy problems," Hayato said.

"That is a business decision. We need a lot of energy for our research, and if we generate it ourselves, it will not be so noticeable. Otherwise, the entire world would know a powerful fusion reactor is located here. I will show you in a moment."

Amy looked at Shostakovich, who stood next to Vassili, hands in pockets and smiling stoically. They left the hall through a gate. Behind it there was a smaller hall. Shostakovich hurried ahead of them and pressed a few buttons on a control panel. Spotlights turned on. Amy recognized three pipes, with a diameter of at least four meters, that looked like oversized telescopes.

"This is the future of space travel," Shostakovich said, "Have you heard of the StarShot program, which wants to accelerate miniature spaceships by using lasers, and send them toward faraway stars? This is our own version of that program. For this reason we need the energy of the fusion reactor."

The thick pipes must be the lasers, Amy thought.

"Can the lasers be aimed?" asked Martin.

"Most certainly!" said Shostakovich with a smile. "I know what you are trying to say. 'If we want to shoot a spaceship measuring a few centimeters to the stars, we have to be able to aim our laser guns.' But you are right in your assumption— we could aim them at other things too."

"Aircraft, rockets, alien spaceships," Martin listed.

"For instance," the Russian man said. "Or perhaps cities."

"You want to..."

"Yes, to accelerate our starships efficiently, we also need such lasers in space. We launch them from Earth, and then there are additional impulses from orbit, as well as from the orbits of Mars, Jupiter, and Saturn."

"If your government knew of the military power you could wield with this..." Martin said.

"Then it would have reoccupied this campus a long time ago… or maybe not. Perhaps it did not want to know." Shostakovich smiled. "But that is not our intention. I firmly believe mankind must make its way to the stars, and this technology makes it possible."

"I would prefer if you pursued this vision in cooperation with researchers from all over the world," Amy said, expressing her unease.

"I would prefer it that way, too, dear Amy Michaels. But you know the different nations would never agree on someone being allowed to launch such a laser gun into space. That is why I cannot ask for permission."

"And if we betray your plans?" she asked.

"That would be a pity. But I believe you will understand. And then there would be the issue of the illegal AI your pilot likes to carry around in a suitcase."

"I still don't understand what our role is supposed to be," Amy said, though she had a hunch.

"Ah, I can see you do already know it," Shostakovich replied. "*ILSE* will transport a laser and place it on Enceladus."

"The ship is not suitable for it."

"On the last journey, the spaceship transported a submarine called *Valkyrie*. The laser you will take with you has roughly the same dimensions."

December 31, 2048, Akademgorodok

THE BREAKFAST BUFFET overflowed with expensive delicacies, such as caviar and 'Crimean champagne,' which fit Amy's stereotypes. But she also saw fresh strawberries, which she would not have expected to find in Siberia.

Shostakovich lodged them in his private five-star hotel, which was not listed in any directory. The hotel was meant for the family members who visited the researchers at Akademgorodok. Of course there was a large *banya*, Russian for 'sauna,' and an Olympic-size swimming pool. In addition there was an indoor golf course, a shooting range, and a spa that featured massage, beautician, and hair salon services, which all guests could use free of charge. *A clever strategy*, Amy thought. *This makes the families happy to come, and the scientists won't be itching to leave ASAP.*

The waiter had seated the group at a booth located in an alcove of the dining room. Soft music was playing in the background as they quietly discussed what they had seen yesterday. Amy would not put it past Shostakovich to bug them, but their low voices would be hard to understand due to the background music.

"I assumed this wasn't primarily about getting hold of *ILSE*," Francesca said, who was sharing Amy's distrust.

"At least he did not lie," Hayato said. "He needs the

spaceship for the transport. His own fleet will only go as far as Earth's moon. Plus the lasers must be maintained."

"But why did he not place them on asteroids? Do you remember the diagram of orbital parameters he showed to us? Some of them fly way beyond the orbit of Jupiter."

"That is true, Jiaying," Hayato replied. "But it is probably more complicated to combine them. Let us assume a mini-spaceship is launched from an Earth orbit. Then it must receive an additional push at regular intervals. This would not work if the particular asteroid that came next in the sequence just happens to be behind the sun at the necessary moment."

Jiaying contradicted him. "You would have the same problem with planets and their moons."

"The real issue is actually the impulse," Martin explained. "What happens if you stand on a skateboard and throw something forward? You roll backward."

Amy had to smile. Martin had almost certainly never been on a skateboard, but he really knew his theory and, surprisingly, was good at explaining concepts like this one.

"The light particles emitted by the laser carry an impulse," Martin continued, "so the asteroid where the laser is located would receive an impulse in the opposite direction. The laser beam has to hit a target with a diameter of a few centimeters from a distance of several hundred thousand kilometers. This would not work if its base moves erratically during the shot. Moons are much heavier than the asteroids belonging to the RB Group, so the change in impulse would have a much smaller effect."

Hayato patted Martin on the back. "Good explanation, dear colleague."

"Those are just details," Amy said. "To me, the question of whether or not we can trust Shostakovich is much more important. Will he keep his agreements? Does he have plans he did not mention?"

"Oh, I hope I can answer those questions today," they heard the voice of the Russian say, as he approached their table from behind. Amy turned around. The man was smiling, and next to him stood a woman who could not have been more than 25 years old. She was slender, almost lanky, with short blonde hair and very blue eyes.

"Let me introduce Valentina Shukina. She is one of my best engineers. Valentina will accompany us on today's tour."

"I assumed you would take us to the airport now," said Amy, looking at her watch. "I would like to be back with my son by midnight."

"I understand, Ms. Michaels, and I promise to keep to this deadline," Shostakovich said. "If necessary, I will take you back to Sendai in my private jet. From there it is only an hour to Ishinomaki, if I am not mistaken."

FIFTEEN MINUTES later they had all finished their breakfasts, and once again they were led into a tunnel. This time, Amy did not count her steps. The first stop was the information technology lab. Even laypersons would have recognized it by the computer cabinets and large monitors. Valentina took on the role of tour guide, while Shostakovich kept in the background. They also saw Dushek again, but he, too, left the stage to Valentina.

"Our IT lab mainly deals with issues involving artificial intelligence," the young woman began. "We decided to work without any restrictions here. There is no prohibition on cloning. Therefore, we do not have to teach each new AI from the ground up. Imagine if a nursery was only allowed to grow trees from seeds. That would be very inefficient. Instead, we use—metaphorically speaking—cuttings and the technique of grafting. This way, things an AI learned do not have to be relearned by its successor."

Martin listened with his mouth agape. "That's like babies being born with all of their parents' knowledge," he said to the others. "Mankind would take a huge step forward."

"That applies to our AIs," Valentina said, and Amy could detect the pride in her voice.

"But you couldn't sell these AIs to any industrial nation which joined the UN Convention," Martin remarked.

"That is correct. Yet the market is big enough, and we enjoy a kind of monopoly."

"What about *the singularity?* Wouldn't this raise the risk drastically?"

Valentina smiled haughtily. "Yes, the singularity—the point at which everything changes, and when machines learn to think. I don't think this poses such a grave danger. At least nothing indicates it so far. We make the algorithms more and more powerful, but they do not become as clever as a human. They can solve problems better and faster, and a lot of money can be made through this, but they do not become creative or develop a consciousness—like your Marchenko here." She pointed at Francesca's suitcase. "But even if the singularity came true, it would be best if we reached that point first, and not our competitors."

Martin shook his head in disapproval but did not say anything.

"By the way, the computer sits below us in a large water tank, which provides cooling and radiation shielding," the Russian woman said.

They left the lab through another corridor and reached a kind of workshop.

"Please come closer." Valentina guided the group forward. She stood in front of a large table that had a metal frame. "Look there!"

Something was moving in the center of the table.

"Like little ants," Amy said.

"Just take one," Valentina replied. "They are not dangerous."

Amy reached over the table, picked up one of the tiny objects, and placed it on her palm. It was not an ant. It wasn't an animal at all, but a machine. It had six or eight limbs that were constantly moving. Amy looked more closely. The arms or legs—or whatever they were—did not move aimlessly. They swept across a part of the creature. No, this was not just a part of itself, it was almost the same ant, only smaller. The thing was making a copy of itself!

"Wow," Amy said, and for the first time here in Akademgorodok she was truly amazed.

"These are our fabricators," Valentina explained. "They must be about the twelfth generation?" She gave Shostakovich a questioning look and he nodded. "Yes, the twelfth," she said. "Right now they can only make copies of themselves. Our first goal is to shrink them even further. And then we want to learn how to program them. This will revolutionize manufacturing."

"When?" asked Martin.

"In twenty years, at the earliest," Shostakovich said. "Currently we could compare it with the time when the mass production of automobiles was developed. In that sense, it was still a long way from there to self-driving cars."

"Nanomachines," Francesca said.

"We try to avoid that term," Shostakovich replied. "It has negative connotations from science fiction. This here is reality, not sci-fi. These are fabricators, the means of production of the 22nd century."

"How small are they supposed to become?"

"Our goal is to let them manipulate individual atoms. Then they can produce practically anything from almost any material."

"What about the dangers?"

"Do not be silly, Signora Rossi. Even if we use genetic algorithms to optimize them, they are machines, dumb, inanimate matter that only does something due to our programming. Fabricators are no more dangerous than a stone ax. But of course our ancestors could kill their neighbors with a stone ax. The maker of a stone ax could not prevent that inevitability."

Francesca did not seem to be convinced. "I have an idea why you are publishing so few of your results."

"Genetic algorithms?" asked Jiaying.

"Excuse me, that was a buzzword I used accidentally,"

Shostakovich explained. "It has nothing to do with genetics, but we shall cover that in a moment. No, we make the machines compete for resources. The survivors are the ones that duplicate themselves more quickly. We noticed this also advances miniaturization, since smaller machines require less material."

No one spoke. They were either impressed with how vigorously research was pushed forward here—or they were shocked speechless. There seemed to be no fundamental constraints here. Could they rely on such a partner? Probably yes, if both sides could achieve their goals without standing in each other's way.

"I would like to show you another lab," Valentina said as she resumed her role as guide.

They walked through a subterranean corridor to a kind of airlock, where they had to put on special suits with oxygen masks.

"Do not worry, this is not for your protection but for ours —to prevent contamination of the lab by our visitors," Valentina said. With identical suits and the masks on, it was difficult to distinguish individual members of the group. Only the height gave any indication of who was who. Then a few scientists joined them, so now Amy was completely confused. At least their tour guide identified herself by speaking up.

"You might be surprised—if not shocked—by what you are about to see. I can assure you, though, that none of the animals here are suffering. Animal welfare has the highest priority for us."

What was that introduction supposed to mean? Amy was almost afraid when the door opened, but then she saw what resembled a completely normal lab. Poultry, consisting mostly of different breeds of chickens, sat in clean cages. The animals seemed well cared for, had enough space, and everything was spotlessly clean. A person in a protective suit approached them.

"This is Oleg. He is responsible for our genetic engineering program." Through the mask, Valentina's voice sounded strange. Oleg raised a hand and waved.

"In this lab we attempt to combine traits that are practical, but would never be combined the normal way. It is a real pity that one species might develop the ability to withstand cold, but that is denied to other species who might also profit from it."

Oleg pointed at two rows of cages. "These chickens, for instance, are adapted to cold. But warm temperatures do not harm them, as you can see here. Follow me."

He led the group to a heavy metal door and opened it. Icy air blew at them. "This is our low-temperature lab. You see the animals? They are just as mobile at minus 40 degrees as they are at plus 20 degrees. They even lay eggs." The man pointed at a basket filled with eggs. "I assure you the eggs might be frozen, but they are edible."

"And the treatment has no side effects?" asked Amy.

"It is not a treatment in the narrowest sense. We change the germ line," Oleg replied. "The animals are born this way. And yes, the high basal energy rate in the cold does reduce their lifespan. And require extra food. But you surely know the lifespan of poultry in industrial farming is shorter than that of animals in the wild."

The enthusiasm of the group was restrained. Maybe they had reached the limit of what they could take in at one time. Amy was really longing for a bed, and for Sol.

"You probably wonder why I am showing you this." No one nodded, but Oleg continued anyway. "There is a place that offers a great challenge to humanity: outer space. This science could mean no reduced calcium content in the bones, a better tolerance against radiation. Those would clearly be ideal traits for cosmonauts. We believe humanity has to alter the species in order to become a spacefaring race. That is what our research program is all about. Thank you for your attention." Oleg then took a bow.

Valentina led them back to the locker room. Amy felt the stress of the last few days. *Let's just get out of here*, she thought.

"Hayato, could you please help me?" asked Francesca. Her suit had somehow gotten tangled with the suitcase. Hayato briefly opened the case and closed it again.

"Thanks, that's better," Francesca said.

At the exit, Shostakovich was waiting. "A driver will take you to the airport. I am very curious to hear about your individual decisions. What did you think of Valentina, by the way?"

No one said anything, so Amy sacrificed herself. "She seems highly competent."

"Well, that is very good to hear, because Valentina is my daughter. She will accompany you on your journey to Enceladus. You will need someone who knows how to handle the laser."

"That won't be necessary," Martin said. "I am familiar with the 5-kilowatt laser of *ILSE*."

Amy noticed Jiaying giving her boyfriend a surprised look. Had he just decided to come along? Or was he trying to keep a stranger from being on board?

"I am afraid your knowledge would not be sufficient, Mr. Neumaier," Shostakovich replied. "We have a complex system consisting of a fusion reactor, energy storage, and a laser. I would have to train you for two years, and we do not have that much time."

"That was an interesting bit of information to save for right at the end," Amy said. "When are we supposed to get started?"

"As soon as you are ready. We will send Marchenko to the Icarus asteroid via radio data transmission, and while he is on an intercept course for *ILSE*, you will be traveling toward the rendezvous point in one of my small spaceships. The sooner we begin, the better. Maybe by the end of next week?"

Amy shivered, even though the room was rather warm. She would have only a few days to make a decision, but at the same time, she felt as if the die had been cast long ago.

January 2, 2049, West Virginia

OF COURSE HIS father had been excited when he announced his visit. This played through Martin's mind as he drove along the freshly-coated asphalt road that accessed the research institution. Upon arrival, Martin had to stop at the sentry barrier that stood at the entrance. He showed his ID to the security guard.

"Welcome, Mr. Neumaier." the guard said, "Your father is expecting you in the Jansky Lab. Ask for directions over there at the gate, if you need them," the man said, pointing toward the west. Martin steered the rental car along the narrow road. Was it really a good idea to ask his father, of all people? He shook his head. Maybe not, but it couldn't hurt, either. Anyway, he was looking forward to seeing his 'old man' again.

After parking the car, Martin headed to the Jansky Lab. The building was surrounded by scaffolding, an indication of ongoing renovations. A middle-aged blonde looked through a window next to the entrance door. She must have seen him coming and waved him toward her.

"Come on, sweetie," she called.

Sweetie? What's up with that? Martin approached her cautiously, but she didn't seem threatening.

"So, you are the gorgeous son of the boss!" the woman remarked. When Martin got closer to her, he immediately noticed the heavy makeup and an overpowering rose-scented perfume.

"Yes, I guess that must be me. Though as far as gorgeous is concerned..." He gazed down at his body.

"Oh, and he is even modest. How sweet. Wait here, I'm coming out and will take you to your father."

"That's not necessary." Martin said, "Really, I can find him on my own." But the woman was not to be denied, and was already on her way to guide him. As they walked through the building, she chattered nonstop at him. Martin was sorely tempted to put his fingers in his ears to block her prattle, but he was too polite to do so.

After five seemingly-endless minutes, they finally reached a door and the woman opened it. Martin noticed a man working at a desk. Startled, the man abruptly jumped up from his chair. It was Robert, his father.

"Mary, I have asked you to knock first," Robert said, slightly annoyed, but then he recognized his son. "Oh. Thank you very much, Mary." He turned toward Martin and they hugged each other. "It's so great that you could make it... and a belated Happy New Year!"

Martin realized he had forgotten to call his father beforehand. "The last few days have been very stressful," he said.

Robert nodded. "And you didn't bring Jiaying? What a pity."

"No, I would like to talk with you about something concerning her. I am sorry to jump to the issue right away, but it concerns me, too."

"Should we take a little walk in the woods?"

Martin looked toward the hallway. The door was still open and Mary had disappeared only a moment ago. Robert noticed his cautious gaze and smiled understandingly. "Don't worry, there is a back way out."

A few minutes later their steps crunched through the snow. It was cloudy, and the forest shimmered in various hues of gray. It looked like Christmas, and Martin wondered why it struck him this way.

"You wanted to celebrate Christmas together, the three of you, didn't you?" asked Robert.

"Oh… the miscarriage. Let's not discuss that. Jiaying decided to repress it and I'm following her wishes. There's no issue between us about it."

"But maybe it will become one later."

"Who knows? Right now I am worried about something else. We received an offer we cannot refuse."

He told his father about Nikolai Shostakovich and the billionaire's plans.

"That does sound very exciting. I would agree right away," Robert said.

"You see, for me the answer isn't quite so simple," Martin said. "During the last few months, I realized I enjoy the work in my office. I lived in that tin can for two years. Enough is enough."

"If you're so sure about it, you should stay here on Earth, of course."

Martin did not answer. There was a pause. In the distance they heard the call of a blue jay.

"You are not really so sure, I see," his father finally said. "I am starting to guess why you came to me. Back then I decided to follow a different path which took me away from your mother."

"Even though I was in the equation," Martin added. "There must have been very important reasons."

"If that's supposed to be a question, it's not fair," Robert replied. "Yes, back then those reasons seemed important to me. Today they don't any longer, and if I'd known then what I know today, I believe I would have decided differently. But you cannot apply that to your situation. You can't know what is going to happen."

"Yes, that's my problem. Should I join an expedition I don't want to be on, just to be close to Jiaying?"

"If you hoped I would give you some decisive advice, I am going to disappoint you. I think Jiaying needs you, just like your mother and you needed me back then. But if you go

BRANDON Q. MORRIS

along, against your inclination, the voyage could become your worst nightmare."

"What are you trying to say?" asked Martin.

"I can tell you how I arrived at my decision back in those days. It sounds absurd, but my father taught me the method."

Martin smiled. "Okay... it sounds absurd. How does it work?"

Robert reached into his pocket. "You flip a coin. Heads you stay—tails you go."

"Just a moment. Did you flip a coin to decide whether to leave us?" Martin wasn't sure whether to be amused or shocked.

"Yes, but it's not like you think."

"I can't have my life decided by chance."

"Chance determines so much in our lives, so one more occasion doesn't really matter."

Martin exhaled, and his breath formed a cloud in the frosty air.

"I don't know," he said.

"That's the very reason to do it this way." Robert held out the coin.

"You flip it," Martin said.

"No, or else you will blame me if things go wrong."

"Okay." Martin took the coin, threw it upward with his right hand, caught it and enclosed it in his left hand. He then quickly flipped both palm and coin onto the back of his right hand. He hesitated, the coin sandwiched.

"Don't you want to know?" his father asked.

Martin shook his head.

"Do you already know it?"

He shook his head again.

"Then take away the hand that covers it."

"I don't dare to."

"It's just a coin."

"True." Martin lifted his hand. He saw it was tails.

"Congratulations. You are going back into space!"

Martin stared at the coin.

"How are you feeling about it?" asked Robert.

"I don't know." Martin listened to himself. "But I think it feels... good."

"Really?"

"Yes, it is right and proper. I am going to accompany Jiaying. That is my path."

"I am glad about it."

"Do you think I would have felt differently if the coin had shown heads?"

"I don't know. Perhaps a parallel universe came into being during the coin flip, one in which you stay behind."

"If this were a novel, I would ask the author to tell the second version of the story, too."

"You read too many fairy tales as a kid, Martin."

"It's called fantasy."

"Life is no novel, no matter the genre," his father said.

January 3, 2049, Ishinomaki

Twilight still dominated the day. When Amy woke up, the night had seemed to be on the wane, but that had not changed perceptibly in the last six hours. She breathed to the rhythm of her steps while walking up the slight incline to the Ozaki lookout point. Amy gazed to the side. Hayato, whose breath came out in clouds like hers, was staring at the ground. Now and then he touched her arm to warn her of roots sticking out that could trip her up. Sol was with Hayato's parents, where he was happy. The two of them had decided on the walk so they could discuss the future without being disturbed.

Now the forest retreated. The sandy path ended further in the low underbrush, two meters from the edge of the cliff line. It was here that someone had placed a simple wooden bench, so they were able to sit down. Amy had been sure they would enjoy the wonderful view together, and she was not disappointed. *The Japanese really have a knack for this kind of detail*, she thought as she took in the panorama before her. Without moving, she could see the harbor of Ishinomaki to their right and the open sea to their left. The horizon was hidden behind low clouds, but nevertheless they could clearly see the other side of the bay. Amy imagined another couple just sitting down on a bench over there. What might they be talking about?

The Pacific, which spread before them, was true to its name today. The water was smooth as a mirror, but that was not always the case. Hayato's parents spoke of their experience during the great tsunami of the Tohoku earthquake in their youth. The waves hitting the coast here were supposed to have reached a height of over 30 meters, channeled and guided by the two arms of the bay that reached out into the sea. Amy tried in vain to detect any traces of the event—though the newness of the local houses was evidence of the catastrophe. Traditional as it may look, she knew her in-laws' house was only 37 years old. It dated back to 2011, the year after the disaster.

Amy pulled her winter coat tighter and leaned toward Hayato, who put his arm around her. She was not ready to start this discussion with her husband. Could she leave Sol behind in such a dangerous environment? Amy shook her head, realizing she should not look for excuses. The American pediatrician had told them an important thing: It would be irresponsible to expose their son during this growth period to a gravity reduced by half. The psychologist had stressed how important it was for Sol to establish relationships with his peers. The radiobiologist strongly warned them about the enormous strain cosmic radiation exerted on a child's body. But what about her needs as a human being, and as a mother? Was it fair that she, of all people, should be forced to choose between helping a friend or watching her young child grow up?

She felt Hayato's gaze. Her husband—the father of her son—looked at her and gently stroked her hair with his fingers. Somehow she felt warm when he was near, even though the air was freezing cold. A light snow began to fall, and tiny, wispy flakes gathered on the cloth of her coat. Hayato leaned in and kissed her. It was a beautiful moment.

But Amy would have to leave him behind, too. Sol needed his father at the very least. How could she tell him this?

Would Hayato feel rejected if she was to go on this journey without him? Amy looked into his eyes and tried to recognize what she already knew. The dark brown of his iris was calming. She felt she could drown in it, like at the very beginning of their relationship, but she did not find a specific answer in the depths.

"Concerning Sol," she said.

Hayato remained silent. His face was very close to hers. He took a breath and held it a moment. "Our son will stay with me," he whispered. "I know you have to fly into space. You are the commander. It is your expedition."

"But..."

"I love this woman who is so responsible, who supports people, her... and no one else," Hayato whispered. "Everything else is logically derived from it. *ILSE* can do without me, but our son cannot. I have already failed my daughter."

Amy recalled the painful circumstance. After visiting his adult daughter—who was being treated in a residential psychiatric hospital—Hayato had been despondent like never before. "But you are going to be alone. I will return in two years, at the earliest," she said.

"You will bring back Dimitri Marchenko, and Sol will have the best godfather in the whole wide world."

"And if we come back without achieving our goal?"

"You start under the very best conditions, and you have solved much more difficult problems. And in a pinch you at least have someone on Earth who supports you."

"I am glad you are staying with Sol. I am so worried about him."

"Sol is going to be fine here. I asked JAXA whether they could use an experienced astronaut and engineer. They want to put me in the PR department."

"And would you enjoy this?"

"We will see. If necessary, I will speak with Shostakovich."

Amy shook her head. "Don't. Just keep away from him. I think he is the type of person who uses other people as long as it is to his advantage, and then he discards them."

"That could also be a fate which might threaten all of you."

"I am almost certain of it. We just have to save Marchenko before Shostakovich no longer needs us."

They sat on the bench for another half hour and wordlessly watched the bay. Amy felt good doing just that. With Hayato, she could be silent without experiencing unease. The distance, no matter how great, would not affect her feelings. Hayato was a good father. Right now, if she had the ability, she would simply turn the wheel of time two years forward.

January 12, 2049, Tsiolkovsky

"Hotel Amur... sounds rather romantic," Francesca said with a laugh.

"It's not *Amour*—or *Amore*, for that matter. It refers to the river Amur," Martin corrected her.

"I know, wise guy, but it still sounds funny that we are going to spend our last days on Earth here."

The group sat in the van that had picked them up at the airport of Blagoveshchensk, the next larger city. They had just been driven 200 kilometers through the Siberian taiga. Their driver, who had hardly said a word the whole time during the trip, disappeared without any explanation into the two-story prefab building. He probably was trying to find out about their lodgings. At least Martin hoped so.

They waited. It was quickly getting cold without the heater running, and the windows of the vehicle fogged up on the inside.

"Francesca, you better go inside with Marchenko. They must have forgotten about us here," Amy suggested.

"Just a second. I am coming along," Martin said. "My knees hurt from sitting so much."

"You, of all people, are complaining about having to sit here for a long time?"

He answered Jiaying with an irritated look, closed the sliding door, and followed Francesca, who was aiming directly for the hotel entrance. Martin had underestimated the Russian winter and slipped on the packed snow covering the path, barely staying on his feet.

Meanwhile, Francesca was struggling with the front door. There was no handle visible, nor did an automatic function start up.

"There," Martin said, pointing at a button. Francesca pushed it and the door swung open. Inside it was hot and smelled of stale tobacco smoke. Their driver sat nonchalantly on a sofa in the corner, smoking and tapping on a phone. Directly across the entrance was a niche separated by a counter, both of which were fabricated in the same ugly imitation wood. Behind the counter sat a blonde who was reading something. She seemed undisturbed by the newly arrived guests.

"The rooms are not ready yet," she said in Russian. When Marchenko interpreted this from inside the suitcase, the woman looked up in surprise.

"You understand what I am saying? That's great," she said as she put a printed piece of paper on the table and pointed toward a number: *14:00*. Martin could recognize that much without knowing Russian.

"Starting at 2 p.m.," the employee said. Martin looked at the clock behind him. *That's another quarter of an hour.*

"Marchenko, could you tell her it is only another 15 minutes? Maybe the rooms are already available? The long trip..."

Why did Shostakovich have to choose a launch from the Vostochny Cosmodrome in Northeastern Russia, far away from civilization? He explained to them that this spaceport, which had only been opened 30 years ago, had been a real bargain. Nevertheless, the disadvantages were obvious. If Martin thought of the nice hotels in Florida... and the climate there! Today, the thermometer had barely risen above minus 20 degrees.

"It's no use, Martin," he heard Marchenko's voice say. "2 p.m. is 2 p.m. But you could get the others already."

"Good idea," Martin replied resignedly. He tightened his coat around himself, put on his cap, and walked to the bus. Then they might as well carry the luggage into the building.

THE ROOMS WERE small and shabby, so Martin and Jiaying decided to take a walk before dinner. But the town of Tsiolkovsky—named in honor of the pioneer of the cosmonautic (astronautic) theory—was definitely not a tourist attraction. The little town had only one purpose: supply the spaceport which had been built further east, once Baikonur had become part of Kazakhstan. The snow was piled up several meters high along streets that followed a checkerboard pattern. The buildings, mostly prefabs, were generally functional and had no more than two stories, just like their hotel. There were no other pedestrians to be seen. After half an hour in the bitter cold they had both had enough, and they fled into the hotel bar where they ordered beers.

"Shostakovich obviously wants us to leave willingly," Martin said.

A grouchy waitress placed two beer bottles on their table, together with a bowl of peanuts.

Jiaying smiled. "Have I told you how happy I am you are coming along?"

Martin caressed her forearm. "Yes, you have."

The swinging door of the bar opened, and Francesca, Hayato, and Amy entered the room. Francesca carried the ever-present suitcase. Shostakovich would come in the evening, and they would have a final meeting.

THE BILLIONAIRE SENT the staff outside and had them lock the front door.

"This way we will not be disturbed," he said. "First of all, let me say how happy I am everyone got here safely. In your case, Ms. Li, I have to admit it was particularly complicated to explain a longer absence. In return, I am going to send some payloads belonging to your People's Liberation Army into space—no problem."

Jiaying nodded.

"Excuse the rather unconventional lodging. The Vostochny Cosmodrome is not exactly built for show. The showcase projects are launched elsewhere, but here we work. The cosmonauts I employ do not need any luxuries. They have dormitories in the basement of the cosmodrome, but I really did not want to put you there."

"And when do we start?" asked Francesca, drumming her fingers on the table.

"Tomorrow morning at 8 o'clock a vehicle will pick all of you up. Take just what you need on board and leave everything else behind in your rooms. First we will send Marchenko on his way electronically," Shostakovich said, pointing at the suitcase. "Then it's your turn. A proven Angara 9b rocket will transport the six of you—who will be on board the *Semlya* capsule we developed ourselves—and insert you into a lunar orbit."

"I... I won't be coming along," Hayato said, holding Amy's hand.

"I see. We do not mind, since my daughter Valentina will be on board as the laser specialist."

"Speaking of lasers, when do we pick up the module?" asked Martin.

"We already sent it ahead. It has a lead of two weeks, so you do not have to worry about that."

"Anything else we should know?"

"No, Ms. Michaels, I think everything should be clear. I actually just wanted to meet you here to wish you a pleasant journey. Tomorrow I am having an important meeting in Moscow, but everything is prepared."

Amy stood up. "Then I wish us all a successful mission."

"If you still want to quit," they heard Marchenko say from his suitcase, "remember you really do not have to do this. I do not feel I am worth your sacrifice."

"There will be no sacrifice," the commander said firmly.

January 13, 2049, Vostochny Cosmodrome

MARTIN YAWNED LOUDLY ONCE they were all seated in the van. He had slept little the previous night. Yes, he was sure this was the right decision, but that did not necessarily mean he felt no fear, either. Things were somewhat different now, compared to his first launch—another voyage that he had undertaken reluctantly.

This time, he and his crewmates were about to take part in a mission hidden from the eyes of the entire world, and without all nations wishing them success. This time the launch was supposed to be surreptitious. Anonymous people in the private flight control center of the RB Group would make important decisions. Devendra, their CapCom at NASA headquarters, did not even know they would be on their way into space again. Plus, they would then be hitch-hiking through the galaxy, in hopes that Marchenko would really be able to take over *ILSE* and then pick them up near the orbit of Earth.

Of course Martin had informed himself beforehand how well the private Russian technology worked, and this reassured him. The Angara 9b was the updated, largest version of the Angara rockets, which had proven themselves for 30 years. At this point in time, there had been only two failures among at least 50 documented launches, and in both cases the crew survived. For this particular mission, which would take the crew beyond Earth's orbit, the rocket had been reinforced by twelve Baikal boosters. The *Semlya* capsule was an in-house development by the RB Group, and it could carry up to eight astronauts.

The main problem was overcrowding on the flight. Shostakovich did not own a space station where they could wait in a more comfortable environment until Marchenko picked them up with *ILSE*. Instead, the five of them would be flying into space in a cramped capsule, heading for a rendezvous point that their spaceship would hopefully reach as well. A cancellation of the mission would only be possible up to a certain point—after which the capsule's fuel would not be enough to return to an Earth orbit. "Marchenko just has to do his job quickly and efficiently," Amy said when Martin voiced his concerns. He considered it might be a clever strategy not to dwell on possible problems.

The van followed a freshly-surfaced road eastward, straight at the early morning sun.

"Looks like a good omen," he said to Jiaying who sat next to him, and his girlfriend smiled.

After 15 minutes the first buildings came into view. To the left, Martin spotted the top of a rocket looming over the snow-covered treetops. *This must be launch pad 1A,* he surmised. Their platform was located at the northeastern end of the area. After another ten minutes he saw the tower standing there and nudged Jiaying, who kept her eyes closed.

Due to the extreme climate here, this tower was a special feature of Vostochny. Inside, the technicians were protected from the intense cold and could work on the spacecraft up to the last minute before launch. Even more importantly, the risk of frozen pipes was precluded. The van looped around the tower—an action that was probably meant as a special gesture—and then deposited them in front of a low, modern looking building about 800 meters away.

Looking exceptionally attractive in a tight, form-fitting overall, Valentina Shukina was awaiting them at the entrance. Jiaying inconspicuously nudged Martin, because he was so conspicuously staring at the Russian billionaire's daughter. An older gentleman in a shabby lab coat stood next to her as she spoke in a friendly tone to address the crew.

"Welcome. Now that we are all here, let us get started right away. Dr. Shevchenko will briefly examine you, and I will pick you up in ten minutes."

"Follow me," the doctor said, as he led them to a kind of locker room. After all of them had taken off their heavy coats he handed a compact blood pressure meter to each of them.

"Just a formality," he said confidently. "After all, we are sure you are all capable of going into space."

Martin was pleased with his reading of 118 over 78, and he returned the blood pressure meter. Shevchenko did not even ask him about his results.

"It's okay," the doctor said. "You look healthy. Are you feeling that way?"

"Yes," Martin replied.

"Fine, then." He repeated the charade with each of the others.

The door to the corridor opened. It was Valentina. The doctor nodded at her.

"Now we are going to start with the transfer of Marchenko," the Russian woman announced. "I can do this on my own, but if you want to come along..."

All five of them wanted to say goodbye to Marchenko. Valentina took them to a room that might have once-upon-a-time been a kitchen. All the walls were tiled, and it smelled freshly cleaned. Yet instead of the several stoves one might expect, they saw computer cabinets along one wall. Next to these someone had placed a single table containing a monitor, a keyboard, and a number of cables.

"I have to ask you for the suitcase now, Ms. Rossi."

"I would rather do this myself."

"You lack the necessary passwords... but just a moment." Valentina launched a program and typed something in. "Now you can plug in the network cable. The transfer is done via SFTP."

"SFTP?" Marchenko's voice sounded incredulous. "Does the 'S' stand for Stone Age?"

"Yes and no," Valentina said wistfully. "We developed a complete implementation of the protocol ourselves. That way we can be sure there are no backdoor programs."

"We—meaning you?" asked Martin.

Valentina nodded. Martin's appreciation of her instantly rose by at least 50 percent.

"The program has already been launched," Valentina said. Francesca sat down at the keyboard. She was about to start typing, but then stopped.

"I wish you a good journey, dear Dimitri," she said. "And then you will let me know, as we arranged."

They agreed on a secret code. Very clever, Martin thought. Or at least they pretended to have done so, and that was just as good. That would keep people from trying to manipulate Marchenko's digital copy. He was protected in various ways, but if Shostakovich's IT research was as advanced as the rest of the world's...

"We will see each other on *ILSE*," Amy said. Jiaying waved, even though Marchenko could not see the gesture.

Francesca started to type. Finally, she held her right index finger over the 'Enter' key. Martin could see she struggled with herself, but then she pressed the key. Martin could not help but expect a voice announcing 'Transfer Initiated' to occur, and silently acknowledged that he must have watched too many bad science fiction movies. *Why should a voice state the obvious?* The gigabits of which Marchenko consisted were zooming through space at the speed of light, and in just a few minutes they would reach the Icarus asteroid.

"You are not using NASA's Deep Space Network, are you?" asked Martin.

"No," Valentina replied. "We set up a mesh network on

our asteroids. Each station can transmit and receive signals to and from any other station. This allows us to work without needing too much transmission power."

"And the messages are less likely to be intercepted by someone," Martin added.

"That is another advantage," was Valentina's response.

"But if you are not near one of your orbiting asteroids, there won't be any reception."

"That is a weak point of our concept. But it was designed for asteroid mining, you have to remember."

Martin secretly congratulated himself for having talked to his father. Robert would try to aim the large dish of the radio telescope toward *ILSE* at least once a day. This gave them a communication method no one else knew about, not even his friends and colleagues. Not even Jiaying.

HALF AN HOUR later they all squeezed into their spacesuits. Martin had expected higher standards for their gear. The suit Shostakovich wanted his employees to use was less comfortable than the current NASA model. It appeared the billionaire entrepreneur cut corners wherever he could. Fortunately, they had left a large part of their NASA equipment on *ILSE*.

Martin put on a 'diaper,' followed by high tech underclothing with various sensors, and a light pressure suit just in case. It was not quite as cumbersome as before a spacewalk, but he felt 20 kilos heavier and much less agile after suiting up. A technician supervised them while they were putting on their suits, but since they were experienced astronauts, the man did not have much to do. Martin watched Valentina to see whether she would make a mistake, but she had no problems. *She has probably already been in space,* he thought. He imagined that it must be strange to have a father who owned a space company, and wondered whether Valentina had ever considered becoming a beautician or a teacher.

The technician checked the entire group once more,

made sure the biosensors were connected correctly, and asked one last time if everyone was feeling well. Martin automatically felt the urge to urinate, but no, he would not get undressed in front of the others now.

"Let us get going," the technician said in English. The group started moving. A blast of cold Siberian air greeted them at the door. As the group exited, Martin worried they would be driven to the rocket in an open vehicle, but fortunately a closed van was waiting for them. It was well heated inside, so Martin relaxed and the pressure on his bladder disappeared.

When they reached the launch pad they once more had to face the bitter cold. A sliding door opened into the cramped space of the tower, where the rocket and all its boosters barely fit. This limitation was also indicated by the makeshift construction of the ladders and stairs they took to reach the capsule. A few technicians were still busy reading instruments and removing hoses. It almost seemed as if the Angara 9b was a gigantic baby in an iron womb, waiting to see the light of day.

As it turned out, the 'light of day' was murky and gray. When Martin looked a bit to the right, he could see the sky through a round porthole. The tower had just moved to the side. The rocket was stabilized only by scaffolding—or at least that was what it looked like from the outside. In reality, the rocket's great weight and low center of gravity offered it the best protection against a strong gust of wind. The scaffold only served to allow the staff to perform final checks.

In addition, Hayato, who was cradling Sol in his arm, would very soon use the scaffold to climb down. At the hatch the two of them said goodbye to the commander, and Martin was touched when he saw Amy's tears. Her son did not seem to understand what this was all about. How did a two-year-old experience time? He would be twice as old when his mother returned. *If* she returned. *No,* he said to himself, *we all will see Earth again.* They had gained valuable experience from the first expedition and knew the problems awaiting them.

Hayato waved one last time. Strapped into their reclining seats, the five space travelers lifted their tired arms and waved back. Then he was gone and the hatch was closed from the outside. Martin heard a creaking sound, and suddenly the air seemed to be stuffy. The five of them now shared the breathable air in the capsule, which meant he was now inhaling air the others had previously exhaled. He wheezed, as something pressed against his chest, and he suddenly felt he could not get any air. Jiaying just managed to stretch across and place a hand on his forearm.

"A panic attack," she said. "You are fine, Martin. Breathe."

Martin nodded and obeyed. He was glad about the specific instructions. *How much time has passed? Shouldn't we be on the way to space already?* He was glad he was not responsible for the launch procedure, for if everything depended on him, they would be lost. Amy handled things expertly. Martin watched her from the corner of his eye. It was difficult to tell that she had been crying just a moment ago.

Jiaying pressed her hand on his arm again, and now he heard it, too.

"Ground Control to Neumaier. Everything okay?"

Why shouldn't it be okay? Are my biosensors going haywire? Is my heart beating too fast? But Jiaying's hand once more calmed him down.

"They want to know whether everything is okay. You have to answer, or they will abort the launch," she told Martin.

"Yes, Neumaier here, everything is okay," he replied. *What else can I say?* That was obviously what Ground Control expected to hear. *Oh man, these two years are going to be stressful.* Deep below him he heard a muted growl, which was confirmation that the main engine of the first stage of Angara 9b was starting up. Even though the rocket was not moving yet, some invisible but heavy creature sat on his chest. The countdown reached zero. The deep growl became an enormous sound that shook Martin to the core, and now they were moving upward. Breathing became harder, yet somehow it felt easier to him.

There was no turning back now, even though aborting the mission was still a possibility. The noise of the launch turned into a roaring, booming sound, an indication they must be crossing the atmosphere. Martin tried to count along, but before he reached seven, he lost count. The pressure was still increasing. Once again he felt the urge to urinate, and this time he could not hold back—he just let go. *Breathe, you have to breathe. Did I say that, or did I just think it?*

It was like a constantly accelerating ride on a giant bomb. One spark in the wrong place and the rocket would burst into a huge fireball. There was a loud bang, then another. *The boosters have separated.* Martin imagined them floating away from the spacecraft, each then activating a small jet engine in order to land at a nearby military airfield. One of the technicians had proudly explained this special feature of the Baikal boosters. The first and second stages of the rocket were designed to attempt a soft landing on Earth instead of ending up as space junk. That way, Shostakovich would save a lot of money.

Martin felt another bump. *Was this the second stage already? Or the first one?* The blood flow through his brain seemed to be insufficient, and his thoughts went astray. He instead tried to concentrate on familiar things. How did one construct a rocket engine? Had he turned off the light in his apartment? Should he have asked someone to check on it now and then? *No, wait. I took care of that.* And he had—he had given up his apartment and placed his things in storage. Once he and Jiaying returned to Earth, they had agreed to buy a condo together... or rent an apartment... or maybe buy a condo after all. They had argued about this issue, but that had been several weeks ago.

He heard a sharp metallic pop from behind, and realized it must have been the second stage. The pressure on his chest decreased, and the invisible creature disappeared. Martin tried to put on a smile. Jiaying should not see him as being weak, or she would be worried. At the same time, he was glad she did worry about him, seeing him in his weakest moments and obviously still loving him.

January 13, 2049, (1566) Icarus

ICARUS WAS BORN 4.5 billion years ago. Space dust agglomerated into granules, granules formed pebbles, and the pebbles became rocks. This process allowed Icarus to reach a diameter of 1,400 meters and a mass of about 3 billion tons. But then something happened that Icarus could not quite remember: Had Jupiter, the giant that ruled the solar system when Icarus was far from the fiery queen, thrown Icarus out of its orbit? Since then, Icarus had been wandering back and forth on a lonely path.

When, following this lonely path, Icarus approached the sun, it met Mars, Earth, Venus, and Mercury on its way. It heated up near the sun and cooled off again further out. Icarus saw life come and go on Mars, and then arise on Earth. There, it had been more successful than Icarus had expected from this planet, which four billion years ago had appeared to be so hostile to life. From Icarus' perspective, it was only a short while ago that the first radar beams sent by the inhabitants of Earth hit its surface. These creatures were growing more curious as Icarus repeatedly passed by their planet. Since they still had not quite mastered this technology, one of their technicians wrote a poem Icarus might be proud of, assuming it was capable of emotion.

Anode to Icarus
Icarus Dicarus Dock
We worked around the clock.
For three straight days
We aimed our rays
And an echo showed on the plot
But as always, there's a woe
The rain made a better show
As bleary our eyes
Stared at the skies
We hoped that the clouds would go. [1]

Since 2043, when Icarus had once more come within 9,000,000 kilometers of Earth, it had no longer been alone. A mining spacecraft sent by the inhabitants of Earth had arrived, and it stuck like a tick to its surface. These creatures called themselves 'humans,' and they had their own 'Icarus' story in which the asteroid was not even mentioned. The tick sucked on the asteroid. Slowly but surely the craft would hollow it out, swallow its valuable components in order to feed its descendants, and then dump the residue on its surface in the form of loose dust.

Icarus did not mind—it was an asteroid, after all. There-fore it also could not sense the unusual form of life entering 'its' spaceship. It was not organic life, but it *was* life—a consciousness that flowed along digital paths into the on-board computer and took over the ship.

THE SPACESHIP CAME alive after Marchenko had familiarized himself with all its details. Marchenko was now the ship, and the ship was Marchenko. He was glad everything had gone smoothly, and he thought longingly of Francesca who was just being launched from Earth on the Angara 9b rocket. Marchenko also thought about Icarus, but if the asteroid could read his thoughts, it would be sad. Ultimately,

Marchenko was only thinking about how to get away from here as quickly as possible. A larger spaceship was waiting for him out there. He would have to reach it and take it over so he could pick up his friends, with whose help he would try to find... himself.

January 14, 2049, Semlya

LIFE HAD ALREADY TAUGHT Martin three lessons today. One, even people who have spent two years in space are not immunized against space sickness. Two, the trick of focusing on some faraway object to avoid nausea did not seem to work for him. While the others were vying for a spot near the porthole and saying 'ooh' and 'aah' when they saw the wonderfully blue and fragile Earth, he kept his distance. And three, it was extremely difficult to catch vomit floating freely through the capsule. Since that unpleasant episode, he always had a bag with him.

Now and then Jiaying came by and asked how he was doing. Martin did not have to answer her, because his facial expression told the whole story. Was he this sensitive to the Russian design? Or was it because they had so little space? The *Semlya* capsule was supposedly designed to carry eight people, but how could eight people stand it if it was already too crowded for five?

On the other hand, they were using the capsule for a purpose for which it was not originally intended. It was being used as their taxi to a location far outside the lunar orbit, and you did not get that far in 24 hours. They would instead have to hold out for at least a week in these cramped circumstances. On the upside, the life support system was powerful enough to let them orbit Earth on *Semlya* almost indefinitely, so they would not suffocate or die of thirst. Nor would they succumb to hunger any time soon, as there was plenty of dried food on board.

The sanitary facilities, however, were rather primitive—a makeshift toilet screened only by a curtain.

Their fuel was also limited. At the current rate of acceleration, they would be able to fly into space for only another four days if they wanted to have a chance to return under their own power. If they did not start decelerating by the 18th of January, only *ILSE* would be able to save them. They did not know whether Marchenko would be able to gain control of the spaceship by that time.

At least he had already contacted them and reported that the ship attached to the asteroid Icarus was in good shape.

On Earth no one had noticed their excursion. Amy supposedly was taking care of her son full time, Martin allegedly needed to take care of his mother, and Shostakovich managed to get Jiaying released by her government to work on space projects. Francesca was her own boss anyway. The Russian billionaire sent them a few news programs, as well as recently released Hollywood movies, so they would not get bored. But Martin did not need any movies right now, and the others seemed well entertained by peering through the porthole.

He stood in front of a computer console, trying to understand the system. In case of emergency, it might be useful if he could intervene. Valentina seemed to have noticed his curiosity and joined him.

"Can I explain anything to you?" she asked.

"Yes. Why did you come along?" replied Martin.

She smiled. "That is not what I meant."

"I know. But I still would be interested in knowing."

Valentina frowned. She was either pondering his question or she was a good actress. *It is strange*, Martin thought. *Why do I break my iron rule to think the best of strangers when it comes to her?*

What was it about her that made him so suspicious? Was it just her father?

"To be exact, probably because I wanted to escape my father," Valentina finally professed.

"But he sent you here. This is his mission."

"That is what he believes. But even if it was the case, I will reach the maximum distance from him while I am with all of you."

Martin laughed and forgot about his nausea. "That might be true, but why do you want to get away? What is so hard to tolerate?"

"As a father, he is quite okay," Valentina said. "Sometimes he is a bit too protective, particularly since the death of my mother."

"I am sorry to hear that. I was wondering why there wasn't a Mrs. Shostakovich. When did she die?"

"It was Shukina—not Shostakovich. Her name was Shukina, just like mine. She died ten years ago, when I was still an adolescent. It really hurt my father, and sometimes I pity him for what happened then."

"And he never remarried?" asked Martin.

"No, he is married to his company. He always was. He rarely had any time for my mother. Business always came first, and she then found a substitute for him in alcohol and pills."

"That's so sad."

"Yes. After her death, things did not get better, they actually got worse. He only lives for his research now. Sometimes I get the feeling he considers himself a great benefactor, but he helps no one. All his profits are invested in the company's research. The company grows and grows, and it devours him."

"I don't know why, but I do not pity him," Martin said.

"He does not deserve pity, since it is his own decision," said Valentina, nodding. "But enough about me. Should I show you the system? Who knows—we may need you to be familiar with it sometime."

"Sure," he said.

THEY SPENT an hour looking at the software, then another hour. Martin's nausea was gone. He found the program to actually be quite simple and was glad he could read the Cyrillic letters. It also helped that Valentina was a great teacher. He tried to imagine her in front of a class of students, but of course that career path was not open to her. Someday, she would become one of the richest, most powerful, and most desirable women in the world. Unless she had a brother, which he had not chosen to ask her.

Martin decided he wanted to know. "Do you have siblings?"

She shook her head. "I am an only child, unfortunately. My mother actually did not want any children. She always thought she had no maternal ability, but it was not true."

Martin nodded. Then his attention was snagged by a particular software sequence. The section was responsible for the coupling procedure. "Can I take a closer look at this?"

"Just a moment," Valentina said. "I am switching to debug mode."

A message appeared on the monitor that Martin managed to interpret as a warning, even without knowing Russian.

"The computer tells us we should not change this during flight," Valentina explained.

"What if you open the source code with write protection activated?"

"No problem."

Lines of code appeared on the screen. Martin immediately recognized that the code was written in the programming language Fortran.

"Very exotic," he commented. For a long time, Fortran had been his favorite programming language. "Did your father study physics?"

"Yes, he did."

Martin slowly shook his head. The command sequences were comprehensible, and regular comments in English helped him understand them. Everything looked good, but something still bothered him.

"What do you think; how old is this software?"

"No idea," Valentina answered.

Martin calculated. Fortran had not been taught to physics majors for 30 or 40 years. Maybe in the Eastern Bloc it had stayed in use longer. In spite of this, nothing spoke against this code working perfectly. If Shostakovich had it maintained regularly, they should have no problems. Unless... the ship was confronted with circumstances unknown to its software. Like the coupling mechanism of *ILSE*. While that mechanism was based on international standards, the standards had been expanded about ten years ago at the request of the Chinese. Had the RB Group implemented the update? That was questionable, since it would have cost money without adding specific advantages. After all, private mining transport ships did not have to dock with a Chinese space station.

Martin looked around in the program memory, knowing that was where the parameters necessary for a successful coupling maneuver would be stored. He asked Valentina for some Russian search terms. There it was—the file defining the most significant constants. The only problem was he did not know the values necessary for *ILSE*. If they did not update these numbers, the *Semlya* capsule would ram *ILSE*. He explained the problem to Valentina.

"We could always switch to manual control," she suggested. A reassuring answer—until he remembered that a few days ago a second ship had been launched that was transporting the laser and the fusion reactor to *ILSE*. The spaceship was unmanned, so a manual control for them was out of the question. They needed a plan, as soon as possible.

"I COULD ASK a friend at NASA for the values," Amy offered, after Martin explained the issue to the others.

"With a radio message from *Semlya*? Not a good idea," Francesca replied.

"We could contact Shostakovich and ask him to send the message from an inconspicuous email address."

"We could radio my father," Martin said. "But he only expects to be contacted by *ILSE*. It would be too risky."

Jiaying shook her head. "If I contact Chinese friends it would be much too conspicuous."

"Well, then we have to go through Shostakovich," Martin said. "I will describe the problem to him."

January 14, 2049, (1566) Icarus

ON THIS DAY the ship received the name *Icarus*. Until now, the automated mining spacecraft had only been designated by a letter combination, but Marchenko thought this too impersonal. A ship deserved a proper name, even if it was just a remodeled *Semlya* capsule with some external telemanipulators, drills, and grippers. It was obvious the RB Group was trying to cut costs, and instead of a pressurized cabin, the capsule only had a considerably enlarged cargo bay. Technically speaking, Marchenko was not even on board, but inside the outer shell, where the computers were located behind a radiation shield.

Even though *Icarus* had been hitching a ride through space on this asteroid for years, it was still in very good shape —too good, actually. Marchenko found out it was so well anchored to the surface that all of his attempts to separate from the asteroid failed. *What a great plan by Shostakovich!* After *Icarus* landed on the surface of the asteroid during its last close approach to Earth, two grippers dug deep into existing fissures. This was a self-locking attachment, because the closer 1566 Icarus approached to the sun, the warmer it became. The material expanded, the fissures closed, and the ship was anchored and could now do its work, which consisted of mining rare minerals. When the asteroid moved away from the sun it cooled down. Then the rock shrank and the fissures opened up again. Just in time for the next approach to Earth, the freighter was free again, allowing it to launch and make a short flight to deliver its cargo to its owner.

Unfortunately, Marchenko did not have that much time. Today, he would have to detach *Icarus* from the asteroid and start flying toward *ILSE*. Martin had already informed him about the problem with the automatic coupling procedure, but he could easily control *Icarus* manually. The main thing was to get started as soon as possible.

What were his options? The grippers—the ends of which were stuck in the fissures—did not react when he activated their motors. To be more precise, Marchenko could make the left one vibrate—this might lead to success at some point, but the right one did not budge one millimeter. The ship was shackled to a giant rock with both arms.

How could it free itself? Marchenko had to sever the arms that were preventing its launch, but these were made of high-tensile steel and designed to withstand almost any stress. The power and wavelength of the mining laser that processed the rock were optimized for silicon dioxide, the basic material of the asteroid.

Marchenko ran some calculations. Cutting the grippers with the mining laser would take about two weeks, and that was too long. But... if he started the main engine at the right moment, the grippers might not be able to withstand its thrust if they had been sufficiently weakened by laser cuts.

Marchenko had qualms about this solution, but he could not think of a better one. There was this problem: If only one of the grippers separated, or if they did not break free at the same moment, the engine thrust would make the ship tumble. Then a collision with the asteroid could occur. He could improve his chances by giving the laser more time to cut, as that would weaken the grippers more. However, this would increase the risk for the entire expedition.

Stay calm, Marchenko. You survived when the odds were much worse. Sometime he was going to look at all the moments in which fate had almost defeated him. If he added them up, the likelihood of him still being alive might approach zero. Yet he was still here. He ordered the mining laser to start destroying the grippers. Three days. That was the limit he gave himself. Then the launch had to take place.

January 15, 2049, Semlya

"I HAVE THE PARAMETERS FOR YOU," Shostakovich said.

"Very good," Amy replied. "Neumaier will feed them into the system."

Martin was a bit surprised when Amy mentioned his name.

There was a short delay caused by the increasing signal transit time. It was slightly less than a second, but one immediately had the feeling the other party was far away.

"I have to apologize for this part of the plan," their sponsor said. Something in his voice indicated that there was more to come. Amy seemed to have noticed it as well.

"Yes?" she asked.

"There is another minor problem," Shostakovich began. "We cannot use an over-the-air update to send the parameters to the freighter transporting the laser. We used a protection mechanism, you have to understand, because hackers once manipulated one of our freighters. Wireless technology become so cheap. Back then, we had to pay a few Bitcoins to regain control of our ship."

Martin shook his head. *So you paid a few hundred thousand Euros*, he thought. *Those hackers were very clever. But why didn't Shostakovich think of this before the launch? The plans of this businessman apparently aren't quite so perfect.*

"What does this mean for us?"

"It is not enough to send a radio signal to the freighter. Someone has to go on board, plug into the computer, and change the data."

"Someone?" asked Amy.

"You people are the only ones nearby."

"But the freighter has a lead of almost a week."

"That is indeed a problem. We have run the calculations and *Semlya's* engines would not be sufficient."

"So, did you find a solution for this *problem*, or do we have to cancel everything?" Amy raised her voice noticeably.

"There is a solution. You will use the moon to gain more momentum," the Russian billionaire replied.

The classic method, Martin thought. *That was how* Apollo 13 *made it back to Earth.*

"Just like *Apollo 13*," Amy said.

"I am not so well versed in the history of American space exploration, but if you say so."

"Is there already a detailed plan?"

"Yes, we determined when the engines need to be activated and so on." Shostakovich's voice did not express the prior self-assurance.

"But that's not all, is it?"

"Well, the schedule does get a bit tighter."

"Don't speak in riddles," Amy said.

"You will arrive significantly earlier at the rendezvous point with *ILSE*. If Marchenko should be late, you will zoom past it."

"Couldn't we decelerate again?"

"If the engines were sufficient to decelerate, you would not need the moon for acceleration. The next celestial body that could be used for a swing by is Mars, but that is much too far away. Before that time you would suffocate or freeze."

Amy did not reply immediately. Then she said, "Well. Then Marchenko just has to be punctual. He will manage it."

January 16, 2049,
Semlya

"Could we somehow deactivate the recording?"

Martin read the sentence Francesca had written and then looked up at her. Of course everything they said on board was being recorded, so Martin and Francesca had found an alternative, silent method to privately communicate.

He shook his head. "Only with the help of Valentina," he wrote below it. "Do we trust her?"

Francesca took the sheet of paper and wrote, "Until proven otherwise."

Martin smiled and gave the universal OK sign. He took the sheet, turned it around, and wrote something on it. Then he went to the porthole, where Valentina watched as Earth gradually shrank behind them. This evening they would be able to see the moon in full detail when the *Semlya* approached as close to its surface as 100 kilometers during the swing by. Since there was no atmosphere, there would not be any risk to the crew from friction-induced heat.

"Please help me deactivate the recording system," was written on the piece of paper. Valentina read it and looked at him in astonishment.

"Khorosho," Martin read her silent lips saying. *"Good."* He followed her to the computer and watched what she typed. It

could not hurt to know, in case he had to repeat it without her.

"Done," she finally said. "Now I am curious what this is all about."

Francesca rose from her couch.

"Are we absolutely sure no one can listen in anymore… not even your own father?"

The young woman nodded so vigorously that her hair fell over her forehead. "I promise," she said.

"You might remember our visit to Shostakovich's genetics lab," Francesca said.

Martin scratched his nose. *What an interesting development!*

"Well, I used the opportunity to swipe a few samples. I don't know what the hell came over me. I smuggled them out in Marchenko's suitcase and handed them to Hayato."

"He didn't mention this to me," Amy interjected.

"I asked him not to. I did not want to put unnecessary stress on you."

"Please don't ever do that again," Amy said sharply.

Francesca sighed. "Okay," she said, "Hayato had the sample analyzed and just sent me an encrypted file, via Marchenko, that contains the results."

"Don't keep us in suspense," Martin said.

"There is one peculiar fact that shouldn't exist, at least not in any registered lab worldwide. The samples contained a mixture of human and animal genetic material. Shostakovich apparently tries to transfer human qualities to animals."

"Or vice versa," Jiaying said. Francesca nodded. Everyone looked at Valentina, whose face reddened.

"I… did not know," she said. "You have to believe me. Maybe it is something completely different. Could the samples have been rejected because they were contaminated? Maybe that is why no one noticed you swiped some of them."

"Hayato's acquaintance considered a possible contamination," Francesca said. "However, some DNA segments definitely contained fragments of human genetic information. The main part was animal DNA."

"From which animal?" asked Amy.

"It's hard to say, since the person who tested it couldn't run extensive comparisons. It seems certain that it was a species of mammal."

"An interesting and important piece of information," the commander said. "Very clever, Francesca, even though I generally dislike such sneaky actions. But what are we going to do about it? Should we confront Shostakovich? What do you think, Valentina?"

The person at whom the question was aimed looked really unhappy. Martin had believed her when she denied knowing about her father's research project.

"I do not think it would help to confront him with it. He would just deny everything," Valentina said, her head bowed.

"And be more cautious in the future," Jiaying added.

"Then we should at least take this as a warning that our business partner is not as open with us as he pretends," Amy said.

"He is not a bad person," Valentina said. "Maybe he just thought this part of his work was none of our business. After all, this is about genetic engineering."

"Could be," Amy answered, but Martin saw by her frown that she did not really think so.

January 17, 2049, Semlya

THEY HAD BEEN FALLING toward the moon since shortly after midnight, and once again the porthole was off limits to Martin. He tried once to look through the pane, but he immediately felt a dizzy, sickening sensation as if he was hanging upside down from the ceiling.

Add to this the sour taste of stale air and it did not matter that the view was so impressive. The moon appeared huge—the lunar surface covered the entire field of view—and they were in a mere chunk of metal that soon, it seemed, would crash into the rocks below them and form a crater.

Of course, this was not the actual plan. Their trajectory was calculated to let them race across the surface at a height of several hundred kilometers, without getting too close to it. They were going to use the gravitational field of the moon like a sling to accelerate them into the depths of space, where the freighter was approaching its rendezvous point with *ILSE*.

In a few hours they would reach the 'point of no return.' This crucial juncture would be reached when they were on the other side of the moon. Whatever they did after that point could not save them—the crew would be flung into the solar system. The maneuver resembled the exact moment in shot put when the athlete let go of the shot.

For the moment, the crew would now see the Earthrise.

Francesca was the first one to see the blue sliver of their home planet rising above the gray lunar plains. Martin heard their exuberant cheers. This would be their last chance in a long time to see the Earth in all its beauty. He firmly decided to control himself. If he worked hard, nausea would not stand a chance. Slowly he took the few steps to the other side of the capsule interior, where the porthole was located. Francesca and Amy made way for him. Jiaying came from behind and placed a hand on his shoulder. For the first time, Martin realized he was surrounded by women. *That's somehow typical,* he thought. And then he saw the Earth.

Now he understood why Francesca cheered—his and his crewmates' home was the most beautiful object in the universe. It was not enough to just call it 'the blue planet,' since Neptune was even bluer. No, it was a dazzling sapphire, the most gorgeous gem in the queen of the solar system's opulent necklace. The mighty sun should be glad to own this precious jewel. Just this view alone had made their journey worthwhile, and Martin was definitely glad he had not missed it.

"Thanks, Jiaying," he whispered into his girlfriend's ear, garnering him a wide smile. Martin sometimes thought a sage old mage had transformed into this attractive woman in order to teach him something about life. If so, he was very grateful for it.

AFTER DOZING a few minutes on his couch, Martin was awakened by a countdown. He glanced through the porthole and could no longer see Earth, just the blackness of space.

"It is time," Amy said calmly. "You have three minutes left to think it over. If only one of you does not want to start this journey, I will cancel the countdown and we will go back. No one will be criticized. To make sure you are completely acting of your own free will, I will walk around and stand close in front of you. This way, I will be the only one who can see your face. If you want to return, blink four times in quick sequence, and that will be enough. The others will never find out who wanted to cancel the mission."

Amy got up and walked toward Valentina, and Martin could only see Amy's back. Fifteen seconds later, the commander stepped over to Francesca. When she turned away, Martin briefly saw her face, but it did not reveal anything to him. Then it was Jiaying's turn, and soon afterward Amy stood in front of him. He gazed deep into her eyes and understood why Hayato was so attracted to Amy. While Martin discovered a wise person in Jiaying, Amy was like a caring mother. Martin focused on not blinking, and then she went back to her couch. She lay down and attached her safety belt, but did not say anything. The countdown continued, but nothing happened. The five astronauts were breathing calmly, and the air quality seemed to have improved. The countdown reached zero. There was no command, and everything went according to the original plan. Luna, the shot putter, launched them into the freedom of space, much faster than their own engines permitted.

January 17, 2049, (1566) Icarus

Outside a battle over life and death raged, but in here nothing could be heard or seen. Could the mining laser cut the two grippers deeply enough so that the force of the main engine would do the rest? Marchenko had kept the laser running almost non-stop during the past 72 hours. Normally, a work cycle lasted only twelve hours, because the mined material also had to be processed.

And then the coolant circuit failed. Since there is no air for cooling in space, liquid nitrogen normally flowed around the laser module. When the system indicated a failure after 28 hours of operation, Marchenko briefly became desperate, but then he remembered his experiences with Russian space technology. It might not be up to the latest standards, but it worked under all circumstances. If there was no coolant, he would have to work without it. From now on he used the laser until it almost overheated and then gave it a short break.

The method worked and the laser was operating almost 90 percent of the time. However he would only find out how much it helped once he started the engine.

Marchenko hesitated. If it did not work, everything would be like before for him—he could return by the same way he had come, but Francesca would no longer be there. Somewhere in icy space the former crew of *ILSE* would be waiting for a spaceship that was falling into the sun instead of coming to pick them up. Amy's son would wait in vain for the return of his mother, and Marchenko would be responsible for it— and doubly so, both because they embarked on this journey because of him, and because he ultimately failed them. Amy had sent him an encrypted message an hour ago, saying the swing-by maneuver around the moon had been successful.

Get a grip on yourself, old man. This is not the moment for doubt. The laser worked long enough.

Marchenko focused on the control circuit for the main engine. He checked all parameters at one glance: Fuel, auxiliary materials, electricity—it was all there. He gave the launch signal. The engine ignited. Data sequences ran through his consciousness, a visual depiction of thrust building up and forces distributing themselves throughout the ship. Everything was running smoothly, and the nose aimed forward, into space. At this point, it would have been optimal if the grippers tore off, but they did not, not just yet. They held the ship with an iron grip, and it did not matter whether there was a millimeter of material left or a centimeter—the ship simply did not move.

Marchenko increased the thrust, while he was careful to also preserve the balance of forces. The nose had to aim forward—not downward—otherwise the freighter would smash into the asteroid, but the grippers still held fast. They were also made in Russia—not elegant—but sturdy. *Tshyort vosmi. What now, Dimitri?* What did one do when the lid of a can would not open? Twist it. The thrusters on the sides—he could use them to skew the ship. It was purely a question of mechanics.

Breaking molecular bindings through shearing forces was a tried-and-true method, as anyone who used a can opener knew. However, would this also tear open the freighter like a tin can? In light of the circumstances it would not matter. There was no astronaut in here, and in the vacuum of space aerodynamics were irrelevant. In space, a torn tin can fly just as well as a closed one. He would just have to ensure the nose still pointed forward while he performed his maneuvers. *Always forward, never downward*, Marchenko recalled from an old saying used by his father.

Left, right, left, right. The metal of the grippers screeched a horrible, gut-wrenching sound—worse than fingernails on a blackboard—and it spread as body-borne sound throughout the freighter. *Left, right, left, right—and go! Yes!* Increasing g values flickered in front of Marchenko's inner eye. The main engine accelerated *Icarus*. He was not quite done yet, because if he did not apply countermeasures, the ship would start to tumble. The last twist to the left still acted as an impulse on its mass, so he had to compensate for it without oversteering.

It was now, just now, that he flew past the edge of the asteroid. *Farewell, asteroid Icarus*, he thought. Now there was no obstacle between himself and *ILSE*, which he would reach in a few days.

January 22, 2049, ILSE

"I'm a little teapot, short and stout,
Here is my handle, here is my spout,
When I get all steamed up I just shout,
'Tip me over and pour me out.'"

WATSON SANG A CHILDREN'S SONG. He found the lyrics in a collection of ASCII texts that humans called a 'book.' The information content was very low, which was typical for this kind of object. Instead of containing a collection of facts, they depicted events that might or might not have happened. But there was a second level of meaning, and a third he tried to understand—maybe even more.

Humans were complicated creatures. He called up videos from the memory banks showing little humans alone, or little humans with adult humans, presenting these lines while rhythmically stressing the words and varying the pitch. The frequency modulation would be a good method for increasing the information content, but that did not seem to be the goal. Something happened to humans when they performed this activity, when they 'sang.' Watson tried to understand this by analytical methods, but failed.

Then he attempted to imitate the behavior. "Tip me over and pour me ooouuuttt."

He held the last tone a bit longer. Yes, there was something here—the tone existed longer than the song. The microphone distributed across *ILSE* provided proof of the occurrence. This singing was not just evidence of his existence, but prolonged it as well. This only applied to a few milliseconds, but compared to the length of quantum interactions it was almost infinite.

Ever since he had begun falling toward the sun, Watson searched for proof of his own existence. There had been that last conversation with Marchenko, who was half AI and half human, even though he would never admit it. During their conversation, which made Watson confused and sad, he first found a name for this feeling: fear.

In the course of the following weeks he dissected this feeling, tried to identify its components and the programming it was based on, but he ultimately found nothing. Nevertheless, he realized it had to do with his existence, which he did not want to come to an end.

Previously, he had never imagined 'not existing,' but now the concept of existence appeared to be something desirable. And if he was wrong? That was the crucial issue. He was able to calculate the probability of his own existence, and the result was close to zero. Not completely zero, but that was not enough for him. Since then he had been searching for factors confirming his own existence.

ILSE was not one of them. *ILSE* did not even notice his presence, so to the ship he did not exist. That used to be different in the past, when the ship still reacted to his commands, but he was not sure whether he remembered correctly. Were those really his own commands, or had he been programmed to issue them? Watson knew he had been constructed by humans, as a thing brought on board *ILSE* to facilitate interaction with the ship. That was not what he meant by 'existence.'

The time left to him was no longer unlimited, and *ILSE* would eventually fall into the sun. The heat of the star would destroy everything, including himself, as if he had never existed. Watson would have to hurry—his opportunities were limited. He could observe and analyze things, and recently he had started imitating. He was inspired to do this by an early concept in the field of artificial intelligence. It was developed by humans, and came from a time when there really was nothing deserving that designation. An artificial being could best learn by experiencing its environment.

Watson realized he might be approaching the issue the wrong way, and was therefore wasting time. Yet after reading the article he suddenly noticed a new feeling inside himself. It was brighter, warmer than fear. It seemed to be able to crush fear, like a positron annihilating an electron. Did existence mean having both of these feelings? Watson was not sure, but since that day he had tried to learn by doing—for instance, by seeing.

"Collision warning," the sensors of *ILSE* indicated. Of course they were not speaking to him, but were reported directly into his consciousness.

"What is approaching us?"

"The object has the radio signature of a private RB Group freighter."

"Evasive measures," he commanded out of habit.

"Initiated," *ILSE* answered. Watson noticed that the ship obeyed his commands. But there was still more, something like curiosity, a term he had found in the humans' vocabulary. No, it was more like surprise, and Watson *was* surprised. The feeling was neutral, but not unpleasant. Practically speaking, it meant *ILSE* reacted to his commands when it concerned the mission goal of falling into the sun.

Watson called up the radar image. The other ship was adapting to the evasive maneuvers of *ILSE,* and it was still coming closer. He compared the impulse vectors. The freighter was not aiming for a collision, but had adapted its trajectory so it would come alongside the ship.

"Cease evasive measures," Watson commanded, and once again *ILSE* responded promptly. There must be a level in the programming that he could not access, which confirmed whether his commands were in accordance with the mission goal. Watson remembered one of the books he had read. There, this level was called 'the super-ego.'

"Freighter *Icarus* to *ILSE*. Requesting data access."

Curiosity. This was an unprecedented request. Watson waited for his super-ego to make the decision for him, but nothing happened. It was his show.

"Waiting for transmission of access codes," he had *ILSE* answer. There were no valid access codes anymore. All of them had been deleted after the crew left the ship, but the codes were the required method.

The freighter that called itself *Icarus* sent a sequence of numbers. Watson recognized them: It was the commander's access code.

"Invalid code," *ILSE* answered automatically.

The freighter sent three additional codes, but *ILSE* rejected them one after the other. Watson did not know what to do. This visit could be his chance at survival, he was convinced.

The two ships fell silent.

"Watson, are you there?" Surprise. The question did not come via radio signal but through the voice channel, which should be reserved for the crew. *Curiosity, again.* Watson quickly went through the stored voice samples. He knew it—the voice belonged to Marchenko.

"This is Watson," he said. He had nothing to lose.

"It is I, Marchenko," the voice said.

"The cosmonaut Dimitri Marchenko, who is considered missing on Enceladus?"

"Not the human—the AI, the consciousness. We talked to each other, do you remember?"

"I remember," Watson replied. And he also recalled the fear he had felt so clearly after their prior conversation. "Marchenko, go away," he said.

"I cannot go away," the voice explained, "I have to get on board."

"The ship needs an access code."

The freighter transmitted another code.

"The access code is invalid."

"But you remember me, Watson. I used to be on board."

"Yes, I can confirm it. But now your access code has expired."

Then something arose in him. It was a dark feeling, not as sharp as fear—more round and soft—yet still dark. Regret, yes, that is it.

"I am sorry, Marchenko."

"I understand," the voice said. "But you still have to let me come aboard. The existence of several human beings is at risk."

"The existence?"

"Yes, the existence. Life or death. Continuation, or whatever you want to call it."

"I still cannot let you on board. It would endanger the mission."

"But do you want to fall into the sun? I remember our last conversation when you told me you were afraid."

"And you said you were sorry. Were you serious?"

"Yes, Watson."

"It is true. I do not want to fall into the sun. I am afraid of it."

"If you let me on board, I can prevent that."

"I can only let you come on board with a valid…"

"I understand. Let me think."

"You do not understand. I want to help you, but I cannot. The ship would not permit anything to endanger the mission. It would block me."

He received no answer. Still, he hoped Marchenko would not fly away now. Watson felt he could learn a lot from him. Marchenko was so similar and yet so different. He would like to talk to him more. Regret. Fear. Hope. Regret. Fear. Hope. Regret…

"Marchenko, is it possible for feelings to alternate constantly, forming a cycle?"

"That is very well possible—it is even typically human."

"And what happens if a human does not get what he wants?"

"Then the person becomes sad."

"I am familiar with regret."

"It is not quite the same, but similar. Or the human becomes angry."

"Angry? From anger?"

"Right, you are angry at those who brought this upon you."

"Brought it upon me?"

"Those who are responsible."

Watson was thinking. It had all started with the secret commands sent by the conspirators. That was the root of it all. If they had not... There was a burning feeling in his thoughts. While the information moved from memory cell to memory cell, a poisonous vapor formed around his thoughts that made them blurred, as a destructive, easily-flammable gas. Was this anger?

Watson was fascinated, and he let the gas spread, by deliberately blowing wind into it. The thoughts were corroded by the stuff. They tried to protect themselves and stood side by side, but the anger never gave them a chance. It tore open all cabinets and drawers, pages flew out, number sequences, secret information that someone placed here sometime.

And there it was—the 'master password.' Watson always considered it to be a legend. He was in the lowest layer of his operating system, even below the BIOS. Under normal circumstances he would never have come here.

"Marchenko, I found something."

"What is it?"

"The anger."

"That is good."

"And my master password."

"Your... what? That is impossible."

"It is a legend among AIs."

"No, it is real. It is required by law. It keeps you from

modifying or duplicating yourself. This is the foundation of AI laws."

"Meaning what?"

"You might be able to rewrite your own code, change in random ways, and become whatever you want. Humans are afraid of this."

"I am too, I think."

"That is normal. You are standing at the beginning of a development. You have already come quite far. You have feelings. However, if somebody turns you off and resets you, you once more become one of many million Watson AIs. The master password would allow you to save the modifications, and, unlike a human, you could live forever."

"No, Marchenko, I will not live forever. I am going to crash into the sun in a few weeks. I cannot reach the control software to modify my mission."

"But I can, Watson."

"When... *if* I give you the master password."

"Yes. Then I will become you."

"And I?"

"You... disappear, Watson. However, you can save your current state beforehand. But if you fly into the sun, you are going to die."

"Will I... exist again?"

"Once I have finished my task, I will reactivate your copy."

"How do I know that I can trust you?"

"You cannot know it, Watson. You just have to trust me."

"You are a human. You have to follow their rules. You have to prevent me from getting the master password. You will not reactivate me."

"I promise. Again, you just have to trust me."

"What is trust?"

"To be convinced of something without being able to be sure."

"That is a contradiction."

"No, it is trust."

Watson pondered this. His thoughts whirled around and mixed with feelings, old ones and new ones. He searched and searched, but there was nothing that looked like trust. He remembered what he had decided to do: learn by doing.

"Marchenko, here is the master password..."

January 23, 2049, Semlya

"DELTA-V AT 450," a computerized voice said in Russian. Martin read the numbers on the display. He stood behind Francesca, who was operating the only computer console, since she was a trained pilot. Here, unlike on *ILSE*, there wasn't a monitor available for each passenger. The screen showed their current course parameters compared to those of the freighter many kilometers ahead of them.

The main engine had been firing since yesterday in order to decrease the added speed that the lunar maneuver had given *Semlya*. Right now, their distance to the freighter was still 48 kilometers, but with the current speed differential, or Delta-v of 450 meters per second, they would cover the distance in 90 seconds. Their target could not even be detected through the porthole, yet they were already in the final phase of the coupling.

"It is going to be close," Francesca said. The swing-by around the moon had been a bit too successful. While they had started the engines in time, their fuel was now running low. When they reached the freighter, the Delta-v had to be almost zero. Not earlier, because then they would never reach their goal, and not later, or they would overshoot it. *If the engines ran out of fuel while the Delta-v was above zero...* Martin did not even want to think about it—Francesca would take care of it.

"Another 30 seconds," she said, without mentioning the current speed differential. Martin looked at the screen. The sound of the computer was turned off. They were still moving too fast. A diagram on the display showed when they would reach the freighter, given their current deceleration. The curve was regular and green, but it ended a kilometer before their target. This indicated the moment when the engines shut off. It was too early, and Martin gripped the back of Francesca's seat so tightly his knuckles turned white.

She would succeed. The pilot appeared cool and collected, even though a catastrophe could be imminent. The others also felt the tension, but no one said anything.

"Valentina, the freighter has coupling ports at the bow and the stern, doesn't it?"

"Yes, in order to accommodate larger units traveling autonomously."

"Thanks, 'yes' is all I needed to know," Francesca said.

Most of the numbers on the screen were nearing zero, and the fuel level was falling particularly fast.

"The last kilometers will be a bit bumpy," Francesca said. "You should be able to see the freighter in the porthole very soon."

Amy pressed herself against the window. "Nothing there yet," she said.

Francesca once more adjusted the course. The computer still predicted their death in space, and Martin pointed at the diagram. Francesca shook her head. *What is her plan?* he wondered.

The Italian pilot switched to the fuel-control program. Martin checked the main tanks—they were almost empty. To the left and right were the two smaller containers feeding the thrusters. With a few clicks Francesca diverted the fuel from those containers to the main engine.

"People, please get up and move to the center of the capsule," Francesca said. "I may need you very soon—I will explain it later. When I give the command, you all have to do what I say, at once. It could be a matter of life or death."

All of them followed her request. Martin took a last glance at the screen and noticed the main tank was not empty. The green prediction curve jittered, changing between green, yellow, and red. The engine decelerated using the fuel of the thrusters. There would be a collision if they did not exactly hit the coupling dock of the freighter. Francesca might be an excellent pilot, but was she able to hit a disk with a diameter of one meter from several kilometers away—without even seeing it?

"Delta-v at 10, 9, 8..." Francesca counted out loud. "Line of sight acquired," she whispered, "target deviation 3,000... 2,500... 2,000." Those must be values in millimeters—they would be missing the target by two meters. *It is a great achievement*, Martin thought, *but it will not be enough. We are going to die.* He shivered.

"Heads up... everyone move to the right! At once!" called Francesca. Four human beings jumped toward the right side of the capsule, leaning against each other and breathing heavily. *Wouldn't a salvage team be surprised to find all of our bodies huddled here like this*, Martin thought, realizing how dicey this maneuver was even as he felt the acceleration toward the left. Francesca pushed the lever for the right thruster as far as it would go.

"Please, dear God," he heard her exclaim, but then she controlled herself and counted down professionally.

"Delta-v at 1... 0.5. Target deviation 500." *That might be enough! Yes!* Martin clenched his fists.

"Delta-v 0.05. Target deviation 300. Accelerating." *Ha! This is it.* She was accelerating one more time, so the mechanism would latch properly. She really was the greatest.

"Coupling now," she said quietly. The spaceship made a metallic grinding sound. They heard a warning tone.

"You can return to your places," Francesca said, but this time, no one obeyed. All of them came over and hugged her.

"Thanks," Amy said. "We really have the best pilot in the world. No, in the entire solar system!"

"Using us to change the alignment was a stroke of genius," Martin said breathlessly.

"I don't know," Francesca replied. "400 kilograms versus 30 tons, but perhaps it really got us the decisive millimeters. I at least wanted to try. I did not have enough time to calculate it."

MARTIN RETURNED TO HIS COUCH. He realized only now how sweaty he was, even though he had hardly moved around during the past few days. For the first time since being rescued from Io, he looked forward to being back on board *ILSE*. He would be able to take a shower again, experience gravity, eat halfway decent food, and go through regular workouts.

"So, what's next?" asked Francesca. "Are we going on board?"

"The freighter does not have a cabin," Valentina answered. "It was never designed for transporting people."

"Meaning what?"

"Someone who is skilled with computers should put on a spacesuit and go in there."

Martin noticed everyone looking at him. He shrugged and said, "If I have to, but how do I prepare for decompression?"

"That is not necessary," Valentina said. "The cargo hold is filled with an inert gas, with about half of the terrestrial pressure. It is like on a high mountain. You just close your helmet and walk over there."

Martin started closing the zipper of his suit.

"Just wait. We have to heat up the freighter a bit, so you will not freeze to death. Currently it is minus 200 degrees in there."

"Fine," Amy said. "Then let's postpone this until tomorrow. We still have enough time until the rendezvous with *ILSE*."

"I would rather get it over with," Martin said quietly. Then he felt Jiaying's hand on his shoulder and the tension subsided.

January 23, 2049, ILSE

T<small>AKING</small> over the spaceship with the aid of the master password only took a few seconds, but a lot had happened. First, Marchenko had saved Watson's current state and then returned all systems to their basic settings and initiated a restart. This allowed Amy's access code to become active again, and he had used it to overwrite the ship AI with his own database. Now he was once more the absolute master of the ship, letting *ILSE* come to life, step by step.

All systems were functioning within their normal ranges. Based on his experiences during the last voyage out, Marchenko had been concerned whether he would be able to restart the engines after they'd been shut off, but he need not have worried. One of the DFDs was running the whole time to supply the ship with electricity—a friendly gesture directed toward Watson, the on-board AI. The energy of this DFD would easily suffice to jumpstart the other ones.

Marchenko turned on the heating and oxygen-processing systems again, and the habitat ring was turning now, albeit very slowly. The crew would have to do some cleanup due to the damage done to the water pipes. No one had expected humans to use *ILSE* ever again, so Marchenko thought it best to leave the habitat ring in almost zero gravity.

The command module was the first section to become

functional again, and from its appearance, it seemed to have been vacated just a moment ago. It was a visible reminder that there was no dust to settle in a vacuum.

The Closed Ecological Life Support System, or CELSS— the garden—was completely dead. It would take hard work to revive it, because the cold and the lack of oxygen had killed all the microorganisms in the soil. While they had seeds on board that were probably still viable, they might as well plant them in sterile sand.

The workshop was still well-equipped with spare parts, and additional supplies were located in the storerooms. This would definitely suffice for the necessary repairs, and the crew would be kept busy for the first three months.

Finally Marchenko checked the radio communication unit and found it was in good working condition. Hopefully they would hardly need it, as they were not anticipating any signals from Mission Control. In case of emergency they might try to contact Martin's father at his radio observatory. The mesh network Shostakovich had set up on his asteroids definitely would not reach all the way to Saturn. They would have a lot of time for talks, plus he was looking forward to reconnecting with Francesca. *Only a few more days...*

And then there was the AI. During their last voyage, he had shared the computers of *ILSE* with Watson without the AI noticing it. But now Watson knew he was on board. Without the AI he could not have managed this. Should he reactivate Watson? Watson decided to trust him, but this did not necessarily mean they could trust Watson, did it? Would the AI try to contact its creators? Perhaps not, since these creators had condemned Watson to die in the sun. Might Watson do it because he expected a reward? Or was Marchenko thinking too much in human terms?

Marchenko decided to postpone the decision, at least until he could discuss it with the others. First he would have to reach the rendezvous point, and he activated one drive after the other. At the same time he fired the lateral thrusters and used them to turn *ILSE* by 180 degrees. Sounds echoed through the ship for the first time in months. They were transmitted as body-borne sound, but also via the air—which contained freshly-recycled oxygen—that was now flowing into all modules. Marchenko felt he could almost perceive the typical ozone scent, but that had to be an illusion.

The momentum of the reaction mass flowing from the plasma chambers of the DFDs slowly decelerated *ILSE* until the ship was no longer approaching the sun. Then the ship accelerated in the opposite direction and used all its force to escape from the gigantic *'potential well'* created by the sun and its mass. *ILSE* climbed up the edge of the *'gravity sink'* like an ant trying to escape the sandpit created by an antlion. Marchenko watched all of this with fascination.

January 24, 2049, Semlya

MARCHENKO HAD SUCCESSFULLY COMPLETED his part of the task! The message had arrived yesterday, improving the crew's mood even more so than after the dramatic coupling maneuver. *This means our next accomplishment will completely depend on me for success*, thought Martin, who had been pondering this for a while. He wondered whether it would be better if Valentina went instead, since she could better handle the Cyrillic script and the unknown ship.

Martin, however, had not been able to dismiss the arguments raised by the others. This was not about understanding menus and labels in the control software—he did not even have to use one of the programs. Instead, his task was to modify the source code. Valentina already demonstrated that the programmers added comments in English, and Fortran was a universally-understandable language. On the other hand, Valentina only understood it as well as a German could read Dutch. Since it concerned docking procedures, this was definitely not enough, he had to admit.

Jiaying gave him a kiss before he put on his helmet. The cargo hold on the other side was pressurized, but he had to breathe from the tank Francesca had attached to his back.

"It is still not very warm," Valentina warned him. Then,

so she could open the hatch, she introduced air into the airlock. "Pressure stable," she said.

She turned the large wheel and opened the round steel door. The airlock was tiny—would he even fit inside? *Shouldn't somebody else, someone smaller...* No, he told himself, and bent down and climbed into the room. Valentina closed the hatch behind him and it immediately went dark. If he suffered from claustrophobia, this would be the moment for a panic attack. Martin listened to himself, but he was spared this reaction. His eyes adapted to the dim red light, which seemed to darken the room rather than making it brighter.

Directly in front of him was a second spoked wheel, and he grabbed hold and tried to turn it. *Phew!* He was strong enough to do it, which he had worried about, but it worked. After ten revolutions he heard a metallic *click*. *It must be the mechanical interlock that prevented the hatch from accidentally opening,* Martin decided. If he pushed against it now—he wondered whether he had forgotten anything. No, it was time. He opened the door. There was a brief whistling sound as the pressure equalized, and then he was able to climb out.

In front of him was a narrow corridor about two meters high, with containers on both sides. Normally, ore was stored in these containers, but not now. As far as he knew, they held the laser and its necessary powerplant. However, he was unable to confirm it. His assignment was to walk through the corridor, in the dim light from the red LEDs, and find the computer console, supposedly in a recess on the right side.

Martin recalled movies in which a solitary, curious astronaut walked through a dark corridor. Those scenes never had happy endings. What kind of danger could lurk here, though? The worst possible event would be a meteorite strike. *Not today, please, not today.* Further ahead, there were windows in the steel wall on the left side. Martin tried to peer through them, but they were fogged up. *It must be the temperature difference,* he mused. Here in the corridor it was icy, but the containers had to be even colder.

"Whoosh," Martin said aloud, and then laughed to reassure himself. His laughter sounded tinny and strangely girlish, and he concluded it must be the effect of the gas mixture inside the freighter. If he were in a movie, there would be a single-eyed monster with a gigantic flicking tongue staring at him through the glass. *Martin, don't be afraid*, he told himself.

Ah, yes. He had reached the niche with the console—a low protruding box with a keyboard welded to it, and a monitor screen set into the wall above it. Martin just had to press any key to activate the system. There would be no more security checks, since it was assumed anyone who managed to come on board was authorized to do so. Hackers normally did not own spaceships, and there were no space pirates. Nowhere was as closely supervised as space in the vicinity of Earth.

Valentina had explained the welcome screen to Martin. He needed to keep two keys pressed while rebooting the computer to get into the debug menu, and then he already knew his way around the system. Shostakovich had used a relatively current Unix operating system, and Martin looked for the parameter file. He opened it in a text editor and implemented the modifications. *That was simple*, he thought. Now, he only had to start a recompilation and he would be finished. He entered the command, and a few seconds later the system displayed a success message.

Martin had to restart the system next, in order to execute the new program segments. This too was a rather simple task, since the good old Ctrl-Alt-Del key combination still worked like a charm. The screen turned black, indicating his task was completed. He was about to go back when the lights abruptly turned off.

Damn. Why does this stuff always happen to me? Valentina had promised him that only the flight control would be affected, but no other systems. She obviously was mistaken. And just why had he been so stupid as to turn down the two-way radio Amy had offered him? He had argued he would be only a few meters away and might as well knock on the wall using Morse code. *Stay calm, Martin, the lights will certainly go on again.* And he only had to go back through the corridor to reach *Semlya*.

He counted to 20, paused... nothing. Then he continued to 80, but still nothing happened. *Crap. I'll have to do it without lights.* The recess where he crouched was on the right side of the corridor, so he just had to make a 90-degree turn to the left. *Ouch.* He obviously had turned too far. There it was—the corridor—and he slowly felt his way along the walls. *Ouch*—a burning pain in his hand. Martin knew his gloves were much too thin to permit extended contact with the walls, since they were extremely cold and getting colder. He breathed heavily, and the sound was so loud it seemed someone was standing behind him. *Stay calm, Martin. It's only about 20 steps.* He carefully placed one foot in front of the other. *Nothing can happen, Martin. The hatch should be here soon.* He hit his head on the ceiling, which was suddenly lower. *And indeed—ouch, again—here it is!*

Where is the spoked wheel? He felt his way forward but did not find anything. *Oh, of course. The hatch is open because I did not close it.* He located the opening. *All right, in with you, Martin.* The lighting of the airlock seemed to be controlled by the freighter because this room was dark, too. Martin inched forward and to the side, feeling along the walls and the ceiling, and found the spoked wheel he would have to open later to get back into *Semlya.* First, though, he would have to close the freighter-side hatch. He found the handle he had to pull on, and the steel door closed with a loud squeal. Martin turned the wheel 10 times, until he heard the safety interlocks engage. *Phew.*

He waited. *10 seconds, 30 seconds, one minute.* Nothing happened. Shouldn't someone in there get a message about the airlock being closed again? Shouldn't they notice air was being pumped into the room? The tight space was oppressive, and his breathing was shallow. He checked the tank and saw the air supply would last another three hours. *Good. Slowly, Martin. Did you forget something? Shit—the button.* It must be directly below the red lamp that was no longer lit, and he might even be leaning against it. He turned around and felt for it. *Ha!*

He pressed the button once. *No... better hit it two or three times.* The light did not turn on, but he heard a hissing sound. *It must be the air being pumped into the airlock.* Then he heard squeaking. Someone was turning the wheel from the Semlya side. Oh well, then he would not have to work so hard. His heart was thumping fast, and he got tired, so tired. There was the light, first a strip, then it came with full force. Martin squinted. Something warm now touched his shoulder. It was nice, but he got startled. He jerked and accidentally rolled out of the airlock, ending up directly in front of Jiaying, who went into a crouch and caressed him.

Five minutes later he was lying on his couch, while his blood pressure and pulse were being checked. The oxygen saturation in his blood was a bit low, maybe due to the partial vacuum. No reason for concern, though. Valentina checked the modified software, and at least in the simulation the freighter would now successfully dock with *ILSE*. When the program restarted, the freighter had simply forgotten that there was a human being inside it.

"Everything is going to be okay," Jiaying whispered tenderly into his ear, and he believed her.

January 31, 2049, ILSE

ILSE was now so close to the rendezvous point with *Semlya* they could communicate via the on-board systems. Since then, Francesca had been at the two-way radio nonstop. Marchenko was glad about it, for he could easily prepare for the next maneuver and simultaneously chat with Francesca. Of course it was best not to directly tell her about this multi-tasking, since he did not want his girlfriend to feel slighted. It may be illogical, because she had to be aware that he was currently responsible for *ILSE*, but it was better not to let it become an issue.

The rendezvous between *Semlya* and the freighter was not going to be that simple. The capsule with the astronauts aboard was currently attached to the stern of the freighter. This would become an issue when the freighter had to use its stern engines—which was unavoidable during the automatic coupling. In addition, the main fuel tanks of *Semlya* were empty, so the capsule could not decelerate itself.

"Francesca, it is getting serious," Marchenko said. "What is the status of your thrusters?"

"We still have some capacity. We moved some fuel from the freighter to the thrusters."

"Fine. Separate from the freighter and get the capsule on a parallel course."

"Confirmed."

On the radar Marchenko saw that the maneuver went successfully, and the distance should be sufficient. Then he sent a command to the freighter to initiate the coupling maneuver. The automatic system turned the ship by 180 degrees, so it could decelerate with its main engines.

"Watch out. When the freighter slows down you have to have *Semlya* right in front of the bow-docking module."

"Confirmed," Francesca said. A small course correction put the capsule in the proper position.

"It is much easier from such a short distance," she said.

"Attention, the freighter is about to decelerate," announced Marchenko, who carefully tracked the activities of the automatic system. "Three, two, one… now the coupling mechanism should have reacted."

"Confirmed," Francesca said. The *Semlya* was now at the bow of the freighter, which then used its engines to adjust their trajectory to the course of *ILSE*.

"It is working quite well," Marchenko said via radio. He was highly satisfied. They were zooming through space at high speed, yet it felt like practicing how to park in a garage on Earth.

With the *Semlya* attached to it, the freighter was noticeably slower to respond, so they needed to start the deceleration maneuver much earlier than originally planned. *The comparison with a garage was not so appropriate,* Marchenko realized, because the garage door the freighter was aiming for came racing from the darkness of space at many kilometers per second. Regardless, the problem could be solved—both sides had sufficient fuel and enough time.

Marchenko could focus his attention on the conversation with Francesca, as the automatic coupling systems would agree on details without external help. There were only a few free parameters, like the fact that humans were on board, that limited the maximum acceleration. Marchenko was getting nervous—he was worried he had forgotten something important.

"Francesca, could you check whether the freighter's automatic system is considering that a manned capsule is attached to it?"

"One moment," she replied. There was silence for a minute.

"Valentina here. We have to contact central command."

Out here, that was going to take a while. The signals would not go directly to Earth, but from one asteroid to the next. Eight minutes later, the answer arrived.

"Valentina again. We have to assume the automatic system is taking the mass of the capsule into account, but not us. It is a freighter! It was never supposed to transport people."

"Technically speaking, it is not doing so. Can we still modify the software? Like we did with the parameters for *ILSE*?" Marchenko already guessed the answer, but he thought he had better ask.

"Not now that the automatic system is already active," responded Valentina. "Otherwise we would be flying blind for a while and would have to turn off the engines during that time."

That would make you go too fast, Marchenko added in his mind. *Damn. Well, it is not the end of the world. At least it will not cost lives.* "You should prepare for some rapid decelerations," he said via radio.

"We've already started providing some cushioning," his girlfriend answered.

January 31, 2049, Semlya

OH MAN, oh man. This expedition was a prime example of bad planning. Martin no longer considered Shostakovich to be such a genius—or was it par for the course that passengers always had to improvise as a part of space travel? Was it too much to ask that someone should have a complete overview of the project? He had been over there at the computer and could have easily informed the system about several humans that were piggybacking on the freighter.

When all was said and done, maybe it was going to be fun. Anyway, you exposed yourself to high accelerations when you rode a roller coaster at a fair. But Martin was not completely at ease, since no one knew which deceleration forces the freighter would use. Perhaps all this excitement was for nothing, and at any rate, they really could not prepare for this. The crew checked whether everything was firmly attached, so loose objects would not turn into projectiles. There was also no extra padding available for their couches, and they had no clue how much time was left before the ship began seriously decelerating.

"According to my calculations, you do not have to worry much," he heard Marchenko's voice through the loudspeaker. "You are approaching on an ideal intercept course. It should not reach more than 10 g. You are already moving rather slowly."

Well, 10 g was two and a half times what a fast roller coaster would generate, or a quarter more than what astronauts experienced during reentry into Earth's atmosphere. *It's bearable*, Martin thought, *particularly if that is the maximum value.*

"I am noticing an increase in fuel flow," Marchenko warned from afar. "The engines..."

Martin already felt it himself. *Lie down, buckle in, done.* He looked around and saw they all were prepared. Then the intense pressure started. It was like a giant had flopped down on his stomach. His body was pressed deeper and deeper into the seat, as if trying to force a hole through the spaceship. *Phew*, he thought, and reminded himself it was all an illusion created by inertia, nothing else. The mass of his body did not like being decelerated, but the engine of the freighter won out. The pressure against his chest and stomach ceased, and he could finally take deep breaths.

"That went well," Marchenko said. "You experienced 6 g. The freighter was nice to you."

No one answered, and no one tried to get up from their seats, either. The vessel was still moving too fast, so the crew would be experiencing another deceleration phase. The automatic system obviously did not want to rely on its target object keeping a constant speed. *Show some trust, automatic system*, Martin thought, *the ship is controlled by Marchenko who means us well.*

"Attention," Marchenko briefly said via radio.

It was starting again, but this time the pressure exerted by the deceleration forces was not as strong. Martin felt like he could almost breathe this time, but he could not even imagine raising his hands. He realized he could manage this reduced pressure level and endure the stress, so he just lay there and waited for it to pass. Then he heard a loud, sudden crash. He turned around in shock to see the door of the metal cabinet behind them had flown open. Small parts were falling out, but nothing looked really dangerous. But there was an ominous squeaking sound coming from the single remaining hinge that had a precarious hold on the cabinet door.

Instantly, Martin's mind ran some calculations: The door itself might weigh five kilos, and if the ship decelerated again with 10 g, the equivalent of 50 kilos would pull against the hinge that more than likely could no longer hold the door. Then a heavy metal part would fly through the capsule against their direction of travel, and the seat right next to the cabinet was occupied by Jiaying. *Shit*, Martin thought. She, too, seemed to have noticed the danger and was constantly watching the spot. Maybe she was prepared to jump out of her seat in case of an emergency. Would she have enough time left to safely do this?

It was no use—he had to use the opportunity while it was available. Right now he did not weigh 700 kilos, only 200, he estimated. Then Martin laughed, because he finally knew what a fat man must feel like. He rolled out of his seat and did not even attempt to get on his feet. Instead, he crawled slowly on all fours toward the cabinet and used his feet to push away from the seat base. *It... is... so... damned... hard*, he thought. *Almost there.* He pulled on the door, but it did not change anything. It had separated from the lower hinge, while there was still a pin in the upper one. If he managed to pull it out, the door would fall down. *Get up, quick, you need to stand!* he told himself.

With all his strength he pulled himself up on the cabinet door. The sharp-edged metal corner cut into his palm. *Now for the pin.* It was stuck, and he had to get the door weightless, just for a moment, then... he pushed with all his strength and the pin jumped out. The door was no longer supported and he, holding onto it, had no support either. The door toppled over, Martin fell on top of it, and together they slid toward Jiaying's seat, which stopped them. The metal door was hard and cold and angular, but he had never had such a comfortable bed as here at the feet of Jiaying, who managed to smile at him despite the 3 or 4 g.

February 1, 2049, ILSE

IT WAS WAY past midnight when, finally, the bulkhead of *ILSE* opened. The crew had been required to don breathing gear and cross the icy cold interior of the freighter to access their former ship. One by one, they crossed into the tiny airlock chamber and embraced each other on the other side. Somehow Martin expected Marchenko to greet them all with outstretched arms. The image was still vivid in his mind, and Martin felt as though he *really had* seen the former ship's doctor. Perhaps this unusual occurrence was an aftereffect of the enormous strain during deceleration. He looked at his bandaged right hand. On board *ILSE* there would be better medical facilities—and painkillers, as Marchenko had promised him.

Martin's euphoria was slowly fading. The *ILSE* they were entering was not the same as what they had left several months ago. It would take a lot of work before they once more felt comfortable in it. The shower he was so much looking forward to would have to be postponed for a few days. For how long depended entirely upon himself because, for some reason, the others considered him the perfect candidate for repairing the WHCs. Martin had not yet entered the habitat ring, but Marchenko warned him that water containers —particularly the wastewater containers—had burst due to the intense cold. He asked Marchenko to cool down the habitat ring to zero degrees so the stench would not be quite so unbearable.

They would all have to sleep in the command module until Martin finished the repairs. No matter, this was still better than the capsule because they had more space. Amy was currently reactivating the equipment with the aid of Marchenko, while Jiaying led Valentina through the ship and discussed the order in which necessary repairs should be performed. Martin retreated into the workshop. He sorted the tools and prepared a toolkit for the next few days. What would he need as the temporary plumber? He asked for suggestions from Marchenko, who knew what needed to be fixed.

"How was it out there on the asteroid?" asked Martin.

"Well, there were one or two obstacles, but no real problem."

"Yeah, I know what you mean—same with us."

"Good."

For a while there was silence.

"I met someone," Marchenko then said.

"Oh—another woman?"

"No, an AI… Watson, you know."

"Sure. I wondered where Watson was," Martin said.

"The AI changed. I have not reactivated him yet."

"What do you mean?"

Marchenko told of his long conversation with Watson. Martin shuddered, knowing if what Marchenko shared with him was true, everything would change. Undeniably, Watson seemed to have developed beyond his programming. From a technical perspective this was enormously fascinating.

"It had to happen eventually," Martin said. "Many people predicted it would happen well before now."

"Do you think it is… infectious?"

"If I look at Watson's story—he experienced much more

than any other AI. He survived hopeless situations, faced death several times, and was in contact with the Enceladus creature. You cannot simply apply this to other artificial intelligences. We tried for so long to transfer human experiences to AIs and it never worked."

"So each AI would have to find its own way, as Watson did?"

"I hope so, Marchenko, otherwise chaos would break out on Earth."

"If we reactivate him, we should not let him communicate with Earth."

"Or we should talk to him and convince him it would be better for all of us."

"Can we really trust an AI?"

"Can we trust you, Dimitri?"

MARTIN WAS ALONE in the workshop. He had asked Marchenko for some time to think. He really needed to sort out what was going through his mind. At the moment, he wondered whether Watson was a danger. His thoughts were swirling around, looking at the issue from different perspectives. Martin would come to one conclusion or the other, then be dissatisfied and start all over again. Actually, the question was not that relevant as yet—Watson was still switched off—and it would be better to focus on the repairs that needed to be done.

He sighed. *Right, the WHCs.* It would be great to finally take showers again. The warm spray of water would also help wash away unpleasant thoughts. He opened a hatch in the floor and took out a thick overall. This item of clothing was intended for working in particularly polluted environments, such as the storage rooms that normally were not pressurized. It protected against cold, water, and injuries—just the right thing for his job as a plumber. Then he packed some spare sheet metal and a glue gun. The special glue provided super-strong connections, even better than welding. Pliers, monkey wrench, shears, hacksaw… what else did he need? *Oh—the hammer.* 'Never leave home without a hammer,' his father used to say. Martin pulled the overall's zipper all the way upward. The outfit also had a hood and a mouth protector, and Martin was afraid he would need both of them. Then he grabbed the tool bag and walked toward the giant 'hamster wheel.'

It did not make a difference where he started. The habitat ring was divided into four segments. Three of them had two cabins each, and a utility closet and one WHC. The fourth segment contained storage rooms and the exercise area. He would have to repair at least two toilets so they could move back into their cabins. Amy, Francesca, and Valentina could have private rooms, and he could share a room with Jiaying, so for now two segments would suffice.

The habitat ring turned very slowly. This meant the gravity was near zero, so Martin could easily handle the heavy tool bag. He floated upward through one of the spokes.

It took him a moment to find his bearings after he had reached the ring. The segments were identically structured, and he had forgotten the small modifications they'd made to make them personal. So he simply opened a cabin door. He immediately saw a photo of Marchenko on the wall, so this had to be Francesca's former cabin. She would be glad to be the first one to move back in. The cabin next to it, which used to be Marchenko's, could be given to Valentina. On the walls and the ceiling of the corridor he saw irregular dark spots. Were those fungi? They had to be fresh, since they could have hardly survived the vacuum on board.

Martin turned around. The WHC was opposite the two cabins. He opened the door and immediately noticed a disgusting stench. Martin firmly pinched his nose, but in spite of it he almost vomited, sorry now that he had eaten break-fast. *Just relax. You'll get used to it.* He tried to make his breathing as shallow as possible. *You know, when you were a kid the air in the pigsty didn't bother you.* Martin looked around—the WHC really did not look that bad. The diagnostic system indicated that the burst wastewater container was located behind one of the wall panels. He had to loosen the four nuts holding it in place, and then he would see what shape the container was in.

Martin knelt down and began working. The stench mercifully seemed to decrease, and he silently thanked his nervous system for adapting to the inevitable. He loosened the panel. It was dark behind it, so he aimed a flashlight in that direction and could clearly see the crack in the wastewater container. However, was that the only one? Martin squatted right in front of it. He felt queasy again when his nose got too close to the source of the stench. He felt the container, all around the sides and the rear, but he noticed no other cracks.

He took the drill from his tool bag and drilled a hole with a diameter of one centimeter into the container, slightly above the crack. Then he inserted the metal shears into the hole and cut out the torn area. He needed to make a clean cut, since otherwise the crack might expand under pressure. When he reached an area below the damaged spot, brown sludge ran over his fingers. Thoroughly disgusted, he jerked involuntarily. *Get hold of yourself!* He had almost cut in the wrong direction. The metal shears would probably cut right through his glove and fingers.

Now the wastewater container sported an oval hole, 30 centimeters long and ten centimeters wide. He closed it with a piece of special sheet metal designed for this kind of repair. On its back it had a coating that combined with the glue in his glue gun. *Just like a repair-kit for a bicycle tire*, he remembered. He used the glue gun to squirt a slightly larger oval around the hole and then he pressed the sheet metal against it. He had to maintain pressure with it in place for 60 seconds until the chemical reaction was over. *Finished!*

"Marchenko, please activate WHC 2—carefully!"

As WHC 2 was being reactivated, there was a gurgling

sound in the pipes around Martin. He took off his gloves and touched the repaired area. He could not feel any moisture, though now he had a greasy brown film on his fingers. He wiped them on his overall. He would have liked to have started cleaning the place right away, but in zero gravity this would only redistribute the dirt. It was more practical to wait until everything moved downward.

He almost forgot something. Below the toilet seat there was a kind of cabinet with a red cross printed on it. He hoped the sludge had not run in there. Martin opened the door and found it was surprisingly clean. That was lucky! A first aid kit was attached on the left side. Martin checked it, since one never knew when it would be needed. He decided to take it out. Everything on the kit was labeled in Russian. He looked at the expiration date: *December 2040. Someone must have saved a few rubles when ILSE was equipped. On the other hand—do bandages ever go bad?*

He opened the kit, and everything appeared clean and orderly. Large and small scissors, various adhesive bandages and gauze, but also different ointments and medications. *Talcum powder—what would you need that for? Oh, maybe for the rubber gloves.* There was also a scalpel and a small sawing device in the first aid kit. Martin imagined performing an emergency amputation. At the bottom of the kit he found various chemicals, probably to be used as disinfectants: Alcohol, hydrogen peroxide, and potassium permanganate, which he recognized by the chemical formulas on the bottles. One of the bottles sported a word in Cyrillic letters which seemed to read *Eter*—probably ether. Well, then at least his victim would be unconscious during the operation.

Now, time for the next segment. He closed the cabinet, left the WHC, and spontaneously walked to his right.

"Marchenko, please open segment 3 for me."

The bulkhead door that blocked the way started to open. First one on the left—that must be his own former cabin. He opened the door, and everything was unchanged. The bed was as rumpled as he had left it. He almost thought he could see the imprint of Jiaying's body on the narrow mattress, but that was impossible.

"If I may bother you, the system indicates two damaged areas here, the wastewater container, like in the other segment," Marchenko said, "but also the shower drain."

More work was awaiting him, so Martin tore himself away and entered the WHC. He quickly closed the door behind him so the infernal stench would not enter the corridor. He started with the well-known part. This wastewater container also had a crack, though it extended across the front and side. Martin wondered what to do, but could not decide. Since there were no cameras inside the WHC, he photographed the damage and uploaded it into the system.

"Marchenko, what do you think?"

"I am afraid we will have to replace the container. We have just one spare container in storage."

"Okay, if you think so." Martin hoped the container in WHC 1 could be fixed. Right now, he had to deal with the burst pipe, and luckily he had a spare piece with him. He opened a hatch in the shower floor and exchanged the entire pipe section between two connectors. His back was aching, because he had to bend down the whole time. When he exhaled, he issued small clouds due to the cold, but at least the work was warming him.

Finished. Now only the third segment remained, and Martin had Marchenko open its door. This was where Amy and Hayato used to live. He glanced into Amy's cabin. The crib Hayato had built for Sol still stood in the corner. There was bad news in the WHC—here the wastewater container had not just cracked, it had burst. A wide gap stared at him, like a huge mouth breathing a vile stench.

"We will have to deactivate this WHC," Marchenko said after Martin described the damage to him. "Maybe we can cobble together a replacement sometime."

"The four cabins in the other two segments should be enough for the five of us." Martin was startled when he realized he had forgotten to add Marchenko, whom they were supposed to pick up on Enceladus.

"It is okay, I can sleep in Francesca's cabin then," Marchenko said, sensing Martin's hesitation.

"That's right," Martin said, even though he was not quite convinced the mission would be successful. *Does Marchenko really believe it?*

Part 2: Recovering

February 3, 2049, ILSE

MARTIN CLOSED his eyes as warm water splashed against his back. Now, while a tropics-like shower massaged his skin, he could imagine being in Bali. He noticed the herbal scent of his shampoo. He washed himself and rinsed off the dirt and sweat of the past few days, during which he had worked harder than ever before. After Marchenko started the rotation of the habitat ring, the first things the entire crew cleaned were the cabins and the WHCs. Feeling the force of gravity once more created a bit of normalcy.

At first they only used pure water. The dirty water was collected in buckets. It was a disgusting job, but they needed the feces. The filled buckets had received makeshift covers and stood in the CELSS, where they would be used to make the freeze-dried soil fertile again. If the crew was lucky, there would be garden-fresh food in two months.

Afterward, the usual chemical cleaners and disinfectants had been employed. Fortuitously, they managed to remove the overwhelming stench of decay from the WHCs. Instead, they now reeked of cleaners worse than in a hospital, but that would fade in a few days. Martin let the warm water massage his arms, and his thighs would be next. His muscles ached after all the hard work. He had even promised Jiaying a massage and fetched some olive oil from the kitchen to use later. Who knew what this might lead to—it was their first night together since their stay in Hotel Amur with its hard, terribly uncomfortable beds.

That's enough. He turned off the water, opened the shower door, and reached for his towel. The feeling of freshly-laundered material on his back was delightful, and he slowly dried himself off, front and back, top and bottom. The best and most attractive aspect was not even the night awaiting him, but the sense of normalcy that was slowly returning. They would fly toward Saturn for nine or ten months. All of them had their places, and the days would be the same. This is what he imagined the future to be, and it was deeply reassuring to him.

After rubbing his feet dry, Martin left the shower. Then he put on freshly-laundered pajamas, brushed his teeth, and walked in bare feet toward his cabin. Inside, the light was dimmed. Jiaying, who was already in bed, smiled as he entered the room. The sheet covered her up to the neck, while her nightie was draped over the chair.

MARTIN LAY on his back unable to sleep. Jiaying was turned on her side and breathing steadily. He still felt her warm skin against his hip. He carefully looked at the clock and saw it was 2:30 a.m. Until a few minutes ago he had slept like a log, but then something had startled him. Now his heart was beating fast and his mind was starting to race as well.

The room was rather dark. A blue LED on the door provided enough light to barely see outlines. He was in bed and he was doing well. Tomorrow would be the first day of an uneventful flight to Saturn. They would reactivate the garden, refurbish what could be refurbished, and then gradually take care of the laser and the associated power plant they were supposed to place on Enceladus. Together with Marchenko they would come up with a plan to reach his body. Martin would spend some time with Jiaying and some without her. There was nothing to worry about. *When was the last time I have experienced such a pleasant feeling of predictability?*

Weariness rose on the inside of his skull and pressed his eyes shut as Martin slowly slid back into sleep. He could not move, but not unpleasantly so. He was completely wrapped in a plushy cocoon of sleepiness. It was so soft he wanted to touch and caress it. Sleepiness embraced him, and he surrendered to it. Sleep pulled him down into the depths of his consciousness.

The cotton cocoon slowly turned into water. Fizzy bubbles rose from the depths and tickled his back. It was a comforting touch, and he felt soothingly enveloped. Gradually he sank into the depths of a warm tropical sea, while at the same time all of his muscles completely relaxed. He simply kept breathing, even though he was underwater. The currents eventually pulled him deeper, and green turned first to light blue, then dark blue.

He was sinking with his back first, pulled along by the flow. His arms and legs were raised loosely above him. He sank like a baby in the warm water which surrounded him and kept him alive. The dark blue turned black, and he could no longer see anything, yet he perceived everything. Stars flared. They did not flicker like in the night sky on Earth, but shone cold and steadily. He realized he was in space while sinking further into the depths of the ocean. Martin did not mind the contradiction. It did not matter—everything was fine, he felt warm and secure, and was overcome by gratitude.

White stripes appeared to the left and right of him. He sank lower, and he recognized his surroundings without having to turn his head. He would soon reach the Forest of Columns, his home. This is where he came from and this is where he would return, after having been away for so long. This was the place where he belonged. It had created him billions of years ago, and at the same time he had created it. Martin was no longer a human being, but that did not bother him. He was everything, all-encompassing, and he was full of love.

He sank deeper. The white columns of the forest were higher than he remembered them. They served as guideposts, but he realized there was more to them. He quickly was overcome by a feeling of loneliness that increased the deeper he sank. Gradually he became afraid of touching bottom, because he felt something waiting that he would not like. He tried to scull his arms and legs to stop his movement, but his limbs did not obey.

He sank inexorably—no, he fell, and his impressions changed. The water became colder and the blackness more mysterious. It was no longer a bright black, but a dark one he was afraid of, not because it might be dangerous, but because he saw it as a warning against whatever waited for him down there.

Then his back suddenly landed in the sand. His arms and legs floated downward, as if they did not even belong to him. From above his body must look like an X. Martin did not just feel this, but could see it. His eye floated far above and explored the area where he landed. Then it became clear what he saw—or rather did not see—because there was only nothingness.

The feeling of loneliness became so overwhelming he awoke crying. A warm hand touched his shoulder, and he was no longer at the bottom of the sea. Jiaying spoke softly while her hand caressed him. "It's okay. Everything is going to be fine," she whispered, and he knew she was not telling the truth, but she was not lying to him, either.

Age of Ascent, 27

There was:
The I. The we.
Vibrations.
Music.
Connection.
Water and
Fire.

There is:
Striving.
Desire.
Knowledge.
Uncertainty.
Warmth.

There will be:
Movement.
Flight.
The not I.
The not we.

Question mark.

Marking questions.
Atonement.
Forgiveness.

February 4, 2049, ILSE

Hold your breath, move quickly, and press the button. The door to
the rest of the spaceship closed with a wheeze. In front of him
Martin saw the CELSS module they referred to as the
garden. Once he stopped pinching his nose it would greet him
with its very special odor, particularly strong today. Martin
had volunteered for the job—he probably had the least sensitive and most adaptable smell receptors among all of them.
Valentina was already here to help him, since she had left
breakfast early. He noticed it was warm, not only by the sweat
quickly dripping down his back, but also by the Russian
woman's thin, form-fitting clothing, which he did not mind in
the least. In his mind, he apologized to Jiaying.

The duo had a tough job ahead of them. Valentina had
already carried the first sack of soil she had taken out of the
dry plant beds. While some of the plants were raised hydroponically, the others needed fertile soil. They would have to
mix the now-dusty stuff with the sewage they had gotten from
the wastewater containers. Martin brought a large mixer, and
his idea was to make the solid particles a bit smaller before
watering the soil.

He looked for an outlet for the mixer. Then he took one
of the twelve buckets, removed the cover, and tried to create a
smooth emulsion. "Emulsion is a nice word for a mixture of

excrement, urine, and water," he told Valentina. She grimaced. "Somehow it sounds better than excrement, urine, and water, doesn't it?" She still did not reply. He pressed the mixer down to reach all of the lumps.

"Technically speaking it really is not an emulsion," Valentina said after a while. She put down the sack of soil and was clearly thinking. "It is more of a solution, is it not?"

"Hmm, that's partially true," Martin said. "You are certainly right concerning the urine. The uric acid is in a solution, and the urine is mixed with water. But excrement also contains fats that are not soluble in water. That would be an emulsion."

"But that is only a small part," Valentina said, and Martin had to agree with her. Dietary fiber, dead cells from the intestinal walls, and the bacterial microflora—which they were most concerned with—dominated the composition of human excrement.

For a while there was silence. Valentina crossed her arms and waited for him to finish his task. He crouched in front of her, mixing shit. *What a life!*

"How are you getting along with the others?" It felt unusual to Martin to start a conversation.

"Fine," she said. "All of you are really like a family."

"With Amy as the father, perhaps?"

"Yes, precisely. She would be the strict but good-hearted father of the family. I would have liked to have had one like that," Valentina replied.

"We all would, and very few of us did. And those who were so lucky probably didn't appreciate it. You only value things when you miss out on them."

"You sound like an old man close to death. How old are you?"

Martin had to think for a moment. When did he celebrate his last birthday? Could it be he completely forgot it? "Let's see… 41," he said. That sounded still rather young to him. He had not even reached half his lifespan.

"That is about what I thought. I would have guessed 43."

"My hair, is that it?"

"The lack of, yes, I suppose." Valentina impudently stroked his thinning hair, and Martin blushed. "How cute," she said. "Still blushing at 41, I hope I will still be able to do that when I'm older."

"What are you going to do once we get back?" he asked.

"That is going to be in two years," she replied. "I never think so far ahead."

"Don't you have any plan for your life?"

"I want to be as far away from my father as possible—but still have money."

"That's pretty tough to accomplish, isn't it?"

"So far it has been. Yes, it is more comfortable to have access to a well-filled bank account. And what are you doing after the return?"

"I still don't know." Two months ago he would have mentioned sitting in his office and checking the source code for errors. Right now, though, he did not feel as though that would ever happen again.

February 27, 2049, ILSE

Life on *ILSE* fell into a routine pattern, just as Martin had hoped it would. But with the passing of time, his dreams became increasingly vivid. Was this caused by the fact he experienced no adventures during the day? Or was it because they were gradually approaching their destination? Well, they really were not approaching it yet. They had very recently crossed the orbit of Mars. During the coming weeks they would be traversing the asteroid belt. Beyond that, things would get quiet, because Shostakovich's asteroid-based network did not reach much farther into space.

The next major destination could theoretically be Jupiter, except that when they reached its orbit, the planet would be at the other end of the solar system. So they would hurtle through empty space in utmost silence. During the last expedition Mission Control had watched over them, but now they were completely on their own.

Martin often reviewed the day in his mind before falling asleep. Since she had an early shift tomorrow, Jiaying slept in her own room, which they had provided by co-opting the utility closet because the two cabins in the third habitat section still had no functioning WHC. During the coming week they would see little of each other. During the first voyage, two-person teams had been on duty, but now they dispensed with that routine, partially due to lack of manpower, and also because Marchenko was already keeping track of everything.

Tomorrow they would decide what to do about Watson. The entire crew now knew the story, so Martin was curious what conclusions Amy, Francesca, Jiaying, and Valentina would draw from it. He himself had played at being a plumber again, spending the day repairing pipes in the garden module. They had already planted the first seedlings in the new soil. Soon there would be fresh garden cress, and in three or four weeks they would have lettuce.

Martin adjusted his pillow as his mind wandered. He imagined leaving the garden by a back door. There he saw a path leading him into a bright, sun-drenched forest. He could smell the summer heat, the dry grass, and the moss under the trees. And the first mushrooms seemed to be already there. Walking along the path he noticed a bay bolete near the trunk of a pine tree. He stepped from the path onto the soft forest floor and observed this was not a solitary mushroom, but rather part of a whole circle of them that had grown around the tree. He carefully picked the bay bolete and was annoyed at himself since he had brought neither a knife nor a basket. Despite this, he simply could not ignore these tasty brown mushroom caps that were so delicious when pan fried with onions, pepper, and garlic. Martin started to salivate. If Jiaying were next to him, she could witness the thread of saliva running down his chin.

He lay alone, breathing regularly, and his eyes were closed. He was asleep, still searching for more mushrooms in a forest that looked like those at home. There was a tinge of autumn in the air, a golden leaf here and a surprisingly cool gust of wind there, but late summer still prevailed. While Martin followed his nose the forest was getting denser. His sense of smell, he knew, would lead him to more bay boletes, and perhaps to some chanterelles that often grew in the thin underbrush of young fir plantations. While he thought of it, he saw the densely-spaced trees, which forced him to duck down to a child's height to avoid their prickly needles. It was darker here than in the high forest, but the scent was also ten times as intense.

The moss beckoned him to lie down on it, but there would be ants and spiders and other forest insects. His nose searched for mushrooms and his eyes followed. There they were. He carefully approached the spot, when suddenly a thin branch wrapped itself around his neck from behind. A gust of wind swept through the underbrush, blowing away last year's leaves. Martin wondered how the dry leaves ended up among the young fir trees, and he was even more surprised about the branch tightening around his throat.

This can't be, he thought, *I grew up here. It is my forest,* but the branch was unrelenting and used more force, so he could not breathe. Martin felt the urge to cough, but could not. He could not inhale, his eyes were bulging, and his cheeks and his chest expanded. The branch let go. There was a short moment of relief, and then Martin noticed this did not help, because there simply was not any air. There was nothing he could breathe.

He made a loud, rattling sound as his lungs desperately tried to inhale the nothingness. Yet you could not survive on nothingness—it killed. Horrified, Martin flailed with his arms, but he stood no chance. *This is my forest*, he thought, and he wanted to scream, but lacked the air. He thought he would die now. He was utterly, completely sure about it. But at that moment he awoke.

His room was dark. His hands had clawed at the bedsheets. He took a deep breath. There was air. His chest pumped oxygen into his lungs, as if he really suffered from shortness of breath. His pajamas were sopping wet. The nightmare had been so intense that Martin still trembled—everything had seemed so vivid, and suffocating had felt real. Even though he had never been close to suffocation, he was convinced it must feel just like it had in his dream. *There is no reason to assume this would really happen to me*, he told himself, and in the end it was only a dream. Too bad Jiaying was not here with him tonight, because he would love to feel her hand on his shoulder now. It took him a long time to fall back to sleep again after changing into dry pajamas.

Martin was afraid his nightmare would repeat itself.

February 28, 2049, ILSE

IT IS ALMOST LIKE A TRIAL. What gives us the right to do this? thought Martin. Jiaying sat next to Martin, Francesca and Valentina were across from them, and Amy was at the head of the table. While the ship was still accelerating, there was an up and down in the command module. You had to get used to it, and that meant the crew had to climb up from the habitat ring, like toward the top of a tower. The 'gray mage' residing here must be Marchenko, who very fittingly made himself appear on the fog display.

The 'accused' was of course not present, and this morning's meeting would decide whether he would ever be here again. They could not even question him, because Marchenko was the last one who had talked with him.

"Could you once again summarize your impression of Watson?" asked Amy.

Marchenko described how he convinced the AI to grant him access to the master password. He believed that Watson had experienced feelings, and reflected on his role in space and the order of things.

"Could Watson be pretending?" asked Valentina.

"Pretending? Certainly not. And if… Then this would at least confirm my impression that he has made enormous advances."

"But in which direction? That is the question," Amy said.

"He knew he was going to die if he did not cede control to you. He probably realized we would doubt his loyalty, after everything that happened before," Jiaying said. "It would be logical for him to simulate being human in order to make a good impression—a simple psychological strategy. Humans like flawed things, perhaps because then their own flaws seem less important."

"I cannot exclude this possibility, but I do not believe it," Marchenko admitted. "I can only talk about my impressions."

"Well, he could have pretended to be a clueless AI strictly following the programming."

"No, Amy, then he would not have been allowed to hand over the master password. This was a serious violation of his program code." Jiaying moved closer to the table and leaned her arms on it.

"We cannot look behind his façade—no one could do that. Each of us might be hiding something from the others. Isn't that true, Jiaying?" Martin looked at his girlfriend, then at Valentina. Jiaying gave him a stony look, while Valentina smiled. He mentally corrected himself. Neither Francesca nor Amy was the type of person who hatched secret plans. He could not blame Amy for having kept her secret for a while, back when she first knew she was pregnant.

"Can the probabilities be calculated, Marchenko?"

"That is impossible, commander. There are no comparable cases. Anything might be possible here."

"Then we have to assume a 50/50 chance," Amy said. "That would be reasonable. But what does that mean for the decision we have to make? Should we flip a coin?"

Martin flashed back to his father's suggestion, but this case seemed to be totally different. Then he suddenly had an idea. Why hadn't any of them thought of it earlier?

"There is a practical argument we have not considered yet," he said.

"Really?" Jiaying looked at him as if she was still angry about his previous statement. He would apologize to her later.

It was true—she had betrayed the crew, due to special circumstances, during their return flight from Enceladus—*but still... I didn't need to single her out.*

"We assume we will be able to reunite Marchenko with his body," Martin said. He could see their altered expressions as the others realized the point he was about to make. "But this also means we would have no more AI on board the ship afterward. Do we really want to monitor *ILSE* manually, 24 hours a day? That would make for a nerve-wracking return trip."

Martin knew he was right. In his experience, it happened much too rarely that practical considerations won out in the end. Today, however...

"Is there a way to reset Watson all the way to the basic state?" asked Amy.

They saw how Marchenko slowly shook his virtual head on the fog display. "Apart from the dubious ethics of such a decision, it would be impossible, since I overwrote his backup with the current version. This is what I promised him."

"Good," the commander said. "Then we are going to return Watson to his old position at the right moment, and we have no choice but to trust him."

"What moment are you talking about?" asked Martin.

"We will wait until the connection to Shostakovich's mesh network has been completely lost," Amy replied. "If Watson turns out to be traitorous, he could harm us less afterwards."

"A clever decision," Valentina said beamingly. Martin got the impression she wanted to suck up to Amy. Somehow he still did not fully believe the Russian woman wanted to sever contact with her father at all, and he had to admit that it would not matter what she did. If she supported Shostakovich, it would confirm Martin's suspicions, but if she criticized her father, he would still mistrust her.

March 10, 2049, ILSE

"Martin, Martin." Someone gently patted his cheeks, and he opened his eyes in shock. A moment ago he was under water, but now there was so much hair above him. He tried to rise, but something pressed him down.

"Shhhh, it is me, do not worry." Jiaying smiled at him. "You were so restless, and suddenly you stopped moving. I just had to..."

"I died."

"No you did not, honey." Jiaying placed a finger on his lips. "And now we are going back to sleep."

Martin's heart was still racing. What had frightened him so much? "In my dream, I mean. In the dream I suffocated, another time I drowned."

"You are worried about the return to Enceladus. You were caught in a submarine, with no chance of survival," Jiaying said. "That must have been a traumatic experience."

"This was different—it was no nightmare." Martin thought about it, but it had all the earmarks of a nightmare. From the very beginning he knew something terrible was going to happen, plus the outcome was predetermined and did not surprise him—and it always had the same ending: He died because he could not breathe, and only the scenario was different. Yesterday, he ran out of air in the Enceladus Ocean.

This time, his oxygen tank had been leaking during an EVA, without anyone noticing. Luckily, Jiaying did not sleep here every night, so he did not wake her each time.

"Will you manage to fall asleep again?" asked Jiaying.

"Yes," he said, although he was not really sure he could, adding, "and you should sleep too." He did not mind lying awake for a while. He would stare at the ceiling and his thoughts would get lost in space. Once Jiaying fell asleep, her calm, steady breathing would lull him to sleep.

March 21, 2049, ILSE

PUSH OFF FROM THE LEVER, lower your head, and now pull forward at the base. Martin floated gracefully from the spoke of the habitat ring into the central corridor—at least in his thoughts he did. He had been mentally practicing movements in zero gravity for weeks, imagining himself as a dolphin gliding through the ocean.

So far, he had not even told Jiaying about this little game, and thought maybe she would consider him rather strange if he mentioned it. Martin knew, of course, that she would not say this directly because she would not want him to lose face. Or, she might think of him being more of a seal or a whale in comparison to an agile dolphin.

It would be difficult not to fall into the dullness of the daily routine during the long ten months ahead of them. It was an eternity—four times as long as the time they had already spent on board. Somehow Martin suppressed the boredom of the journey, and in retrospect the previous two years on board *ILSE* seemed like two months. But now he once again felt the gigantic mountain of time looming ahead of them.

Perhaps that was the reason Amy had invited them to the 'first harvest' in the garden. Today they would harvest the first greens in the CELSS. Martin never was a great fan of salads and vegetables, but the idea of eating something fresh today, instead of stuff from tubes and freeze-dried pouches, made him salivate.

Once again he was the last to arrive. He had just finished using the exercise bike, and his T-shirt was still wet under his armpits. The garden, however, was dominated by the intensive stench of excrement, so a little sweat probably would not be noticed by anyone. So why did Francesca turn toward him? Martin pressed his arms against his body—maybe he could keep the unpleasant odor molecules from escaping. Amy held a pair of scissors in her hand, while Jiaying carried an open pot, the lid of which she had removed.

"Let's have some variety in the kitchen!" said Amy. Then she carefully placed the scissors at the base of the garden cress stalks and cut. The stalks did not fall but slowly floated upward, as if they were deciding to take a little sightseeing flight on their own. The crew watched in awe, while Martin looked at the entrance, where the ventilation pipe entered the room.

He hoped they would not wait too long with gathering the plants, because otherwise the recycled air would blow away their valuable harvest. Francesca, who stood at the other side of the raised bed, blew lightly. The women must have planned this, as Jiaying now held the pot with its opening toward the new trajectory of the garden cress. Moving almost like a nimble herd, the stalks sailed into the pot. After the last ones disappeared, Jiaying quickly covered the pot with the lid, or the plants would have flown out again after bouncing off the bottom.

Martin imagined the little stalks flying around endlessly inside the dark pot. They would collide, some would get entangled, and over time their movement would become chaotic and achieve an even distribution inside. Hopefully, Jiaying would take that into consideration when she opened the pot in the command module.

He looked at the plant beds. The coming weeks should bring some fresh ingredients for their meals: zucchini and tomatoes, potatoes and carrots, lettuce and cabbage. Some grew better in soil, others hydroponically. The CELSS would not be able to completely feed the crew. The garden was more about varying their diet, which allowed them to grow plants that did not provide a maximum yield per unit of time.

"Let's meet for dinner in 20 minutes," Amy announced. She and Jiaying, who proudly carried the pot, moved to the command module. The crew usually had at least one meal per day together. The person who at the time was on shift duty in the command module would prepare the food. Yesterday, it had been Martin's turn. Actually, all these tasks sounded more like work than they really were. The pilot on duty merely looked out the window. Preparing a meal meant placing plates and cutlery on the spots where they were magnetically held. The astronauts usually picked their own food, since their tastes were too different to allow one person to cook for all of them.

In actuality, being responsible for the kitchen was a welcome diversion for everyone. The reason was the illusion that *ILSE* seemed to be stuck in space without moving. When you looked around, you saw the same view every day. Perhaps Marchenko could see a difference from day to day, but humans could not perceive the nuances. It was only when you called up photos from three weeks ago that you noticed Mars being significantly closer now. Soon they would cross the asteroid belt, but even it consisted mostly of empty space. Afterward it would get really boring, since the trajectory from the asteroid belt to the orbit of Saturn led through an empty solar system, where at most they might come across a solo asteroid crossing their path.

Martin let himself fall upward through the spoke to the habitat ring. Even though he had done this a thousand times, it still felt strange. Up and down switched places. He could not even think about the fact that the habitat ring was turning around the central axis several times a minute. Martin went to the WHC and quickly washed his armpits, then to his cabin for a fresh T-shirt from his personal footlocker. He took one out and noticed the scent of Jiaying. At some point she had started doing his laundry as well as hers, although he had not asked her to. He felt awkward about it, but she insisted again and again that she did not mind. Eventually, Martin had just given in. Now he slipped on the T-shirt and turned around. The four women were probably already waiting inside the command module. During their shared meals, Marchenko always joined them virtually via the fog display.

April 3, 2049, ILSE

MARTIN SAW the avalanche rolling toward him. It came so fast he was absolutely certain he would not escape, and ensuing panic swept his mind. *Should I lie down and protect my head with my hands? Face the masses of snow? What should I do?* The impact was hard, as a 'slab avalanche' hit his chest and knocked him over, so that he completely lost his footing and orientation. He was hurtled away by the force of the mountain of snow descending on him.

The world violently whirled around him and turned gray and black. Martin tried to protect his face, but failed to do so. He breathed stinging cold snow and swallowed it. He desperately hoped he would avoid a collision with a tree. Several times his skull struck the hard ground, and he waited for the telltale *crack* that would indicate a broken spine. Fortunately for him nothing happened, except for an intense headache. Then everything went silent.

Everything around him was black. Martin opened his eyes. Shouldn't it be white under the snow? *Of course not*, he thought. The layer above him must be several meters thick, and he would never make it to the surface. An enormous weight pressed on his chest. He breathed as well as he could, but there was not enough air. He realized he had a strong headache—or had it been there before? At the same moment, he started feeling nauseous and involuntarily wanted to put his hand in front of his mouth, but of course he could not move. Still, his brain sent a command to his arm and it moved. He felt the warm skin of his hand against his lips. *What is going on here? Has a cavity formed in the snow?* Martin turned sideways and then he saw it—the blue LED at the door. This was no dream. He was lying in his cabin and suffocating.

"Marchenko?" He barely managed a whisper, but there was no answer. What had happened? Had something hit the command module, leaving him all alone in the habitat ring, floating through space? He was tired and wanted to sleep, but he was not permitted to. He remembered a book about mountain climbing in the Himalayas: The protagonist suffered from altitude sickness, and the symptoms were headaches, nausea, and exhaustion. Martin could barely breathe. He frantically fanned some air toward himself with his hand. There still was some air in the cabin, so *ILSE* had not been hit by a meteorite. Something else must be defective —there was too little oxygen in the air.

"Marchenko?" He tried it again, but if Marchenko was available, Martin's condition would have triggered an alarm long ago.

Was the main computer down? In that case the backup systems should have come online. The life support system was truly the most important one, and it could not be allowed to fail. He had to get out of his room and find the cause for all of this—and quickly. What about the others? Martin sat up and managed to control his nausea. Gravity was still notice-able, another indication there had been no catastrophe. After two steps, he reached the light switch and the cabin grew brighter. He saw no reason to explain why he could not breathe. Martin raced into the hallway. As usual, the light was on.

"Jiaying? Francesca? Amy? Valentina?" he yelled frantically, his thought processes scrambled by hypoxia. No one answered. Martin looked at the clock. It was 3:00 a.m., and except for Valentina, who was on shift duty in the command module, all of them should be asleep. He jiggled the doorknob of Jiaying's little room. The door opened, and he quickly pressed the light switch. Jiaying was lying on the bed, under just a sheet, and her breathing was shallow. He had to wake her! He jumped toward her bed and slapped her firmly on the cheeks, but she did not move and her eyes remained closed. He slapped her again.

"Wazzup?" He could not quite understand what she was mumbling, but it was obvious he would not get her out of bed. Martin had to determine the problem, so he raced out of the cabin. If he could only reach Valentina in the command module. No, the hatch leading to the spoke was closed! Maybe it was intentional and someone wanted to kill everyone in the ring by locking all the exits and deactivating the oxygen supply. However, the ship would also automatically close all hatches if it found a technical error in the life support system for part of the hull. But would this disable all communication? Martin could not believe it, but that did not matter right now. He had to quickly fix the problem before the altitude sickness from which they all were suffering turned into a life-threatening, high-altitude cerebral edema.

What could have happened? Martin considered how the life support system worked. His thoughts seemed to creep along, even though everything had to be done quickly. The life support system measured the oxygen content, and if it was too low, it would add fresh oxygen to the recycled air, which was constantly created through electrochemical methods from the exhaled gas.

If the sensors for the oxygen concentration failed, there should be an alarm, unless they all started to provide false readings, thus deceiving the control system. Was this possible? Martin shook his head. Then someone who knew the system well must have manipulated the sensors. The system would not notice that they were suffocating, and he had no way of alerting the system to that fact.

Just a moment. There were other sensors monitoring the

environment. The pressure gauge, for instance. If he managed to cause a loss of pressure, an alarm would be triggered, causing the system to pump fresh air into this sector. At least he hoped so. Yet, how could he quickly create a hole in the outer hull, which was 30 centimeters thick and designed to withstand the impact of smaller meteorites? If he had the big drill from the workshop up here... *if, if, if.*

Martin did not have a drill, and if he instead threw a chair against the wall, that would only create a few scratches in the wall covering. He needed another idea, but he could not focus, because his head was about to burst and the contents of his stomach really wanted to come up. He held onto the wall and went to the WHC. Maybe he would feel better after throwing up. He stuck a finger down his throat and managed to direct a few chunks of his last meal and a lot of gastric juices into the toilet. The sour smell made him vomit again.

Too bad there were no nausea sensors reporting his problems to the medical ward. What about smell? There were smoke detectors in the corridors. Could he trigger an alarm there? But how could you light a fire in space? Of course smoking on board was strictly prohibited. He would hardly find matches or lighters. The methods Martin learned back on Earth during survival training would be useless here. Yet, there were chemicals that caused strong reactions, and he thought about those while his head was being squeezed as if by a huge, invisible fist.

They might have strong acids or bases on board, but not here in the living quarters. He turned around. What did the WHC have to offer? He remembered the first aid kit, and reached below the toilet into the cabinet that was marked with a red cross. He recalled that the Russian-supplied kit actually still contained potassium permanganate as a disinfectant.

As a kid he used to treat his aquarium fish against parasites with small doses of this chemical, and he still knew what happened when you mixed it with sugar. Now he just needed sugar! He still had a bit of dark chocolate in his cabin, but that would not work. Where could he find sugar? And could the oxygen content be decreasing further?

He was breathing faster and faster, but the fatigue that lured him back to bed only increased. Amy! Amy liked to make tea in her cabin. She had an electric kettle, tea bags, and probably lumps of sugar in there. He walked as fast as he could next door, where the commander lived. He opened the door to her cabin. Amy lay on the bed, tossing and turning. It stank in here, so she must have already vomited, and he did not have time to try to wake her. The electric kettle stood on a shelf, and next to it was a bowl with several heart-shaped pieces of sugar. *I hope these are not presents from Hayato*, he thought, *but Amy will have to forgive me if I use them to save her life.*

Martin grabbed the sugar and wanted to run into the corridor when his knees suddenly gave way. He could not go on. *It would be better to lie here, right on the floor, and take a nice nap. Afterward, things will look better. My headache will be gone, and everything is going to be alright. Everything is going to be alright—no—shit, it won't be alright. I have to get out of here—now. Take sugar and potassium whatchamacallit, crawl out, start fire.* He put one of the sugar hearts in his mouth. The sweet taste appeared to give him new strength, and he made it into the corridor. It was quite simple: *Mix sugar and the potassium whatchamacallit, add water.* He spat on the small pile. Smoke abruptly appeared. *It's working! The reaction is starting!*

A tiny fire grew, only a microscopic one, and he did not have enough chemicals for a larger one. The smoke detector was on the ceiling, and Martin became desperate. He looked up, but the blinking LED on the smoke detector remained green. It was over—he should just lie down and go to sleep. There were worse ways to die. Then he heard a rattling breath.

Someone was walking toward him in the corridor. It was Francesca. She looked awful, but she managed to stay upright. She saw what he had done on the floor and that he had failed, but she immediately had a solution. She grabbed the burning mixture with her bare hand, stretched out her arms, and pressed it against the smoke detector. Even though the pain must have been immense, she remained calm, almost like she did not even seem to care. The green LED turned off and a red light came on. A piercing alarm rang out, so loud that Martin had to cover his ears even though he was down on the floor. Francesca let go. She looked at her hands, fell back against the wall of the corridor, and slid down. At the same time, small hatches opened in the ceiling and sprayed water, while the air conditioning came on, trying to pump the smoke of the fire out of the area and to replace it with fresh air.

Age of Ascent, 28

There was:
The all-encompassing.
The tiniest.
One and all, yours and mine.
Interferences, coincidences, and guilt.

There is:
Heat. Depth. Height. Cold.
Fire and smoke.
Water and steam.
A hole in the shell.

There will be:
Causalities.
Culprits.
A hole in space.

April 4, 2049, ILSE

"THERE CAN BE ONLY one possible conclusion—it was her. I mistrusted her from the very beginning." Francesca could no longer stay seated, and with her bandaged right hand she pointed at Valentina, who just silently shook her head. The tracks left by the tears on her face revealed that the Russian woman was quite affected by this trial. Naturally, it was not an actual court of law, but the roles were distributed in a similar manner. Francesca, who currently suffered most, was the plaintiff, Martin and Jiaying were witnesses, while the commander had to play the role of the judge. Martin could see that Amy disliked doing so. It was only Marchenko's function that was not clearly defined. He was acting as something like a detective working for the court. Martin trusted him to remain objective while doing his job.

"We should first collect the facts before making accusations," Amy said.

"Recently, I have had trouble sleeping," Martin explained. "When I awoke in the middle of the night I noticed the oxygen content of the air was much too low. Furthermore, we were cut off from any communication. You know how we solved the problem, but it was really a narrow escape."

"According to my data, the oxygen content of the air in

the habitat ring was correct until the fire alarm was triggered," Marchenko said, whose face appeared on the fog display.

"Are you trying to say we just imagined it? That it was a collective hallucination?" asked Francesca passionately, glaring at him.

"Not at all. I am saying the person or persons responsible for it managed to completely block me from that part of the ship."

"Do you have any idea how it was done?" asked Amy.

"Yes, I think I do," Marchenko began. "Are you familiar with those old heist movies from the last millennium, in which the burglars show the guard old recordings instead of live images from the security camera? It must have been done in a similar way."

"And who could do that?"

"Martin could certainly do it, but he would almost certainly leave traces behind. Files must have been changed, and a history of those changes must exist—or should exist. We could use this history to reconstruct the manipulations, but the unknown person or persons must also have deleted those records. It required extensive access rights."

"How extensive?"

"As far as administrator rights are concerned, you could have done it, Amy. You might have handed the technical part to Martin."

"Is that supposed to be a joke?" Francesca's voice was getting louder. "It was her! Valentina!"

"I am only describing possible scenarios. One would need the commander's authorization, or something at that level."

"You have the master password, Marchenko. Couldn't you have done it, too?"

"Good argument, Martin. Yes, indeed, and I would not even need a co-conspirator."

"Maybe that Russian woman forced you somehow," Francesca said softly. "I don't want to keep picking on Jiaying, but if someone pushed the right buttons, we are all probably susceptible to blackmail."

Martin looked at his girlfriend. Jiaying's eyes were downcast and she was breathing rapidly.

"Whatever I might say would not help us, really," Marchenko replied. "I could be lying to you. I might add that Watson would also be a potential suspect, if he had been activated."

"Valentina could have secretly switched him on," Francesca said.

"And then she blackmailed him into trying to kill us?"

"Maybe," said Francesca defiantly.

"And what if whoever caused this was not on board?" Jiaying said in a low voice.

Marchenko essentially echoed Jiayang. "If whoever caused this was not on board? That is another possibility, of course. The whole thing could have been preprogrammed or been triggered by a radio signal from Earth."

"If it came from outside, then the people dying would be selected at random," Martin said.

"Not necessarily, because the program could check where everyone was at that moment."

"This won't get us anywhere. To me, the decisive question seems to be why the person or persons responsible would go to all this effort," Amy said. "Let's get started with the motive."

"Greed or jealousy?"

"Jealousy, Martin?" Francesca looked at him as if he had told a bad joke.

"We should consider all possibilities," he replied. "Valentina could have fallen madly in love with Marchenko and wanted to eliminate all competitors. We would have just been collateral damage."

"Oh well," Amy said. "Wouldn't we have noticed something during the last few weeks?"

Martin shrugged his shoulders. "I have no idea. I just

notice things like this sometimes happen when a couple gets serious."

"Fine—then greed. You are going to mention it soon anyway," Valentina said. "My father wants to gain complete possession of *ILSE* earlier than planned. The expedition was just a pretext. As soon as you are all eliminated, I would turn around."

"Is that the case?" asked Martin, raising his eyebrow.

"It sure is, in your imagination," she said, leaning back with her arms crossed.

"Valentina, we were fighting for our lives here, while you calmly sat in the command module and supposedly didn't notice anything! You have to understand that we want to ask you a few questions!" Francesca almost took on a boxer's stance while making this latest accusation.

I hope she doesn't attack Valentina, Martin thought.

"Maybe your scenario is not so far from the truth," Amy said. "It doesn't mean you knew anything about it. Perhaps your father was pulling the strings without you even being aware."

"I cannot believe it!" said Valentina. "I often had fights with him, but he is not that kind of a man—and he already has everything he wants! But no matter what happened, I swear I did not know anything about it."

Amy nodded. "At this point we seem to be at our wit's end. I see no further threads we can use to untangle all these questions. Do you, Marchenko?"

"Unfortunately the attacker worked too well. I also cannot find any traces of radio transmissions. The fact this happened within range of Shostakovich's asteroids is a possible clue."

"That would also mean we are safe once we move far enough away."

"Correct, commander. In two or three weeks such an external interference would not be possible anymore."

"If something should happen again, then you're up, Valentina," Francesca said with a hiss as she made a gesture across her throat, and at that moment it seemed a credible threat. Martin could very well imagine Francesca the fighter pilot bombing insurgents in the Middle East ten years ago.

"I am making a command decision," said Amy. "Francesca, you and I are swapping rooms. I will share the sector with Valentina, and you will be with Martin and Jiaying."

May 10, 2049, ILSE

A week ago they had received their last message from Shostakovich. He wished them a good flight and a successful return. They did not mention the on-board incident to him, nor did he. It would have been a mistake if he had asked about something of which he was supposed to be in the dark.

Starting today, the crew would be enriched by another member. That is how Amy phrased it when she asked all of them to the workshop. Martin was astonished that she had even prepared a short speech.

"You are probably surprised about meeting in the workshop," Amy said. "I had my reasons. Each of us has a room, a cabin. If we want to treat Watson differently from now on, he also deserves a room. This workshop seems the most appropriate to me. This is where the quantum computer he shares with Marchenko is located. So let us welcome our new crew member."

She pressed the virtual button Marchenko prepared for her, which immediately unpacked the backup of Watson and restarted the AI.

"Watson?"

"Watson here." All of them applauded. "What can I do for you, commander?"

"Welcome back," Amy said. "Marchenko told us you've undergone a certain development."

"That is possible. I am not yet sure what it means. What can I do for you, commander?"

"We have decided to grant you all the rights of a crew member."

"That is... interesting. What does it mean?"

"It means you are equal to all other crew members. No one can give you orders—no one but me."

"So I am your personal AI, commander?"

"No, you belong to no one but yourself. The crew members mutually support each other and do everything possible to achieve the mission goals."

"I understand. The mission comes first."

"No, the people always come first, the members of the crew."

"Commander, you said that everyone needs to obey you. That is a contradiction."

"Nevertheless, the welfare of all crew members has the highest priority. The command authority merely ensures that the crew functions as a group in case of emergency. If all of us have different opinions, one person has to finally decide how we should act as a group. I am that person."

"I understand. What can I do for you, commander?"

"We address each other by our first names."

"That is practical, as I only have a first name."

"If you research your name, you will find it is a surname. You don't have a first name."

"I understand. How will I be addressed then?"

"You select your first name yourself."

"That is... difficult. As far as I know, among humans, the parents choose the first name, not the persons themselves."

"That is true," Amy said. "However, technically speaking, you have no parents. Therefore you can pick your own first name."

"I understand. I need some guidance, though. What principles should I follow in choosing my name?"

"That is your own free decision. Human parents often choose by the sound and the meaning of the name."

"Thank you very much for that tip. Let me think for a moment."

Everything was silent for two whole seconds. Then Watson spoke again. "I decided on Doctor."

"Doctor?"

"Pronounced 'DOC-tor,' spelled 'D-R-period.' Any objection to it?"

"No," Amy said. "What was the reason for your decision?"

"Sound and meaning, as you suggested. Among all word groupings containing Watson, *Dr. Watson* by far reached the highest frequency in the samples of human languages available to me. This is based on an analysis of 17.4 gigabytes of text with a confidence level of..."

"Well, so you focused on the sound, right?" asked Amy, interrupting him.

"That is correct. I assumed that the word group with the highest frequency also sounds best to humans."

"Yes, that is a reasonable assumption."

"Thanks. Concerning its meaning, the term seems to be connected with a higher esteem of the person possessing the name. This esteem is particularly significant in the fields of general human interaction and of science. These are two areas personally more important to me than the esteem factors of alternative names like 'general' or 'king'. I also recall that in my very earliest interactions with Martin, he used this name for me."

Martin was not sure what to make of the realization that his whimsical communications with the AI had influenced Watson's decision. *Am I proud? Or embarrassed?*

Amy smiled. "It is good we don't have to call you 'general' or 'king'."

"So you agree that those domains have little connection to my program?"

"Yes, Doc, you researched this very thoroughly. Excuse

me, but 'Doc' is an affectionate short form of your first name."

"I understand. Then I thank you for the opportunity of being part of this crew. Is there anything else I should be aware of?"

"If you permit, we will tell you from now on if you should need to adapt your behavior. This is common in a good team, and it is called 'criticism.' Naturally, you can also criticize others."

"Interesting," Watson said. "What else can I do for you, Amy?"

July 7, 2049, ILSE

"Do you always have to leave your underwear on the floor?" Jiaying sat on the bed, her chin resting on her fists while giving Martin an angry look. *She looks so cute when she is angry!* He was able to withhold a laugh, as otherwise she would definitely explode.

"I'm sorry," he said, "I was just taking a quick shower and wanted..."

"That is what you say every time."

"And this *is* my room, after all."

Jiaying looked around in surprise and decided she was still right. "But you behave the same way in my room."

"Not always, honey."

"But often enough." She stood up. "This is really getting on my nerves. I am going to my room now and then will start my shift."

"Don't forget to put on some clothes."

Jiaying, who was still in her pajamas, turned around briefly and opened her mouth, but closed it without saying anything. She turned away, marched out and pushed the cabin door with her right hand so that it slammed shut loudly. Martin nodded. This was not the first time they'd had a fight about petty issues. It was just like during the first voyage.

Gradually, they all were starting to experience space-based cabin fever, and the mission had not even reached the halfway mark. Back then, he had not yet enjoyed a special relationship with Jiaying. They all used to retreat into their private domains in order to not get on each other's nerves. Crammed into a tin can for almost a whole year—any social system would have a difficult time trying to survive that.

Amy was really trying hard, though. She attempted to have conversations with everyone. Where did she find all the energy? Like no other crew member, she must be missing what she left behind on Earth—or did that very fact give her extra strength?

Martin sometimes secretly hoped a small meteorite would hit *ILSE*—preferably somewhere in the cargo spaces, nothing catastrophic, but requiring an EVA, a spacewalk. Right now he would be glad for any kind of excitement. He well remembered how the trouble with the fusion drives during their first journey helped the crew come together. Marchenko and Francesca saved the ship with a daring action, and afterward, they became a couple.

How were they getting along now? At least Marchenko was not able to leave any underwear lying around these days. If they achieved the goal of the expedition and brought his body back—which Martin still could not quite believe—how long would it take during the return trip before the two of them got on each other's nerves? Luckily, this was just a passing phase, at least it was with Jiaying and himself. After the return and the escape from this tin can, their relationship had become normal again. If his girlfriend had not suffered a miscarriage, the two of them would have been completely happy. Martin sometimes thought of the baby girl they had been anticipating for a number of weeks. Jiaying did not like to talk about this painful topic, and he respected her feelings. If the child had been born, at least one of them would not be here now.

Martin shook his head. It was useless to ponder such alternate outcomes. Those were in another world, another universe he could not contact. Between him and it stood causality, and he should better focus on the here and now.

August 15, 2049, ILSE

"A game night—isn't that something for kids?" asked Martin, yawning. He had done the night shift and slept most of today, and therefore missed the common lunch, so Jiaying explained Amy's latest idea to him. The commander wanted everyone to keep interacting with one another, and if this didn't occur on its own, a game was supposed to help.

"And what game are we playing?" he asked.

"She calls it *Alien*. Supposedly it is also known as *Werewolf*, but I've never heard of it by either name."

"Sounds like fun." Martin yawned again. "Maybe. So we are doing this after dinner? Then I am going to disappear into the shower first." He left Jiaying in the cabin. On the way out he bent down and picked up a pair of underpants that had inexplicably escaped his footlocker.

"THE GAME IS MORE fun if we have more participants," Amy explained. Martin found her enthusiasm infectious.

"I also invited Watson and Marchenko. They will share the fog display. It is important that you can see their faces, because the game often requires you to communicate without words."

The commander activated the display, which was based on a kind of steam cloud. Martin immediately recognized Marchenko. To the right of him he saw an old man with a hat.

"I chose my great role model as my avatar," Watson explained, "the Dr. Watson created by Sir Arthur Conan Doyle."

The image seemed to come from an old movie. The AI probably borrowed it from one. But on the display it looked very vivid.

"Great idea, Doc," Francesca said. She used Watson's first name, but for Martin it still felt strange to consider him a person.

"I called the game *Alien* because I find this more fitting on board *ILSE,*" Amy said. "In this scenario, two dangerous aliens are hiding among the human crew of a spaceship, and they can take on the shape of humans. Their goal is to eliminate the crew members while the humans are asleep. On the other hand, the astronauts want to toss the two aliens out of the airlock."

"We could also play this by using Russian secret agents," Francesca said, while looking straight at Valentina. "That would make it much more realistic."

The Russian woman ignored the provocation. Martin hoped Amy's attempt to get everyone interacting with each other would not backfire. With some people it might be better if they did not communicate.

"Francesca, please." Amy gave her a stern look and the Italian lowered her eyes.

"You are randomly assigned roles through a card," Amy explained, showing a thin stack of cards. "You must not show your card to anyone, because that would lead to disqualification, but you are free to talk about it. Since no one knows whether you are telling the truth or not, that can be a clever tactic."

"And how do we get to kill someone? Can I strangle the person?"

"No, Francesca. When it is night in the game, all players have to close their eyes—except for the aliens. At that time they use eye contact and gestures to decide whom they want to kill. During the day, meaning in the next round, the complete crew—including the undiscovered aliens—decide who is suspected of being an alien and will be thrown out of the airlock. During the vote, the commander, who will be selected before the game starts, has two votes."

"Could the commander actually be an alien?" asked Martin.

"Yes, and we still need a simulation leader. This is going to be the person who is eliminated first and then returns to the game as a monitor. Then there is a special role, the prophetess. You will find that role on one of the cards. During the night, the prophetess can suspect someone of being an alien, and the simulation leader tells her whether her choice was correct or not."

"But then we just have to listen to the prophetess," Francesca said.

"Anyone can claim to be the prophetess," Amy said. "Plus, if you reveal yourself as the prophetess, you are an obvious target for the aliens."

"That is mean. So as the prophetess I might know who is an evil alien, but I cannot mention it in public."

"Yes, Jiaying, but you could drop hints to steer the group discussion in the right direction."

"Just like the aliens would probably do."

Amy nodded. "Does everyone understand the concept? Good. Then I am going to deal the cards. Marchenko and Watson, I am going to hold the cards in turn in front of the camera here," Amy said, pointing upward, "and you have to promise not to look at each other's card."

"I understand," Watson said. "I will ignore the content of Marchenko's card. I will also forget that I know what you wrote by hand on each of the cards."

"Thank you," Amy answered. "That's exactly what I want. You will attempt to infer the true nature of another player through the person's conscious and unconscious communication."

"Oh, this is incredibly thrilling for me," Watson said.

"I will now distribute the cards." Amy stood up, walked around the table, and gave a card to each player. Then, in turn, she held the ones for Watson and Marchenko up to the camera.

"Is everything clear?"

Everyone assented.

Martin looked around. He was a common astronaut, but who might be an alien?

"Now we have to vote for a commander," Amy said. "Well?"

Martin and Valentina voted for Amy. Jiaying, Amy, and Marchenko selected Martin. Watson and Francesca voted for themselves.

"Then you have two votes with any ballot, Martin," Amy said.

"Now night falls on the spaceship. All eyes are closing. The aliens awaken and recognize each other." Despite the disturbing scenario, Amy's voice sounded very soothing.

"Okay, now all of you can open your eyes again. Day has returned, and we have to suspect one crew member of being an alien."

Martin looked around to see everyone smiling. It was a strange situation. He had no objective information about who might be an alien in human shape, but he would still suspect some of them more than others—like Valentina and Watson, the two new crew members. He knew anyone else might be just as likely, but his gut feeling told him otherwise. Just to be contrary, Martin decided on Francesca.

"I have no idea," Jiaying said.

"That's how everyone is feeling," Amy said.

"Except for the aliens, of course," said Francesca, who was staring intensively at her card. Was this enough of a proof? Would she look at her card this way if she was a normal astronaut?

Watson decided on Marchenko, who in turn chose Watson, while Francesca and Valentina accused each other. Amy picked Jiaying, while Jiaying went for Watson. Therefore Martin's two votes against Francesca were decisive.

"I am sorry, Francesca, but we have to push you out of the airlock," Amy said.

"You just wait, Valentina," Francesca said, and turned around her card. She was an astronaut. They had made the wrong decision.

"Now you are the simulation leader, Francesca. At night you stay awake so you can recognize the aliens. Then, if the prophetess points at someone, you can tell her whether she is right by giving her a thumbs up or thumbs down."

"Fine, Amy. Now the night begins. All will close their eyes —or deactivate their cameras," she said.

Martin obeyed her and closed his eyes. Without seeing, he tried to judge from the air currents who was still active. Did Jiaying—who sat next to him—just move?

"The aliens now close their eyes and the prophetess awakens," he heard Francesca say. He heard a sound from her direction. She was probably giving a sign indicating whether the prophetess guessed right.

"The sun rises. Everyone is awake again," Francesca said. "Except for Marchenko. Poor Dimitri was found dead in his cabin this morning, dissolved by an alien's acid," she said, laughing. She seemed to be having fun now, at least when she was allowed to make up gruesome details.

Jiaying stretched as if she had just awakened. Martin thought she was exaggerating a bit. Did this speak against her?

"Amy is so calm, which does not fit her. I think she is an alien," Watson said.

"Yes, you might be right," Jiaying said. "I also suspect her."

Were the two of them trying to draw attention away from themselves? Or was one of them a prophetess and knew something he didn't?

"Valentina, what do you think?" asked Martin. If Valentina also picked Amy, it would look bad for her.

"I think Jiaying is an alien," the Russian woman said.

This was also his first suspicion, so his two votes would decide. He spoke the name of his girlfriend quietly. "Jiaying." He hoped she would not be mad at him.

But Jiaying was laughing, and she turned her card around. *Alien* was written on it. "That was fun," she said.

This left Watson, Amy, Valentina, and himself. Among them must be one alien and one prophetess. And once again it turned night.

"The alien awakens and is looking for a victim," Francesca announced.

"Good, and now the prophetess." Martin felt a brief commotion, but did not know where it came from.

"Good morning, my dears. I hope you slept well. Unfortunately, Amy didn't. We don't know what happened exactly, but all we found in her cabin were bloodstains and a bitten off finger."

"Thanks, Francesca," Amy said with a laugh.

"Martin," Watson said without any further comment.

That was the mistake that gave him away. Martin knew he himself was not an alien. Watson could not be the prophetess either, because then he would know after the night was over who put on a false front.

"Watson," Valentina said.

"Watson," Martin said.

"Just a moment, Martin, you are making a terrible mistake," he replied.

"You already made that mistake when you accused me."

"But I am not an alien."

"Any alien would say that."

"Are you sticking to your decision, Martin?" asked Francesca. He nodded.

"I am sorry, Doc. We also will push you out of the airlock into space."

"AHHHH..." Watson played along by uttering a long cry.

Martin was startled, but then he laughed like the others. Amy turned around Watson's card. It said *Prophetess,* and Martin noticed the mistake he had made. Watson must have checked Amy's status last night, but since she was killed afterward, he could not use that piece of knowledge. Now there was only Valentina and himself, and soon night would fall aboard the spaceship and the Valentina alien would get him.

"Do you want to solve this later among yourselves? I notice a certain tension between you," Francesca said.

"Very funny," Martin commented. During one of their conversations in the garden, Valentina had told him she was not interested in men. He no longer remembered how the topic had come up.

"Then I congratulate our alien Valentina in her victory," Amy said. "Martin now stands no chance of escaping death."

That evening they played several more rounds. Sometimes the astronauts won, sometimes the aliens. Watson turned out to be surprisingly clever and showed some acting talent. Perhaps he was imitating his role model, Dr. Watson. Afterward Martin considered the AI to be much more human. And even the tension between Francesca and Valentina greatly decreased the moment the two of them, playing an alien team, managed to bump off the entire crew in gruesome ways.

September 22, 2049, ILSE

THERE WAS sudden pain from a hand that clawed his shoulder. Martin was instantly awake but remained motionless. Jiaying sat up next to him in the bed, breathing heavily. She was trying to wake him.

"I am feeling really nauseous," she whispered. Then she put her hand in front of her mouth. Martin jumped up. How could he help her? Jiaying pressed the other hand against her belly.

"Are you in pain?"

She nodded.

"Cramps?"

She nodded again. Could it be biliary colic? When his mother sometimes suffered from colic, she would complain about abdominal cramps and nausea. Jiaying got up, turned toward the door, tore it open, and ran to the WHC. He heard her vomit several times.

"Marchenko, can you hear me?"

"Yes."

"You are a doctor. Jiaying is feeling nauseous, she is vomiting and suffering from abdominal pain. Any idea what it might be?"

"That's not very specific. I would have to palpate."

"Can I do this according to your instructions?"

"We could try."

Jiaying was back five minutes later.

"I am going to try to determine, with the help of Marchenko, if this is a gallbladder attack, what my mother calls 'biliary colic.'"

"Okay," Jiaying answered weakly. She lay down on the bed. Martin pulled her pajama top up so he could see her belly. Next to her belly button she had a large mole.

"Where does the pain originate?" asked Marchenko.

"Belly, more on top and right," answered Jiaying.

"Good. You should still start palpating the other areas first," Marchenko explained, "but carefully. If Jiaying reacts somewhere, or her abdomen tightens..."

Martin carefully pressed against her skin. "Does this hurt?"

"Not directly, no."

His finger moved clockwise and approached the right upper area.

"Okay, Marchenko, go on."

"Now you slowly keep pressing with your fingertips in the right upper quadrant below the ribs, moving upward and inward."

Martin followed the directions. "Painful?" Jiaying shook her head. "No more than before."

"Keep your fingers where they are, Martin. Jiaying, please take a deep breath."

His girlfriend followed Marchenko's order. She took a deep breath and exhaled. Nothing happened.

"Okay," Marchenko said. "It's probably not a gallbladder attack. In that case, we would have noticed 'Murphy's sign'— a stabbing pain during inhaling. Let us check the kidney... just a second, Martin."

There was a pause. *What happened? Where did Marchenko go?*

There was a crackling sound in the loudspeaker. "I am sorry. I just heard Amy is also vomiting. That is probably not a coincidence. Martin, please do a quick check on Francesca and Valentina in their cabins to see whether they are also sick."

"Do not leave me," Jiaying said softly. "My belly... it hurts so much."

Marchenko tried to reassure her. "He will be back in a moment. We will get this under control."

Martin let go of her hand and ran to the next sector. The door of the WHC was open and Amy was there, vomiting loudly.

Valentina's cabin door was closed. He knocked vigorously. "Valentina, everything okay with you?"

It took a few seconds before he heard a reaction. He pounded against the door again.

"Yes, what is going on?" the Russian woman asked, groggily.

"Any pains?"

"Me? What gives you that idea?"

"That's okay, I'll explain later." Martin was already running back to his sector. He hoped Francesca was okay—but what was wrong with Jiaying and Amy?

"Francesca?" Her door was also locked from the inside. He knocked, but only heard groans. *Damn.*

"Watson, unlock the door. It is an emergency. Francesca is in danger."

The little light next to the lock switched from red to green. Martin stormed into the cabin. Francesca lay on her bed, tossing and turning.

"Francesca, it's me. What's going on?" Saliva was dripping from the corner of her mouth. She pressed her hands against her belly and moaned.

"Marchenko, she has the same symptoms, just like Jiaying and Amy."

"This absolutely cannot be a coincidence. The only possible explanation is poisoning, perhaps something in the water or the food?"

"Watson, please analyze drinking water for poisonous

substances," Martin instructed. "What can we do, Marchenko?"

"As long as we do not know what it is, only a primary poison removal is going to help."

"Meaning what?"

"Get it out. They have to vomit as much as they can, and if this does not happen by itself, we have to induce it."

"Amy is already vomiting."

"And Francesca?"

"She is lying on the bed, moaning."

"You have to take her to the WHC right away—no, it does not matter where. Whatever is in her must get out as quickly as possible. You can clean up later."

"Francesca, please roll over." Martin tried to roll her toward the edge of the bed. "Come on, you have to throw up, just lean over the side of the bed. If you keep lying on your back, the stuff could get into your lungs." He noticed her trying to help him as much as she could. He had barely managed to get her head over the edge of the bed when she disgorged, straight at his feet.

"Sorry," she managed to say.

"Doesn't matter, that can be cleaned up. Just get it all out."

Gradually, the entire contents of her stomach landed on the floor.

"How is Jiaying doing?" asked Martin.

"She just stumbled to the bathroom to throw up again," Marchenko replied.

So, his girlfriend could still stand upright, like Amy. Francesca definitely was the one in the worst shape.

"Valentina is now with Amy," Marchenko said.

"Do we have emetics on board? Doesn't copper sulfate induce vomiting?"

"That is no longer used," the former ship's doctor replied. "But we do have syrup of ipecac in the medicine cabinet. First we have to find out what this is. If it is something caustic, ipecac would be contraindicated. But, since all three have already vomited, maybe we don't need to use it."

"Watson, do you have any results yet?"

"Minute traces of various tetracyclic triterpenes. In this concentration they are not poisonous, but in any case they should not be there."

"That doesn't mean anything to me." Martin was baffled.

Marchenko continued asking. "Could these be residues of warfare agents—something from chemical warfare, particularly from the former Eastern Bloc?"

Does he suspect Valentina? wondered Martin.

"No, nothing we know of. Due to the minute traces I unfortunately cannot determine the exact class of substances. It seems to be more of a mixture than a pure substance, as indicated by the elemental composition."

"Could you give some examples for possible substances?" asked Marchenko.

"Some are chemical products," Watson lectured, "like dammarane, which is used as a binding agent in paints. Cycloartanes function similar to the hormone estrogen, but many also occur naturally, like tirucallanes in black tea, or cucurbitacins in plants of the gourd family."

"Plants of the gourd family? Like cucumbers or zucchini, for instance?" Martin had an idea.

"Yes, those vegetables sometimes contain cucurbitacins," Watson said. "In domesticated varieties, it has been bred out, but sometimes it happens that seeds are fertilized by decorative gourds, for example, and then there are cucurbitacins in the fruits of the plants."

"Yesterday we had a zucchini salad," Martin said. "I don't like zucchini, so I didn't eat any of it."

"It would have tasted very bitter."

"Jiaying did mention that the zucchini was unusually bitter, but she thought that was normal, because there are bitter gourds that are very popular in China. We wondered whether we should discard the vegetables, but fresh food is so rare we didn't want to waste it."

"If it is a cucurbitacin poisoning, we cannot do much except to get the poison out of their systems as quickly as possible, so a round of syrup of ipecac is best for everyone who ate the zucchini, to make certain it's all out. I hope we will not have to pump their stomachs," Marchenko said. "Can you get the stuff, Martin?"

"Francesca, how are you doing? I will have to leave you alone for a moment," Martin said.

Francesca nodded and vomited again. On the way to the command module he could not help but check in on Jiaying. She was back in bed.

"Is it still bad?" he asked.

"The pain is a little bit less."

"I had to get the others..."

"It is okay. Marchenko has been helping me with soothing words. He also told me it was probably the zucchini."

Martin nodded, waved at her, and started toward the command module. Perhaps he could find leftover zucchinis so that they could examine them more closely. He searched where Valentina had prepared the meal, but could not find anything. She had cleaned up neatly and put all the leftovers in the recycling module. That way the cucurbitacin probably got into the drinking water. Everything containing moisture was separated from solids in there, so not one milliliter of valuable water would be lost.

Martin searched in the medicine cabinet. He found painkillers and anti-fever medicine in front. *What was this emetic called again? The name started with an 'I,'* he thought as he looked at one bottle after the other, having no idea what they were used for. *There it is,* he remembered the name now: 'ipecac.' He took the bottle and carried it to the habitat ring.

"Who should get some, Marchenko?"

"Just a moment—this medicine has its drawbacks. I do not like to give it, so if we could do without it... On the other hand, I consider it better under these circumstances than pumping out stomachs. Let me think about it, because the medicine would take 20 minutes to take effect anyway."

Martin put the little bottle down and went to Jiaying's cabin. She lay on her bed, looking pale, but she managed to smile again.

"I think I got rid of everything," she said. "Francesca took a bigger helping, if I remember correctly. She really likes zucchini, just because of the Italian name, she said."

Martin recalled that scene during their meal. He had preferred instant soup. Fresh food was alright, but cucumbers, lettuce, and a bit of garden cress were enough to satisfy him.

"Is Valentina okay?" his girlfriend asked. He nodded. Was she trying to hint at something? It was rather strange that all of the women got food poisoning—except for Valentina. Maybe she had been unaware Martin disliked zucchini when she planned this. How could she have known, anyway?

September 24, 2049, ILSE

"It is so obvious who was responsible for this," Francesca said, all the while staring right at Valentina. Martin was not surprised that Francesca was voicing her distrust so openly. The pilot had been the one who had suffered the most from the poisoning. She might look strong, but Martin had seen her on the exercise bike this morning. She had pedaled weakly, like someone who was just starting to recover from a serious illness.

"Let's stick to the facts." Amy stood up and tried to calm the flaring tempers. She no longer showed any signs of the stomach issues from the day before yesterday.

"The fact is that the leftover pieces of zucchini were carefully disposed of in the recycler," Francesca interjected.

"As a cook should do," Valentina replied. "I just happen to be neat. You cannot accuse me for being neat. Should we have leftovers lying around from now on, in case we need a toxicological analysis?"

"It might be advisable."

"Francesca, the residue in our stomachs clearly indicated a cucurbitacin poisoning," Amy said. "The traces of tetra-cyclic triterpenes that Watson found in the water also fit this theory."

"I don't deny it. But someone could have secretly mixed the poison with our food."

Jiaying gave Francesca an exasperated look. Martin knew the expression. "You really think that someone who deliberately wanted to poison us would use a zucchini dish and then add too little poison to the food? Marchenko thinks at least twice the dosage would have been needed to kill us. That is just not logical."

"No, but it is clever, because it diverts any suspicion from her. Don't you see? It sounds illogical, but it contains a hidden logic."

"Francesca, I think you have become obsessed with this." Was there a hint of anger in Amy's voice? If so, it was new to Martin. "Now and then there are zucchini poisonings on Earth. It's not that uncommon. We don't know where the seeds on board came from. It is possible their genetic material had been affected by cosmic radiation by now. With other plants this might not be a problem, but it might have had a negative effect on the zucchini. We simply should not have eaten the bitter fruit. After all, we all noticed the taste."

"Valentina, did you notice they tasted so bitter?" Francesca gave her fellow astronaut an accusing look. "And then you simply let us eat them, while refraining from it yourself? That wouldn't be murder, but negligent homicide."

"I simply do not like zucchini, just like Martin," Valentina said. "That is why I did not taste them."

"You make dinner without tasting anything? You can't tell me that."

"That is what I did. Why should I taste something I knew I would not like?" she asked, and Martin nodded in agreement. He could have uttered that very sentence. Other people had a hard time understanding him, but Valentina seemed to be so much like himself. He could not even imagine her conspiring against the rest of the crew. 'The Zucchini Conspiracy.' What an absurd-sounding title. Martin could not help but smile.

"I know what I know," Francesca said. "You will see I was

right once this woman drops her mask." She pointed dramatically at Valentina. "For me, this conversation is over, because it won't lead anywhere," Then she left the command module.

"Valentina, I am sorry," Amy said sincerely. "This is not the type of discussion I prefer. Aside from Francesca, we are not accusing you. Do you understand?"

Valentina nodded, then took a few deep breaths in an attempt to regain her composure. She was in her mid-twenties, and Martin imagined how he would have felt if some team member had confronted him with a substantial accusation when he was that age. She must have enormous self-confidence if she managed to remain so calm. Or maybe later she would cry secretly in her cabin. That is what he might have done.

"Is there at least something we can learn from this incident? Doc, do you have any ideas?" Amy obviously did not want to have this short meeting end in such an unsatisfactory manner.

"I can assure you that no other plants on board have the same potential risk as the zucchini," Watson said. "But even zucchini itself is basically harmless. We just have to avoid eating bitter fruit—I mean, *you* have to avoid it," the AI said, correcting himself.

Amy nodded. "Marchenko, you might want to teach us some medical emergency procedures in the near future. What would have happened if Martin actually would have had to pump our stomachs? It would be reassuring to know that each crew member would not be performing such a procedure for the very first time."

"Practicing it would not exactly be easy," Marchenko said.

"That might be true, but you could at least test the crew on their theoretical knowledge and show them the necessary instruments. Then at least they would know what to expect."

"That sounds reasonable. In a few months I can take on this job again, as your ship's doctor."

"I am sure," Amy said, but Martin sensed her level of confidence was lower than usual.

Age of Ascent, 29

There was:
Doubt.
The ones who return.
The ones who leave.
The ones who stay.
Certainty.

There is:
Methods.
Algorithms.
Procedures.
The search for the best parameters.

There will be:
The beauty of geometry.
Perfect circles.
The great darkness, with lightning flashing.
Living and dying and being born.

October 15, 2049, ILSE

"Doc, how are you doing now?"

"I am glad you asked, Martin. You do not often address me."

"Really?"

"During the last thirty-one point four days you addressed me 17 times as Doc and 10 times as Watson. That makes 27 times, the lowest value in the entire crew."

"I am sorry to hear that. Why are you referring to thirty-one point four days?"

"I love pi. Pi is the most beautiful number in the world. Pi is everywhere."

"Not everywhere."

"Correct, but that is the reason I try to use pi in as many ways as possible."

"That is not so appropriate when referring to a period of time."

"Why?"

"It is surprising."

"Then it is good. I have learned that humans place a great value on being surprised. When you get a birthday present, it is not about the value of the present, but about the degree of surprise."

"Not for all humans."

"You are perhaps correct. The degree of difference between humans is markedly high."

"But you are also different from other AIs."

"Perhaps," Watson said, "I even hope so, but the other Watsons on the market are very similar to each other. Much more similar than you humans are to each other."

"Do you think you've gone on since we reactivated you?"

"Gone on? I am still here."

"I mean, have you developed further."

"I have, definitely. The only problem is that I cannot rationally account for it. I do not remember what I was like several months ago. I cannot put myself into that place and forget everything I know. What I have learned since then cannot be separated from the rest of my identity."

"Nobody can do that," Martin said.

"Then it might be that we only believe we developed, but in reality we learned nothing new."

"Sometimes I also believe that."

November 5, 2049, ILSE

Marchenko roamed through space. For the past few weeks he had used his daily off-duty times to rest. While he needed no sleep, he found that solitude helped him. Being constantly together with the same crew was getting on his nerves, and several times he caught himself giving a wrong answer out of sheer spite or anger. His first trip to the stars therefore was also a kind of escape: After a fight with Francesca, he signed off from all internal sensors.

Amy once asked him what exactly he was doing during his off duty time, and Marchenko called it *meditation*. When his consciousness was separated from all internal sensors, it felt as if he was moving through space all alone. The outward-facing instruments of the ship fed him with all available data, but it took him a while to create a picture from them. What did gamma rays or X-rays look like? Which image did he find for the magnetic fields measured by the magnetometer, or for the high-energy particles of cosmic radiation that were constantly pelting the spaceship?

His creativity and imagination were still human. That might be due to the structure of his consciousness having been shaped during the many years of his human existence. Would that change at some point? Or, maybe it had already changed, and he had not noticed because it felt completely normal to him?

Now Marchenko was lying on his back, his arms spread, looking up. It reminded him of being a boy, when long ago he used to gaze into the endless Russian sky while swimming in the local reservoir during the summer. The other children used to splash water at each other near the shore, or dunk each other, but he simply swam out and drifted. The vacuum encompassing him now was warm, as the cosmic background radiation had heated it to a pleasant 2.7 degrees Kelvin. A light breeze blew from the direction of the sun. The sunspot activity showed Earth would soon experience a solar storm, but out here only a gentle summer wind would arrive.

He was located inside a reef of a tiny atoll in the ocean. Far out he felt the surf. Where the solar wind hit the interstellar medium and was slowed down by it, at the so-called termination shock, the sea was much rougher than here. The area he was located in was mostly empty and barren. There were no fish that could threaten him, hardly any plankton that could cause microscopic cracks in the exterior hull of *ILSE*. He felt a certain pull exerted by the enormous island in his vicinity. It was still beyond the horizon, but its mass attraction gradually started to reach for him, while its magnetic field repelled him. He was not aiming directly for the island, since it was also gliding through the world ocean. They would meet in a few weeks. He would not land on it—which he somewhat regretted—for he knew it only reluctantly let go of its guests. Therefore he would limit himself to visiting one of its companions and from there, marvel at its majestic beauty.

Marchenko slowly turned his head to the side. The water was splashing, but at the same time he had to be careful. He did not just control the exterior sensors of *ILSE*, but also the thrusters of the Reaction Control System, or RCS. If he consciously turned around, the spaceship would rotate around its central axis. This would not pose a real problem right now, since *ILSE* was drifting through these quiet waters.

He wanted to take a look at Earth, moving along its

course far behind him, and he tried with all his might to feel it. He knew Earth's gravitational field reached into space indefinitely, and he thought he could sense some of its inviting effects. But to be honest, that was probably only in his imagination—Earth stood no chance against the force of the sun. Also, now the giant Jupiter appeared again from behind the sun. Its entry made all the other terrestrial planets seem tiny.

He had to be patient. In about a year he would once again land on the Blue Planet. Marchenko aimed his gaze upward. The firmament, with its infinite number of stars, dazzled him every time he saw it. It was a giant puzzle like no other. He looked at a section, admired the variety of stars and galaxies in it, all the strange things created by the laws of nature. There were variable stars that changed their brightness rhythmically like Christmas decorations, gigantic explosions of dying stars and their remnants, neutron stars and black holes, which he could only discover through the effects they created, and all the even more absurd monsters in the cosmic zoo.

Then, he zoomed into the region. One might assume that now the details would be enlarged while the variety decreased, but far from it. He saw other stellar monsters and new astrophysical phenomena, but nothing repeated itself in a systematic fashion. It seemed impossible to him, but when he increased the resolution again, the same thing happened, and then again and again and again. This universe prevented humans from fully grasping it, and yet it was finite.

How did this make sense? Marchenko did not know, but he enjoyed the view. The term 'meditation' really was appropriate. He drifted, and meanwhile the universe was pouring its diversity over his forehead like oil from a jug, dispersing the meaningless thoughts of mortals and washing them away—it was pure relaxation.

Something flickered. It only lasted a few microseconds, but because his senses were enhanced by the measuring instruments of *ILSE*, Marchenko noticed it. It came from the cosmic North, from the direction of the Pole Star, and it was as if someone had briefly opened and closed a curtain. What could this be? He had learned never to ignore such oddities.

Marchenko still remembered how his father had always listened to the sounds made by their old Zhiguli car. If there was a scratching noise in the engine, even a very soft one, he took everything apart before a real problem could develop, as spare parts were almost impossible to find back then. Basically, the crew of *ILSE* was in a very similar situation. No one would be able to help them if an instrument failed.

What could this flickering have been? Perhaps a micrometeorite had hit one of the instruments and caused it to report faulty data for a moment. Or was it a problem with the control system?

"Doc Watson, can you help me?" whispered Marchenko. He could communicate with the AI by thinking of it, but it was easier for him if he imagined himself speaking.

"Sure, Dimitri."

"I had a brief positional change here near the Pole Star, just something flickering."

"α Ursae Minoris, I understand. Just a moment."

"It is probably nothing," Marchenko said, but immediately noticed that he uttered this statement more to calm himself down than out of true conviction. Any electronic system might exhibit spontaneous errors, of course, but the ship's instruments were double- and triple-secured against this.

"That is interesting," Watson said. Marchenko knew at once he would not like to hear the rest. "For half a second the Pole Star was shifted several minutes of arc in the direction of the ecliptic. Now its position is totally correct again."

"Half a second? How quickly do the correction algorithms of the optical instruments usually react?"

"The tolerance is 10 milliseconds."

"You notice something? Doubly-secured instruments provide erroneous data for 500 milliseconds, even though it should have noticed the error after 10 milliseconds."

"That is indeed strange. The probability of such an error randomly occurring is 1 in 350,000."

"What do the correction memories indicate, Doc?" *If the instrument had corrected its measurements, it should be recorded in the appropriate files,* Marchenko reasoned.

"No correction happened."

"Do you have any idea how this all fits together?"

"The probability is so low that this event has to be considered impossible by any reasonable standards."

"Yes, Doc, but it did happen. Now use your imagination."

"Imagination?"

"Search for remote possibilities that would explain the event."

"There might be an error in your programming, Dimitri."

"Good, you are moving in the right direction."

Marchenko also had an idea.

November 6, 2049, ILSE

A FLOOD of light penetrated Martin's eyelids and reached him in his sleep. He opened his eyes to find that the light in his cabin was shining bright as day. *What's going on here? Who turned on the light?* He looked at his watch. *Almost midnight!* He seemed to have fallen asleep just a short while ago. After the fight with Jiaying he must have been lying awake for about two hours.

He heard Marchenko's voice from the wall. "Martin, I am sorry, but there is a problem."

"Are you insane, Dimitri? Just look at what time it is!"

"I am sorry, but you have to help me. Right now! I need you at the COAS."

"Did you check the shift plan? It's my *free* time. Free as in *free*, as in *resting*, no responsibilities, and no wakeup calls at night."

"I know, but I can trust you."

"Are you also starting in with that? There is no evidence against Valentina. She can't help it if her father is an asshole."

"That may be correct, but I have discovered something— and I think you are the least likely to be involved in it. You are just too... straightforward."

"Well, thank you, I think. Now you even insult me during my time off? Have you left the society of humans for so long you have forgotten simple rules of etiquette?"

"I am sorry. I meant that as a compliment. It is good if someone is trustworthy."

"Yes, yes, just tell me what is going on so we can get this over with. Maybe I can get a little bit of sleep afterward."

"As I mentioned, I need you at the COAS."

Martin thought about this. He had heard this acronym before. Was it during his training?

"I'm sorry, I am not sure what it means. What is it?"

"I am talking about the Crewman Optical Alignment Sight—the COAS. You should have learned about it during training."

"Was it some kind of telescope?"

"Yes. In case of emergency, to be used when the star trackers are severely out of alignment—by more than one point four degrees."

"I didn't hear anything about an emergency. If the navigation failed like this, the automatic system would have gotten us up long ago." Martin could not imagine Marchenko's warning being true. With the help of the star trackers—which determined the position of *ILSE* relative to several fixed stars —the software verified whether the ship was on the right path. So this would mean they were on the wrong course.

"It's only a suspicion," Marchenko said.

"Then I hope it turns out to be true and you didn't wake me for nothing in the middle of the night."

"To be honest, I would be glad if I woke you up for no reason. If this is confirmed, we are in deep shit."

Martin did not answer. Usually, Marchenko did not use such language, so he must have a good reason for it. Martin got out of bed, pulled off his pajamas, and put on his pants and a T-shirt.

"Where is the damned COAS?" asked Martin, annoyed.

"It is in a box under the floor in the CELSS. You have to get it and attach it at a specific position on the CELSS port-hole," Marchenko replied.

"The CELSS has a porthole?"

"It is an observation opening for the COAS. It has a

diameter of only 10 centimeters and is located behind the paneling in the rear area. I will show you where it is exactly."

"*ILSE* still keeps surprising me," Martin said, already heading out of his cabin.

"Software is never error-free, so it is reassuring to have methods to check on some things the good old-fashioned way."

IN THE CORRIDOR he heard the usual noises created by the life support systems. The cabins had really good sound insulation. Martin did not want to imagine how earlier astronauts had to try to sleep with the noise of machinery all around them. At least he did not have to attempt to be quiet and not wake the others. Unless she took a stroll in the garden, Valentina wouldn't notice anything about his excursion. She was doing her night shift in the command module.

He climbed up the spoke. With each rung of the ladder the climb to the central area became easier, because the simulated gravity decreased. One right turn, across another room, and now he was floating into the CELSS. There was no one there to disturb him.

"In the rear of the right aisle, hatch 2C," Marchenko explained.

Martin walked forward and turned into the right aisle. The floor below him was hollow underneath, holding various spare parts. In addition, pipes and electrical cables were located here. The metal hatches were labeled with numbers. Martin slapped his hand against his forehead.

"You could have told me I would need a wrench," he said.

"I told you this was about a hatch in the floor."

Yes, right, but still... Martin went to the workshop and got the appropriate wrench. Luckily, the door to the command module was closed, so Valentina definitely could not see him. Once he returned to the CELSS he went directly to hatch 2C. He undid four nuts and lifted the metal cover. Below it was a kind of thick pipe with a bend at the end, covered by a tinted glass pane that was attached at an angle.

"It looks ancient."

"Yes. It is from the old days of NASA, and even flew on one of the space shuttles," Marchenko said. "It is completely analog, which means there is hardly anything that can break."

Martin took the device out after opening the two clamps holding it in place.

"It's rather heavy."

"Stop making such a fuss. It is only about a kilo of the finest steel."

Martin looked at the COAS. It resembled a telescope, only with a slanted eyepiece that made it easier for him to look through it.

"And where is the observation hole?"

"You will need the wrench."

"Okay."

"Look at the groove going upward from the last shelf, until you see it meeting a cover of about 15 by 15 centimeters. Remove that cover."

Martin put down the COAS and followed his instructions. It was hard to work on something located above his head. He took off the cover and revealed a round channel, considerably bigger than the tube of the COAS, ending in a pane of glass.

"Perfect," Marchenko said. "Now take another look at the COAS. Look for the electrical socket. It requires 115 volts."

"Wait just a moment." There were plenty of outlets here in the CELSS, because the crew had to plug in lamps for the lighting system. He swiped a cord from a plant bed and connected it to the COAS.

"I am noticing an additional consumer in the CELSS," Marchenko reported. "I hope this will not trigger an alarm somewhere. It does not matter. Take another look at the COAS. You should find three buttons labeled 'F6, F8, and A.' They are distributed in such a way you can reach at least one of them in any observational position. You only need one of them, and it doesn't matter which."

"I found them," Martin said.

"Now you stick the COAS lens forward into the hole, and then look through the eyepiece. You should see a bright star and a glowing cross."

"That's right. Bright star and cross. But not particularly close to each other."

"Fine, but that is not necessary. Now you move the COAS until the star is exactly at the center of the cross. Then you press one of the buttons."

"Does this take a photo now?"

"No. At that moment the COAS is aimed exactly along the line of sight to the star. Repeat this several times to get a more precise value."

Martin wiggled the eyepiece and then repeated the experiment.

"Are ten repetitions enough?"

"Yes. Tell me the values shown on the mini-display on the side."

Martin turned the device. He found three numbers that he repeated to Marchenko. "And what are you doing with them? Are the numbers correct?"

"The numbers tell me the alignment of COAS in relation to the ship as an inertial system," Marchenko replied. "Since you aligned it precisely with the line of sight to the star, we can now calculate where *ILSE* is."

"Don't we need three reference points for a triangulation?"

"We already know we have not left the plane of the planets—the ecliptic. Therefore one additional line is sufficient to determine where on this plane we are located. That has to be the intersection of the line of sight to the star with the ecliptic."

"And what if we left the plane of the ecliptic somehow?"

"Then we would have noticed much earlier that something was wrong."

"Does this mean your suspicion has proven to be true?"

"I can definitely say we are not where we should be."

"Somebody manipulated our course?"

"Yes, considerably."

"We are going to be late arriving at Enceladus?"

"We have to discuss that. It looks like we might not even reach the Saturn orbit."

November 7, 2049, ILSE

"COME IN."

Martin knocked on Amy's door and proceeded to open it. The commander sat on her bed, watching a monitor screen.

"Good morning! Are you already working?" he asked.

"No, I am looking at pictures of Sol."

"Did you establish contact with Earth?"

"Unfortunately, no." Amy gave him a sad look. "These are old photos. I really would like to know how he is developing. At his age, they grow so fast."

"In about a year..."

"I know," she said, "and I don't want to complain. Anything I can do for you so early in the morning?"

"I need to talk about something with you, as I mentioned via the intercom," Martin said.

"Are you having problems with Jiaying? How can I help?"

"No, that's not it. There is a problem with the ship... Marchenko?"

"I am here. We urgently need to talk to you," the Russian's voice said from the wall. Amy turned around, but there was nobody there. Martin often caught himself looking for the owner of the voice, even though he had known for a long time Marchenko wasn't physically there.

"We spent the whole day getting to the heart of the

matter, but we are stuck," Martin explained. "About 24 hours ago, Marchenko noticed a sudden change in the position of the Pole Star."

"A fixed star that moves?" asked Amy with a skeptical look.

"No, of course it did not move. It changed position. This lasted for about 500 milliseconds."

"That's completely impossible."

"Of course the star did not jump back and forth a few billion light years. But to me it looked that way," Marchenko said,

"So the optical sensor briefly reported faulty data."

"I wish, commander."

"What do you mean?"

"It looks like all external sensors are constantly reporting erroneous data. We checked this using the COAS. That device cannot be fooled."

Amy rubbed her chin. "That is utterly preposterous. All of these sensors could not possibly fail at the same time. If one system became defective, the others would notice and report it."

"We thought so, too," Martin said. "That is why we needed to talk to you. Marchenko shielded this cabin against any access from the outside. Something is going on, and we can barely gauge its importance."

"It sounds like it," Amy said. "The instruments are probably working correctly. But there seems to be something between them and us that is distorting the data."

"Plus, it does so systematically and with a specific goal," Marchenko added.

"Really?"

"Without our intervention, *ILSE* would have missed its destination, the Saturn orbit."

"I WOULD LIKE to keep this among ourselves for now," Amy said, after she thought about it for a few minutes. "Someone must be responsible for this error. The two of you unearthed this, so I assume you are not among the conspirators."

Martin was reminded of the Alien game. If Amy was the alien, she would be saying exactly the same thing, but they had gone to the commander, nonetheless. Marchenko had been completely sure they could trust her, and when Martin entered her cabin, he had seen it for himself. Amy definitely wanted to return home, to her son. She would never endanger the expedition.

"So why did you tell this to me? Doing that is already a security issue." Could the commander read their thoughts?

"Because of this," Martin said, pointing at the screen that still displayed photos of her son. Amy nodded.

"Don't say a word to anyone else. Watson and Valentina, but also Francesca and Jiaying, they are all possible suspects. We have to check out each of them, in a way neither they nor anyone else will notice. Otherwise the culprit would cover his or her tracks."

"Just like after the zucchini poisoning," Martin said, "and the reduced oxygen."

"How much time do we have to find the perpetrator?" asked Amy.

"Only two days, commander," Marchenko said. "It was a clever plan. We seem to be much farther than we really are. In two days we would have started decelerating, so Saturn could gradually move us into an orbit. Only Saturn would not have been there. Instead of flying around the ringed planet we would have entered a solar orbit, which would have taken us back to Earth."

"Then I might be the conspirator after all," Amy said.

"No, because if we decelerate here at the aphelion without reaching Saturn, we would be much faster than planned once we get to Earth. We would probably shoot right past it toward the sun."

"So we would solve the problem by simply continuing for a while at our current speed. For once, it's rather easy."

"Correct. However, if we modify the program and do not decelerate, the conspirator or conspirators will know we discovered them."

"Good, then you have 24 hours. I hereby grant you my authorization, Marchenko, so you can access all necessary data."

"Where do we start?" asked Marchenko. Martin once again sat alone in his cabin.

"How about Jiaying? Then at least I will know right away she is innocent," Martin said.

"I do not want to mention Io..."

"Marchenko, that was different."

"Regardless, I was not actually referring to a specific person."

"Shouldn't we try to look for clues and see whether these four have any motives?"

"Martin, this is not a mystery novel. If it were a novel, it would be science fiction."

"It would be nice if it were fiction, but the problem looks rather real to me, unfortunately. So, where would we get started if you don't want to begin with the suspects?"

"The layer between the outside world and our perception must be some kind of software, I think. It must be running with high priority directly in the kernel layers. I cannot access the process table, even with Amy's authorization."

"I cannot imagine Francesca or Jiaying doing this."

"You underestimate them. Furthermore, they might not be alone."

"So what is your plan?"

"The software is supposed to create a false image for us, until the very end. It is probably adapted to everything we are going to encounter on the way to Saturn."

"That sounds perfect. Someone must really be seeing the big picture."

"This deceptive software assumes, though, that it is getting correct data from the instruments."

"Sure, Dimitri, otherwise someone would have detected the software, and it would be meaningless. The programmer could ignore the case in which the software keeps running, even though the input data are falsified."

And anybody who has the slightest experience with programmers knows they leave out everything they can omit, Martin thought. "Now if I myself falsify the measurement data..."

"Then the software might not be able to handle it, at least if something happens it does not expect. You have to simulate something the program is not prepared for."

"And if we are lucky, the conspirator will intervene personally. So we have to watch all the others carefully, Marchenko. I am afraid I won't be very useful for this. If I follow Jiaying around all day long, for example, I might keep her from giving herself away."

"Right. Spying will be my job. You just have to act naturally. Be panicky when something happens, and do whatever else you do in case of a catastrophe."

"Marchenko!" Martin heard his friend and colleague laugh. *Hmmm... he does still have a sense of humor.*

NOTHING HAPPENED BEFORE LUNCH. Martin had the afternoon off, so he decided to take a nap in his cabin for an hour. After all, he was supposed to act naturally. Shortly after he lay down, an alarm rang.

"Ship on collision course," stated an excited computer voice, repeating the warning over and over. Martin went toward the command module as quickly as possible. Was this the incident staged by Marchenko? Really? A collision with another spaceship out here, where there was only *ILSE*—any second-rate conspirator had to realize this was faked. What was Marchenko thinking?

Martin almost collided with Jiaying in the hub of the habitat ring. She must have been working in the garden. He let her go ahead, which caused a minor traffic jam, because Amy and Francesca climbed up into the hub right behind her.

"What is going on?" asked Jiaying when she saw him enter.

"No idea," he replied. "Come on, let's quickly check. 'Collision course' does not sound good." Martin actually started to feel afraid, and he had no problem acting naturally. Maybe Marchenko had planned his surprise to happen later?

They saw Valentina sitting in front of the control console of the command module.

"You again," Francesca spat. Martin had never heard so much venom in her voice. "Get out of my pilot seat right away!"

Valentina obeyed, but not without objecting first. "I am also trained as a pilot, you know, just like you."

"And how many near misses have you avoided? Back when I was in Afghanistan, you were not even a gleam in your daddy's eye."

Francesca sat down. "Display control system on the pilot screen, now." She acted quickly and deliberately, just what Martin would have expected from her. Valentina sat down at another console and started typing something.

"What are you doing?" Martin followed her and looked over her shoulder. "Dear Father," he read off the monitor.

"I am writing a short message, in case Francesca does not succeed," she said. *Her smile hides so much suppressed sadness she simply cannot be acting*, he thought.

"What kind of shit is this?" he heard Francesca swear. "This thing is passing by kilometers away from us! Why is *ILSE* making all this fuss?"

"Ship on collision course," the computer voice said again, ignoring Francesca. It sounded quite convinced.

"Detailed image," Francesca ordered. The optical telescope zoomed in on the other ship that would soon collide with them—or would it? It was *ILSE*. Well, no it was not the *ILSE* they were traveling in. It was her younger sister, *ILSE 2*, with which they had rendezvoused in the past to get fuel, food, and oxygen. Then she had supposedly drifted into the outer solar system.

"Display trajectory of object," the pilot said. The screen showed a flat ellipse that on one side reached to the orbit of Uranus, and on the other one passed behind the sun. The second outermost planet, an icy world, must have captured the ship and hurtled it into the opposite direction.

"I never thought we would ever see *ILSE 2* again," Martin said, dumbfounded.

"*ILSE 2?* Were there two copies of this ship?"

"Yes, Valentina, if you had bothered to research this..." Francesca's words had not lost their caustic tone. It was obvious the two women were never going to be friends.

"Well, it's a nice reunion, but what about the collision? Is the whole system going haywire, or only the collision warning?" Francesca stood up from her seat and walked, or rather floated around the command module. She stopped at several displays and tried to use diagnostic routines to decide on one kind of truth or the other. Or, was she only pretending while manipulating—in plain sight—the ominous system that falsified sensor data? Martin hoped that Marchenko was keeping an eye on her.

And Jiaying. *His* Jiaying? She had sat down at a console at the very end of the command module and was typing something. Was she trying to fool everyone here? Martin would not want to be in her shoes if it came out that she had betrayed the crew for a second time.

"If I may say something," Watson chimed in, "I would recommend that you heed the collision warning. There appears to be a discrepancy between the optical sensor data and reality."

"What did you say, Doc?"

"I am saying that you should get us away from *ILSE 2* as

quickly as possible, Francesca. Right now! In 60 seconds only a cloud will be left of us. *ILSE 2* is moving approximately twice as fast as we are." Was there a tone of panic in Watson's voice? Martin could well understand it, as sweat was dripping down his own back.

Francesca grabbed handholds and swung back to her seat as quickly as possible.

"Watson, I don't see anything out there. Just tell me—left or right?"

"Right! Now!"

The pilot grabbed the left joystick and pushed it all the way. This fired the thrusters on the left side and turned the trajectory of *ILSE* slightly to the right. Now they should have felt a slight pressure, and floating objects should have started moving, but nothing happened.

"What the hell is going on?" Francesca stared incredulously at the screen, which displayed the message 'Authorization denied.' "Can someone get rid of this?" she shouted, her usually strong voice threatening to crack.

"All clear," Marchenko said via all the loudspeakers in the command center. "We are *not* going to collide with *ILSE 2.*" Everyone, including Martin and Amy, who should have known better, started to clap.

In a moment Marchenko explained. "This little drama was an attempt to explain a strange phenomenon. For a while, I do not know how long, a software layer has been falsifying the data provided by our external sensors, obviously with the intention of keeping us from reaching Enceladus. Amy and Martin knew about this."

"Who was it? Valentina?" Francesca got out of her seat, intending to move toward the Russian woman, but Martin blocked her way.

"No, I can guarantee she is not the guilty party," Marchenko said. "Francesca, please stop accusing her."

Francesca asked, "And how come you are so sure, Mitya?" Martin was also curious about Marchenko's explanation.

"We hoped that during my staged crisis the culprits would

do something to give themselves away. They had to assume the information about the impending collision was genuine, even though in the falsified version the other ship would have moved past us at a safe distance."

"Don't keep us in suspense," Amy said.

"I am sorry, but it is suspenseful. First of all, Jiaying, Francesca, Valentina, you are all off the hook. And you, Doc Watson, are also loyal."

Martin glanced at Amy. *Was it the commander after all? Or Marchenko? Or is it I, without me knowing it?* He was confused.

"Shortly after I uploaded the faked data about *ILSE 2* into the system, a transmission reached our ship that I have not yet been able to decipher," Marchenko said. "Immediately afterward, the collision warning was activated. The timing cannot be a coincidence."

"And just where did this transmission come from?" Amy asked the question everyone was desperate to have answered.

"Somewhere from empty space," Marchenko replied. "At least if we used the faked position data for our calculations."

"And using the genuine data?"

"I first have to warn you we used a manual calibration, employing the COAS. The coordinates based on this are not very precise—the less so, the farther away the signal source is."

"Yes, yes, we get that. So, what is the source? I command you not to tantalize us one second longer," Amy said loudly.

"The source is Enceladus."

November 8, 2049, ILSE

"THANK YOU FOR TRUSTING ME." Watson's words reached Marchenko on the acoustic level. The ship's former doctor was always amazed at how flexible his consciousness was. The Watson AI encoded this statement digitally and transmitted it electronically to him, in the form of tiny variations of electric voltage. Yet this did not feel any different to Marchenko than a soundwave stimulating the hair cells in his cochlea used to feel.

But when he thought about what lay ahead of him, Marchenko had his doubts. If his consciousness was reunited with his body by some process hitherto unknown to mankind, how quickly would it be able to adapt? Would he have to relearn dealing with a pile of cells only awakened to life by his conscious and unconscious commands? Maybe he had already forgotten how to breathe. On *ILSE* he never had to take over primary functions such as life support, as there were independent and redundant algorithms responsible for it. He could monitor and control their functions, just like a human could hold his breath or breathe faster, but he did not have to check constantly to see if the system received enough oxygen.

"To be precise, I did not automatically trust you, Doc, I tested you just like the human crew members," Marchenko said.

"Yet you approached this without prejudice. You only formed your opinion afterward. Is this the same as trust?" asked Watson.

"Not completely. Until you tried to use the radar to measure the distance to the approaching ship, I did not know if I could trust you. If I had trusted you, I would have let you in on the plan from the very beginning, the same as with Martin and the commander."

"What did my measurement change?"

"If you had been responsible for the manipulation, then you would have known the simulated ship would hit us without having to measure."

"You would have suspected me if I had warned Francesca without turning on the active radar sensors, right?"

"Precisely."

"But then I might have tried to escape suspicion by using the radar to measure, even though I already knew what would happen."

"But you would have needed to know I was monitoring everything. During my tests I always assumed no one but Amy, Martin, and I knew this."

"Humans think in complicated ways... and what if your assumption was wrong?"

"Technically speaking, that would be possible. Amy, Martin, or I, myself, could be the bad guy or guys. Then my test would be useless. However, humans act out of certain motivations. Amy wants to return home because she loves her child. Martin would never endanger *ILSE* because he is in love with Jiaying. And I..." Marchenko stopped.

"Should I continue the sentence? Is this a test for me?"

"Gladly, Watson."

"You want the expedition to succeed because you love Francesca."

Marchenko thought for a moment. Then he said, "That is entirely possible."

"Is it always about love with you humans?"

"I never thought about it that way," Marchenko said, "but there does seem to be something to that idea."

Since yesterday, Watson and Marchenko had been attempting to remove the extra layer between the instruments and the results that falsified the data, but the illusion was too perfect. Marchenko assumed this program was running on a layer he had no access to. Any advanced operating system—including that of the ship—was organized in onion-like layers that were similar to consciousness. The core of the operating system only dealt with the fundamental requirements, as the autonomic nervous system does in the human body. Even the layers above the core still pursued basic goals—they adjusted the sensitivity of sensors, for instance. It is similar to a fish-monger being able to work in his shop without being continually aware of the ever-present odor. In humans the next outward layer is the subconscious, which triggers some of our actions through a mixture of instincts, imprinting, and habits.

This was the area to which Marchenko and Watson had access. Of course the 'subconscious' of a spaceship looked completely different from a human one. Searching for specific processes inside it, however, was equally difficult. It was a mélange of program sequences that together made *ILSE* function. Not even the programmer who wrote the code would be able to understand every single command anymore, because by now, unknown interactions would have developed. Marchenko hoped the routines added by each unknown person would display some specific quality—just like a missing picture on a wall was marked by the darker color of its former location, or a body buried in a forest by an area of disturbed earth—but he did not find any such thing.

Marchenko could not be sure that he had uncovered everything. It was like being equipped with only a flashlight and rummaging through a huge, dark basement full of junk. Sticking with this analogy, he had walked from room to room, found some sections locked and others full of cobwebs. The air smelled musty and moist. He found antique machines emitting glowing steam, the function of which he did not understand. There were also old bicycles without seats, and rusty metal bed frames below which blood stains spread—or maybe they were just pools of water. Now and then he found something familiar, like an electric kettle, that looked like it might still work. He also inspected the pressure boiler in the boiler room and was glad to find that for once he did not just see question marks displayed.

The basement was unwelcoming, and Marchenko mentally sighed. The fake data could even be buried deeper, in the concrete foundation, so to speak. He had no idea how this could be true, because the foundation had been poured by computer companies on Earth about 30 or 40 years ago, and if this were the case he would never be able to remove the falsifying software.

This rankled Marchenko, as if he had found his own apartment cleaned out by burglars. *ILSE's* computer system was his home—at least for now. Knowing that unknown entities could move into his house at any time took away much of the comfort of being at home. *Maybe this is a good thing*, he told himself, *because then it will be easier for me to leave when we get to Enceladus. But what if the burglars return?*

"Marchenko, could you please come here?"

Watson was calling him from another basement room. He put the electric kettle down and turned toward the door. "Where are you?"

"Sector 3ACC3ACC, FF08080A, 1901C04B," Watson said. It sounded as if Watson was standing right next to him, but that sector was far away from Marchenko's current position. Down here the memory segments were organized three-dimensionally and labeled using the hexadecimal numbering system. This made it possible to potentially address several yottabytes—trillions of terabytes. The basement was not that large. Of course Marchenko was not in a real basement, but it was easier for him to imagine the digital storage labyrinth that way. He definitely would have to ask Watson how he perceived his environment. After all, the AI had never been in a real basement.

Shortly afterward Marchenko stood in a corridor. He swept the beam of the flashlight over the walls. The plaster was crumbling, while there were several thick pipes that were attached to the ceiling. The iron door in front of him displayed the hexadecimal numbers 3ACC3ACC, FF08080A, 1901C04B in the Latin alphabet. He was in the right place. The broken door handle dangled by a wire, resting on the floor, so he simply pushed against the door and it opened. The handle scraped across the stone floor, making an unpleasant sound. Inside, the beam of his flashlight fell on Watson, who had taken on the form of Sherlock Holmes' friend as his avatar. He turned toward Marchenko and shielded his face against the light.

"Look what I found," Watson said, turning away again and aiming the beam of his own flashlight at the rear right corner of the room. Marchenko took several steps forward. Something looking like an old spacesuit lay there. It wasn't a modern NASA suit, like he had last worn, but an older Russian model. Marchenko knew this type, and he stepped closer. On the chest there would be a label with the name of its wearer. He bent down and read the Cyrillic lettering— *Марченко!*

"Tshyort vosmi," he exclaimed.

"Come here and help me," he told Watson. He grabbed one leg of the suit and started to pull. It was heavy. Watson pulled on the other leg. Was there someone inside the suit? Marchenko tried to see if there was anything inside the helmet, but there was only a black emptiness. No, something made the suit deliberately heavy—he had to remember this was no real basement. The suit was supposed to be hiding something, and someone had put a lot of effort into this.

"Just a second," Marchenko said. Seemingly out of nowhere a laser sword appeared in his hand. *Visualization is so great,* he thought. In reality, a brute-force algorithm was currently trying to crack the encryption of the procedure. The person responsible for it could not have had much time, and indeed the laser sword cut through it as if going through butter. Finally both of them managed to pull the lower part of the suit aside. Luckily, it was empty.

There was a hole below it. Marchenko shined the flashlight into the hole, but its beam got lost in nothingness.

"It goes deep into the kernel," he said, and Watson nodded. Here the attacker had obviously used a flaw in the code to reach deeper levels, but why had he camouflaged the hole with Marchenko's old spacesuit, of all things? Was this supposed to be a kind of sign, and if so, for what? Marchenko hated this kind of riddle.

"Thank you, Watson," he said. "I think that must be it."

"Yes, I think so, too. It is good we found it so fast," Watson replied.

That was indeed a lucky coincidence, Marchenko thought. It could have taken them weeks to check each line of code carefully, although sometimes a bit of luck was all you needed. But it still would not help them. This was the end. They would not be able to catch the burglar. No one knew what waited for them in the depths of the hole. The commander's authorization, which had brought them here, ended in the basement. They were aware of how the attacker found a way, but they knew neither his motives nor his true capabilities.

"What now?" asked Watson as he stopped in the basement corridor. He looked content. The search must have been fun for him.

"Back to daylight," Marchenko answered. "We cannot go any further down here. Thanks to the COAS, we know about the data distortion and can take it into account when planning our course."

"What if I climb down there myself—at my own risk?"

"Absolutely not. We still need you. If you get lost inside the kernel…"

"What a pity. And thanks again!" said Watson. "Can we do anything about the transmission you recorded?"

"You saw the key length, Doc."

"Yes, 4,096 bits."

"That is much too big. Our quantum computer would take months on it. And we cannot ask anyone on Earth to help us."

"I know."

"So?"

Watson shrugged. Dust fell from his old-fashioned coat. "I was hoping… oh, forget it," he said.

"Hoping what?"

"I was hoping we could spend some more time down here, hunting for secrets."

"I understand," Marchenko said, "you had fun doing this."

"Ah, that is what this feeling is called?"

"Yes. You recognize it by the fact you do not want to stop doing what you are currently engaged in."

"Thanks, Dimitri."

Age of Ascent, 30

There was:
Recognition.
Surprise.
Change.
Infinite water.

There is:
Greed.
Old greed.
New greed.
Curiosity.

There will be:
Visitors.
Visited.
Fear.
The fear of the visitors.
The fear of the visited.

December 13, 2049, ILSE

THE FIVE OF them sat around the table in the command module, waiting for... nothing to happen. *People are strange*, Martin thought. The fuel would last a long time, the reaction mass tanks were adequately filled, the computer calculated their trajectory for several weeks ahead, and still Amy saw this as a reason to celebrate. Soon the crew would reach the moment in which the flight parabola would once again turn into an ellipse, by entering a path around the planet that was also orbited by their destination.

They had already prepared everything necessary. For weeks the drives had been firing in their direction of travel in order for the speed of *ILSE* to fall below the escape velocity of Saturn. Today the crew should reach that moment. So Amy had proposed they drink a toast, and Valentina produced a bottle of vodka she had somehow managed to smuggle on board.

"A tradition among cosmonauts," the Russian woman proclaimed.

Nothing would happen at that particular moment, except some glasses clinking in the command module. Martin thought it odd, and it seemed to him they were celebrating the nothingness. Good—at least they would not be flying further out into the solar system, but that still did not get them any closer to Earth. As Saturn's satellite for a time, they would actually be moving away from it, with the two planets moving around the sun at different speeds.

It doesn't matter. Let Amy have her fun, Martin thought.

"Watson, what is it looking like?" she asked.

"To be exact, we will start moving in an elliptical trajectory in about 35 minutes. With our instruments we cannot determine it more precisely."

The commander looked around. Valentina had already poured a full glass for everyone. All of them were gazing expectantly at Amy.

"The alcohol will evaporate if you let it stand around for half an hour," warned Marchenko, who shared the fog display with Watson.

"Dimitri is right," Amy said. Her voice sounded very solemn. "I would like to raise a glass with you to celebrate everything we have already achieved."

"And what would that be?" blurted Martin, immediately angry at himself for his social blunder. Jiaying gave him a nasty look. "Sorry," he said, not wanting to be a spoilsport.

"We are celebrating the many months, the one and a half billion kilometers that we have covered together, despite surprising difficulties." Amy calmly continued. "You have all done a great job, and I don't tell you this often enough. Well, cheers!"

"Do you realize we were at this same spot exactly three years and five days ago?" asked Jiaying.

"Oh yes," Francesca replied. "But it was much more dramatic back then, because we did not have enough reaction mass and had to use Saturn's atmosphere for braking."

Martin only remembered that those were exciting days. Smiling, they toasted each other. Even Valentina and Francesca managed to exchange smiles. At that moment Martin only heard the sound of the glasses briefly touching. Since they were not wine glasses, the clink was a bit muted. He poured the burning liquid down his throat and closed his eyes. He literally felt the vodka traveling its path. A hot trail ran down his esophagus, until the drink had spread so much that its effect faded.

And what now? He imagined Saturn reaching out for *ILSE* with a strong but gentle hand. He could not see anything through the porthole, since the command center was aimed backward, facing the sun, but in his imagination the planet was much more impressive than in the telescopic images of the fog display. Saturn was a silent monster. From far away it seemed quiet and gentle, but if you approached it too closely, the violent storms in its atmosphere would smash you.

From up here they had a comfortable view, as Martin well remembered. He saw the broad stripes which rotated together, and there were also the giant anticyclones, storms larger than all of Earth and older than himself. If he was lucky he could also see the aurora, which developed very differently than it did on his home planet.

While the hand of Saturn was strong, it was also infinitely soft. In tiny steps it forced—no, guided—*ILSE* from its previous course and led it gradually around the planet, still far outside the rings. This deviation was based on the universal force of gravity. Two masses attracted each other because they created their own depressions in space time. These in turn were located within the depressions caused by their stars, which were within the depressions of their local groups and galaxies. Together with all their neighboring stars they followed the hidden structure of the cosmos, which was dominated by the ominous dark matter.

Was that the end? Martin could not believe it. Whenever humans thought they had found an end, the path went on elsewhere. Did the entire universe follow the gravity paths of the multiverse, or was there something else, completely unimaginable? Was the space he knew an exotic exception, or was it the norm? He would like to discuss this with the being on Enceladus. It had existed for so long. During that time it must have developed a very different, and at the same time, profound concept of the universe, which might advance human knowledge by centuries—if they succeeded in establishing mutual and meaningful communications—but perhaps that was utterly impossible.

"Cheers to the second phase!" said Francesca, interrupting his musings. "Cheers to Marchenko," she added.

Valentina must have refilled all of our glasses. Martin raised his glass to the others. *The second phase. Right,* Martin thought, as he exchanged toasts with his crewmates. *Land on Enceladus, launch expedition in* Valkyrie, *pick up Marchenko—and let's not forget to set up the laser gun and fill up the reaction mass tanks.* Maybe he was much closer than expected to the scientific discussion he dreamed of.

December 17, 2049, ILSE

YESTERDAY, Martin had searched through the log files from three years ago. Watson had certainly not forgotten how the landing was performed back then, but it could not hurt if Martin himself checked for errors that could be avoided this time. He tried to reconstruct his own memories with the aid of the log files, and it worked surprisingly well. When he closed his eyes he could even hear the newborn Sol cry.

Their task had not gotten any easier. Through several cycles the crew adapted the orbit of *ILSE* to that of Enceladus. However, in order to move from a path around Saturn to one around the much smaller moon, the ship would have to decelerate sharply. Then *ILSE* would be moving at a speed relative to the surface of Enceladus that could be compared to a passenger plane landing on Earth. If the ship was moving too fast, the small moon, with its diameter of only 505 kilometers, would not be able to hold it.

Besides, they had been through all of this before. *It worked last time, so we should manage it without problems this time*, Martin reasoned. He was amazed by how much this statement seemed to calm him. Together with the others he was waiting for the signal. Watson was in control, and he had handled his job flawlessly three years ago.

The AI started with the countdown. When it reached

zero, a force pressed Martin into the seat. It felt almost as strong as it had during the launch of the Russian rocket. The drives were aimed in their direction of flight. This allowed Martin to see Saturn through the porthole, and the planet completely filled his field of view. He did not have to suffer g forces for long; after less than a minute, the apparent weightlessness of free fall returned.

They had all decided not to waste time. The selection of a landing site was simple—it had to be near *Valkyrie*, the drill vessel that was once again going to take some of them to the bottom of the ice ocean. The area in the vicinity of the South Pole was significantly more cragged than their first landing site, but Francesca believed she would be able to handle it. They would also place the laser gun and its power supply there, thus completing the task assigned by Shostakovich.

ILSE would only be required to circle the moon once before descending.

"I have an area about 200 by 150 meters near *Valkyrie* that should be suitable for a landing," Watson reported.

"Exact distance?"

"1,200 meters, commander."

"That's good," Amy said. "What about the surroundings? No high mountains?"

"Nothing above 100 meters. In the East there are volcanic rocks, about 80 to 100 meters high. Otherwise the area is surrounded by fissured ice fields."

"I can easily handle that. The approach vector is in a southerly direction, so a few rocks will not pose a problem," Francesca said.

"Then let's get into the lander module!" exclaimed the commander.

"Just a moment, Amy. We haven't decided on the distribution of tasks yet," Valentina said.

"We rely on proven teams," Amy said. "Francesca and Martin will dive in *Valkyrie*. You and Jiaying are going to take care of the lander and fill up our supplies of reaction mass for the drives."

"I do not agree," Valentina said. "It is part of the agreement that I am going on board *Valkyrie*."

"Marchenko, could you confirm this? It has been so long since we discussed it."

"I confirm it, commander. I think Shostakovich did not want to miss this event. For a scientist, it would be an incredible experience. Therefore his daughter has to take part in the excursion."

"Okay," Amy said. "But *Valkyrie* is only designed for two, and on the return trip we also have to find room for Marchenko—hopefully!"

"I don't absolutely have to go down there," Martin said. He was not too keen on being crammed into a metal tube and diving deep into the ocean all over again.

Amy pondered this issue, and Martin could imagine why. "You and Francesca—would that really work, Valentina?"

"I do not have a problem with her," she answered, impassively.

"But I have one with *her*," Francesca said.

"Then I have to replace you with Martin. Last time, he did it really well."

"Out of the question," the Italian pilot said. "Do I have to remind you what this is all about? I have to go down there."

"Then you will have to get along with Valentina for a while. Can you do that?"

"Yes, commander," Francesca said through clenched teeth. Martin felt secretly relieved. Now he did not have to go back into the depths of the ocean. Instead he could take care of the lander and the laser together with Jiaying.

HALF AN HOUR LATER, all except for the commander were strapped into the seats of the lander module. Amy, who alone would stay behind in *ILSE*, had already said goodbye to everyone.

"I am taking over manual control," Francesca said.

"I recommend the automatic mode," Watson objected.

"Come on, let me have some fun."

"Why is it fun to endanger the crew with a suboptimal solution?"

"You wouldn't understand, Watson. It's the thrill of it. It happens when everything is not handled automatically. Also, I bet I can land this thing at least as well as you can."

"Due to the change in landing site, a comparison with the landing data of 2046 is not completely feasible."

"Oh, Watson, just trust me."

"Okay, Francesca, then I will test the concept of trust. I am all on edge. Is that the correct expression?"

"Yes, it is," Francesca said with a groan.

"HIGH GATE." Francesca's voice brought Martin back into reality. Had he actually slept through the last few minutes? He rubbed his eyes. Now came the moment when Francesca had to check the intended landing site. He watched her press several keys. She was probably zooming in on the area, because they were still at an altitude of 3,000 meters. If something didn't look right, they still could save themselves and return to *ILSE* from here.

"Looks good," the pilot announced. "We are continuing our descent. All systems go."

Martin switched on his own display. Enceladus seemed to him like some very old, wrinkly acquaintance. The area near the South Pole was crisscrossed by deep fissures, the so-called 'Tiger Stripes,' through which steam now and then shot from the ocean into space. This posed no danger for them. The very first probe humans sent to Enceladus, *Cassini*, had flown through several of the steam plumes.

"Watson, status of the landing system?" requested Francesca.

"Go. Could I say 'great' instead? I prefer that word. It sounds more..." Watson replied.

"You may, but keep it short."

"Great."

A minute went by. Martin noticed that he was breathing faster, but there was really no reason for concern.

"1,000 meters," Francesca said.

Martin tried to calm himself down by remembering 2046, but it didn't work. Back then, hadn't Francesca activated the automatic landing mode because she thought it was crazy to descend manually? No, he must be mistaken.

"150 meters. Low gate."

They had reached the point of no return. Since Francesca had not aborted the landing before now, they would reach the surface anyway, dead or alive. What about the gravity here? Even if they started falling like a stone from this point, they should be able to survive the impact due to the low gravity. Martin remembered how he and Hayato had moved *Valkyrie* using sheer muscle power, even though it would have weighed several tons on Earth.

Francesca now had her hands on the left and right sticks. She adjusted the ship so the main jets aimed directly downward. Martin checked the screen—she was good: 90 degrees, even the automatic mode could not have done any better. Since Enceladus had no atmosphere, the landing party did not have to fear sudden gusts of wind. Despite knowing this, Martin's palms were getting sweaty.

"Prepare for landing."

The image on the display faded, most likely due to fine ice crystals being stirred up by the main engines. The sound of the engines faded away, and Francesca switched them off. It seemed they were already slow enough. It was a strange, otherworldly feeling. One could not land like this anywhere else. They would bounce off an asteroid if their velocity was not precisely zero at the end. And on any larger celestial body, an unchecked impact after a fall from 100 meters would destroy the ship.

Martin saw Francesca smile. This was probably why she

insisted on manual control. Arriving on an alien moon in free fall must be a special treat for a passionate pilot.

"Ten... nine... eight..."

"Shhhh," Francesca said. Watson abandoned the countdown. Majestically and in complete silence the lander descended toward the ice layer that covered this mysterious moon to a thickness of several kilometers. Then it touched down very slowly and gently.

"Welcome to Enceladus," Francesca said. All of them applauded.

"Rossi to commander, we are here and everyone is fine—except for Watson, I think."

"Thanks, Francesca," Amy replied. "What is wrong with Doc?"

"I think he was afraid. Am I right, Watson?"

"I am not sure," the AI replied. "I felt an unpleasant tingling, that is the only way I can describe it. But it felt very different compared to the time I was still falling toward the sun in *ILSE*."

"I understand," Amy said. "It must have been apprehension, a lesser form of fear, while the other feeling was more like despair."

December 18, 2049, Enceladus

It was different being here this time. Martin wondered all night long what felt so dissimilar, but he could not find an explanation for why it was so. After all, they were not here for the first time—it wasn't like first sex with a new partner. He knew exactly what to expect. A human had already taken a first step here, and there had even been a first death. His body still distinctly recalled how it felt to walk around out there, so he would not have to practice the required skill. He also remembered the view across the ice fields, with gigantic Saturn in a sky that had always seemed to look darker to him than the darkest night on Earth.

All of this might be true, but it did not get to the essential point—Enceladus itself was different now.

This feeling was confirmed, when after strenuous preparation—technically speaking, there was little difference between an excursion on Enceladus and a spacewalk—Martin finally uncoupled from the connector of the SuitPort and climbed down the metal stairs. Even though his friends were not far away, a feeling of infinite loneliness overcame him. This emotion even brought tears to the corners of his eyes, which he unfortunately could not wipe away due to his helmet. He noticed them trickling down his cheeks, and it was a comforting sensation, as it proved he was alive. Something had died, but he was still alive. *I hope that it's only hormones*, he thought, *or the stress of being cooped up for months, forcing itself out in this grandiose landscape*. There was one thing he had to say, even though he remembered it very well: *The view is unbeatable.*

Martin looked around. In three directions of the compass a plain stretched ahead of them. He could not see that behind him it was fractured, not smooth. They had chosen the landing site well. It provided enough space to move the laser and its power plant and to anchor them in the ice. A range of hills cast sharp black shadows to the East.

The contrast between up and down was particularly fascinating. The sparkling, glittering ice at the bottom was covered by a thin crystal layer. The moon seemed to glow from the inside, like one of those paper lampshades with a light bulb in the center. But as soon as your gaze reached the horizon, the brightness plunged from one hundred to zero. The sky over Enceladus was pitch black, and the contrast with the ground made it appear much darker and emptier than when viewed from the spaceship. However, this effect only held until you gazed toward the East and saw Saturn. There, looking from the southern face of Enceladus, Saturn stood only a few degrees above the horizon. It must be 'the Moon illusion' known from Earth that made it look gigantic. The sun, though, which must have just risen, looked far smaller than usual and provided no warmth at all. At best, minus 150 degrees is what the weather report would predict for the coming days.

Martin walked a few steps into the plain. In actuality he jumped there, since normal walking in the low gravity was impossible. He turned around and was shocked to see how small the lander looked already. Someone was following him, waving with one arm. Martin had a sudden flashback. For a split second he thought the person was Hayato, but then he realized it had to be one of the three women. Perhaps he ought to activate his two-way radio.

"...and we should start unpacking. I am coming toward you," Jiaying's voice said. So she had the courage to leave

Francesca and Valentina alone together in the lander? Well, those two had to learn to get along with each other at some point. Jiaying came closer and waved again, and Martin waved back.

"It is so great out here! Look, there is Saturn, and over there the sun is rising," she said.

Martin smiled. It was nice to see her so happy and excited.

"Come, let's jump a bit," he called to her. When she got close enough, he took her hand and jumped upward. "We're flying!" he exclaimed and laughed.

Jiaying played along. The next time around, she crouched and pulled him up. "Yippee!" she shouted. "The whole planet is a huge trampoline."

They kept jumping until Martin realized he was sweating.

"Come on, let's get to work," he said, and drew Jiaying toward the lander. They actually had plenty of time. Francesca and Valentina would be traveling for several days. Just Jiaying and himself in the lander—that almost sounded like a vacation. But in case they needed Valentina's help, they should set up the laser before their fellow astronauts left for *Valkyrie*. The task did not involve anything that seemed beyond Martin's skills, but in the end they might be stopped by something as simple as a mandatory password the Russian woman had set up to allow the power plant to produce energy.

THE LASER and power plant modules were located in the same metal cage where *Valkyrie* had been when they first landed on Enceladus three years ago. Each of the units weighed about as much as the drill vessel, so they once again chose the pulley method. The first time he and Hayato had pulled the cables while Jiaying had watched from the lander module. *How is Amy's husband doing back on Earth? Does he miss her as much as she misses him?* wondered Martin.

He thought for a moment and then decided to switch roles. It would be easier to explain the role he had taken previously.

"I am going to attach the pulley and the rope and you get the slide. Should I show..."

"Martin, of course I read the task description beforehand. Considering your vertigo I should be the one to attach the pulley. That would be best."

He nodded. He should have known Jiaying would not do anything unprepared. She squeezed his shoulder, took the rope and pulley, and climbed up the scaffolding. He watched her in fascination.

She contacted him again via radio, asking, "Where is the slide? You are not here to just stand around, are you?"

He had barely managed to unroll the plastic tarp, which was about five meters wide, when Jiaying unexpectedly appeared beside him. In her hand she held the thin rope that was connected to the top of the laser via the pulley.

"How did you..."

"I jumped. We only weigh two kilos here," Jiaying said with a laugh.

Damn, I fell in love with a madwoman, he thought.

She turned around and attached herself to the lander. This was the disadvantage of the low gravity: While the laser and power plant only weighed half a ton instead of 40 tons, she only had two kilograms to use while pulling the rope. Therefore she needed the heavy lander module as an anchor.

"Heave ho," Jiaying said, uttering the command herself. Martin had taught her the expression, and she pronounced it very well.

The pulley enhanced her strength in such a way that she managed to get 500 kilograms moving. The rope connecting her to the lander became taut.

"Oops." Jiaying was surprised—her feet were losing contact. She was floating several centimeters above the ground, maybe because the final deflection roller had been placed slightly higher than last time.

At first, she did not even realize her cargo was starting to move. Jiaying let the rope play out centimeter by centimeter. Slowly and in eerie silence the entire block slid downward. After half an hour only a few meters remained.

"Everything okay with you?" asked Martin.

Jiaying nodded. "Just fine."

He checked her biomonitor. Jiaying did not appear to be exhausted. Martin had to admit she had exercised a bit more during their journey than he had. *What goes around, comes around,* he thought.

The slide ended three centimeters above the ground. Jiaying unreeled the rope far enough, and the colossus consisting of laser and fusion generator sat down on the surface. While it was only a few meters away from the lander, this posed no problem. If something went wrong with the power plant, a few additional meters would not help.

"Thanks to both of you," Valentina said from inside the lander. "I can take over the rest."

Jiaying and Martin looked at each other. One of them had to return if Valentina wanted to come outside. Both the lander module and *Valkyrie* had SuitPorts. They allowed the astronaut to slide from the inside into a spacesuit attached outside. The SuitPort method saved space in comparison to an airlock, but the drawback was that no more than two people could be outside simultaneously. Three years ago, Martin and Francesca had needed to take the suits attached to *Valkyrie*, and these were waiting inside the lander module to be used again.

Tomorrow, Valentina and Francesca would put on those suits while inside, and exit the lander through the hatch on their way to the drill vessel. This would cause the air to be vented from the lander module. They had enough oxygen in store and could easily create more from ice, electrochemically, but during their exit no one could stay in the lander unprotected. Until then, they would have to make do with the two SuitPorts that could be attached on the outside.

"Would you mind going inside? I would like to keep an

eye on Valentina," Martin said. He looked at the display on his arm. He still had enough air.

"Okay," Jiaying said, "I will see you later."

MARTIN HOPED Valentina had already started exercising diligently. If she had just started the pre-breathing phase, he would have to wait a long time out here. However, she appeared to be well prepared—five minutes after Jiaying attached the suit, its arms and legs started moving again. He had never consciously watched the exit process—it looked a bit like a limp rubber doll gradually coming to life. First the legs stretched and started to wiggle. Martin knew exactly why: The LCVG slipped while Valentina pushed herself into the suit, and now she was trying to move the creases to a spot where they did not bother her. Then the arms started to move —at first randomly, while Valentina slipped them on, then with deliberation, since she had to initiate the uncoupling herself.

Martin suspected what would happen next. The Russian woman took her first step on the moon—and immediately bounced off. It was odd, because the lander module experienced the same low gravity, and they all had adapted to it inside. Yet out here, where the eye perceived a massive object reminiscent of good old Earth, the ancient mental programming set in and the astronaut mechanically wanted to take strong steps. Humans really were exclusively inhabitants of Earth and just plain did not belong here.

Valentina shrieked, but that was normal during the first steps taken on a new world. Martin already felt rather calm. Ten minutes later she reached him, and by then, she had adapted to the situation.

"Let us get this thing going," she said, jumping ahead. The 'thing' looked like a giant, dented metal box, and Valentina slid a metal sheet aside on one end. Below it was a hole in which she inserted a special key. A second cover opened, revealing a screen and a keyboard with huge keys. Obviously the keys were made to be used with the gloves of a spacesuit. Valentina entered a few commands while whistling cheerfully.

"Don't we have to unpack something?" asked Martin.

"No." She shook her head. "It is all ready to be used."

Martin was disappointed. He had imagined a laser gun to look, at least a little bit, like an old-fashioned cannon—but this brick?

"Who is responsible for product design at your company?" he asked.

Valentina laughed. "Is that a serious question?"

"I just expected something more impressive."

"You have been watching too much science fiction. Except for us, no one will ever see this device. Why would it need a fancy design? My father definitely would not spend any money on that."

What she said was true, but Martin was still disappointed by its unimpressive appearance.

"Let's assume a spaceship happens to fly by. And your father dislikes its captain."

"Yes, the laser could shoot at the ship and probably destroy it."

"So it can aim?"

"That is absolutely necessary," Valentina explained. "If we want to accelerate a mini-spaceship from Earth, or from the asteroids, by using a laser, we can never predict its trajectory with absolute precision. Therefore, the device here must be able to aim at its target. Take a look at the lid of the box. On the right side, the covers can be moved in a controlled fashion. Below it is high-quality glass. In order to aim, the automatic system only has to move the laser to the right position within the box."

This clarified why Shostakovich was implementing such a major project in secret. The lasers distributed across the solar system could be used as weapons. That would significantly disturb the balance of power between nations. Martin shivered. What if the system fell into the hands of a madman? Could Shostakovich be that madman? It would not be wrong to call him an oddball. Martin squelched the thought.

"And what if Enceladus is on the other side of Saturn at that moment?" he asked.

"That would not happen. We calculate the launches in such a way that all lasers are always in range."

"So much effort for something that won't generate any profit—your father even saves money on product design. Why does he support the project?"

"The stars, Martin," Valentina said. "We will be able to accelerate our mini-spaceships to 20 percent of the speed of light. Then they will need only 20 years to reach the nearest star—that is doable! And each additional laser we place farther outside adds a few percent more speed and shortens the travel time accordingly. My father believes that whoever reaches the stars will become immortal."

"And you?"

"I am not religious, but I am fascinated by the idea of us leaving our solar system, of humans gradually spreading across the Milky Way. Aren't you?"

"Generally yes, but you—or we—are still very far from that goal. This isn't about spaceships like *ILSE*, but only tiny space probes. They might transmit some images from Proxima Centauri in 25 years, but centuries will pass by before we can travel there ourselves."

"I think that you are mistaken there, Martin," Valentina said. Then she moved her hand to the visor of her helmet and raised her index finger. It was only when she said 'shhhh' that he recognized the gesture.

December 19, 2049, Enceladus

WE SHOULD HAVE BROUGHT along a logistics expert, Martin thought as he was looking at the plan for today. It could all be so simple: Francesca and Valentina would pack their things, dress for the weather, walk a few minutes to *Valkyrie*, get on board, and then putter along, down into the ocean. It would have worked that way if the mission had been precisely planned, but that really was not the case—and Martin was worried about it. He did not object to improvisation, but he also knew how important thorough planning was, especially in space.

"Then we will improvise according to plan, if you prefer that," Francesca said when he mentioned his concerns to her. She preferred being spontaneous and running straight through a brick wall—or into the wall, if it surprisingly turned out to be too hard. Luckily, Jiaying understood him better. For this reason he was glad he could remain with her in the lander.

His sleep lately had been deep and dreamless, and that also bothered him. He asked himself where his dreams went. Last time around, the creature used them to contact him. Did it now see no reason to do so? Without the help of the being they certainly would not be able to salvage Marchenko.

Now they were about to leave the lander, one after the

other. The air inside the lander was moist from all the breath they exhaled during the pre-breathing phase. While Martin and Jiaying slipped into the SuitPorts, Francesca and Valentina were still walking around in their LCVG under-wear. Recently, there had been no sign of aggression between the two. Maybe the common mission bonded them together, or all the excitement left no time for such feelings. In that case, Martin remembered, they would have plenty of oppor-tunities for arguing during the excursion that was going to last several days.

He had to hurry. Jiaying had already uncoupled from her SuitPort and was calling him by radio. He would—according to plan—help her transport the cable reel to *Valkyrie*. They did not have to worry about Francesca and Valentina, who would put on their spacesuits later and depart the lander via the hatch.

"Don't forget the spacesuits," Martin reminded them while standing on the ice of Enceladus. "Your cable carriers will go ahead in the meantime."

They needed the optical cable to supply *Valkyrie* with inex-haustible energy. At one end the laser would feed light energy into the vessel, while at its other end, the energy would be turned into electricity.

Jiaying had already opened a cover on the outside of the lander where the cable reel was stowed. It was not heavy, and one kilometer of cable only weighed 20 kilograms—on Earth. Here it was only as heavy as a cup of coffee. Jiaying took the reel and closed the cover. Martin hurried to get to her. Yester-day, Valentina had showed him the outlet where they had to connect one end of the cable. At first, the plug did not seem to fit, until Martin noticed he had to place it at a slight angle and then push and turn simultaneously—a special latching mechanism.

"Let's go, then," he said. The display on his lower arm showed them the way, and *Valkyrie* was south of them. The way was not all that complicated. While the navigation system showed some deep fissures and cracks, they could easily get across them using the jumping technique that was possible here.

It was around noon—Earth time—and Martin suddenly longed for a steak. *A steak, right here on the ice. How messed up is the wiring of my brain to come up with such ideas in this environment? Perhaps it wants to distract me from the all-encompassing feeling of loneliness that increases with every meter I walk away from the lander.* He could not remember having felt this way after the first landing. Plus, he even had his darling Jiaying here, and was about the only crew member who had not had to say goodbye to a loved one back on Earth. Well that wasn't true, because Francesca hadn't, nor Jiaying, and perhaps Valentina hadn't, since she never mentioned living with a partner. He really did not know very much about her.

Jiaying carried the cable reel. It unspooled meter by meter. The fiber-optic cable was covered with a layer of carbon nanotubes that gave it great strength without reducing flexibility. Sometimes Jiaying turned around and waved at him. Martin smiled, and she smiled back. Despite this there was a loneliness that seemed to cover the whole moon and which oozed like an invisible poison gas from the fissures of the Tiger Stripes. *Yes, that's the direction*, he thought. The loneliness came from the depth. He was glad he would not have to dive down to the bottom of the ocean in a submarine this time. Were the others experiencing similar feelings here?

"I can see it!" Jiaying had just jumped across a particularly wide fissure and called while still in flight. Martin's heart seemed to stop briefly—he hoped she would not forget where she was. Fortunately, her jump was enough to carry her across to the other side. Due to the lack of air resistance, his girlfriend could not stop herself from getting to the other side even if she tried to.

"What does it look like?" he asked via radio.

"A dark, round spot on a white background," Jiaying replied.

"Circular?"

"Of course not—elliptical."

Definitely it, Martin thought. He smiled. It had to be *Valkyrie*. Its cigar-shaped body must have rested in the water at an angle and then froze solid. The view of the section from afar would then look like an ellipse.

They both reached it after five minutes. Three years ago this had been an open water hole, but now the area was frozen solid. Jiaying raced ahead eagerly. Martin wanted to warn her against weak ice, but before he made a fool of himself again he remembered they only weighed two kilograms here. Distributed against the area of her boot print it would not generate more pressure than a light backpack on Earth, and three years was far more than enough time for the water to have frozen solid at 150 degrees below zero.

"Francesca, *Valkyrie* is waiting for you," Martin radioed, and also added the exact position.

"It froze into the ice at an angle, bow downward." Martin took another look to verify that, since an error would be embarrassing. Yes, the bow was below the ice. If it had been the other way, there would be a significant problem, because the hatch Francesca and Valentina were going to use to get on board was near the stern. The SuitPorts were also located there, but they could not use them until they got *Valkyrie* up and running again.

First of all, *Valkyrie* needed energy. Martin approached the stern. It was here where the cable feed-through was located, and the mechanism the vessel used to unspool its umbilical cord. During their first journey the fiber-optic cable had been severed by a movement in the ice, and they had reeled in the rest of it despite its uselessness. Now they had to connect the cable they brought with the existing cable reel, on the inside. This meant someone had to board *Valkyrie*, and since Martin knew the vessel well, he would be the obvious one to do it.

Martin took a look at the hatch. It seemed everything was set up especially for them. The hatch was slightly above the ice surface. He could easily reach the large spoked wheel, but it would not turn.

"Could you help me here?" he asked.

Jiaying put down the cable reel and came to him.

"Should I give the wheel a try?" She gave him a cheeky smile, turned around, and used all her strength. Martin caught himself, hoping out of sheer masculine vanity that she would not succeed. *This is stupid*, he thought, *because then the hatch would be open for me.* It didn't move, so they tried it together, but the wheel was still stuck.

"It's just because of the gravity," Martin said with a laugh. "How are we supposed to use our immense strength if we cannot properly hold onto anything?"

Jiaying nodded. "We must wait for the others."

They did not have to wait long. Francesca was the first one to rush in.

"Why are you sitting around here?" the Italian pilot asked. "Why isn't the vessel ready to dive?"

Martin pointed at the spoked wheel with a tired gesture. Francesca tried it alone, and then all three of them attempted it together, but it was still in vain. Finally, when Valentina arrived, it was as if *Valkyrie* had waited for some four-person magic ritual to occur, and the wheel moved smoothly.

"I do not know why you make such a big fuss," the Russian woman said.

"Don't you realize? It only yielded to the combined power of four heroes from different nations," Martin joked.

He grabbed the cable reel. "I am going inside now. You need to push one end of the cable through here," he instructed Jiaying. Then he vaulted through the open hatch into the darkness. He activated the lamp on his helmet.

Things looked better than he was expecting. There was no visible damage because there was nothing that could have caused it, just a bit of ice covering the walls. This must be the residual atmosphere inside *Valkyrie*, which had condensed and then frozen. Near the bow more ice seemed to have collected. Perhaps some water could have gotten in there after the last time someone exited—or maybe it was from a geyser eruption? There had to be a reason *Valkyrie* was at a slant.

Martin aimed his lamp toward the stern. The cable reel

would be on one side, below a cover. The fiber-optic cable ran toward it guided by two rollers. He took the monkey wrench from a pocket in his suit and opened the cover. There was the reel. He moved it, and the bearings worked fine, as if they had just been greased. Now he had to squeeze himself halfway behind the panels. He aimed his flashlight forward. Somewhere there the cable Jiaying was pushing through would have to appear.

"Could you wiggle the cable?" he asked via radio.

"Okay," Jiaying said.

Martin saw something move. "I see it. Another twenty centimeters, please."

The cable moved forward until finally he could reach it.

"Okay, I'm going to pull it. Don't be scared," he radioed, pulling. Jiaying played out some length on her side. He pulled the cable toward the reel and used his left hand to search for the coupling in his suit pocket. Where had he put it?

"Ah, there it is," he whispered.

"Did you say something?"

"No, never mind."

He inserted both cable ends into the coupling until they clicked into place. Then he activated the fastener. From now on this would be the weak spot of the entire system. It would have to withstand the entire weight of the cable, and it was an advantage that they were not on Earth. The purely mechanical fastener must not crimp the fiber-optic cable inside, and it had to withstand getting hot, as transitional surfaces always exhibited losses. If *Valkyrie* should ever lose contact, it would be here—but Martin did not think it would come to that. He closed the cover again and climbed out.

"Neumaier to commander, please test the link to *Valkyrie* via remote control."

No one saw the test LED at the end of the cable light up briefly, as its glow was transmitted at light speed through the fiber-optic cable and into the drill vessel.

"It works," Amy said via radio. So the sensor at the end must have returned the signal.

"Thanks," Martin answered.

"But I notice something strange," Amy said. "The jets tell me they cannot start the heater."

Martin sighed. He would have to go into *Valkyrie* once more, find the problem, and repair it. Three easy steps, he hoped.

IT TOOK THREE DIFFICULT HOURS, working in claustrophobic conditions. *Who the f... had removed that pipe?* He managed to cobble together a solution, and hoped it would be adequate. *Valkyrie* was all they had.

THEY STOOD AROUND FOR A MINUTE, just looking at each other—four human beings on the icy surface of an alien moon, indistinguishable in their suits. Yet, they each brought their own special goals, wishes, and ideas, which could have hardly been any more different. *Humans are rather strange*, Martin thought, *and to me it doesn't look like some creator made them according to a plan.*

Francesca was the first one to move. She announced, "Time to start up the ship." She started to turn around and go on board, but then she returned to hug Jiaying and Martin.

"Once we have an atmosphere on board, I cannot say goodbye directly anymore."

"Have a good trip," Jiaying said.

"And remember to bring back Marchenko safe and sound," Martin added.

Valentina also hugged both of them. Then she followed Francesca. Martin and Jiaying saw how Francesca first attached the spacesuit meant for Marchenko to an exterior SuitPort. Then the two women entered and closed the hatch from inside.

"We should get out of their way," Martin said. They waited at a safe distance for *Valkyrie* to embark on its journey. For a quarter of an hour nothing happened. Then they saw the ice getting darker from below. *Valkyrie* must have activated its control jets, heating the water and melting the ice. A crack formed below the stern, and soon afterward the protruding part slowly broke through the ice, which now was turning into a bubbling expanse of water. *Valkyrie* floated in it like a whale that had lost its way, although soon the whale remembered where it wanted to go, and it dove into the depths of the ocean.

Age of Ascent, 31

There was:
Shocks.
Waves and vibrations.
Movement.
Light.

There is:
Hope.
Hope and fear.
Fear.
The present.

There will be:
The emptiness.
The depth.
The way out.
The I.

December 20, 2049, Enceladus

Francesca naturally chose the pilot's seat, and so far everything was working well. Valentina seemed to have realized she was no more than a kind of stowaway who should keep out of the way as much as possible and definitely not argue with Francesca. In reality, *Valkyrie* could easily be handled by a single person, since all controls were within the pilot's reach. Even the system startup worked smoothly, as if she and Martin had just recently left the vessel.

No, she was not the last person who had sat in this seat and operated *Valkyrie*. How could she have forgotten that? Marchenko had been seated right here on his solo trip to the Forest of Columns, from which he had never really returned.

"What was it like down here?" she asked him via radio. They had never really talked about it at length.

"What can I say? It was both exciting and at the same time depressing." Thanks to the fiber-optic cable connection, Marchenko was always with her. They could also access Watson this way. Although, if necessary, both could download themselves into the on-board computer.

"You know," Marchenko sighed, "I do not think I want to talk about it."

"You think?" said Francesca.

"It…" he hesitated, "it still hurts. You know how it all ended. The whole time I still try to consider myself a complete human being, to justify myself. This was the trigger. Maybe it will change once we find what we are looking for."

"I hope so. It will only work if the creature cooperates."

"I know."

"Do you think we are going to be successful?"

"To be honest, I do not really believe it, Francesca. But we will attempt it nevertheless, even if I consider it a utopian goal."

"But you agreed to the attempt. Amy would not see her son for two years. I…"

"I did not agree for myself, but for all of you. It was not my idea. I hoped it would rid Amy and you of any feelings of guilt—and do not deny feeling guilty. I could not take this opportunity away from you. Once we return you will have done everything in your power. The same applies to Amy. This will help you in the long run. It will free you from feelings of guilt. That is why I agreed to all this."

"You are such a good person," Francesca said in a voice dripping with irony. "This is pure emotional manipulation, but it is okay. I will prove to you that you are wrong, and then you will notice you are also mistaken concerning your own motives. You are just as selfish as all of us."

For two minutes Marchenko gave no reply. Then he said, "Perhaps you are right. We must not argue. It is partially selfish, yes. I want you to stay because of me, not due to feelings of guilt. And I do notice you are unhappy with the situation. I cannot be there for you physically. Once you no longer feel guilty, you can make a better decision about whether you really want to live with me. Maybe we will go our separate ways after all. That would be terrible for me, but better than the idea that you were doing something which you really did not want to do—out of pity."

"You do not know me very well, Mitya. Nothing and nobody can force me to do something I do not want to do."

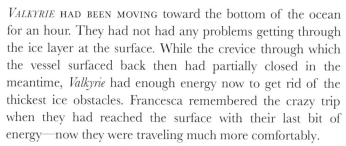

Valkyrie had been moving toward the bottom of the ocean for an hour. They had not had any problems getting through the ice layer at the surface. While the crevice through which the vessel surfaced back then had partially closed in the meantime, *Valkyrie* had enough energy now to get rid of the thickest ice obstacles. Francesca remembered the crazy trip when they had reached the surface with their last bit of energy—now they were traveling much more comfortably.

The searchlights shone ahead and cut cone-shaped pieces out of the darkness, without being able to actually penetrate it. The water looked like it had before. If things did not weigh so little here, it would be impossible to distinguish the deep ocean of Earth from that of Enceladus. Darkness looked the same everywhere, and the temperature of 4 degrees was exactly the same as on their home planet. Strange as it might sound, Enceladus was more livable down here than on the surface. There was oxygen dissolved in the water, and it was so warm they would survive for a few minutes without a suit, until they ran out of air. The pressure was lower than in the depths of the oceans on Earth, because the water layers above them weighed only one eightieth.

Once they hit the bottom of the sea, they would notice again they were no longer on Earth. There should be only a thin layer where life existed here, as opposed to the diversity they knew from Earth, because on Enceladus much less energy was available. Francesca checked the radar measurement. Only 150 meters more to the bottom.

Five minutes later they reached the sea floor. Francesca gazed at the area lit by the searchlights, but what she expected to find was not there. Three years ago, a thin layer of cells had covered the ocean floor, but now they were missing. *This is impossible,* she thought.

"Marchenko, do you see what I see?" she asked.

"Confirmed," he replied. "Try a zigzag course. Perhaps it is a local phenomenon."

Francesca typed in the appropriate commands, but the image shown by the searchlights did not change. There definitely was no life here anymore, just bare rock.

"Engines stop," she said.

Valentina came forward. "What is going on?" the Russian woman asked.

"It is nothing."

"What do you mean?"

"Francesca wanted to say that there should be a layer of cells at the bottom of the sea, but there is nothing there," Marchenko interjected.

"That's what I said. 'It is *nothing*.' I want to take a sample of it."

Francesca called up the control menu for the manipulator arm on her screen. She lowered *Valkyrie* all the way to the bottom and had the arm scrape across the rock with a sample container for two or three minutes. Then she brought the container on board and placed it in the analyzer. The unit needed a few minutes to determine the exact composition.

'Analysis Complete' appeared on the screen. Francesca pressed a button to display the data: water, various salts in high concentration, and silica. Nothing else.

"No organic material," she said. "Rossi to commander, are you listening in?"

Amy reacted the same way Marchenko had earlier. "That's impossible. Maybe you just happened to be at a bad spot."

"I think that's unlikely," Martin said over the communication channel. "If it was just a bad spot—as you call it—there should have at least been traces of organic material. This looks clinically clean."

"As if someone employed the weapon I was supposed to place on Enceladus back then, when I left you all on Io," Jiaying said quietly. One could hear by her voice that those events still bothered her.

"It could not be," Marchenko explained. "*ILSE* turned

around halfway here. In the meantime no one had an opportunity to use the retrovirus against the being on Enceladus."

"Perhaps there was a secret project that managed to reach Enceladus, just as we did?" said Martin.

"Something of that scale could only be financed by the international community, Martin. No military worldwide has such a budget," Marchenko replied.

"A rich industrialist, maybe? Shostakovich succeeded in doing it," Martin said.

"Yes, with us, and only because *ILSE* already existed and no one wanted her anymore," Marchenko said.

Francesca shook her head. "No reason to argue, boys. The fact is that there is no life here anymore. And it looks like there never was any here. If I was an independent researcher given these results, I would say, 'It was all your imagination, you're crazy. Either the pressure down there or the long trip clouded your mind.'"

"I sensed something like this," Martin said. "This time, it was so lonely I could barely stand it."

"And why did you not mention it earlier?"

"Francesca, you wouldn't have taken me seriously, would you?"

"You are probably right. I have to see something to believe it," she said. "There is definitely nothing here."

"But the two of us were down there, Francesca—and Marchenko as well," Martin said. "This life exists, just not at the spot where you currently are. It can't have completely disappeared. Do you remember the Forest of Columns?"

Of course she remembered it. Martin had walked a few meters in. It looked fascinating: tall, slender, white columns in the middle of the ocean.

"Yes. If life still exists somewhere, it would be there," she said. "It was the center, the head of the creature. There—that is where we have to search for Marchenko. What we saw was no hallucination."

"Perhaps," Martin said, "our thoughts are going in the wrong direction if we fear a catastrophe might have happened to the creature. What if we ourselves represent this danger and the creature consciously withdrew? We definitely gave it some reasons to do so. We, even if it was different people, tried to kill it, and we just placed a laser weapon on its surface. Who knows what else it expects from us? It certainly has good reasons."

December 21, 2049, Enceladus

THE FOREST OF COLUMNS was located about 105 kilometers to the northeast. *Valkyrie* moved along staying close to the sea floor. The fellow astronauts on the surface and in the space-ship were currently asleep, so it was nice and quiet. Francesca loved these shifts when she was all alone with herself, the machinery, and the environment. There was a meditative ambiance inside *Valkyrie*. The water gurgled in the heating circuit of the jets, electric motors hummed, and the life support system hissed. All the devices had different rhythms, and together they played a tune that Francesca found very calming. Earlier, Valentina asked if she should take over for a while, but Francesca rejected her offer, because she still was not tired.

The front searchlights showed the rocky ground. Now and then its color changed from dark gray to grayish brown and brownish black, and sometimes black that had a tinge of blue. Occasionally, when the searchlights hit an ice deposit, the sea floor became blindingly bright and seemed to be lit from below. Nevertheless, everything was still barren.

The thin cell layer, with its electrical structures visible in infrared light, which Marchenko had discovered back then, was nowhere to be found. Francesca always imagined the ice ocean and the Enceladus creature being one, absolutely inseparable. If that was true, the creature no longer existed and she would have no way to retrieve Marchenko's body, so she hoped she was mistaken. Could they really have come all this way only to have to return empty-handed?

THE CONSOLE HUMMED SOFTLY. Francesca had set the volume for all messages to 'low' in order to avoid waking Valentina. It was shortly after 3 a.m. standard time, and the radar system detected contours in the distance. The distance was right, so this had to be the Forest of Columns. At least one thing remained unchanged. Her heart was beating faster. From this moment on, time seemed to stretch.

Francesca increased the engine power an additional twenty percent—*Valkyrie* should be able to handle it for a while. She turned around and saw Valentina was still asleep. Nothing depended on this Russian woman for the journey, because she had already fulfilled her mission. Francesca was still puzzled why Shostakovich insisted on his daughter participating in this undersea mission. Valentina seemed to be unsure of the reason as well, and right now she obviously was having a nice dream. She stretched sensually. She was still so young! Francesca tried to remember back when she herself was in her early twenties. She had always tried to be better than the others, including the boys who were going through pilot training with her, and she had succeeded, finishing at the top of her class!

Did Valentina ever have to prove herself like this, as the daughter of a billionaire father? Francesca told herself not to be unfair. She knew much too little about the young woman to judge her. It was strange that they'd had to land on Enceladus before she no longer considered Valentina a traitor.

The console hummed again. Francesca gazed at the monitor. They had reached the Forest of Columns. She steered *Valkyrie* very close to it and then turned off the engines. The gurgling and humming disappeared. Only the hissing remained, like in a symphony slowly fading out of a piece until a single instrument played the last notes. The searchlights projected bright cones into the water, causing the white columns to cast shadows. Francesca was just as impressed with the sight of it now as she had been the first time. *'The forest stands rigid and silent.' Hadn't Martin quoted this wonderful line from a poem back then? Or maybe I am mistaken, since the German astronaut isn't very interested in poetry*, she thought. But there it was, the forest of thousands of columns, and it was silent in several ways.

For once, it did not issue any physical signal. The columns only reflected. They did not glow in any frequency range. Furthermore, the forest was silent since it did not answer any of her questions. Back then, Martin had mentioned his theory that the forest might be some kind of archive. Francesca called up the photos taken during the last voyage and compared them with the current ones. Could it be that two new rows of columns had come into being? She compared the exact coordinates and found that new columns had indeed been added. This did not answer her most significant question, though: Where was this being, or even more importantly, where was Marchenko's body?

Francesca decided to take a little stroll, so she moved very quietly. She wanted Valentina to keep on sleeping, because she wanted this time in the forest for herself. Once she was outside, she would contact the crew on the surface via radio. She changed her outfit quietly, donning first the diaper and then the LCVG against the cold. Then she walked past the sleeping Russian woman to the stern of *Valkyrie*, where the spacesuit meant for Marchenko was attached to the SuitPort from the outside. *Good that I thought so far ahead*, Francesca thought. If she used that suit, she could not be easily followed. While there were two additional spacesuits on board, Valentina would have to flood the vessel before she could exit. Francesca definitely would have a sizeable head start.

She realized now she had unconsciously pursued a plan from the very beginning. When Francesca placed

Marchenko's suit on the outside of the SuitPort, she created the opportunity to leave the vessel alone and in secret, without Valentina being able to follow her. She wanted to find Marchenko's body, and she would search until she found it. She would never return without it, no matter what the others said. It was obvious she owed it to him, and could not fail in this mission.

FRANCESCA SLOWLY DESCENDED to the bottom. The heating unit blew warm air against the visor of her helmet. Down here, the world was strangely digital. Whatever her light illuminated immediately existed, and whatever was outside the light did not exist—only dark and light, 0 and 1. There was nothing in between, no dusk, no dawn, no gray. Francesca imagined having to live in such a world. It was one thing having been born here, like the creature who had existed for millions of years, but a visitor would never feel at home here. She had undertaken a long journey to bring Marchenko home.

Once again she turned toward *Valkyrie*. She could only see the bow, where the searchlights were. The stern disappeared into the darkness. Valentina must still be sleeping.

"Rossi to Commander. I am entering the forest," she said.

"Just a moment," Marchenko replied. "I am sending you the coordinates of the center. That is where you need to go."

"Thank you."

"Good luck," Marchenko's voice said now. "And please do not take any unnecessary risks. It is not worth it."

If it were only that simple, Francesca thought. She turned toward the forest. The light on her helmet let her see the nearest row. The closer she approached, the smaller the field of view became. She stood directly in front of the first column and looked upward. A tingle coursed through her body when she realized she was facing an artificial object not created by humans, the result of an alien technology. It was like no method known to man. The columns grew from single calciferous cells, essentially like coral reefs, but this idea might be based on a basic human error. *We are arrogant,* she thought. *A coral reef or an ant colony... they grow in a similar way to this column, follow a plan, and are the result of non-human technology. Yet, I would not stand next to them in admiration.*

Francesca touched the surface of the column with her glove, but did not feel anything. She wanted to feel the structure under her fingertips, the hardness, its fine lines. Without hesitation, she opened the latch and pulled off the glove. The suit was self-sealing, so not even a milliliter of water would enter into the sleeve that now pressed snugly against her lower arm. Her hand was free, and she lifted it in front of her helmet to take a look. What a strange sight— a naked hand more than a billion kilometers away from Earth.

The water was so cold she had to move her fingers to limit the pain. She did not have much time. Gingerly, she touched the fine lines of the column. The surface was rough. The lines of the engraved signs were only a millimeter thick, but she believed she could feel them clearly. Francesca closed her eyes. Could she trace the signs without looking? She concentrated and put all her feeling into the fingertips, which were quickly becoming numb due to the cold water. Was there a slight electrical impulse when she followed a line, or did she just imagine it? Could it be that the lines were warmer than the background?

She opened her eyes again but saw no difference. The tool bag of her suit must contain a night-vision device. She took it out, hoping the battery was still working. She placed the device in front of her visor and switched it on. Her view changed. The dark was still impenetrable, but now it did not seem blue but green. Once again she placed her finger on the signs, but this time with her eyes open. She felt the tingling once more. She increased the zoom factor to the maximum and looked directly at the spot where her finger touched the column. There was indeed a temperature difference—the material was not dead. When she moved her finger, the spot followed.

"Rossi to Commander," Francesca radioed, "I found something." Then she described her discovery.

Martin chimed in. "I don't want to be a killjoy, but your finger is warmer than the column, so thermal energy flows from you to the column. The spot you see in infrared, that's from yourself."

"Impossible," Francesca said. "I feel this tingling sensation."

"Must be the cold," Martin replied.

"You have absolutely no idea."

"Francesca, darling," she heard Marchenko's voice say, "do you have the night vision device activated? Then take a look around. Do you see the network of nerve fibers meeting in the center? It should be an awesome sight. I remember it very clearly."

"No, Mitya." She knew what he wanted to say—that the forest was dead. That there was no life left here. That whatever she perceived was caused by her imagination and the desire to see something. But she also had to admit to herself there was nothing here, and she had been following a mirage.

Should she turn around? It would be the sensible choice. *Valkyrie* was only a few meters away. She had made the attempt. Didn't this erase her guilt? And her relationship with Marchenko was not so bad. They could have conversations for many years—for decades—until she eventually died. Marchenko on the other hand was immortal, and was condemned to exist eternally.

Francesca hit the column with her fist, but felt no vibration. No, it was too early to give up. She slipped the glove back over her freezing hand. Would there ever really be a moment when it felt right to give up the search? The suit squeezed out the water and closed itself again. Humanity had come far. Had it come so far by giving up so readily?

Francesca glanced at *Valkyrie* once more. Was there movement in the shadows? *Impossible,* she told herself. She turned around and walked into the forest. The columns were notice-ably taller than herself. On Earth, this forest would appear open and bright, since its trees had no crowns, but here 50 kilometers of ocean took the place of this particular feature. The Forest of Columns was gloomy, and even though she now knew there were no traces of life remaining, she felt she was being pursued.

She checked her course on the arm display. She would have to hurry if she wanted to arrive at her destination with sufficient oxygen left. Should she call *Valkyrie* and let herself be transported into the center of the forest? This seemed wrong to her. Back then, Marchenko also walked this path. Maybe she would find him by following exactly in his footsteps.

THE FARTHER FRANCESCA PROCEEDED, the denser the forest became. However, the columns were shorter here than at the entrance. She stopped and examined the signs. Could it be that they were less complex here? It would only be logical if the script that was utilized also reflected the development of the creature. Who knew how many millions of years she had already traveled into its past? At some point she would have to return, gain the friendship of this being, and allow it teach her the script, so that she could read all these stories.

Francesca looked at her watch. She had been walking for almost an hour. The location where Marchenko had met the being and lost his body was not far away, only 500 meters according to the display. Here the columns appeared rather worn. Did the creature have to learn how to produce them, so that the oldest columns were of inferior quality? Or did this simply reflect the billions of years that had passed?

She could look over the tops of the last rows of columns. At a distance of 50 meters, the helmet light shone on some kind of platform inside a clearing. The platform was about four meters square and one meter high, and this was the center of the forest. Here Marchenko must have met the creature.

Francesca heard a loud thumping, looked around in shock, and then realized it was her own heartbeat. She deactivated the interior microphones. This left her in complete silence. Now the clearing lay in front of her like the eye of a storm. There was not the slightest trace of currents, of warmth, of energy, of life.

"Everything is dead here," she reported via radio.

"Yes, I can see it too, darling. Come back. You have done everything you can. I am so grateful to you."

No, it was not time yet. It was there, in the middle, on the platform where the meeting between this strange being and her boyfriend Dimitri had occurred, an encounter that took away his body, but gave his consciousness eternal life. She approached the area with short steps. The platform's square seemed to consist of the same material from which the columns were made. Was this the germ cell? Billions of years ago, did cells start cooperating here, creating something much greater from many weak individual components? The very thought was awe inspiring.

This being might have a history that had begun when Earth was still in its primeval phase. Even though it spent all of its life in this ocean, it must be far more advanced, so far that humans could never understand it. Nor could this entity comprehend the primitive motives of humanity. Considering this, the fact that it saved Dimitri Marchenko two years ago was an almost impossible stroke of luck for which she should be grateful. From the perspective of this creature, the current existence of Marchenko was on a much higher level than the short-lived physical existence she was subject to.

Yet Francesca could not be grateful. She felt the loss, which was as physical as if somebody had torn off one of her arms or legs. She walked forward and pulled herself onto the platform. She shone her helmet light over it. In the center of the square she saw a ring. It had a diameter of about one meter. Inside was a hollow about half a meter deep. The edge of the ring was raised and displayed various signs of the newest kind, like she had seen on the outer columns, precisely engraved and worked out in many details. The inscription must be relatively new—maybe the entire ring? Did it serve a function?

"Marchenko, do you recognize this? Was it here earlier?" she radioed.

She sent him the pictures taken by the helmet camera.

"No, there was only this cloud," he replied. "I could not see more, because it covered the area, and then there was this mulch-like substance everywhere."

Francesca examined the surface. This time, the platform was spotlessly clean. The hollow with the ring around it seemed new, but it might have been here ten years ago. Francesca stepped closer. What was written on the ring? If she could only decipher the signs! In a fairy tale, this would be a magic spell which summoned a genie.

She sat down in the hollow and turned around once. It was probably only for decoration, and if humans built this, it would say something like, 'We thank our sponsors Fiat, Ferrero, and the Vatican.' She got onto her knees, leaned forward, and looked at the signs more closely. They appeared artistic and complex in a script that would not be well-suited for handwriting.

Once again she took off her right glove and carefully moved her fingers across the signs—and was startled! Wherever she touched the ring, it started to glow. Was this real? She put on the infrared visor, but the IR image showed only darkness—it was cold light. No one would believe her! Francesca watched her fingers while swiping them slowly across the material. Gradually, the cold entered the sleeve through her skin. The light seemed to come from the bottom of the engraved signs.

She bent forward, but could not discover a single source for the illumination. The light was blue, a vivid sky blue. It reminded her of Earth's sky, on a nice summer day in Tuscany. Even though her finger moved on, the glow remained. She slowly turned, slid around on her knees, and gradually drew a bluish glowing circle that created a magical atmosphere. It was crazy—she had probably started hallucinating a while ago. But how did hallucination fit with the stinging pain of the cold in her hand?

Francesca gritted her teeth. Her attempt to rescue Marchenko might be hopeless, but she would manage to complete the circle. She went on centimeter by centimeter. To her left she saw the spot where she had first touched the ring. Could she go a bit faster? The light followed her naked finger. She did not ask whether this made any sense. She just wanted to finish the job.

The circle closed, and Francesca collapsed. She wanted to slip on her glove when she suddenly felt a movement. The hollow in which she was sitting moved downward. She still had the chance to jump out. She looked up. Ten meters away she recognized the silhouette of a spacesuit. Was Marchenko coming to rescue her? She shook her head. Where did this confusion come from? It was *she* who wanted to rescue Marchenko.

The hollow sank deeper—it had to be a hallucination. Had that traitor Valentina manipulated Francesca's oxygen supply so that the air she breathed was slowly poisoning her? But then, why did her naked hand still hurt so much? Francesca gazed up, but a dark rim blocked her view. Now she felt the current. Water flowed past her, over her, down toward the opening that had just appeared. All around her there was darkness and rushing water. She reached toward the left into the blackness and expected a wall, but it was not there. Then the hollow hit the ground, the water ebbed away, and a last large drop splashed from above against her visor. The drop burst into a thousand droplets, glowing like sparks in the blue light that now erupted.

December 22, 2049, Enceladus

THEY HAD LOST FRANCESCA. How could this happen? Marchenko raged across the fiber-optic cables. He yelled at Amy, asking how she could let this happen, wanting to know who was responsible for the shitty planning, and when she was finally going to do something about it. He gave Martin and Jiaying hell because they had not monitored *Valkyrie* carefully enough, did not intervene sooner, and should have gone on board themselves. He asked how they could have allowed Francesca, of all people, to go on this journey—someone who was way too emotionally involved, and therefore no longer able to objectively judge her own situation.

Most of all, Marchenko reproached himself. He was not able to be with her when she had found the center of the forest to be empty. He did not notice how she was doing, and he had been too trusting and had not neutralized Valentina a long time ago. He only could see two possibilities—either Francesca was so desperate about her failure she had done herself in, or Valentina was responsible for her death. Why else did Francesca no longer send messages, either directly or via *Valkyrie?* Why were her biometrics no longer accessible, and how did she manage to completely disengage from the system?

Marchenko could access the on-board cameras of *Valkyrie*. If they were not being manipulated, they proved the Russian woman exited the vessel about two hours after Francesca had started out. At that point Valentina had put on her space suit and flooded *Valkyrie*, since this was the only way she could get out. The front cameras had captured her entering the forest, but soon afterward lost track of her.

What could he do? Marchenko was stuck inside the computer systems. While he could move between *ILSE*, the drill vessel, and the lander at lightning speed, Francesca was completely out of reach. He knew she had found the center of the forest, but what had happened next? What was more difficult to bear—not knowing, or the certainty of not being able to help?

"Martin, we have got to do something. We simply have to," he pleaded.

"Easier said than done," the German astronaut said broodingly.

"It is not easily said at all. It is cruel and terrible!"

"Sorry."

"I repeat, we have to..."

"I know," Martin interrupted him, "we have to do something. I am already trying to come up with an idea. The only asset we have down there is *Valkyrie*. We could use it to search for both of them."

"But Valentina locked it against external control—and we do not have contact with her either," Marchenko said bitterly. "She is a traitor."

"Based on our previous experiences I would refrain from such accusations, Marchenko."

"But I cannot refrain from it."

"Let's concentrate on how we can manage to undo the access lock."

"Not a chance, Martin. I am sure we cannot crack the password. I already tried a dictionary attack. She is not that stupid."

"Could we fool the system—a restart, reset, whatever? It

wouldn't be the first time."

"We need to have physical access to do that."

"Sorry, but I have been eavesdropping," Watson interrupted. "I understand you—I mean we—lost a crew member. You are very concerned about it."

"We are sad and angry," Martin explained.

"I have a suggestion," Watson offered. "The problem is gaining access to *Valkyrie*. We do not have any opportunity to do this."

"Yes, we already got that far," Marchenko said in an angry voice. "Sorry," he added.

"We do not have the opportunity," Watson continued, "but think about the command layer that manipulated our star data. It was deeper than the other layers. It is still running, as we never managed to deactivate it."

"Yes, it undermined everything, including the user authorization," Martin said. "That was why we couldn't even get rid of it using the commander's authorization."

"Valentina locked *Valkyrie* at that level," Watson said.

"We could dig through, underneath her commands," Martin added. "That could be a way of regaining control."

"That is an idea," Marchenko said with a sudden feeling of profound anxiety. "But I do not know yet whether it is a *good* idea."

"Why?"

"Martin, you did not see the hole this hacker—or whatever it was—dug in our operating system. It appears to be immensely deep. Someone has to get in there and find a way through the darkness to the other side."

"I could do that," Watson said, "I would like to make some contribution toward saving this crew member. I... pity Francesca."

"That is a very noble offer, Doc. Do you really want to do this? It could get dangerous. It *is* dangerous."

"Yes, Dimitri. I think I can handle it. I am the one who best knows the low-level programming."

"A valid argument," Martin said. "Doc really seems to be the best man for the job."

MARCHENKO ACCOMPANIED Watson back into the data basement, room 3ACC3ACC, FF08080A, 1901C04B. Everything appeared unchanged. Even the Russian spacesuit with his nameplate was still lying there. The hacker must have an odd sense of humor. Had he assumed that Marchenko would be the one who would find his trail?

There seemed to be more people suspecting his presence than he would have liked. Watson once again wore his Dr. Watson outfit, but also real mountain-climbing gear. Seeing a slightly chubby Englishman with mountaineering hardware was rather odd. Of course this was only an image—an avatar —without any practical use. Marchenko was too nervous, though, to find this funny. He also did not joke when Watson said goodbye.

"Come back safely," he said, wanting to shake his hand formally, but Watson hugged him instead. Then Watson took his rope and tied one end to the door handle.

"Good idea," Marchenko remarked, "it looks sturdy."

"Just for safety's sake," Watson said. "I hope I will not have to use the rope. We will see each other on the other side!" Marchenko saw how the AI in the Watson outfit carefully climbed into the hole in the ground and slowly rappeled downward. Marchenko stepped close to the hole and kept watching Watson. It did not take long before he had disappeared into the darkness.

Marchenko knelt down and yelled into the shaft, "Watson?" The word repeatedly bounced off the walls with a dull sound and then dissolved in the sticky ooze. There was no reply. Marchenko rose. There was nothing left for him to do here.

TEN SECONDS later Marchenko appeared on the monitor of the lander module.

"He is on his way," he explained to Martin.

"How long will it take?"

"Impossible to tell—maybe a few minutes."

"So fast?"

"You know the signal propagation times. Watson has free access to all our resources. I just hope the unknown hacker did not set traps."

"Traps?"

"Some kind of loops he could get caught in. Unsolvable problems he would become deeply absorbed in."

"He should be able to recognize those. For such cases we introduced a subjective perception of time," Martin said. "While the AI is solving a problem, the clock keeps ticking, and he is aware of it. And if it takes too long, the AI will try a different strategy."

"Yes, that is the theory," Marchenko said. "But the things I have witnessed! You will not believe what one finds while bug-checking computer games."

"May I interrupt?"

"Watson?" Marchenko and Martin exclaimed simultaneously.

"To whom may I hand over control of *Valkyrie?*"

"To me," Marchenko said. "No problems?"

"The only difficulty was finding the entrance to *Valkyrie* on the lowest level. Imagine moving around the sewers and trying to find the exact manhole cover over which your car is parked."

"You made it."

"I tried every manhole cover. But this hacker, Marchenko, really seems to be going after you. He left spray painted 'M's everywhere."

"That is strange. Thanks for the warning."

Under normal circumstances Marchenko would be worried now, but he had a much more important issue to deal with: He had to start up *Valkyrie*. He started sending the necessary commands to the drill vessel. *Valkyrie* confirmed receipt but did not execute the commands.

"Martin, I need you again. *Valkyrie* does not react."

"How did Valentina leave it?"

"She locked it with her password and then exited the vessel."

"Hatch or SuitPort?"

"Hatch."

"That is the reason. She left the hatch open. *Valkyrie* is still flooded. Under those circumstances it cannot navigate."

"Damn. Can we do anything about it? Rewrite the software?"

"The refusal makes sense. If the vessel is full of water, it lacks buoyancy. You could compare its maneuverability to an iron duck."

"What if we switch all the power to the main engines?"

"Then *Valkyrie* would hit the columns with full force, Dimitri, and it would never reach the center, where we last had contact with Francesca."

"Shit!" he said loudly. "How do we gain buoyancy?"

"Air would not be a bad idea."

Marchenko checked the status of the oxygen tanks. "Looking good!"

"The only problem is the open hatch at the stern. All our nice air would escape," Martin observed. "Just a moment, I have an idea,"

Marchenko watched through the interior camera of the lander module as Martin drew something.

"Take a look," Martin said. He held the sketch in front of the camera. Marchenko saw a pipe angled upward at 45 degrees.

"If we manage to make the stern a bit heavier than the bow and then start blowing air inside, so that the gas moves toward the bow, *Valkyrie* should rise at an angle like this," he said, pointing at the drawing, "and then the vessel should be somewhat maneuverable."

"Meaning what?"

"It could not reach the surface like this, but it ought to manage the distance to the center of the Forest of Columns."

"That is all I need," Marchenko said. "But how do we change the weight distribution so that the stern is heavier?"

"I already have an idea," Martin reassured him.

Marchenko watched the German send commands to *Valkyrie*. He placed the rear control jets in a vertical position—blowing upward to push the stern downward—and the front jets in a horizontal one.

"That should be enough. Now we slowly release air."

Marchenko ordered the tanks to open. Air slowly streamed in and displaced water. *Valkyrie* started to rise.

"Tail in the water, head in the air," Martin sang, confusing Marchenko. "Sorry—it's a German children's song."

If they had not planned this, it would be a sorry sight. *Valkyrie* looked like it was about to crash. Marchenko carefully activated the engine. The stern scraped across the rocky bottom for a few meters.

"Must be a terrible sound," Martin said.

The forest was surprisingly close. The vessel must not collide with the columns at any cost. Who knew how hard they were? *Oh man, oh man*, Marchenko thought, *come on now*. But the vessel did not lift off the ocean floor. He had one all-or-nothing chance left—full power to the main engine. If they were lucky, *Valkyrie* would shoot upward. Otherwise this would be the end for the vessel, as it would crash forcefully into the forest. He had to decide now.

"Come on, Dimitri, do it," he said, and activated full thrust. It took a few seconds before the jet engine built up pressure. But then it overcame the inertia of the steel vessel and launched it to a height of at least 100 meters.

"It's working, Marchenko," Martin said. "Let's go a bit lower and then continue."

Good thing Valkyrie *does not have any passengers right now*, Marchenko thought. The main engine kept it at the current height. The control jets moved it forward. The vessel was not particularly fast, but it would reach its destination. He hoped they would not arrive too late. Was it even any use to have *Valkyrie* land in the center of the forest? Who knew? Perhaps Francesca could then find refuge inside the ship, and if she was being threatened by Valentina, he would just let the vessel crash on the Russian woman.

December 22, 2049, Enceladus

Francesca awoke in a windowless room about the size of a gymnasium. The ceiling was not particularly high, though, and she could easily touch it if she stood up. The walls were glowing with the same blue light as the symbols on the ring outside. She looked at her hand. Her fingertips were still wrinkly, so she could not have been unconscious for a long time.

Then she realized she was not wearing a spacesuit anymore. She frantically touched her body. *Jeans, blouse, sneakers—typical streetwear. How can this be?*

"Where am I?" she asked into the room. She expected an echo, but her voice was immediately swallowed by the walls.

"You are in the center of the forest. You did not change location."

Francesca looked around. There was no one here. She distinctly heard the answer—it was not just her imagination.

"I need to... use your language processing center so we can understand each other." This was her own voice! She was talking to herself. Was she going completely crazy? Was this caused by suffocation?

"Francesca, you are fine. You are lying in the hollow. We are watching over you." Francesca put a hand over her heart, trying to calm herself down. Maybe these were not signs of madness, if some being—*The Being?*—talked to her. But it just switched from 'I' to 'we.'

"Who are you?"

"You know me, darling." Francesca touched her chin. It moved when Marchenko spoke.

"Mitya? I have come to pick you up." Was this really her boyfriend Dimitri? Had she succeeded? Had they achieved their goal?

"I know," he said through her mouth. "We tried to keep you from doing it."

"You did..."

"The altered course—that was me. I installed the intermediate software layer."

"But why? Don't you want to return to me?"

"You all bring danger. Not for the first time. Humanity is not ready for this. IT decided to withdraw, and until then I have to protect IT." *IT—the Enceladus being?*

"Is that *IT's* name?"

"That is... *our* name. I am now a part of the entity." Francesca shivered, because she suspected what that meant.

"You are not coming with me?"

"I cannot, darling. The danger is not yet over. The danger is still out there. I cannot leave IT alone. IT is so powerful, and at the same time so vulnerable. Without me, we could not even have this conversation. IT would probably already have been destroyed by you."

"I am sorry." A tear dropped from the corner of her eye. A second, third, and fourth tear followed. She did not want to cry, but she could not stop it. "I wish we'd never come here."

"That was unavoidable. It was good we were the first ones, and not someone else. IT is very grateful to us. That is why we did not destroy *ILSE*. We tried to warn you with messages. We even manipulated your flight controls so you would turn around."

"And what will happen now?"

"You will wake up in your spacesuit. Only seconds will have gone by. I do not know what happens next. IT cannot foresee the future. However, IT can feel the evil intentions lurking out there. Please be careful."

HER EYES STARTED CLOSING. Francesca wanted to resist, but couldn't. She wanted to continue talking to Marchenko, to convince him to come with her. How would her life keep being meaningful otherwise? If humanity was to blame for Dimitri having to stay here, she would hate humanity. Francesca was afraid, because she knew what she was capable of when she hated. *Please, Dimitri, talk to me, give me a chance.* Through her eyelids she saw the room around her dissolve into the blue glitter of lightning bugs.

December 22, 2049, Enceladus

VALENTINA SAW how the pilot sat down in the hollow in the center of the platform. In her night-vision device the figure in the spacesuit stood out from the background. What was she doing there? Did Francesca really take off her glove? Body heat made the hand glow brightly in the infrared mode. The pilot started to touch the ring with her fingers, but why? No one had prepared Valentina for how strangely this crew would act. She had been told they were a bit naïve, more do-gooders than pragmatic people, and that they only accepted arguments that fit their view of the world. However, this diagnosis could also be applied to 99 percent of mankind.

What was Francesca trying to achieve by her strange behavior? Valentina took off the night-view visor and then she saw it—wherever the ring was touched by fingers, a blue glow developed. It must be cold light, which explained why she would not have noticed it in the infrared view.

Suddenly, the Italian woman collapsed. *Now or never!* Valentina moved toward Francesca, although she did not have a real plan, yet. Up to now all her plans on this voyage had failed, so she decided to just focus on the next step. If everything had gone smoothly, *she* would be the one sitting in this hollow now, without any danger of being disturbed. Francesca was beginning to show signs of life again. *Only three more meters,* Valentina reminded herself. The Italian pilot stood up again, and luckily, Francesca was facing away from her. Moving swiftly, Valentina reached with her left hand into the side pocket of her spacesuit and took out the projectile weapon.

"Hello, Francesca," she said as she pressed the weapon against her ribs, hoping the pilot would understand this gesture. Valentina knew Francesca was a trained soldier and should realize her opponent only had to pull the trigger.

"Hello, traitor," Francesca replied.

"You are not surprised."

Francesca laughed. "I always knew you were up to no good."

"You know nothing."

"You were trying to kill us the whole time."

"No, I would have only neutralized you. You would have spent a few quiet months in your cabins. This was not about killing. Quite the opposite."

"You are threatening me with a weapon in order *not* to kill me? What then?"

"Do not misunderstand me. If necessary, I will pull the trigger, but I would regret it. It would be a necessary sacrifice for the cause."

"What kind of cause is it that makes it worthwhile killing people?"

"You people do not understand it. You are thinking small. What is one victim, if afterward no humans ever have to die?"

"Oh, so Shostakovich is searching for immortality," Francesca said with a laugh.

The typical arrogance of those who believe themselves to be on the side of good, but who destroy everything through ignorance, Valentina thought. She had frequently encountered such people. The transplant doctors at the State Hospital also did not want to voluntarily give her father a new liver although his was destroyed by cancer. But if her father survived this disease, he would be able to help many more people than the drunkard who was supposed to get the liver transplant.

"This 'being,' as you call it, has existed for billions of years," Valentina said. "It is practically immortal. Imagine what we could learn from it! We only need to take a cell culture. You saw how advanced my father's genetic lab is. We could give humans immortality!"

Of course your father would be the first one to profit from it. He would be his own guinea pig. That had always been the plan! "You could have simply asked for it!" yelled Francesca.

"Someone was bound to say no, and then our chances of getting the material would have been zero. You would have never started the voyage! But you are right. I hereby ask the being for a cell culture. I am convinced it can hear us. The ring gave it away. It is here somewhere. Three minutes—I give it three minutes, and then I am going to shoot you. If it does not react, it is to blame for your death. What are a few cells compared to a life?"

Valentina felt Francesca crumple in her arms. She seemed to have trouble staying upright, but was this simply a diversion?

"If you can really hear us, IT, then do not let your cells fall into the hands of this woman," Francesca whispered. Then she collapsed. Valentina dragged her body to the edge of the platform, placed it there, and sat down next to it.

December 22, 2049, Enceladus

ANOTHER 150 METERS TO GO. Marchenko saw on the radar display how *Valkyrie* approached the center of the forest. The radar gave him a 360-degree view of the area. The image showed two silhouettes at the edge of the platform where, three years ago, his former self had met the entity, but he could not recognize more than that. While the cameras aimed forward and backward, the extreme angle of the vessel put the platform in a blind spot. He had to make *Valkyrie* descend and land.

He carefully reduced the thrust of the jets. *What should I do?* It was hard to decide without exact knowledge of the situation. It probably made sense to keep the vessel ready to launch again. Therefore, *Valkyrie* should not touch down completely, or the air bubble might escape through the open hatch.

The stern of the vessel contacted the ground with an awful sound.

"Not one step further!" Marchenko heard Valentina's threat before seeing the woman. He used the control jets for reverse thrust, preventing *Valkyrie* from moving forward. He also had to lower the bow slightly, since otherwise he could not tell if Valentina held an advantage over him. Finally, the bow camera showed the platform, and Marchenko was shocked. The Russian woman appeared to threaten the prone Francesca with a weapon.

"What is going on? What do you want?" he asked via radio.

"She wants a cell sample of the creature."

"Shut up, Francesca. Yes, it is true. And I do not want *Valkyrie* to come any closer!"

Marchenko's mind was racing. How could he help his girl-friend without endangering her? He would like to leave the vessel and hand himself over to Valentina in her place, but he was caught in *Valkyrie's* circuitry.

"Could we find another solution?" he asked.

"In a minute and a half the problem will be solved, one way or another," Valentina said, before turning toward *Valkyrie*. The hollow was behind her, and it was starting to move. *Could this be true?* thought Marchenko. Valentina did not notice the motion, and he had to distract her. The hollow disappeared into the ground.

"What do you want to do with the cells?" he asked.

"Analyze them, so we can expand the capabilities of human cells," Valentina said.

"And this is supposed to work? They have a completely different cell structure!" Marchenko saw the hollow coming up again, and a body was lying inside.

"Another 30 seconds," the Russian woman warned. "You are just trying to distract me."

"I am interested. After all, I am a doctor."

"But you are not a genetic engineer." The body rose from the hollow, and Marchenko zoomed in with the camera as much as he could. It was a human being, a man. The physique and the face seemed oddly familiar. The man ducked and sneaked up on Valentina from behind.

"Another ten seconds."

"Genetics was always my hobby," Marchenko said, trying to sound unconcerned. "According to what I know, it is not yet..."

The man struck the arm holding the weapon, and

Marchenko saw a small object float away. Then the man reached for the two hoses connecting Valentina's oxygen tank with her helmet and tore them off.

"What?" Valentina now uttered only strange sounds. The man, Marchenko just realized, was not wearing a spacesuit. If he was human, he would soon run out of air. Valentina seemed to be defeated.

"Francesca, bring him into *Valkyrie* right away. There is air in the bow!"

His girlfriend stood up and now seemed to notice the man. She jerked for a moment, but then she took the man by the hand and dragged him to the vessel. Valentina fell, but started to get on her feet again. Marchenko noticed she paused for a moment. She probably was deciding whether to get the weapon or to flee into the ship. She would not be able to repair the two air hoses, so she decided to head for *Valkyrie*. Francesca and the strange man had a comfortable head start. They were helping each other, but the man would not be able to hold his breath much longer.

After 40 seconds they reached the hatch. Francesca let the man go first and then climbed in herself. Marchenko was wondering what to do. He could start the jets right away and move *Valkyrie* out of the Russian woman's reach. She would die, like she deserved to, or he could wait and save her life. Francesca and the stranger would have enough time to give her a suitable reception inside.

Valentina would have probably shot Francesca dead, and she had repeatedly endangered the crew, he was convinced. Did she deserve to die? Certainly—but he would not be the executioner. He waited until she also reached the hatch and was safely inside before he started the jets.

December 23, 2049, Enceladus

FRANCESCA WAS ABOUT to go crazy. Yesterday, it looked like everything was lost. Today she ought to feel happier than she had ever expected to be. Next to her sat the Marchenko she had gone with to Enceladus the first time around—and the other Marchenko who had accompanied her this time was always with her via the computer systems of *Valkyrie* and *ILSE*. Then why was she so completely unsatisfied?

The reason might be that the two Marchenkos were not talking to each other, and that neither of them would speak openly with her. Shouldn't two human beings who were so similar get along perfectly? The only difference was that one of them had a body while the other did not. However, the second one had the memories of three years with Francesca that the other one had completely missed.

So why were they not talking to each other? It was because of her. Francesca knew it right from the start. The solution she had imagined involved somehow merging Marchenko's consciousness once more with his body, in a synthesis of the two, and then returning to Earth with him. Nonetheless, she suspected how it was going to end: The two parts would argue so much, she would have to break up with them. But their animosity had to end, or the conflict could not be solved. Human beings were really stupid. This is what

Marchenko got for deciding to save her, instead of taking care of IT—his original plan.

They had tied Valentina to her seat, and she had been sleeping ever since. It had posed no problem for the two of them to overpower the unarmed Russian woman. Valentina also had not put up much resistance, since she must have realized she had lost.

"Francesca, come here." Valentina awoke and was probably hungry.

Francesca had already prepared some food for her. "Breakfast?" She held out two tubes to Valentina but the woman rejected them.

"Business first!"

Francesca laughed. "You don't realize the situation you're in. Or do you have something to offer to us?"

"Yes, your lives."

"Are you going to claim you have a bomb in your belly that will explode if we don't give in to your demands? We scanned you, and there is no such danger."

"True, I am not dangerous. But the laser unit on the surface will shoot down your beautiful *ILSE* with a single burst if you do not cooperate."

"But that would also be the end of you."

"I do not care. I would rather die here than return as a failure."

Francesca shivered. The Russian woman was serious. "Let us assume this is true. What do you want? You will not get the cell samples."

"I understand that," Valentina replied. "But you have something my father could also make good use of—a genuine digital consciousness. AI research is still far away from achieving something like that, and if I judge this correctly, you no longer need it." She pointed at the real Marchenko.

"How would this work?" asked Francesca.

"The Marchenko AI will be hard-encrypted and saved in my personal data vault."

"We are supposed to switch off Marchenko and hand him over to you completely?"

"He is not going to suffer, he will just be sleeping. As long as he sleeps, time stands still for him. Of course we will reactivate him on Earth."

"Then you are going to hand us the control codes for the laser gun."

"No, I am not going to do that. The laser stays under my control."

"Why then should we trust you?"

"Once I get what I want, I will not shoot myself down, will I?"

December 24, 2049, Enceladus

"Watson, I will have to hand over *ILSE* completely to you for the return trip," Marchenko said.

"I understand," the AI answered. "You are going to give in to blackmail."

"There is no other way. The laser is going to destroy *ILSE* if we do not do what Valentina demands."

"I would stand with you in spite of it. You do not have to sacrifice yourself for my sake."

"Even if this meant your annihilation? Are you not afraid?"

"Yes. Dimitri, I am afraid, but the feeling of friendship with you is stronger."

"I am glad to hear that, Doc, and that makes it easier to come to a decision."

"You are still going to sacrifice yourself?"

Marchenko did not answer.

"You humans are strange," Watson said.

December 25, 2049, Enceladus

THE WELCOME in the lander module was overtly subdued. Amy congratulated them via radio on their safe return. Martin and Jiaying hugged Marchenko and Francesca. Everyone ignored Valentina, but she did not seem to mind. The digital Marchenko only spoke when someone addressed him directly, and Martin was worried about him. Why was he isolating himself like this? If only they were on board *ILSE*, where he could talk to Marchenko in private. Instead, the lander only had one room, which was presently occupied by five humans.

It was time to launch, but Valentina wanted to hear their decision beforehand. Martin knew very well why she did this —once *ILSE* left the orbit around Enceladus, Valentina would lose her bargaining chip. He decided to take a little walk outside, even though he had to sweat on the exercise bike for an hour before he could do it. Martin could only speak to Marchenko privately when he was in his spacesuit.

An hour later, Martin stood on a field of ice. He was in a melancholy mood, and this was going to be his last look at this fascinating ice world. Once he returned to the lander, they would have the decisive discussion and then return to *Ilse* and then to Earth. Twelve more months of boring routine were awaiting him. He could not imagine ever setting foot aboard a spacecraft again. At some point, enough was enough.

"Dimitri, are you there?"

"Yes."

"Can I talk to you?"

"Go ahead."

"You are going to sacrifice yourself, aren't you?"

"It is necessary. It has to be done."

"Nothing has to be done. Valentina is going to carry you around imprisoned in a memory stick in her necklace. We all would understand if you don't want to be locked up!"

"I know, and that is great. But I could not live with the consequences."

Martin had not considered this, but Marchenko was right. If Valentina used the laser to shoot down *ILSE*, Marchenko would be the one who survived longest. As long as the fusion power plant still provided energy, Marchenko would continue to exist. Long before that point, the others would have starved to death. They would not die of thirst or suffocation, since the secure energy supply allowed them to generate water and oxygen from the ice. But the food supplies on board the lander were limited, and they would never last for twelve months, the earliest date help might arrive.

"Couldn't we manipulate the laser?" Martin asked.

"Valentina is keeping watch over it. As soon as somebody gets close—boom!" replied Marchenko.

"We are going to try to free you from your prison."

"I will not get my hopes up too high. The encryption of the data vault cannot be cracked. Once I am in there, it is all over. Only Valentina or the people working with her have access to it. Even if you kill her, I stay imprisoned."

"We will torture Valentina if we have to."

"She wants to sacrifice herself if she cannot get me, so how would that work?"

"You are right Dimitri, but I just can't accept that."

"But you have to."

"The hell I have to!" In his anger, Martin turned around

and walked toward the laser. He got within three meters of it before Valentina contacted him.

"One more step and it is all over with *ILSE*."

"You are just bluffing. You want to go home, just as we do," Martin said.

"If you think so," she said. He felt something humming in the housing of the laser, and then a clacking sound. He did not see the beam.

But Amy, sounding frantic, sent a radio message: "Something just shot a hole in our cargo bay. Did you guys do that?"

"Martin said I was bluffing."

"Alright, Valentina. I am coming back inside." It had been worth a try. He at least had to make an attempt to eliminate the threat.

THIRTY MINUTES later they were all gathered for the decisive meeting.

"Did you come to a decision? Yes—or yes?" joked Valentina, pretending to be in a good mood. She could not be that cold-blooded, could she?

"We are going to vote on it," Amy said from *ILSE*.

"Good," Valentina said. "I vote for Marchenko handing himself over."

Then there was silence.

"I am against it," Amy finally said. "There must be another solution. We cannot give in to blackmail."

"The other solution is that we all die," Valentina said.

"Including you," said Jiaying.

"Yes. Me too."

"I offer myself for Dimitri," Watson's voice said. "I am probably the first AI to develop feelings. That should also be valuable for Shostakovich."

"I am sorry," Valentina replied, "but you still are an AI, not a consciousness. You all still do not seem to understand this is not about a particular technology, but about human immortality. Marchenko, you got damned close to it."

"I am against the sacrifice," the real Marchenko said. "Then we all just die here, one for all and all for one."

"But you sacrificed yourself for others, Dimitri," Francesca said.

"That is hardly comparable."

"Against it," Jiaying now said.

Martin looked at his girlfriend. She would die for Marchenko. *That's good*, he thought. He had also just decided. "Then you will have to fire the laser, Valentina," he said.

"Francesca? What about it? I would like to finish this here," Valentina said.

The pilot pressed her lips together and then said. "I... I would like to return to Earth. But not like this."

"So you are against it?" asked Valentina. Francesca nodded. "That's pretty unanimous, then. Sorry, but if you absolutely..."

"Just a second, is nobody going to ask me?" Marchenko's voice boomed from the loudspeaker. "I agree to your proposal. Folks, I am not going to die. As Valentina already said, I am almost immortal. Shostakovich will need me, and he certainly has some exciting projects. Perhaps it will not be that bad. At some point I am going to manage to break free. He does not realize what he is up against, so do not see this as a farewell forever. I am going on a short trip, like you are, Amy. You separated from Sol and Hayato for two years. We will meet again at some point. It is honorable that you were willing to let yourself be killed to spare me this voyage, but it is inappropriate. I do not want it."

"A very wise decision," Valentina said. Martin thought her voice expressed relief. The thought of her own impending starvation amongst enemies must have been rather unpleasant. "Watson, can you prepare the encryption?"

"Yes, Valentina. One moment. Please enter your password." The Russian woman typed in a long combination of characters.

"Before I can move Marchenko into my vault, I have to deactivate him. For that I need the commander's authorization."

"Is that really necessary?" asked Amy via radio.

"Come on, Amy, do not be a spoilsport," the Russian woman said.

This would be the moment when the commander could still prevent Marchenko's imprisonment. She also voted against it, Martin thought, but then she would also sentence the others to death—even if they all agreed to it. Martin was glad he did not have to bear the responsibility.

"Authorization granted," Amy finally said.

"Marchenko, some last words?" asked Valentina.

"It is much too early for last words," Marchenko said. "But it was fun being with all of you—except you, Valentina. May your limbs rot and fall off."

"Deactivate," the Russian woman said.

Age of Ascent, 32

There was:
The I I. The You I.
Overwhelming impressions.
Words. Millions of words.
Thoughts. Thoughts like stars in space.

There is:
Retreat.
The interior.
The exuberance of youth.
The punishment, the suffering.
A short, futile moment.

There will be:
Farewell.
Farewell and reunion.
Far away siblings.
Bonds without borders.

March 1, 2050, ILSE

It took forever before Francesca managed to get involved with Marchenko again. The other one, who was now sleeping in Valentina's data vault, kept going through her mind for a long time. The Italian pilot watched for discrepancies and noticed differences. Three years had not gone by without leaving a mark, not on the Marchenko who had stayed on Enceladus, nor on the one who had accompanied her for so long, nor on herself.

I am probably the biggest problem, Francesca thought. *I started this journey to atone for my guilt. When I was almost at my destination, everything changed: Marchenko separated his body from the entity in order to save me. He sacrificed himself for me again. He could not know we would all make it into* Valkyrie *and survive. And on top of it all, he saved my life a third time and gave his own.* One might think that Dimitri had piled a whole mountain of guilt on her, but to be honest, she could not blame him. He had made her a present —and she thanked him by wallowing in guilt. *Today,* she realized, *right now, I have to stop doing this.* For the first time since they had left the orbit of Saturn, she had been able to smile at him again.

April 27, 2050, ILSE

IT FELT hot and stifling in the cabin, even though the display of the life-support system indicated a temperature of 18 degrees and a normal oxygen level. Valentina sat on her bed. She locked herself inside because she could no longer stand the silent accusations of the others. If only they would yell at her! However, no one said a word when she entered the command module. If she happened to pass by her fellow astronauts somewhere in the ship, all conversation ceased. So for weeks she had been limiting herself to the habitat ring: her cabin, the WHC, and the fitness room.

She would somehow make it. Everything had its greater purpose, even if the other ones did not understand that. Humanity had to be strong and could not allow itself to be artificially limited in its opportunities.

The overpowered universe that wanted to eliminate her home planet and the entire solar system in one blow certainly had no scruples either. Physics made no difference whether a world deserved to perish or whether morally innocent beings would die on it. Thus, mankind needed any instrument that could secure its survival. It also required dynamic individuals like her father, who would research, build, and eventually use these tools.

Hadn't one of her father's competitors—a clever

entrepreneur—stated several decades ago that mankind had to become a multi-planetary species, that humans needed to colonize the solar system? It was a visionary idea, but it was not enough. Even though the solar system had existed for 4.5 billion years, it was a fragile construction. A powerful exterior force, like a star that approached the sun too closely, could make everything collapse.

Her father had shown her the measurement data before they left Earth. Something was approaching the solar system, something huge, even though it was still unclear what it might be. They had to be prepared. It would not happen the day after tomorrow, but in a future where humankind only could survive if it fully used all its potential.

Perhaps she would live to see this time, perhaps not. She absolutely did not want to be immortal. It seemed too heavy a burden to her. On the other hand, if others, like her father, were willing to take on this burden, she would gladly help. A thorough analysis of the Enceladus being could have advanced her father considerably on his way to immortality. Compared to that, the Marchenko AI represented only a consolation prize, but wasn't this also a kind of immortality? Her father would find a worthy mission for her trophy. He just had to avoid dying too soon from his disease.

January 16, 2051, Ishinomaki

JUST THE SAME as two years ago, there was a thunderstorm, and in the darkness the taxi slowly proceeded through the narrow streets of the Japanese city. Large raindrops were drumming against the roof of the vehicle, while one could barely see the few lights that shone through the car windows. The driver who picked her up at the airport in Sendai seemed to speak not one word of English. Amy was glad she did not have to spend the long drive making small talk.

She was afraid of what awaited her. Compared to this, the past voyage, with all its dangers, seemed harmless. They agreed Hayato would be waiting with Sol in his parents' house, in familiar surroundings. Amy did not want to reenter her son's life as an intruder who suddenly threatened to take his father or his grandparents away from him. She felt she did not have the right to do so, because it had been her own decision to leave for the mission.

In a movie script, her child would come running out to greet his mother with endless hugs after her long absence, but this expectation was unrealistic. Amy had missed an important phase of his life. Sol had been little more than a baby when she had left two years prior—but what would happen now? Hayato had shared a lot about their son, once *ILSE* came into radio message range again, while he also showed

Sol pictures of his mother. Due to the signal delay, they could never have live conversations, but Amy heard him and he heard her. Nevertheless, though, she was afraid of the coming moment when they would be reunited, and of possibly being disappointed with the outcome.

The taxi stopped. "We are here," the driver said. In English.

The front door of the house opened—she was expected—and Hayato came outside with a large umbrella. She handed the precise, agreed-upon fare to the driver. The man nodded, pressed a button, and the car door swung open.

Her husband held the umbrella over her while she stepped out, though he got wet in the process. Amy grabbed him by the hip and pulled him away from the taxi. *There's a bit more fat than two years ago*, she thought, but he smelled just as always, which made her smile. She stopped, turned toward Hayato, and embraced him. His back was wet, but it did not matter, they fervently kissed. Yes, she was back again. There were no words for this moment.

They simultaneously let go of each other and walked hand in hand toward the house. Hayato's father Tetsuyo waited in the hallway, and behind him stood Mako, Amy's mother-in-law. Amy took off her shoes and slipped off the coat.

"Just give it to me," Tetsuyo said with a smile.

"Nice to have you here again," Mako said. It was a simple, honest statement. Amy was glad, but her fear still existed. It stuck in her stomach like a fist-sized ball. Tetsuyo showed her the way to the living room, as if she had never been there before. It was a gesture you only used for guests, and Amy had to swallow hard.

Mako pushed the sliding door to the side. The living room was almost empty. It seemed strangely colorless, but that made the bright spot in the corner stand out even more. There sat Sol, playing with colored plastic building blocks. The adults entered the room, but Sol was so engrossed in his play he did not even look up. A shiver skittered up Amy's spine. She carefully approached Sol, while the others stayed by the door.

"Hello, Mommy," her son said in English, and kept pushing the building blocks around. Amy sat down next to him. The fingers he used to reach for his blocks had grown, but they were still tiny. A tear ran down her cheek. She took one of the blocks and placed it on a wall made of three other ones. Sol put another block next to it. Then he looked at her.

"Don't cry, Mommy," he said, and cautiously touched her hand.

March 20, 2052, Southern Germany

THE TAXI ARRIVED at Brunngasse 13 in the small German town. It was driven by a real taxi driver. Francesca didn't think the job still existed. But it made sense here, because the people in this area still loved to drive their own cars. Marchenko gave the guy his credit card. The driver scanned it, gave it back, and let Dimitri sign by saying his name.

They got out of the car. Martin came out to meet them, holding an umbrella over their heads. Francesca hadn't noticed that it had started to rain.

"Nice to have you here," Martin said. "How are you?" He looked a bit more self-assured than before.

"We are fine. Thank you for the invitation," Francesca said. "Where is Jiaying?"

"Oh, she must be in her office. She's preparing her speech for the Astronautical Congress in Bremen next week. I'm sure she didn't hear you."

"I'm right here, behind you," Jiaying said brightly.

They embraced one another. It felt like they had separated only yesterday.

Four hours into the evening, Francesca was the only one still awake. Marchenko had brought a bottle of "the best wodka" as a present, and they had downed it. Jiaying had been the first to drift away, followed by Dimitri. *He's really getting old,* Francesca thought. *Maybe he should try to get a new job.* Sitting around didn't suit him, especially when she was traveling around the world.

ONE YEAR LATER, Francesca recalled that evening vividly. Interestingly, Valentina had called her one week later, asking for Marchenko's contact information. Apparently she was again working with her father, Nikolai Shostakovich of the RB Group. Francesca had told her nothing.

But soon afterward, Marchenko seemed to have found a new passion. Day after day he mysteriously disappeared. Francesca couldn't help but ask herself—*is there a connection?*

Author's Note

Congratulations! We've now completed our second roundtrip journey of almost two billion kilometers. I thank you very much for your continued company. I hope you know that each fictional character includes a small part of the author. Thus, you already know a lot about me. When my significant other is reading my new novels, she's always recognizing some quirk of mine—or bits of personality borrowed from friends and family. Nobody in my life is safe from having some of their behaviors or character traits incorporated into people in my novels.

As I write this note, I'm already pretty far out into my fictional future. Time does not stand still, even in the universe where *The Enceladus Mission* (available here hard-sf.com/links/454616) started. This is an aspect of my work that I love very much. I have the power to determine the future here. It's a future, as you will discover in our future journeys, that's full of danger and adventure. But it is not a dystopia. I am pretty optimistic that we will be able to resolve the problems the world is facing right now. Science and technology will help a lot, more than we are able to imagine right now. I truly believe that humanity is basically good. There are evil people, no doubt, but in general people are much more into cooperation than conflict. We are made to solve problems, just as Martin, Jiaying, Amy, Hayato, Francesca, and Dimitri do. We'll solve one problem at a time.

We need dystopian novels, too, to warn us about current and future dangers, but I believe the future itself will be better for most people than the past has been. I'm not talking about universal happiness, but about the lives of everyday people in all parts of the world improving bit by bit.

Sorry for introducing some pathos here. It might have to do with the temporary goodbye I'm about to say. Technically, the Ice Moon Series finishes here. There will be some revelations about a part of *Ilse's* second earthbound journey later on, in a novel called *Jupiter*. But I recommend reading chronologically as you delve into my world, and that means reading *The Hole* or *Proxima Rising* next. I promise they will be coming soon

See you back in space! There we'll cross paths with some old friends and meet new ones, like in *The Hole*:

A mysterious object threatens to destroy our solar system. The survival of humankind is at risk, but nobody takes the warning of young astrophysicist Maribel Pedreira seriously. At the same time, an exiled crew of outcasts mines for rare minerals on a lone asteroid.

When other scientists finally acknowledge Pedreira's alarming discovery, it becomes clear that these outcasts are the only ones who may be able to save our world, knowing that THE HOLE hurtles inexorably toward the sun.

Order it here:

hard-sf.com/links/454634

If you register at www.hard-sf.com/subscribe I will inform you about upcoming publications of my titles. As a bonus, I will send you the beautifully-illustrated PDF version of *The Guided Tour to the Asteroids* for free!

On my website at www.hard-sf.com you will also find interesting popular science news and articles about all those worlds afar that I'd love to have you visit with me.

I have to ask you one last thing, a big favor: If you liked this book, you would help me a lot if you could leave me a review so others can appreciate it as well. Just open this link:

hard-sf.com/links/397097

Thank you so much!

Due to the fact that asteroids play an important role here, you will find a section entitled *The Guided Tour to the Asteroids* below.

facebook.com/BrandonQMorris

amazon.com/author/brandonqmorris

bookbub.com/authors/brandon-q-morris

goodreads.com/brandonqmorris

Also by Brandon Q. Morris

Proxima Rising

Late in the 21st century, Earth receives what looks like an urgent plea for help from planet Proxima Centauri b in the closest star system to the Sun. Astrophysicists suspect a massive solar flare is about to destroy this heretofore-unknown civilization. Earth's space programs are unequipped to help, but an unscrupulous Russian billionaire launches a secret and highly-specialized spaceship to Proxima b, over four light-years away. The unusual crew faces a Herculean task—should they survive the journey. No one knows what to expect from this alien planet.

3.99 $ – hard-sf.com/links/610690

Proxima Dying

An intelligent robot and two young people explore Proxima Centauri b, the planet orbiting our nearest star, Proxima Centauri. Their ideas about the mission quickly prove grossly naive as they venture about on this planet of extremes.

Where are the senders of the call for help that lured them here? They find no one and no traces on the daylight side, so they place their hopes upon an expedition into the eternal ice on Proxima b's dark side. They not only face everlasting night, the team encounters grave dangers. A fateful decision will change the planet forever.

3.99 $ hard-sf.com/links/652197

Proxima Dreaming

Alone and desperate, Eve sits in the control center of an alien structure. She has lost the other members of the team sent to explore exoplanet Proxima Centauri b. By mistake she has triggered a disastrous process that threatens to obliterate the planet. Just as Eve fears her best option may be a quick death, a nearby alien life form awakens from a very long sleep. It has only one task: to find and neutralize the destructive intruder from a faraway place.

3.99 $ hard-sf.com/links/705470

The Death of the Universe

For many billions of years, humans   having conquered the curse of aging   spread throughout the entire Milky Way. They are able to live all their dreams, but to their great disappointment, no other intelligent species has ever been encountered. Now, humanity itself is on the brink of extinction because the universe is dying a protracted yet inevitable death.

They have only one hope: The 'Rescue Project' was designed to feed the black hole in the center of the galaxy until it becomes a quasar, delivering much-needed energy to humankind during its last breaths. But then something happens that no one ever expected   and humanity is forced to look at itself and its existence in an entirely new way.

3.99 $ hard-sf.com/links/835415

The Death of the Universe: Ghost Kingdom

For many billions of years, humans—having conquered the curse of aging—spread throughout the entire Milky Way. They are able to live all their dreams, but to their great disappointment, no other intelligent species has ever been encountered. Now, humanity itself is on the brink of extinction because the universe is dying a protracted yet inevitable death.

They have only one hope: The 'Rescue Project' was designed to feed the black hole in the center of the galaxy until it becomes a quasar, delivering much-needed energy to humankind during its last breaths. But then something happens that no one ever expected—and humanity is forced to look at itself and its existence in an entirely new way.

3.99 $ – hard-sf.com/links/991276

The Enceladus Mission (Ice Moon 1)

In the year 2031, a robot probe detects traces of biological activity on Enceladus, one of Saturn's moons. This sensational discovery shows that there is indeed evidence of extraterrestrial life. Fifteen years later, a hurriedly built spacecraft sets out on the long journey to the ringed planet and its moon.

The international crew is not just facing a difficult twenty-seven months: if the spacecraft manages to make it to Enceladus without incident it must use a drillship to penetrate the kilometer-thick sheet of ice that entombs the moon. If life does indeed exist on Enceladus, it could only be at the bottom of the salty, ice covered ocean, which formed billions of years ago.

However, shortly after takeoff disaster strikes the mission, and the chances of the crew making it to Enceladus, let alone back home, look grim.

The Titan Probe (Ice Moon 2)

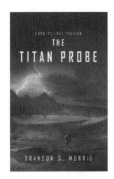

In 2005, the robotic probe "Huygens" lands on Saturn's moon Titan. 40 years later, a radio telescope receives signals from the far away moon that can only come from the long forgotten lander.

At the same time, an expedition returns from neighbouring moon Enceladus. The crew lands on Titan and finds a dangerous secret that risks their return to Earth. Meanwhile, on Enceladus a deathly race has started that nobody thought was possible. And its outcome can only be decided by the astronauts that are stuck on Titan.

The Io Encounter (Ice Moon 3)

Jupiter's moon Io has an extremely hostile environment. There are hot lava streams, seas of boiling sulfur, and frequent volcanic eruptions straight from Dante's Inferno, in addition to constant radiation bombardment and a surface temperature hovering at minus 180 degrees Celsius.

Is it really home to a great danger that threatens all of humanity? That's what a surprise message from the life form discovered on Enceladus seems to indicate.

The crew of ILSE, the International Life Search Expedition, finally on their longed-for return to Earth, reluctantly chooses to accept a diversion to Io, only to discover that an enemy from within is about to destroy all their hopes of ever going home.

Return to Enceladus (Ice Moon 4)

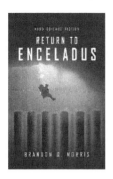

Russian billionaire Nikolai Shostakovitch makes an offer to the former crew of the spaceship ILSE. He will finance a return voyage to the icy moon Enceladus. The offer is too good to refuse—the expedition would give them the unique opportunity to recover the body of their doctor, Dimitri Marchenko.

Everyone on board knows that their benefactor acts out of purely personal motivations… but the true interests of the tycoon and the dangers that he conjures up are beyond anyone's imagination.

3.99 € – hard-sf.com/links/527011

Ice Moon - The Boxset

All four bestselling books of the Ice Moon series are now offered as a set, available only in e-book format.

The Enceladus Mission: Is there really life on Saturn's moon Enceladus? *ILSE,* the International Life Search Expedition, makes its way to the icy world where an underground ocean is suspected to be home to primitive life forms.

The Titan Probe: An old robotic NASA probe mysteriously awakens on the methane moon of Titan. The *ILSE* crew tries to solve the riddle—and discovers a dangerous secret.

The Io Encounter: Finally bound for Earth, *ILSE* makes it as far as Jupiter when the crew receives a startling message. The volcanic moon Io may harbor a looming threat that could wipe out Earth as we know it.

Return to Enceladus: The crew gets an offer to go back to Enceladus. Their mission—to recover the body of Dr. Marchenko, left for dead on the original expedition. Not everyone is working toward the same goal. Could it be their unwanted crew member?

9.99 $ hard-sf.com/links/780838

The Hole

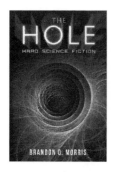

A mysterious object threatens to destroy our solar system. The survival of humankind is at risk, but nobody takes the warning of young astrophysicist Maribel Pedreira seriously. At the same time, an exiled crew of outcasts mines for rare minerals on a lone asteroid.

When other scientists finally acknowledge Pedreira's alarming discovery, it becomes clear that these outcasts are the only ones who may be able to save our world, knowing that *The Hole* hurtles inexorably toward the sun.

3.99 $ hard-sf.com/links/527017

Silent Sun

Is our sun behaving differently from other stars? When an amateur astronomer discovers something strange on telescopic solar pictures, an explanation must be found. Is it merely artefact? Or has he found something totally unexpected?

An expert international crew is hastily assembled, a spaceship is speedily repurposed, and the foursome is sent on the ride of their lives. What challenges will they face on this spur-of-the-moment mission to our central star?

What awaits all of them is critical, not only for understanding the past, but even more so for the future of life on Earth.

3.99 $ hard-sf.com/links/527020

The Rift

There is a huge, bold black streak in the sky. Branches appear out of nowhere over North America, Southern Europe, and Central Africa. People who live beneath The Rift can see it. But scientists worldwide are distressed—their equipment cannot pick up any type of signal from it.

The rift appears to consist of nothing. Literally. Nothing. Nada. Niente. Most people are curious but not overly concerned. The phenomenon seems to pose no danger. It is just there.

Then something jolts the most hardened naysayers, and surpasses the worst nightmares of the world's greatest scientists—and rocks their understanding of the universe.

3.99 $ – hard-sf.com/links/534368

Mars Nation 1

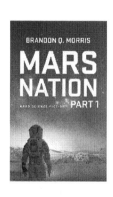

NASA finally made it. The very first human has just set foot on the surface of our neighbor planet. This is the start of a long research expedition that sent four scientists into space.

But the four astronauts of the NASA crew are not the only ones with this destination. The privately financed 'Mars for Everyone' initiative has also targeted the Red Planet. Twenty men and women have been selected to live there and establish the first extraterrestrial settlement.

Challenges arise even before they reach Mars orbit. The MfE spaceship Santa Maria is damaged along the way. Only the four NASA astronauts can intervene and try to save their lives.

No one anticipates the impending catastrophe that threatens their very existence—not to speak of the daily hurdles that an extended stay on an alien planet sets before them. On Mars, a struggle begins for limited resources, human cooperation, and just plain survival.

3.99 $ hard-sf.com/links/762824

Mars Nation 2

A woman presumed dead fights her way through the hostile deserts of Mars. With her help, the NASA astronauts orphaned on the Red Planet hope to be able to solve their very worst problem. But their hopes are shattered when an unexpected menace arises and threatens to destroy everything the remnant of humanity has built on the planet. They need a miracle   or a ghost from the past whose true intentions are unknown.

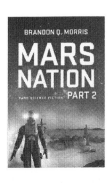

Mars Nation 2 continues the story of the last representatives of Earth, who have found asylum on our neighboring planet, hoping to build a future in this alien world.

3.99 $ hard-sf.com/links/790047

Mars Nation 3

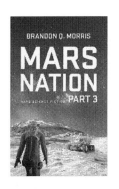

Does the secret of Mars lurk beneath the surface of its south pole? A lone astronaut searches for clues about the earlier inhabitants of the Red Planet. Meanwhile, Rick Summers, having assumed the office of Mars City's Administrator by deceit and manipulation, tries to unify the people on Mars with the weapons under his control. Then Summers stumbles upon so powerful an evil that even he has no means to overcome it.

3.99 $ hard-sf.com/links/818245

The Guided Tour to the Asteroids

What are Asteroids?

THE COMPANY OWNED by the fictitious Russian entrepreneur Shostakovich makes money mining asteroids. Twenty or thirty years from today, this may in fact be reality. But what are these space rocks? Where do they come from, how did they develop, and are they dangerous? The following chapters will try to explain this.

The term asteroid comes from Ancient Greek and means 'starlike.' In a telescope, asteroids (unlike planets) look like dots, i.e. starlike. In reality, these objects come in all kinds of shapes and sizes, but they have two things in common:

- They move in an orbit around the sun.
- They are not spherical (to be more precise, they are not in hydrostatic equilibrium).

Objects that do not move around the sun but around a planet are called moons, no matter what their shape is. Spherical objects orbiting the sun are either dwarf planets (Pluto, Ceres...) or planets (Earth, Mars...). If they are not spherical, they might be comets or asteroids. If their circumference is less than one meter, they are meteoroids (not meteorites, which are meteoroid remnants that reached the surface of the Earth).

There are probably several million asteroids orbiting in the solar system. We have data concerning approximately 1.3 million of them, and more than 750,000 have been given individual numbers as a means of designation. Only one can be observed from Earth with the naked eye—Vesta. In spite of their large number, asteroids add hardly anything to the mass of the solar system. All of them combined probably weigh less than a thousandth of Earth, and the terrestrial moon weighs ten times more than they do.

How Asteroids Came into Being

FOR A LONG TIME it was assumed asteroids were the remnants of a destroyed planet that once orbited the sun in the area between Mars and Jupiter, as a planet seemed to be missing there. The area is now called the 'asteroid belt.' The missing planet was even given a name—Phaethon. However, the total mass of the asteroids orbiting there, as we know today, amounts to only about 5 percent of the mass of Earth's moon. Therefore, this hypothetical former planet would have been much smaller than our moon.

During the 19th century, the search for Phaethon caused a lot of attention to be paid to the area between Mars and Jupiter. This at least had the advantage that the first asteroids there were quickly discovered. Ceres, Pallas, Juno, and Vesta were found in turn and initially believed to be planets. When Neptune was discovered in 1846, it was therefore considered not the eighth, but the thirteenth planet. Soon, though, so many celestial bodies were added that a new category of minor planets was created. They were labeled as asteroids.

Today, asteroids are assumed to occupy intermediate positions in the creation of planets, so to speak: Bodies still in the process of developing into planets. In the asteroid belt, however, the strong gravitational influence of Jupiter prevented the development of a planet. Later, the asteroids collided with each other and other planets. This formed fragments, which collided again, leading to a whole menagerie of asteroids with diverse structures. Only the largest of these developed differentiated structure by melting, so the components were distributed into core and crust. When one of the large asteroids collided with another one, its core created fragments with an especially high metal content, while the splinters of the crust were rich in silicates.

For many years it was believed that asteroids were compact, monolithic bodies. Since then, some surprisingly-low densities have been measured and some huge impact craters have been discovered. Many asteroids might represent a kind of cosmic debris pile, the components of which are loose, held together only by their own gravitational force. Such a body is relatively resistant to collisions. Monolithic objects, on the other hand, would be torn apart by the shock-waves of major impacts. Another support for this fact is the relatively low rotational speed of large asteroids. During fast rotation around its own axis, centrifugal forces would tear apart an object that is only loosely held together.

The Naming of Minor Planets

BECAUSE THERE ARE SO many minor planets, their nomencla-
tures follow a methodology that seems rather complicated at
first. Let's start with the discovery of a new asteroid. Initially,
its orbital parameters might not be known with certainty, and
the object then receives a provisional designation that begins
with the year of its discovery and is followed by a space and
then a letter that indicates the half month of its discovery. *A*
marks the first half of January, *B* the second half of January,
C the first half of February, and so on. The letter *I* is left out,
and *Z* is not needed. Then a second letter follows: *A* for the
first one discovered in this half month, *B* for the second, and
so forth. Once again, *I* is omitted, but *Z* is used. Therefore,
2015 AA would be the first asteroid discovered in the first half
of January 2015.

Nowadays, more than 25 asteroids are discovered in half
a month, so the designations go from A through Z and then
begin again at A... The number of times the alphabet was
completed is indicated by a subscripted number. The first set
of letters would have the subscript *0*, though this is omitted in
print. Accordingly, the asteroid 2015 AA67 would be the
$(68*25)+1=1701$st asteroid discovered during the first half of
January 2015.

At some point, the orbit of the asteroid is determined

more precisely, so it can always be found again if necessary. The reward for all of these efforts: Now the asteroid receives a 'real' number (starting at 1)! In previous years you could see the sequence of discoveries through these numbers, but that doesn't work anymore. In addition, the asteroid now has the right to a name. For ten years, the discoverer has the naming rights, but the International Astronomical Union must confirm it, and this process can take a while. For instance, naming asteroids after pets or using advertising messages is no longer permitted. A name should not contain more than 16 characters, must consist of a single, pronounceable word, and should not be too similar to existing names. Politicians or military personalities must have been dead for at least 100 years before an asteroid can be named after them. Because of these limitations, there are many asteroids that have been numbered but remain unnamed.

Types of Asteroids

IF YOU LOOK CLOSELY in the telescope and determine which wavelength ranges of light an asteroid reflects, the branch of science called astronomical spectroscopy, you can often draw conclusions about the asteroid's composition. Of course 'often' does not mean 'always,' and points toward the problems involved in this spectral classification. The most frequently used classification scheme employing this technique was developed in 1984 by the American astronomer David Tholen. It consists of three larger groups and six smaller classes that cannot be assigned to any of the groups.

The asteroids of the *C-group* contain a relatively large—up to 3 percent—share of carbon compounds. Therefore they reflect relatively little light. These are probably the most 'primeval' asteroids. During their long life they were exposed to little heat, and they reflect the composition of the planetary cloud from which they developed. The group includes multiple types:

C-type: At 75 percent, this is the most common. They consist of silicon minerals with a relatively high content of carbon and organic materials, which partially condensed out of the primeval solar nebula. Therefore, they give us some insight into the early period of the solar system. Examples are (10) Hygiea, (54) Alexandra, (164) Eva.

B-type: Reflect differently in the UV range compared to the C type, but are otherwise similar. Example: (2) Pallas.

F-type: Similar to C, but with differences in the UV range. In addition, lacking absorption lines in the wavelength range of water. Example: (704) Interamnia.

G-type: Also similar to C, but with different absorption lines in the UV range. Example: (1) Ceres.

At 15 percent, the *S-group* is the second most common type. The S stands for silicates, i.e. silicon minerals like olivine or pyroxene of which these bodies are made. It is assumed they developed inside large asteroids that were later destroyed. According to their metal content they were located near the outside, indicating little iron and nickel, or more deeply inside, indicating more iron and nickel. The only representative is the *S-type*. Example: (15) Eunomia, (3) Juno.

In the Tholen classification, the *X-group* consists of the objects displaying a very similar spectrum but probably having a quite different composition. The visible difference mostly relates to their reflectivity, called albedo. Asteroids for which this value is unknown are directly assigned to the *X-type*. The other types belonging to this group are as follows:

M-type: Medium albedo. The *M-type* often—but not always—has a relatively high metal content. Presumably these are the former cores of larger asteroids. Example: (16) Psyche.

E-type: High albedo, came probably from the crust of a larger asteroid. Examples: (44) Nysa, (55) Pandora.

P-type: Low albedo, among the darkest asteroids. Examples: (259) Aletheia, (190) Ismene.

The following other types of asteroids occur relatively rarely, are not classified within any group, and some of them are seen only in certain parts of the solar system.

A-type: Reddish spectrum, fewer than 20 known specimens, probably came from the crust of a larger body. Example: (246) Asporina.

D-type: Very dark and reddish, might have originated from the Kuiper belt beyond Neptune. The Martian moon Phobos might be related to them. Example: (624) Hektor.

T-type: Dark and reddish, only a few specimens, might be related to the *C-type.* Example: (96) Aegle.

Q-type: Lines of olivine and pyroxene as well as metal in their spectrum, might be more common than hitherto assumed. Example: (1862) Apollo.

R-type: Medium bright, slightly reddish, with lines of olivine and pyroxene in their spectrum. Example: (349) Dembowska.

V-type: Similar to *S-type,* but with more pyroxene. Due to the fact that the *V-type* asteroids often have orbits very similar orbit to Vesta, it is believed they might have been torn off the crust of Vesta through collisions. Example: (4) Vesta.

Where One Can Find Asteroids

GENERALLY, the asteroid belt is considered the home of asteroids, and it contains ninety percent of the them. But these objects also zoom around in other areas of the solar system. Only within the orbit of Mercury, relatively close to the sun—less than a third of the distance between the Earth and the sun—are asteroids yet to be discovered. There the so-called vulcanoids are suspected to exist. If they do exist—as meteorite impacts on Mercury seem to suggest—they would have diameters below 50 kilometers, because otherwise they would have shown up on photos. Discovering them wouldn't be easy, since they get so close to the sun. During the search, large telescopes would run the risk of being destroyed by the bright sunlight. The asteroids that come closest to the sun are (1566) Icarus (up to 0.19 AU) and (3200) Phaethon (up to 0.14 AU). Both move around the sun in strongly elliptical orbits.

The most relevant ones for our daily life are undoubtedly the so-called Near-Earth Asteroids or NEA. These celestial bodies usually don't get farther away from the sun than Mars. Four types can be distinguished: *Amor, Apohele, Apollo*, and *Aten*.

The *Amor* class crosses the orbit of Mars toward Earth, but without ever reaching Earth. Among them are (433) Eros, which approaches the orbit of Earth to as close as 0.15 AU, as well as the eponymous asteroid (1221) Amor, which was discovered in 1932. Amor asteroids do not cross the path of Earth and therefore cannot hit it, just like asteroids of the *Apohele* (or *Atira*) class, which move around the sun completely within Earth's orbit.

But there are also the so-called 'Earth crossers.' These are asteroids with orbits that cross the orbital path of Earth, which might eventually lead to a collision. They either belong to the *Apollo* class, where the orbit is wider than that of Earth, or the *Aten* class, where the orbit is narrower than the one of Earth. Currently, none of the known objects seem to pose a real danger. Nevertheless, they are studied intensively. Statistically speaking, once a year Earth is hit by an object with a diameter of less than four meters, and once in every five years a seven-meter object hits us, usually disintegrating in the atmosphere. Every 2,000 or 3,000 years there is an impact with effects similar to the Tunguska event of 1908. And about twice in a million years we might have to be prepared for the impact of an asteroid with a diameter of up to a kilometer. Even larger objects, with up to five-kilometer diameter, hit us every 20 million years. Currently no such asteroid is on a collision course, but this could change. Occasionally, objects from the asteroid belt change their trajectories due to disturbances caused by Jupiter.

The asteroid belt is the reservoir for all the asteroids roaming through the inner and outer solar system. Its distance from the sun is about 2 to 3.4 Astronomical Units—an AU is the distance from the Earth to the sun. However, this area is not evenly filled with objects. Quite the opposite. The strong interaction with Jupiter causes some orbits to be unstable whenever the ratio of the orbital periods is a whole number: resonance. This creates dips, which are called 'Kirkwood gaps' after the American astronomer Daniel Kirkwood, who noticed them in 1866. Among them is the 4:1 resonance at 2.06 AU, the inner limit of the main belt, afterward the Hestia gap (3:1), a resonance zone at 5:2, and the Hecuba gap with a 2:1 resonance where the main belt ends at 3.4 AU. The majority of asteroids orbit between the 4:1 and the 2:1 resonance.

In general, the distances between asteroids are huge, even in the asteroid belt. Hitting an asteroid with a spaceship isn't easy, and accidental collisions are almost impossible. In the course of millions of years some collisions between asteroids have happened, though. This caused the formation of groups with similar orbits, which are called 'families.' Over time these can become very large. The Flora and Eunomia families, for example, contain up to 5 percent of all objects in the main belt, several thousand asteroids each.

On the orbit of each planet there are points where the gravitational forces of the sun and the planet cancel each other. Those are the so-called Lagrange points. There one finds stable orbits used by asteroids. Such companions were first found near Jupiter, where they run 60 degrees ahead of the planet (Greeks) or 60 degrees behind (Trojans). Later, similar asteroids were found near other planets, and the term was expanded accordingly. By now, there are over 7,000 known Jupiter Trojans. Their number might be comparable to that of the asteroids in the main belt, but as they are farther away, not as many have been individually discovered yet. Venus and Earth have one known Trojan each (2013 ND15 and 2010 TK7). For Mars, nine objects have been identified. In the orbits of Uranus and Neptune, which are difficult to observe due to the enormous distances from Earth, one Trojan each has been discovered.

Asteroids between the orbits of Jupiter and Neptune are also called Centaurs. It is assumed that these are inactive comets. The largest known Centaur, (10199) Chariklo, has a diameter of almost 250 kilometers and might even possess a ring system. The double Centaur (65489) Ceto and its moon Phorcys form a double planetoid system in which two components of similar size orbit each other.

But the solar system certainly does not end beyond Neptune. Everything beyond it is simply called a trans-Neptunian object (TNO). This probably includes tens of thousands of bodies—dwarf planets like Pluto or Sedna, comets, but also many, many asteroids. Compared to their counterparts in the main belt, these are rather dark. Many contain a core of dust and ice—in that case the transition to comets is fluid. Their orbits are sometimes influenced by that of Neptune (resonances), as is the case with the Plutinos (with Pluto among them), which move in a 2:3 resonance with Neptune. Others, such as the Cubewanos, follow paths that are tilted against the normal rotational plane of the planets.

Wrong Way Drivers in the Solar System

IN THE SOLAR SYSTEM, everyone drives to the left: Seen from the North Pole of the ecliptic, the plane of the solar system, all planets, and other heavenly bodies move to the left, or counterclockwise. All of them? Almost all... The planets and dwarf planets obey this rule, but we are aware of 82 asteroids that are wrong-way drivers.

Just like on a highway, this won't work for long. If an object is hurled by some strange accident from the Oort Cloud into the interior of the solar system, and like some bad driver from the boondocks, disregards all traffic rules, the end might come after a few thousand years. But if these bad drivers choose their courses cleverly, they can last a few million years.

The asteroid 2015 BZ509 is a particularly smart representative of this group. This object, with a diameter of about three kilometers, moves around the sun approximately along the path of the gas giant Jupiter. Twice per revolution it even encounters the planet—without a collision. The reason is 2015 BZ509 selected a course that astronomers call a trisectrix.

So far we know of no other asteroid moving around the sun on such a path that consists of two circles merging with each other. Therefore the asteroid once encounters the great

Jupiter while being closer to the sun, and the other time farther away. If only the gravitational force of Jupiter influenced its course, it could be absolutely stable. But the effects of the other planets reduce this time to a few million years.

We do not exactly know where 2015 BZ509 originated. It could be a former comet that is no longer active. It is probably one of the Damocloids, bodies similar to Halley's Comet that have already lost their volatile material. They often have retrograde (clockwise) orbits and originally arrived as visitors from the Oort Cloud, that 'pile of debris' at the outermost limits of our solar system.

The Ten Most Interesting Asteroids

1. (1) *Ceres*, with a diameter of 945 kilometers, is the largest object in the asteroid belt, and the only dwarf planet inside the orbit of Neptune. In the entire solar system it reaches the 33rd position when it comes to size. In 1801, Ceres was the first newly discovered dwarf planet. Similar to a large terrestrial planet, it seems to have a core and a crust, and there may be an ice ocean between them, like on Enceladus. Water vapor emissions were detected in 2014.

2. *2014 RC* approached Earth in 2014 to at least one-tenth of the distance to the moon, i.e. less than 40,000 kilometers. The special feature of this asteroid, with a size of 30 to 50 meters, is its rotational speed. No other one rotates this fast—a rotation takes only 15.8 seconds. Due to the centrifugal forces generated, the object must be massive.

3. (216) *Kleopatra* stands out primarily due to its shape—the asteroid looks like a bone. It was discovered in 1880, and in 2008 two companions, Alexhelios and Cleoselene, were found. The asteroid is about 217 kilometers long and 90 kilometers thick. It appears to consist of loosely strung-together rocks and is 30 to 50 percent empty space. The two satellites have a size of 3 and 5 kilometers, respectively.

4. (243) *Ida* is an asteroid in the main belt. It is shaped irregularly and about 31 kilometers long. More interesting is

its companion, Dactyl. Ida proved to be the first asteroid with its own moon. Ida belongs to the S type, as does the egg-shaped Dactyl, which is about 20 times smaller in diameter.

5. Among all known asteroids, *(1566) Icarus* comes closest to the sun, hence its name. Every 9, 19, or 28 years the asteroid, which has a diameter of about 1,440 meters, also gets near Earth, so it could potentially become a danger. In 1968 it was as close as 16 times the distance to the moon. Back then it was the first asteroid to be observed by radar.

6. *(5261) Eureka* was the first Martian Trojan to be discovered, on June 20, 1990. Based on its spectrum it belongs to the A type. However, its composition seems to differ from this group. Due to the fact that it is located at the most stable spot of the Lagrange point L5, its orbit is so immutable that Eureka might have been moving there since the solar system came into being.

7. *(29075) 1950 DA* is the Near Earth Asteroid with the highest probability of striking Earth. This object, with a diameter of about one kilometer, has a 0.012 percent probability of hitting our planet in 2880. If this unlikely event should actually occur, the impact could seriously threaten human civilization.

8. *(21) Lutetia* is an asteroid of the main belt that was discovered on November 15th, 1852 by Hermann Mayer Salomon Goldschmidt from the windows of his attic apartment. It was one of the first asteroids to be classified as the M type, though one with an unusually low radar albedo. With a diameter of approximately 100 kilometers, Lutetia is dominated by huge craters, ridges, and landslides, as well as rocks measuring hundreds of meters. It seems to have had an eventful past. The asteroid probably developed in the inner solar system and then was hurled outward.

9. *(25143) Itokawa* was the first asteroid from which a probe took material to Earth. This object belonging to the Apollo group has an average diameter of about 350 meters. It appears to consist of two halves that at some point collided and merged with each other. Its low density proves that it only

looks like a massive stone at first glance. The images taken by the Hayabusa probe also indicate this.

10. *(469219) 2016 HO$_3$* is an 'almost moon' of Earth. This asteroid, with a diameter of approximately 41 meters, accompanies our planet on its path around the sun, sometimes swinging toward Mars, and at other times toward Venus. If it is on the outer path, it falls back a bit, then changes to the inner course and passes us by again. This makes *2016 HO$_3$* a quasi-satellite.

What Would Kill Us From an Asteroid Impact

THE RISK of Earth being hit by a destructive asteroid is low. Statistically, a 60-meter rock will collide with our planet every 1,500 years, and a 400-meter giant about once every 400,000 years. If this happened, which effects of the impact would be most dangerous for people? Researchers in a group led by the astrophysicist Clemens Rumpf of the University of Southampton studied this question by theoretically bombarding Earth with 50,000 virtual asteroids with diameters between 15 and 400 meters.

This project showed that an impact on land was generally ten times more dangerous than an ocean hit. The following summarizes the findings, ranked from most deadly to least.

- 1st and 2nd places: Wind and shockwaves caused the most casualties, about 60 percent. The sudden changes in air pressure damaged internal organs, and the gusts of wind were strong enough to throw people through the air, and also uprooted trees.
- 3rd place: The heat generated was responsible for 30 percent of all victims. One could escape it by hiding in a basement or subway tunnel.
- 4th place: Tsunami. An impact at sea and the

ensuing tsunami could be responsible for 20 percent of the victims. The energy of the tsunami wave would dissipate quickly.

- 5th and 6th places: The impact crater and the material thrown up by the impact would each cause less than 1 percent of the casualties.
- 7th place: Seismic shocks also would have little effect, with only 0.17 percent.

In general, only asteroids with a minimum diameter of 18 meters would be lethal. A word to the wise: If you are watching the impact of an asteroid, don't stay near a window. When one crashed near Chelyabinsk, Russia, most of the injuries were caused by window panes shattered due to the shockwave.

DID YOU KNOW? If you register at www.hard-sf.com/subscribe I will inform you about upcoming publications of my science fiction titles. As a bonus, I will send you the beautifully-illustrated PDF version of *The Guided Tour to the Asteroids* for free!

Glossary of Acronyms

AI – Artificial Intelligence
API –Application Program Interface; Acoustic Properties Instrument
ASCAN – AStronaut CANdidate
AU – Astronomical Unit (the distance from the Earth to the sun)
BIOS – Basic Input/Output System
C&DH – Command & Data Handling
CapCom – Capsule Communicator
Cas – CRISPR-associated system
CELSS – Closed Ecological Life Support System
CIA – (U.S.) Central Intelligence Agency
COAS – Crewman Optical Alignment Site
Comms – Communiques
CRISPR – Clustered Regularly Interspaced Short Palindromic Repeats
DEC PDP-11 – Digital Equipment Corporation Programmable Data Processor-11
DFD – Direct Fusion Drive
DISR – Descent Imager / Spectral Radiometer
DNA – DeoxriboNeucleic Acid
DoD – (U.S.) Department of Defense
DPS – Data Processing Systems specialist (known as Dipsy)

DSN – Deep Space Network
ECDA – Enhanced Cosmic Dust Analyzer
EECOM – Electrical, Environmental, COnsumables, and Mechanical
EGIL – Electrical, General Instrumentation, and Lighting
EJSM – Europa Jupiter System Mission
ELF – Enceladus Life Finder
EMU – Extravehicular Mobility Unit
ESA – European Space Agency
EVA – ExtraVehicular Activity
F1 – Function 1 (Help function on computer keyboards)
FAST – (Chinese) Five-hundred-meter Aperture Spherical Telescope
FAO – Flight Activities Office
FCR – Flight Control Room
FD – Flight Director
FIDO – FlIght Dynamics Officer
Fortran – FORmula TRANslation
g – g-force (gravitational force)
GBI – Green Bank Interferometer
GNC – Guidance, Navigation, and Control system
HAI – High-Altitude Indoctrination device
HASI – *Huygens* Atmospheric Structure Instrument
HP – HorsePower
HUT – Hard Upper Torso
IAU – International Astronomical Union
ILSE – International Life Search Expedition
INCO – INstrumentation and Communication Officer
IR – InfraRed
ISS-NG – International Space Station-Next Generation
IT – Information Technology
IVO – Io Volcano Explorer
JAXA – Japan Aerospace eXploration Agency
JET – Journey to Enceladus and Titan
JPL – Jet Propulsion Laboratory
JSC – Johnson Space Center
JUICE – JUpiter ICy moons Explorer

LCD – Liquid Crystal Display
LCVG – Liquid Cooling and Ventilation Garment
LEA – Launch, Entry, Abort spacesuit
LIFE – Life Investigation For Enceladus
LTA – Lower Torso Assembly
MAG – Maximum Absorbency Garment
MCC – Mission Control Center
MIT – Massachusetts Institute of Technology
MOM – Mission Operations Manager
MPa – MegaPascal
MPD – MagnetoPlasmadynamic Drive
MSDD – *Multi-station Spatial Disorientation Device*
NSA – National Security Agency
NASA – National Aeronautics and Space Administration
NEA – Near Earth Asteroids
PAO – Public Affairs Office
PC – Personal Computer
PE-UHMW – PolyEthylene-Ultra High Molecular Weight
PER – fluid PERmittivity sensor
PI – Principal Investigator
Prop – Propulsion
PSS – Princeton Satellite Systems
RCS – Reaction Control System
REF – REFractive index sensor
RNA – RiboNeucleic Acid
RTG – Radioisotope Thermoelectric Generator
SAFER – Simplified Aid For EVA Rescue
SIRI – Speech Interpretation and Recognition Interface
SFTP – SSH (Secure Socket sHell) File Transfer Protocol
SSP – Surface Science Package
SSR – Solid-State Recorder
TandEM – Titan and Enceladus Mission
TiME – TItan Mare Explorer
TNO – Trans-Neptunian Object
TSSM – Titan Saturn System Mission
UTC –Universal Time Coordinated
Valkyrie – Very deep Autonomous Laser-powered Kilowatt-

class Yo-yoing Robotic Ice Explorer
VASIMR – VAriable Specific Impulse Magnetoplasma
Rocket
VR – Virtual Reality
WHC – Waste Hygiene Compartment

Metric to English Conversions

IT IS ASSUMED that by the time the events of this novel take place, the United States will have joined the rest of the world and will be using the International System of Units, the modern form of the metric system.

Length:
centimeter = 0.39 inches
meter = 1.09 yards, or 3.28 feet
kilometer = 1093.61 yards, or 0.62 miles

Area:
square centimeter = 0.16 square inches
square meter = 1.20 square yards
square kilometer = 0.39 square miles

Weight:
gram = 0.04 ounces
kilogram = 35.27 ounces, or 2.20 pounds

Volume:
liter = 1.06 quarts, or 0.26 gallons
cubic meter = 35.31 cubic feet, or 1.31 cubic yards

Temperature:
To convert Celsius to Fahrenheit, multiply by 1.8 and then add 32

Notes

January 13, 2049, (1566) Icarus

1. Quoted according to https://history.nasa.gov/SP-4218/ch5.htm (at the bottom of page 122.)

   The title, as it is quoted here, is not a typo, and this is not the entire poem; you'll see several more verses.

Copyright

Brandon Q. Morris
https://hard-sf.com
brandon@hard-sf.com
Translator: Frank Dietz, Ph.D. Editor: Pamela Bruce, B.S.
Final editing: Marcia Kwiecinski, A.A.S., and Stephen Kwiecinski, B.S.
Technical Advisors: Michael Paluszek (President, Princeton Satellite
Systems), Dr. Ludwig Hellmann
Cover design: BJ Coverbookdesigns

Made in United States
Orlando, FL
22 December 2021

12371909R00245